DEAD MAN'S PRAYER

Jackie Baldwin practised as a solicitor in a rural town for twenty years, specializing in family and criminal law. She then trained as a hypnotherapist and now works from home. She is married with two grown-up children and loves to walk with her two dogs in local forests. She is an active member of her local crime-writing group.

Dead Man's Prayer is her first novel.

@JackieMBaldwin1

Dead Man's Prayer

JACKIE BALDWIN

HarperCollins*Publishers*

HarperCollins*Publishers*
1 London Bridge Street
London SE1 9GF

www.harpercollins.co.uk

This paperback edition 2016
1

First published in Great Britain by
HarperCollins*Publishers* 2016

A catalogue record for this book is available from the British Library

ISBN: 978-0-00-820096-1

Typeset in Minion by Palimpsest Book Production Ltd, Falkirk, Stirlingshire

Printed and bound in Great Britain by
CPI Group (UK) Ltd, Croydon CR0 4YY

MIX
Paper from
responsible sources
FSC C007454

FSC™ is a non-profit international organisation established to promote
the responsible management of the world's forests. Products carrying the
FSC label are independently certified to assure consumers that they come
from forests that are managed to meet the social, economic and
ecological needs of present and future generations,
and other controlled sources.

Find out more about HarperCollins and the environment at
www.harpercollins.co.uk/green

For Guy

JUNE 2012

Father Ignatius Boyd lifted the crystal tumbler to his mouth and gulped greedily at the brandy, his shaking hand causing the glass to knock unpleasantly against his teeth.

The ruby velvet curtains and gas fire did nothing to dispel the chill he felt in his soul. It had rattled him seeing Frank Farrell at Mass this evening. His past mistakes had been haunting him of late as his body began to fail him. It would not be long until he met his Creator, and he had a feeling he would be found wanting. He had recently travelled to Rome to confess his sins to an anonymous priest but it had not brought him any comfort. His penance had not been the anticipated repetitions of the rosary, but a harsh command to reveal what had been hidden and to make what restitution was in his power. Until he completed that penance, his immortal soul remained in peril.

When he had seen Farrell at Mass this morning he had felt it was a sign. Before his courage failed he had hurried after him but his shouted greeting had fallen on deaf ears.

Another letter had been waiting on the mat when he returned home. For a moment he had the insane idea it might have been left there by Farrell, but on reflection he acknowledged it wasn't his style. He picked it up from the floor, where he had flung it in a rage, and studied it helplessly for some clue as to the sender's identity. The paper was cheap and flimsy, but the words meant business.

It was eleven o'clock. He walked over to the window and moved the curtains a fraction so he could peer out. The darkness pressed against the window as though it was trying to get in. He opened his bedroom door and listened intently. All was quiet and as it should be. Father Malone and the housekeeper did not keep late hours and had already retired to their rooms. Remembering the stricken expression of the young priest earlier, he felt a slight pang of remorse. He could have handled the situation better.

Suddenly the insistent trill of the phone pierced the silence. He swiftly ran down to answer it, his plain black cassock whispering on the stairs. With trembling hands, he picked up the phone, the colour draining from his face as he heard the menacing voice on the other end of the line.

Slowly he replaced the receiver on the hook. With a lingering backwards glance, he opened the back door and slipped out into the still night. It was clammy and not a breath of air disturbed the overhanging trees as he hurried up the narrow lane to the church, his heart thudding uncomfortably against the confines of his chest.

He went in the small door to the rear of the church and paused to listen. All he could hear was the sound of his own breathing and the thump of his heart. As his eyes acclimatized to the darkness he walked slowly towards the confessional box, resisting the urge to flee with every step. He paused outside the Priest's door. The handle wouldn't yield. He walked to the Penitent's door and swung it open. As he sank onto the kneeler the metal grille flew open and Father Boyd reared back with a shout of terror, hearing the sickening crunch of bone against unforgiving stone.

CHAPTER ONE

Detective Inspector Frank Farrell glanced around the tiny imper-
sonal room with its beige walls, grey carpet, and cheap wooden
desk strewn with files. Not for the first time he wondered whether
he'd done the right thing in accepting a transfer back to Dumfries
from the murder squad in Edinburgh. The rain drummed relentlessly on the window behind his desk. He looked out over the
town. The swollen grey clouds had leached colour out of the
landscape. The first early morning shoppers were dumping their
cars in the car park across the road from the station. Beyond the
rooftops the Lowther Hills were shrouded in mist.

Turning round, he folded his long body onto the chair behind
the desk and, with a frown, pulled a pink slip of paper towards
him. It was a message from Father Ignatius Boyd, dated yesterday;
the day before he started his new job. Farrell's jaw clenched. The
cheek of the man daring to phone him after all this time! Boyd
had even tried to engage him in conversation after Mass yesterday
morning, but Farrell had been having none of it. Impulsively he
screwed the message up into a tight ball and lobbed it into the
wastepaper basket. He had better things to do than pander to an
elderly priest whose Christian charity could be measured in nega-
tive numbers. Ignoring the niggling voice in his head that said

he was being unprofessional, Farrell pulled the nearest file towards him and started reading.

He'd almost finished when the phone rang. A nervous voice asked him to go along to Detective Superintendent Walker's office on the top floor.

Farrell moved quickly knowing that if you got on the wrong side of the super it cast a long shadow. He knocked firmly and a clipped voice bid him enter. The large airy office contained a small compact man behind a large desk. His sleeves were rolled up and Farrell could just make out the tail-end of a tattoo on his left arm. Tufts of fiery red hair stuck out in all directions above milky-white freckled skin. Walker ignored him, continuing to rustle the papers on his desk. Farrell waited patiently. Some men never leave the playground. Eventually, when the silence had started to stretch between them like a steel cable, Walker looked up and treated Farrell to his best ballbreaker stare.

'Now, Farrell, I hope you realize that we'll not tolerate any funny business at this station.'

'Sir?'

Whatever Farrell had expected it wasn't this. He could feel amusement welling up and struggled to keep his face impassive.

'You know what I mean, don't play the innocent with me, lad. I don't want any papist mumbo jumbo interrupting the smooth running of this station. No speaking in tongues, no Bible-study lunches, and absolutely no bloody exorcisms! Do I make myself clear?' Walker thundered, looking every inch a candidate for a heart attack.

'Crystal, Sir.'

'You want to get up to that sort of thing you do it in your own time, got it?'

'Yes, Sir.'

'Now we've got that out the way, welcome aboard.'

Walker proffered a meaty paw, and Farrell shook it. Walker snatched his hand back as though he'd been stung.

'Why you …'

'Sir?' said Farrell.

'Dismissed!' bellowed Walker, pale eyes bulging.

I really shouldn't have done that, thought Farrell, walking away. He'd been so incensed by Walker's ill-judged assumptions about him that he'd been unable to resist giving him a Masonic handshake as a parting shot. Only his first morning and already he'd landed in hot water.

It wasn't as if it had been a real exorcism. Last year a complete loony tune had escaped from the local hospital and managed to bag a couple of hostages. As the guy had thought he was possessed by the devil, Farrell had pretended to exorcise the evil spirit and got him to surrender. It had been the quickest way to get the job done. Since then he had never heard the end of it. The big brass in Edinburgh had been falling over themselves to avoid him, like he had something unsavoury they might catch.

Ten minutes later, Detective Chief Inspector Lind stuck his head round the door. Farrell recognized him at once. Although he was only forty-three, the same age as Farrell, Lind was all but bald with a few remaining wisps of blond hair clinging on perilously to the side of his head. Farrell resisted the urge to run his hands through his own thick mop of hair just to check it was still there. Lind's face cracked open into a wide smile that seemed to light up all the dark corners of the room. Farrell was amused to note that his lean fitness-fanatic friend now had the beginnings of a pot-belly.

'Frank, welcome to the wild South West.' Lind plonked himself down in front of the desk. 'So, how have you been?'

Farrell thought about telling him then decided against it.

'Oh you know, buried under a mountain of paperwork. Thought I'd see if there was any action down here or if it's still all cattle rustling and two cop bops.'

'You're well behind the times there, sunshine,' snorted Lind. 'Breach of the peace is the least of our problems now.'

Farrell smiled warmly at his new boss and old school pal.

'How's Laura these days? Not sent you packing yet?'

'I'm keeping her barefoot and pregnant, just in case.'

'Another one!' laughed Farrell. 'When's it due?'

'The middle of September,' said Lind. 'You must come over for dinner soon. Laura would love to see you; be just like old times.'

'Sure,' said Farrell, smiling until his jaw ached. Even the mention of her name after all this time was enough to unsettle him.

Lind leapt up. 'Got to dash, I've got a departmental meeting. The briefing is at nine thirty.'

Farrell wasn't sure how he felt about having Lind as his immediate boss. On the one hand, he knew Lind wouldn't give him any hassle. In fact, he'd probably be falling over himself not to rub his nose in it. On the other hand, he felt a bit uncomfortable having someone around who had once known him so well.

Laura McCarron: the biggest sacrifice he had ever made. Her lingering presence had occasioned him both grief and comfort over the years. To confront the reality of the woman she had become might finally restore some equanimity.

A little cheered, he applied himself to the files again until a few minutes before the scheduled briefing. As he'd suspected, the subject matter was fairly tame compared to what he'd been used to dealing with in Edinburgh.

Wandering down to the briefing room Farrell cast an expert eye over the loose assortment of officers inside. Within a few days they would differentiate into clumps of good cops, bad cops, smart cops, lazy cops and … attractive cops. He looked quickly away but not quickly enough. She'd noticed him staring and was headed straight towards him.

A pair of reserved grey eyes looked up into his and a dainty hand, cool to the touch, reached out to shake his.

'DI Kate Moore; you must be DI Farrell?'

'Guilty as charged,' he said with a warm smile.

A faint blush coloured her cheeks and she slid her eyes away from his.

'If I can be of any help while you're settling in, don't hesitate to call on me,' she replied before walking off rather too smartly to the other side of the room.

Farrell became aware of covert glances from other women dotted around the room. It made him feel uncomfortable and gave him the urge to retreat into himself. He did nothing to encourage female interest. His manner of dressing was low key and he doubted if he could flirt if his life depended on it. It was just a cross he had to bear. A joke by God at his expense.

An old boy with the ruddy complexion of a hardened drinker and hair like a pot scrubber wandered over next to make his acquaintance.

'DS Stirling; I hear you're a local man,' he said.

'That's right,' replied Farrell.

'And would you be related to Yvonne Farrell, by any chance?'

'She's my mother.'

'Is she now?' said DS Stirling, gazing at him. 'I know her from the bowling. I didn't know she had a son. It's a small world, eh?'

'Some might say too small,' Farrell replied, feeling the tension in his jaw.

'Come and meet one of the other sergeants: DS Byers.'

Farrell followed Stirling across the room to where a man in his early thirties with the gym-sculpted body of the truly narcissistic was trying to impress DI Moore. Farrell was amused to note that she looked unmistakably relieved at their approach, which enabled her to extricate herself.

DS Byers then turned and pumped Farrell's hand so hard his fingers lost their blood supply.

'DS Byers at your service, Sir, or should I say Bless me, Father, for I have sinned?'

There was a collective intake of breath as the eyes of all those in the room nervously flicked their way. Farrell, making them sweat, coolly looked around them all and then back at the hapless Byers, who was already regretting his foray into levity.

'I don't know, Byers, should you?' Farrell asked.

Just then DCI Lind entered and the confrontation was over as soon as it began. Farrell took a seat at the back, the better to observe his fellow officers.

'The tourist season is starting to kick off now so we're going to have to clamp down on Jimmy McMurdo's wee gang on the Whitesands,' announced Lind.

There were a few snickers at this from which Farrell deduced Jimmy McMurdo was filed under 'local colour'. Lind held his hand up for silence and continued.

'Scintillating repartee with the local winos won't be at the top of anybody's holiday wish list. The byelaws are there so use them.'

They all listened fairly attentively as Lind briefed them on ongoing enquiries and allocated actions for that day. Farrell was impressed; his old friend seemed to run a tight ship.

Behind him there was a minor commotion as a somewhat dishevelled young woman with bloodshot eyes entered. She tried to slip into the seat beside him only to drop the folder she was carrying with a bang. Malicious eyes pivoted to her and then back to DI Lind. Lind paused mid-sentence and glared, his expression a few degrees before zero.

'Nice of you to join us, DC McLeod,' he said.

'Sorry, Sir, the bus—'

'I don't want to hear it. Just make sure it doesn't happen again. We're public servants and as such we're paid to work, not to get up and wander in when we feel like it.'

'No, Sir,' said the unfortunate constable.

'Moving on then …' said Lind.

Farrell tuned out and studied his new neighbour. A faint whiff of stale booze and cigarettes wafted over him causing his nose to prickle in distaste. Her hair looked like it hadn't been combed and there was a small ladder in her tights. Sensing his scrutiny, she turned and scowled at him. He tried a rueful grin but she was having none of it.

Suddenly, a young police officer burst through the door with such force that it banged against the wall. Lind opened his mouth to give him a roasting then stopped, taking in the lad's white face and serious expression.

Farrell stiffened. Something bad had happened. He could smell it. Lind took the constable to one side, his expression becoming graver as he listened to what he had to say, and then motioned for him to sit.

'Listen up, people. PC Thomson has just informed me that there's been a murder down at St Aidan's: the elderly priest there, Father Boyd.'

Farrell could feel the blood drain from his head and forced himself to surreptitiously take deep breaths until the dizziness receded. He became aware that he was being watched curiously by DC McLeod and gave her a savage glare that caused her to redden and turn away. He brought his whirling thoughts back under control just in time to hear Lind appointing him as Senior Investigating Officer.

CHAPTER TWO

Farrell parked across the road from St Aidan's. Despite the fact that it was June dark clouds still glowered in the sky, sending down a grizzling lament of rain. The sandstone church occupied an elevated position within landscaped grounds, looking down with unfeeling eyes on the flotsam of humanity washed up onto its steps. A tall spire reached for the unobtainable.

Feeling unnerved by the prospect of what was to come Farrell forced himself to quit the car. PC Thomson was waiting for him. His face had the waxy pallor of a mannequin. Probably the lad's first murder scene, thought Farrell. He quickly posted the assembled uniforms to search the surrounding area and guard all entrances and exits, then, motioning to PC Thomson to follow him, he reluctantly entered the church. Automatically he extended his fingers to dip in the holy water, but stopped himself in the nick of time. Hardly appropriate; he was here as a copper not a priest today, and he'd do well to remember it.

'Over here, Sir.'

Farrell saw DS Byers, DS Stirling, and DC McLeod standing behind the outer cordon of blue-and-white tape. Striding over he nodded an acknowledgement and addressed DS Stirling.

'Right, Sergeant, I'm appointing you Crime Scene Manager on this one; you know the drill?'

'Yes, Sir,' replied Stirling.

Byers looked sour. Stirling posted PC Thomson on the outer cordon with strict instructions to let no one past except on Stirling's say so. Stirling and Farrell carefully suited up, covering their whole bodies, including feet and hair, in blue plastic.

'Any sign of the perpetrator?' asked Farrell as they stepped through.

'No, Sir. The church and grounds have been searched.'

'Any sign of forced entry?'

'None, Sir.'

Both officers ducked under the second line of tape. Silently Stirling swung the door of the confessional open. Farrell sucked in a breath and held it. Whatever he had expected, nothing could have prepared him for this … this … obscenity. Acid flooded his mouth and he forced it back down his throat. Stirling swore under his breath then looked mortified. An unmistakable whiff of incense overlaid other more noxious smells emanating from the confined space.

Farrell shoved away feelings of revulsion and steadily regarded the crime scene. Father Ignatius Boyd was propped up on his knees in the small confessional; his hands bound tightly together with rosary beads in a parody of prayer. From his bulging eyes and protruding tongue it looked as though the cause of death may have been strangulation, though there was also a fair amount of blood with its unmistakable rusty odour. Underneath the dead priest's hands was a white sheet of paper, but Farrell didn't dare disturb anything until the police surgeon and the Scenes of Crime Officers had done their stuff.

A man in his fifties with a ruddy, weather-beaten complexion came hurrying into the church.

'Bill Forster, Sir, police surgeon,' said Stirling at Farrell's elbow. Farrell thought the man looked more like a farmer than a doctor. Although he would be no stranger to dead bodies, Farrell was willing to bet Forster had never seen anything like this before. As the confessional door swung back on its hinges the doctor gave an audible gasp, seemingly rooted to the spot; then getting a hold of himself he conducted a brief examination with meticulous professionalism, careful to disturb the body as little as possible. He then straightened up and followed Farrell back through the cordons into the interior of the church.

'What can you tell me, Doctor?' asked Farrell.

'Well, I can confirm that life is extinct; no surprises there.'

'Can you give me a preliminary cause of death?'

'I'm not qualified to comment on that, Inspector. You know the limitations of my role here.'

Farrell ground his teeth in frustration but knew better than to press him further.

Two SOCOs arrived, as the doctor was leaving, laden with the paraphernalia of their trade. Nodding in recognition to Stirling, they introduced themselves to Farrell as Phil Tait and Janet White. Quietly and efficiently they then got to work under the capable direction of Stirling, as CSM. Farrell dispatched five pairs of uniforms on door-to-door enquiries. He asked them to complete Personal Description Forms for everyone they interviewed. This murder was undoubtedly Category 'A', and he was leaving nothing to chance.

Farrell's concentration was interrupted by a heated altercation between PC Thomson and DS Byers. Rolling his eyes skywards he went to investigate. Byers was clearly struggling to hang onto his temper. The young constable was flushed but resolute.

'What seems to be the problem?' snapped Farrell.

'This impudent young bugger won't let me through the cordon,' blustered Byers.

'You mean you're bitching about the fact that he's doing his job? You know as well as I do that cross contamination of the scene is to be avoided at all costs.'

'I thought it would help if I saw the set-up with my own eyes,' muttered Byers.

'Afraid you'll have to make do with the video, like everyone else.'

Byers marched off in high dudgeon, and Farrell winked at PC Thomson.

'Well done, lad.'

'You might want to come and see this, Sir,' yelled Stirling.

Farrell swiftly approached. Janet was holding something up in her gloved hands for him to inspect. It was the white piece of paper that had been trapped under the hands of the deceased. Written on it, in what appeared to be blood, were the smudged words 'mea culpa, mea culpa'. The paper was carefully bagged, signed, and then sealed.

'Looks like a real whack job,' said Stirling.

'You got that right,' replied Farrell. 'Did you notify the duty fiscal?'

'Yes, Sir, but, if it's OK with you, I decided not to let him view the scene,' replied Stirling.

Farrell nodded acquiescence then stepped out of the church. He couldn't even begin to get his head around this. Seeing the incident van, he walked over. Together with a number of uniforms, DC McLeod was questioning members of the public. Word had evidently got about and a sizable crowd was gathering, kept at a distance by hastily erected barriers. An opportunistic burger stand was setting up on a patch of waste ground. Hungry coppers were turning a blind eye.

A media truck arrived and started to send cables snaking around. Two young public-school types with trendily sculpted hair started walking around importantly with big furry microphones held aloft. A young blonde woman in skyscraper heels and a powder blue suit descended and glanced around, selecting her prey. To Farrell's horror she started to approach him with a determined expression on her painted face. This he could do without. Fixing him with a basilisk stare and thrusting out her hand, she left him with no choice but to advance reluctantly and shake her hand. Where the blazes was the civilian press officer?

'Sophie Richardson, Border News,' she said, drawing her lips back over impossibly white teeth.

'DI Frank Farrell, Senior Investigating Officer.'

'Can you confirm the identity of the deceased, DI Farrell?'

'Not until the family has been informed.'

'What can you tell us?'

'Simply that enquiries are ongoing. We are treating this matter as a suspicious death. Excuse me, I'm afraid I'm needed elsewhere.'

Farrell turned on his heel and started to walk back into the church. The crowd was growing in size and becoming more vocal. The local hacks looked ecstatic at the prospect of a juicy murder to report on for once. Did no one actually care that a man had lost his life today?

An alarm on Farrell's watch beeped. Glancing round to make sure he was unobserved he surreptitiously popped a pill into his mouth and swallowed. Straightening his shoulders, he then pulled open the heavy oak door and strode back into the church. If only he had swallowed his pride and spoken to Boyd yesterday. He was tormented by the thought that he might have been able to prevent his murder.

CHAPTER THREE

Farrell glanced at his watch. His stomach growled with hunger. It was about time he went and interviewed the remaining parish priest and housekeeper. He cast around for someone free to accompany him and his eye lighted on DC McLeod, who was looking pale and drawn. Time to get her out of here. He beckoned her over.

'Sir?'

'Come with me, DC McLeod. We're going to interview Father Malone, the other parish priest.'

'I didn't know there were two of them, Sir. I'm not of the, er ... same persuasion.'

Farrell led the way round the back of the church and up a narrow paved lane that led to a detached sandstone house. It had been many years since he had called it home. He knocked firmly on the door.

A slight young man, who looked to be in his late twenties, opened the door. He was clean-shaven and formally dressed in an immaculate black suit with a clerical collar. There were dark shadows under his pale blue eyes that were suggestive of more than one sleepless night.

'Father Malone?' asked Farrell. 'We'd like to ask you a few questions.'

'Yes of course. Please, come in,' the priest said in a flat voice.

He swung the door open and they followed him along a dark hall into a comfortable, if rather old-fashioned, living room. Farrell felt a sense of dislocation as though he had inadvertently stepped back into his own past. The carpet and drapes were the same. The only addition to the room since he had lived there appeared to be the small flatscreen TV, positioned self-consciously in the corner as though apologizing for its existence.

'Won't you sit down?' the priest said, gesturing vaguely to a well-worn leather sofa, as though his body was going through the motions but his mind had retreated elsewhere.

Farrell leaned forward, making eye contact, trying to force him back into the room with them.

'I understand you were the one who found the body?'

'Yes, that's right. I had gone over to prepare for morning Mass at 9.30. I hadn't seen Father Boyd at breakfast but I assumed he had taken a tray up to his room as he sometimes does. He's not that keen on morning chit-chat. I mean he wasn't ...'

'I know this is painful but can you tell me how you happened upon the body? I mean I presume you weren't hearing confessions that early in the morning?'

'No. I was walking up the aisle ready to open the front door when I noticed the confessional door was slightly ajar. I went over to nudge it closed but something was stuck behind the door. I opened it to get a better look and that's when ... I saw ...'

'Did you disturb the scene in any way? Maybe check if he had a pulse, move him, or something else – in any way?'

'No. It was quite clear to me that he was dead. I simply ran back here and phoned the police.' He looked ashamed. 'I was afraid the killer might still be there. I should have stayed and prayed over him, attempted the last rites ...'

Farrell could see the priest's guilt escalating.

'He had already passed. It was too late for any of that. If you had lingered any longer all that would have happened is that the crime scene would likely have been contaminated, making it all the harder to bring his killer to justice.'

There was a tap on the door and a plump middle-aged woman entered the room carrying a laden tea tray. When she saw Farrell the cups began to rattle and she choked back an exclamation. Father Malone rose at once to take the tray from her and seated her in a chair.

'Mary, these officers have come to question us about anything we know that might help them catch the person who did this terrible thing.'

'He was a good man. He didn't deserve to die like this,' she said. 'I hope whoever did it rots in Hell.'

Father Malone looked troubled.

'Mary, Father Boyd would expect us to forgive his killer.'

'Father Boyd believed in an eye for an eye. He wasn't like the namby-pamby young priests they turn out of the seminary these days,' she added, darting a contemptuous look at Father Malone.

Farrell looked at the portly woman sitting across from him, lines of bitterness scored into her face. He tried but failed to find the woman she had been when they first met, beneath the layers of fat and anger. What had happened to her? He might get more out of the priest if she wasn't there. He doubted there was any degree of collusion between them, but best to interview them separately for now.

'DC McLeod, could you please take Miss Flannigan to the kitchen until I am ready to interview her and also obtain details of Father Boyd's next of kin, please.'

At a gesture from Farrell, McLeod gently helped Mary Flannigan to her feet and went off to the kitchen with her.

The priest sat silent, his face grey to match his socks.

'When did you last see Father Boyd?'

'It would have been around ten p.m.,' he murmured. 'I left him sitting here, reading a book, while I went to bed. Mary had already gone upstairs and he told me he'd lock up.'

'Did he mention any plans to go out?'

'No. It was just an ordinary night.'

'What did you talk about?'

The young priest looked unaccountably furtive.

'Nothing in particular, just bits and pieces.'

Farrell sat back and stared at Father Malone thoughtfully. What wasn't he telling him? The silence lengthened. Through the wall he heard the tap running in the kitchen and the clatter of dishes. The young priest continued to avoid his gaze, two spots of colour now staining his cheeks.

'No unexpected visitors, late phone calls?'

'Wait, I did hear the phone ring. It woke me then I dozed off again.'

'Any idea what time that might have been?'

'I couldn't say.'

'Had he seemed himself lately?' asked Farrell. 'Anything appear to be worrying him?'

'He'd received a few crank letters: three, I think. He tried to brush it off but I could tell he was upset by them.'

'What was in them?'

'He wouldn't say, and I didn't like to pry. He's … he was a very private man, liked to keep people at a distance.'

'And you didn't try and sneak a peek?'

'Certainly not! I probably wouldn't even have known about them had I not got up before Father Boyd on one occasion. I saw something lying on the mat and was about to pick it up when Father Boyd yelled at me not to touch it. He was clearly upset. I remember his hands were shaking and he stumbled back against the wall as he was reading it,' said the priest.

'These letters, were they posted or hand delivered?'

'Hand delivered, I believe. Do you think they've got anything to do with …?'

'Time will tell,' said Farrell. 'Where did Father Boyd keep the letters?'

'I really have no idea,' said the priest.

'Do I have your permission to search the house?'

'Yes, of course. Do what you have to,' said the priest.

'One more thing. Did Father Boyd keep an appointment diary? It might help if we can track his movements prior to the murder.'

The young priest leapt to his feet with an air of relief and fetched a leather-bound diary from the hall. Farrell turned to the weeks before and after the killing. His eyebrows shot up as he noted that Boyd had met with Father Joe Spinelli, Farrell's own spiritual adviser, the Friday before he died. Turning the next few pages, Farrell spotted the name Clare Yates. His pulse quickened. She was still here after all these years then. Worse, he was going to have to follow this up.

Still scowling, Farrell went into the kitchen and found DC McLeod sitting beside two mugs of tea on the table. Instantly, he tensed.

'Where'd she go?' he demanded.

DC McLeod looked surprised at the urgency in his voice. 'She said she needed to go to the bathroom. What's up?'

Farrell didn't reply but tore out the kitchen and took the stairs two at a time. Hearing the sounds of drawers banging shut he raced past the unoccupied bathroom, followed by a perplexed McLeod, and crashed through the door the noise was coming from. The housekeeper was standing with her back to him. He strode over and spun her round, his suspicions realized. She was holding a piece of paper to a cigarette lighter. Farrell snatched the charred bit of paper off her but most of it had been destroyed. Father Malone arrived at the open door and took in the scene.

'Mary, what have you done?' he remonstrated.

Farrell was furious. He pulled out a pair of handcuffs from his pockets and unceremoniously handcuffed the housekeeper, whose bravado was now overlaid with apprehension.

'I am detaining you on suspicion of attempting to pervert the course of justice. Anything you say will be noted down and can be used in evidence against you,' Farrell snapped.

'I won't have you lot trying to blacken his name. He was a good man,' Mary mumbled, refusing to meet his eye.

'Did you get that?' said Farrell to McLeod, who was busily scribbling away in her notebook.

'Yes, Sir.'

Father Malone gestured helplessly to the handcuffs.

'Look, is all this really necessary?'

'Too right,' said Farrell grimly. 'She's destroyed a major piece of evidence.'

'I didn't even know she knew about the letters. Father Boyd must have confided in her,' the priest said, sounding surprised.

At that point two uniforms came in, having been summoned by radio, and led the now sobbing housekeeper away. Farrell followed them out to the waiting squad car. As she was about to get into the back seat she whipped round to face him. It took the combined efforts of the two young officers to hold her steady.

'They had an argument last night, Father Boyd and that apology for a priest in there. I heard them shouting while I was in bed.'

'You heard Father Malone shouting?' asked Farrell, his gaze sceptical.

'Well, I heard Father Boyd shouting at him, and he must have done something to rile him up so much. There's a black heart under that cassock, I'm telling you ...'

Farrell tried to hide his distaste and looked at her impassively, though he could feel his temper rising.

'Did you hear what the argument was about?' he asked.

'I couldn't hear from my room.'

She looked down furtively and Farrell resisted the temptation to roll his eyes.

'Did you get up, perhaps, for a drink of water?' asked Farrell.

'As it happens I did,' she said.

'And?' snapped Farrell.

'It was all over by the time I got downstairs. Father Malone brushed past me without so much as a by-your-leave so I got my drink and went back to bed. Poor Father Boyd was never very lucky with his priests now, was he?' she added for his benefit.

Farrell itched to retaliate and wipe the malicious grin off her face, but instead indicated to the officers that they should proceed, turned on his heel and walked back into the house.

He had intended to ask Father Malone about the argument there and then but the young priest looked about fit to keel over. It could keep. Knowing Boyd and his temper as he did it was probably something and nothing anyway.

'I'm afraid we're going to have to turn this place over. Is there anywhere you can go and stay meantime?'

'There is a couple I'm friendly with. I'm sure they would put me up,' Father Malone replied, looking as though his legs might collapse from under him at any second.

Farrell glanced at DC McLeod.

'On it, Sir,' she said, and escorted the young priest out to more waiting uniforms.

She was holding up well, thought Farrell. It wasn't at all common for officers in Dumfries to be faced with a murder of this nature. Perhaps there was more to party cop than he'd thought.

Farrell ran an expert eye over Boyd's bedroom, scanning for likely hiding places. The room was large and comfortably furnished with a liberal smattering of antiques and the odd expensive-looking oil painting. The rich reds and greens of the Axminster carpet threw the drabness elsewhere in the house into sharp relief. The double bed was piled high with a sump-tuous quilt and scatter cushions. So much for the vow of poverty, thought Farrell, picking up the lid of a fine cut-glass decanter and sniffing the expensive brandy it contained. He rifled through the good quality suits in the wardrobes, raising an eyebrow at some of the labels. Boyd had clearly developed a taste for the finer things of life. Relentlessly he pressed into every nook and cranny with probing fingers. Nothing. He turned his attention to the walnut bookcase where there were many scholarly theological volumes. On the bottom, pushed self-consciously to the back of the shelf, were a number of paperback thrillers. He flicked briskly through each of these, looking to see if anything was hidden between the pages. Again, nothing.

His eyes turned to the ornately carved crucifix above the bed; the figure on which seemed to be following his progress disapprovingly round the room. Averting his eyes and feeling slightly foolish he took the wooden plaque on which it was mounted and removed it from the wall. He tapped the back. It sounded hollow. Hardly daring to breathe he prised off the back and removed two sheets of paper. Bingo. He yelled for McLeod and she ran into the room. Carefully, he opened a folded sheet of paper. In crude capitals were the words:

I KNOW WHAT YOU DID

Farrell opened out the second sheet of paper.

IF IT HAPPENS AGAIN I'LL TELL
YOU'RE GOING TO BURN IN HELL

Farrell carefully bagged the letters in an evidence bag, and DC McLeod co-signed the label. What on earth had Boyd been up to, he wondered? It was a shame there had been no envelopes with the letters. It might have been possible to obtain a DNA match from any saliva used to seal the envelope.

Just then PC Thomson walked in. 'Sir, they're ready to take the body to the mortuary.'

Farrell considered him.

'Someone needs to go with the body to the mortuary until it is signed in and sealed. Do you think you can hack it, son?'

PC Thomson seemed to go even whiter.

'No problem, Sir,' he said.

'Good lad; Sergeant Stirling will sort you out with the right forms to take with you. We'll be down in a minute.'

Farrell turned round to see DC McLeod regarding him with a thoughtful expression. She gestured to the wooden crucifix lying on the bed ready to be removed as evidence.

'Trade secret, Sir?' she asked.

'Something like that,' answered Farrell and turned to leave.

As he supervised the body being loaded into the hearse in its inscrutable black bag, Farrell felt a sense of foreboding. Evil was afoot in his old hometown.

CHAPTER FOUR

Farrell regarded the last sandwich in the canteen dubiously. It purported to be ham salad but he had his doubts. His stomach gurgled. He grabbed the sandwich, coffee, and a squashed satsuma. Thin pickings. A case like this required physical as well as mental stamina so he scoffed the lot in five minutes and headed back upstairs. It was his responsibility to get this investigation up and running without delay.

He found DC McLeod already hard at work, brow furrowed in concentration. He picked up the sheaf of papers beside her.

'Are these the statements from the door-to-door enquiries?'

'Some of them, Sir.'

'Anything interesting so far?'

'One man was out walking his dog around 11.30 p.m. when he saw a figure slipping out of the church. It was someone tall with a long dark coat on. Unfortunately, he only got a view from behind. He assumed it was a visiting priest.'

'It's a start,' said Farrell. 'Sergeant Byers should be in the Major Crime Administration room. Bring all the statements.'

As they entered the MCA room, McLeod made a beeline for the civilian scribes already assembled to input the information gathered into the Home Office Large Major Enquiry System.

Farrell started writing bullet points on the whiteboard, ready for the first briefing of the case. They didn't have a lot to go on.

An hour later the room was a hub of activity. Farrell walked across to the whiteboard and held up his hand for silence. He pointed to a graphic photo of the murdered priest attached to the wall.

'To solve this case we need to look into the past of the deceased very carefully. Although we can't yet rule it out, this murder doesn't feel at all random to me. It looks personal. In light of the anonymous letters it may well be that the priest was being black-mailed by the killer prior to his death. However, blackmailers don't usually kill their meal ticket. We need to talk to members of his parish. Some of these old biddies can recall events fifty years ago but not what they did yesterday. Find out who had a grudge against Boyd. We need to know his movements over the last few weeks. McLeod, have you tracked down the deceased's family yet?'

'Yes, Sir, both parents are dead but he has an elderly sister, Emily, who lives in Edinburgh. She's coming down tomorrow afternoon, and PC Thomson is meeting her at the station.'

'DS Byers, I believe it was you who interviewed the dog walker?'

'Yes, Sir.'

'I'd like you to organize pairs of officers to interview members of the parish. We'll get a list of names and addresses from Father Malone. He'll be in shortly to give a formal statement. Also, get the dog walker together with one of the identikit guys. I know it was only a rear view but it's all we've got to go on at the moment. Any questions?'

'What about the housekeeper?' asked Byers. 'I hear the Custody Sergeant has a headache with all the shouting and bawling going on.'

There were a few titters at this. It was common knowledge that the Custody Sergeant, Donald Sloan, liked a quiet life and felt sorely aggrieved if he didn't get it.

'We'll be interviewing her later this afternoon. Her solicitor's in court this morning and can't make it in until 4 p.m. She'll be up before the Sheriff tomorrow morning with the rest of the custodies,' Farrell replied. 'The procurator fiscal has no objection to bail subject to a condition that she doesn't go near the house. We don't want her destroying any more evidence.'

'The press is going to have a field day with that one,' said Stirling.

'No more than she deserves,' said Farrell.

'Was there anything going on between them, do you think?' asked Byers.

Farrell's jaw tightened. Get a grip man. Why, after all these years, did he still feel a compulsion to protect the reputation of the dead priest, despite all that had happened? He became aware of the silence. Everyone was staring at him.

'She was willing to risk her own neck to protect his memory. Whether she was also sleeping with him, who can say? However, as Father Malone lived in the same house, I would suggest that it's unlikely. You can do a bit of digging, if you like. A bit of subtlety wouldn't go amiss though, if you think you can manage that?'

Byers looked offended. However, there were knowing smirks around the room.

'Right, if there's nothing else, everyone get to it. I don't need to remind you all that the clock's ticking. Every hour that passes makes catching the murderer that bit harder.'

Farrell headed for the sanctuary of his office and closed the door. He craved solitude like a junkie needing a fix. Sinking into his chair he inhaled deeply. Closing his eyes did not make the nightmare images of Boyd kneeling before him recede. Rather, they seemed to be burned onto his retina. He glanced over at his wastepaper bin and saw the crumpled pink message slip lying where he had hurled it only this morning. The worm of guilt burrowed deep within him. Maybe Boyd had been reaching out to him for help. If he hadn't been so pig-headed maybe he could have done something to save him.

The phone rang. It was PC Thomson informing him Father Malone had arrived for questioning. He headed for the interview room, collecting DS Stirling on the way. Maybe now the young priest would be more forthcoming than he had been this morning.

Opening the door, he saw that the priest was still deeply shocked. His hands were clasped together in front of him as if in prayer but Farrell suspected it was more to try and stop them shaking than anything else. His left eye had developed a slight twitch that wasn't there this morning.

Once the tape recorder had been switched on and introductions made Father Malone pushed over a chunky folder, filled with names and addresses.

'Here's the parish register. Most of our active parishioners should be included but there are also a fair number of people who turn up to Mass week in and out but don't seek to become further involved. If they haven't been baptized, married, or confirmed in the Church, they won't be noted down anywhere.'

'Thank you; that's most helpful,' said Farrell.

DS Stirling settled back in his chair, letting Farrell take the lead, as agreed earlier.

'Father Boyd was an old-school priest, very black and white in his views, wasn't he?'

'You could say that,' said Malone, swallowing hard.

'Not exactly tolerant?'

'No, he believed very firmly in upholding the teachings of the Church.'

'A man like that must have made some enemies along the way, surely?'

'Well, yes, up to a point but nothing to incite a crime of this … magnitude or depravity. It was all small stuff, really.'

'Maybe not to the people involved?'

'The kind of thing I'm talking about is refusing religious

instruction for kids whose parents want to send them to a secular school rather than the Catholic primary or refusing to do a Requiem Mass for lapsed Catholics. Nothing worth killing over.'

'So, you're saying he was petty?'

'He would see it as principled: setting a strong moral compass for his congregation.'

Petty, vindictive, and narrow-minded, thought Farrell, feeling his ire rising. He pushed the thoughts away and resumed, now with a hard edge to his voice.

'What were you and the deceased arguing about the night he died?'

Colour flamed in Malone's face and he dropped his eyes.

'Well?' demanded Farrell.

'If you must know, he said that he doubted my vocation and that I should give some thought to leaving the priesthood. Yes, we argued. For once I stood up to him but I didn't kill him. In fact, I tried to forgive him … I'm still trying,' he said in a low voice.

Farrell regarded him. Malone's version of events certainly tallied with his own memories of Boyd. In any event, they had nothing tangible to suggest he might be a suspect so probably best to cut him loose for now and not antagonize him further. He glanced over at Stirling, who gave a micro shrug in response.

'Interview terminated at 15.46,' he said for the benefit of the tape.

He escorted Malone back out to reception and watched until he was out of sight. Stirling had clearly thought the priest was on the level but he still had a niggling feeling he might be missing something. But what?

Feeling his energy levels starting to flag once more he grabbed more coffee and a Mars bar on the way back to the MCA room. His stomach grumbled in protest. This case was giving a whole new meaning to the phrase baptism of fire.

CHAPTER FIVE

Mary Flannigan sat across the table from Farrell, refusing to look him in the eye. The duty solicitor, a lad who looked barely old enough to drink, sat beside her. This time, Farrell had felt it politic to let Stirling conduct the interview and had instructed him to go on a charm offensive at the outset.

Stirling got everyone present to introduce themselves for the tape.

'I would like to remind you that you are still under caution and that anything you say may be used in evidence against you in court. Do you understand?'

'I'm not stupid,' she retorted.

'Miss Flannigan, aside from these proceedings, first of all let me offer my condolences. I know that this must be very difficult for you. I understand that you had worked for Father Boyd as his housekeeper for some twenty years?'

'Twenty-three years.'

'What did you do before that?'

Farrell realized even he didn't know the answer to that question. Mary Flannigan looked shifty, embarrassed.

'I don't see how that's relevant?' she countered.

'Just answer the question, please,' insisted Stirling.

Struck a nerve there, thought Farrell.

'On the advice of my solicitor, no comment.'

Her young solicitor looked somewhat startled, and she tapped the side of her nose at him.

'Would it be fair to say that Father Boyd relied on you heavily?' asked Stirling, laying it on with a trowel.

'Of course he did; the poor man would have been lost without me to take care of him,' she replied, dabbing at red-rimmed eyes with a tissue.

'Would you say that you were close?'

The shutters came down.

'Just what are you insinuating?' she snapped.

'Did he confide in you?'

She took her time to reply.

'No, not really. He was a very private man. Father Boyd took his duties as a man of the cloth very seriously. He didn't unburden himself to me or to anyone else as far as I'm aware.'

'In that case, how do you explain the fact that you knew about the anonymous letters he had been receiving? Did he tell you?'

An expression flickered briefly across her sullen face. Shame? Fear? If so, then why?

Her solicitor was signalling that she shouldn't say anything, but she ignored him.

'I was putting away his laundry one day and I found them.'

'Found them where?' Farrell interjected.

'In his sock drawer,' she said, unconvincingly.

'Why did you destroy the letter we found you with?' asked Stirling.

'I wanted to protect his memory,' she said. 'I'm sorry, so very sorry. I should never have …' She started weeping, seeming genuinely overcome.

At a nod from Farrell the interview was terminated and she was escorted back to the cells.

Farrell was still getting the feeling that something didn't ring true but he couldn't pin it down. Maybe his objectivity was being compromised by the past. Stirling again hadn't noticed anything amiss. He'd thought her behaviour was consistent with the loyalty of a faithful old retainer. Was he imagining things?

Back in his office, he settled down to make some bullet points for the next briefing at 6 p.m., keen to ensure that nothing was overlooked. He weighed up the pros and cons of making it known that Boyd had tried to contact him the day he died but, on balance, decided to keep it to himself for the time being. It would have been different if they had actually spoken but as things stood at the moment there was nothing it could add to the investigation. He didn't want his past dragged into the present if it could be avoided.

Farrell updated the rest of the team at the next briefing about his impressions of the evidence garnered from the priest and the housekeeper. As an afterthought, he asked DS Byers to try and ascertain what Mary Flannigan had been doing with her life before she worked for Boyd. She had seemed unnecessarily cagey. He also approved for circulation the identikit image of the man seen by the dog walker; although, given that it was a rear view, it didn't take them much further forward. Finally, having done all that he could think of and with exhaustion settling like sediment in his body, he forced himself to leave and go home.

As he drove along quiet country roads on his way out to the tiny hamlet of Kelton, Farrell lowered the windows to allow the cool night air to chase away the tiredness that was slowing down his brain. The earth smelled moist and rich with unidentifiable scents on the periphery of his memory.

Turning right into the small lane, he dipped his headlights so as not to disturb his neighbours in the surrounding cottages. The stones crunched under his wheels and the tang of salt water from the River Nith drifted up to greet him. Farrell could feel his clenched muscles finally start to unknot.

What on earth …? As he reached the cottage his headlights had picked up a shadowy figure slinking round the side wall from the rear garden. The light illuminated a white face with glittering eyes briefly turned his way.

Farrell skidded to a halt and flung himself out the car and down the lane in hot pursuit. As he stumbled onto the muddy banks of the Nith, running perpendicular to the lane he had just left, the darkness closed in on him. He could only hear the sound of his ragged breathing and the sucking noise of the tidal river. After a couple of minutes, he paused to listen, trying to control his laboured breathing. Someone coughed behind him. He spun round, heart hammering.

'Police,' he yelled. 'Don't move!'

As he shone the thin light of his torch in the direction of the sound, he met the interested gaze of a belted Galloway cow.

From ahead the faint sound of mocking laughter drifted towards him on the back of the slight breeze that had got up. He spun round to give chase but it was one bit of nifty footwork too many. His feet went from under him, and he landed face down in the brackish mud.

Squelching home, he noticed more than one curtain twitching. Grabbing a torch from his car he circumnavigated the cottage checking for signs of forced entry, but there were none. At least he interrupted the burglar before he had a chance to break in. Not that he had anything worth taking.

After a long hot shower Farrell pulled on a faded pair of jeans and a navy roll-neck sweater. He padded through to the sitting room in his bare feet and inserted some Gregorian chants in the CD player. Pouring himself a generous measure of whisky, he sank back onto the leather couch and lost himself in the soothing rhythms of the music.

Later, as he got up to change the CD Farrell noticed something out of the corner of his eye. Through the door of the sitting room he could see downstairs to the front door. Something was poking out from under the doormat. Warily he went down the stairs and pulled out a single piece of paper. In ragged capitals, it said:

I'M TEMPTED TO CONFESS
YOUR GUILT WILL GROW AND GROW
ONLY YOU CAN STOP ME NOW
JUST LIKE BEFORE

Farrell sucked in his breath. What did it mean? He paced up and down the confines of his small cottage for half an hour before dismissing the letter as a crude prank. It was just a shot in the dark. Everyone had a guilty conscience about something, didn't they? It clearly had nothing to do with Boyd's murder at any rate and that was all he was concerned with right now. The lettering was completely different, and Boyd's anonymous letters had been unambiguously threatening in tone, whereas this one was more couched as a sort of riddle. Probably just some yob who'd figured out he had a copper living near him and decided to have a laugh at his expense.

Utterly exhausted he climbed into his pyjamas and glanced at the towering stack of books on his bedside table. He flicked through the latest sci-fi offering from his favourite author. Tempting though it was, he didn't have the mental energy to enter another world tonight. Instead, he picked up a well-worn leather volume. Lips moving silently, he read *The Divine Office* until sleep claimed him.

CHAPTER SIX

Promptly at ten the following morning, Farrell and McLeod entered Dumfries and Galloway Royal Infirmary. Farrell glanced at McLeod and saw that she was looking apprehensive. For the first time he wondered if he should have brought her along. He'd figured she could use the experience. As they went down in the lift to the mortuary, it felt as though they were descending into the bowels of Hell. As soon as they arrived they were issued with robes and masks then bade to enter the post-mortem room.

As usual, the first thing that hit Farrell was the smell of formaldehyde, although it was the pungent smells creeping under the edges that really did for him. Feeling light-headed, he breathed shallowly and tried not to gag. Boyd's body was laid out on the slab, and Farrell had to struggle not to avert his eyes. This was the first post-mortem he'd attended where he actually knew the victim. As he saw the pitiably frail body that had been disguised by the magnificent silk vestments of the Church he felt like the worst kind of voyeur. He glanced at McLeod. She was pale but bearing up.

The pathologist gave them a brief nod before starting to dictate. As it was a murder investigation, Bartle-White was assisted by an independent visiting professor of pathology from Glasgow.

After a while the officers were beckoned over by an imperious gloved finger. Bartle-White pointed to the neck of the deceased.

'Cause of death, I would say, has been strangulation. The ligature seems to have been some kind of chain; see those indentations?'

'Could it have been a rosary?' asked Farrell, feeling sick to the pit of his stomach.

The pathologist stepped back, thought for a moment. 'I suppose it's possible, although it would have had to have been very strong to withstand the force applied.'

'How about this?' asked Farrell, pulling an evidence bag out of his pocket. 'This was wrapped round the victim's hands.'

Bartle-White studied the rosary carefully and turned once more to the deceased.

'Yes, I should say that in all likelihood that is the murder weapon. Did it belong to the deceased?'

Farrell slapped his head in annoyance.

'McLeod, once you're done here, go and see Father Malone and get him to confirm whether or not this rosary belonged to Boyd.'

'I would say that death occurred between 10 p.m. and midnight and that, judging by the lividity of the corpse, the body was not subsequently moved. There is a depressed fracture of the skull, which is the source of all the blood, but that was not of sufficient severity to have killed him outright,' continued Bartle-White, in the manner of one discussing the vagaries of the weather.

He then picked up a scalpel, and Farrell tried not to flinch as the first incision was made. The pathologist continued his work dispassionately; his dry words punctuated by the unseemly squelches of a body giving up its secrets.

'Hang on a moment, what do we have here?'

The pathologist held up a small silver object covered in blood and other gunk.

'This was lodged in the victim's digestive system. I would say it is likely it was consumed immediately prior to death,' he said, sounding bemused.

It appeared to be a small religious icon of a baby Jesus. Bartle-White cleaned it up, popped it into an evidence bag, and signed the label. Farrell co-signed the label and gave it to McLeod.

'When you go to see Father Malone ask him about this as well. Don't let on where it turned up; just ask him if it belonged to Boyd or if he's seen anything like it before. If that draws a blank, then get on to ecclesiastical suppliers; see if there's anywhere locally it could have been purchased.'

'Yes, Sir,' said McLeod. 'Should I get on it right away?' she asked hopefully.

Farrell took pity on her.

'Go on, then, scarper.'

She didn't need to be told twice.

The post-mortem threw up nothing else out of the ordinary. It transpired that Boyd, like so many priests, had turned to the bottle. His liver was shot through with cirrhosis. If he hadn't been murdered, he would likely have been dead within the year.

As Farrell drove away from the morgue he reflected that, had it not been for Boyd taking the action he did, in another twenty-five years he too might have been a lonely old man seeking solace in a bottle. Although it was out of his way, Farrell drove slowly by St Aidan's, feeling heartsore at the way things had turned out.

The church was located in a predominantly working-class area. It was a busy parish with a catchment area that took in ghetto-style housing estates where drugs spawned crime and poverty as well as the determinedly genteel areas of those who were either climbing up or sliding down the social scale: a true microcosm of society. Many here turned to religion as a means of combating their despair at the hopelessness of their situation. Others turned their back on God, rejecting Him with all the angry defiance of which they were capable. This could have been his parish had things turned out differently, had Father Boyd not ... but the man was dead. It was a matter for God to judge his actions now. As for Farrell, he must now bring his murderer to justice, regardless of his feelings about the man.

CHAPTER SEVEN

DC Mhairi McLeod shuddered as she turned the key in the ignition and quit the hospital car park with squealing tyres. Note to self. Never ever attend a post-mortem again. It was one thing reading the eventual report couched in dry medical terms, most of which she had to look up in the medical dictionary she kept in her drawer. It was another thing entirely actually being present. She wondered how the pathologist could stand to do his job; day after day, hacking into people like they were just pieces of meat. Desperately she tried to delete the images of the dead priest from her memory, but they were there to stay. Dammit. It had been a helluva couple of days. She felt her nerves were stretched as taut as a violin; one good twang and they would ping apart.

Before Farrell came along she had been aware that the other detectives had stopped taking her seriously and felt that she had failed to live up to her earlier promise. Ever since Ewan had run out on her on the eve of their wedding six months ago, she had been all over the place, more interested in having a good time than in forging ahead in her career. The career that had meant everything to her until it lost her the man that she loved. Ewan had struggled with her crazy hours, not to mention the fact that from time to time she might be placed in harm's way. What had given him the final push to end things was when she had failed to turn up for their rehearsal dinner because she had to talk a young drug addict down from the roof of the local hospital. Farrell had been loading responsibility on her from the day he arrived. Maybe he hadn't heard yet that she was a flake?

Parking outside St Aidan's, Mhairi quickly walked up the lane to the priests' house. She banged the heavy brass door-knocker. The curtains were still shut in a few of the rooms and there were smudges on the brass plate. There were no signs of life. Growing impatient she knocked again. This time, after a few seconds, she heard a door opening deep in the interior of the house accompanied by the sound of urgent footsteps. The door was flung open and a slightly dishevelled Father Malone stood there, blinking almost comically in the sunlight.

'DC McLeod … er, sorry to keep you waiting. No housekeeper, sometimes I forget …'

'No worries,' Mhairi said, smiling at the young man, who resembled a badger woken up from hibernation too soon.

'Come in,' he said, throwing wide the heavy wooden door and causing it to creak alarmingly on its hinges.

Father Malone rushed ahead of her into the same room they had been shown a few nights ago. He threw open the curtains and whisked away a pile of newspapers from an upright chair, gesturing for her to sit down. The carpet looked like it could do with a good hoover.

'Aren't there any ladies of the parish who could come in to give you a helping hand until Mary is able to return?' she asked.

'Too many, that's the trouble. If I let one in to help they'll all want to do it and then it'll be …'

'Needlepoint at dawn,' Mhairi finished with a grin.

'Something like that,' he said.

Mhairi fished in her handbag and brought out the two evidence bags that Farrell had given her. Father Malone saw what she was doing and started to look anxious.

'Do you recognize this rosary?' Mhairi asked, passing the sealed bag to him.

The priest looked at it carefully then handed it back.

'No, it's not one I've seen him use.'

'How about this little ornament?'

She handed him the other bag, feeling nauseous again as she remembered where it had been found.

Again, Father Malone stared at the item intently through the plastic.

'It looks like it might have been removed from a nativity scene but I can't say it's ringing any bells with me, I'm afraid,' he said.

'If you need any religious items, like rosaries or statues, can you tell me where you would get them?' asked Mhairi.

'Well, there's a place in Edinburgh I know we have used. Let me just look up the address.'

He retrieved a battered address book from the old-fashioned sideboard and flicked through the pages. He then wrote an address down and handed it to her.

Suddenly, the door-knocker sounded with a thump causing them both to jump. Father Malone went to answer it, and Mhairi put the items carefully back in the zip compartment of her bag before standing up and following him out.

Father Malone was having a whispered conversation with a craggily handsome man in jeans and a fisherman's sweater. As she approached silently there was something in their body language that made her feel uncomfortable, as though she was intruding.

'Look, it's not a good time. The police are here. You have to leave …'

'Don't mind me,' Mhairi said behind them.

Father Malone sprang back from the door as though he'd been stung, his face flushing deep red. An expression of annoyance flitted across the other man's face but Mhairi couldn't tell if he was annoyed with the priest or annoyed with her for interrupting them.

Mhairi thanked Father Malone and walked down the steps, resisting the impulse to look back and see if the man had been ushered inside. What was that all about, she wondered?

Back at the station, Mhairi checked in the evidence bags. As she went past DCI Lind's office he glanced up and beckoned to her to come in. Although she'd been pulled up by him a few times, she had a lot of respect for the DCI. He always strived to be fair and, unlike a lot of the blokes in the station, he had never tried to come on to her.

'Come in, Mhairi,' he said. 'How was the post-mortem?'

'Absolutely gross, Sir.'

'It's something you never quite get used to, which is probably a good thing. Anything useful come out of it?'

'It looks like he was strangled with some rosary beads. He also had his head bashed in, er, I mean a depressed fracture of the skull, but that wasn't the cause of death, Sir.'

'What else?'

Mhairi's face screwed up in remembered disgust.

'They pulled out an ornament of a baby from his digestive tract, Sir.'

Lind raised his eyebrows.

'And I thought this case couldn't get any weirder,' he sighed.

Mhairi returned to her desk, called up the digital images of the rosary and religious icon she had taken earlier, and emailed a query to the address Father Malone had given her. This case was really freaking her out. She'd never known anything like it.

CHAPTER EIGHT

Farrell sat behind his desk and pulled an overflowing basket towards him. So much for the concept of a paperless office. The reports on his desk were multiplying like bacteria. He pulled a sheaf of brightly coloured charts that had been sent up by the civilian intelligence analyst towards him. Quickly scanning them, he soon realized that they told him nothing new. There simply wasn't enough data available yet to pinpoint any specific patterns forming. He took a sip of the mud-coloured coffee he had grabbed on the way up and pulled a face. Pure gut rot. He glugged it down anyway. Needs must. If they could uncover a motive in this case it might lead to the killer. What had the dead priest done that had been so heinous it had led to his murder? Could he have interfered with somebody's kid? Farrell thought back to his own years as an altar boy and couldn't recall a single instance when Boyd's conduct had made him uneasy. It didn't fit the mode of killing either. An outraged father would have charged at Boyd like a bull at a gate. There would have been no finessing at the crime scene. Unless, of course, the killer had dressed it up to look like a nut job to throw them off the scent. It was no good. He was going round in circles. Glancing at his watch, Farrell realized it was nearly time for the final briefing of the day.

On the way to the MCA room he decided to pay a visit to the tiny fingerprint lab, where any prints from the murder crime scene would be undergoing analysis. A middle-aged civilian woman was hard at work with her back to him, and he couldn't for the life of him remember her name.

'Hi there, er …'

She spun round to face him and was wearing a name tag. Saved.

'Barbara, how's it going?' he said, aiming for a jovial tone. Name tags might be the answer to his prayers, on the one hand, but he always felt uncomfortable having to read it off a woman's chest. That was a whole other can of worms in the hermetically sealed politically correct goldfish bowl they all had to operate in these days.

Not being inhibited by any rank she promptly shot him down in flames.

'Now then, Inspector Farrell, it'll take as long as it takes. There's no point going out of your way to try and butter me up. When I get something you'll be the first to know. Now, was there anything else, or will I be getting on with my work now?'

'Yes, just you carry on,' said Farrell, turning swiftly on his heel. Talk about taking no prisoners. Feathers distinctly ruffled he headed for the MCA room.

The alarm on his watch beeped. He reached into his pocket automatically, to pop a pill, then withdrew his hand. Surely one day wouldn't hurt? He was already shattered and didn't want to take anything with a sedative effect, however minimal.

In the MCA room, Farrell started briefing the Investigation Team, which got bigger and bigger all the time as more and more officers became involved. Initial door-to-door enquiries had drawn a blank. No one had seen or heard anything. Time to widen out the search.

'DS Byers, any leads thrown up by HOLMES?'

Byers gave a hollow laugh.

'Are you kidding, Sir? All the initial statements have been fed into the system and it's throwing out names, cars, and streets like there's no tomorrow.'

'Keep on it with the rest of your team then, Byers. Let me know if anything interesting comes to the fore,' said Farrell. He'd put Byers in charge of an eager team of young constables figuring it might make him more motivated.

'DS Stirling, how did your meeting with the sister go this afternoon?'

'Different to what I expected, Sir. She's quite a formidable lady. It was as if she was more bothered about the embarrassment of him being murdered than the fact that he was dead. A real cold fish.'

'Any idea of who might want to kill him?' asked Farrell.

'Not a clue, Sir,' said Stirling. 'Her precise words were … I don't exactly move in those sorts of circles.'

A ripple of hilarity wound round the room, dying down as Farrell's face remained expressionless. He gave them all a hard stare. Some shifted nervously in their seats.

'So,' he said slowly, 'what you're telling me is that we don't yet have a single hot lead in this investigation?' He paused for effect and then thundered. 'That's not good enough. Get back out there; keep interviewing till you uncover something worthwhile. Interview parishioners, the sewing circle, the postman. I want no avenue of enquiry left unexplored. A man has died a horrible death. We owe it to him to apprehend the killer and by God that is what we're going to do.'

Farrell swept out of the room and there was a flurry of activity as the door shut behind him. He was troubled by the lack of progress in the case. The first forty-eight hours in a murder investigation were crucial and so far they had next to nothing to go on.

CHAPTER NINE

Farrell was hard at work compiling charts in his office when DCI Lind burst through the door like a tornado startling him out of his concentration. He could see at once from Lind's face that it was bad news.

'John, what's happened?'

'It's Laura.'

Farrell felt his heart scud against his chest like it was trying to get out.

'She's been taken up to the Infirmary. They called me from the ambulance. Seems she had a fall. The baby … might not make it.' Lind sagged against the side of the desk, as though his legs were going from under him.

'John, I'm really sorry.' Farrell felt helpless. He awkwardly patted his friend on the shoulder.

'Laura's mother is still in Carlisle, shopping. I can't get hold of her. I was wondering—'

'Anything, anything at all,' butted in Farrell.

'Do you think you could nip to my place and babysit the kids? A neighbour is minding them just now but she has to leave soon. I don't have time to find anyone else. I need to get to the hospital right away.'

'Sure,' said Farrell. 'Now get yourself off, I'll sort the kids out.'

Lind handed him a key and started to rush out the door then paused and slowly turned round.

'One more thing,' he said.

'Name it,' Farrell said.

'Could you … pray for us? I know I'm being a hypocrite, being an atheist and all that but …'

'Try and stop me,' said Farrell. 'Now, away you go.'

Lind tore off, every muscle in his body taut with tension.

Twenty minutes later, Farrell pulled up outside a semi-detached Victorian house in a leafy street in the old part of town. The warm brown sandstone had tendrils of pink clematis and sweet-smelling honeysuckle probing randomly into nooks and crannies. A homemade swing hung from the spreading branches of an ancient beech tree over the well-maintained lawn. Tucked in one corner was a sandpit with a bunch of buckets and spades.

As Farrell inserted the key into the lock, he felt his skin crawl with envy at the thought of John coming home each night to find Laura waiting for him. Annoyed with himself, he pushed the unwelcome thought away.

Inside, the house was warm and welcoming, as he had known it would be, with sanded wooden floors and brightly coloured rugs. From the hallway a palette of warm reds and yellows led into the various rooms. The neighbour, her eye on the clock, rushed past him apologizing for not being able to stay longer. As he shut the door behind her and found his way into the living room he was immediately clocked by four pairs of eyes. Crikey, kids weren't exactly his specialist subject. At a guess he'd say the girl and three boys ranged in age from eighteen months to six years with the girl being the eldest.

Adopting a falsely hearty tone that convinced no one, he introduced himself, babbling inanely all the while like an Energiser Bunny. The children sat motionless on the couch saying not a word; their behaviour good to the point of scary. The only sound was the youngest sucking rhythmically on an old cotton blanket when Farrell paused for breath. He regarded them quizzically. They stared at him. One of the youngest boys started to speak, but was immediately shushed by his older sister.

'We're not allowed to speak to strangers,' she announced in a clear voice.

'Quite right too,' said Farrell. 'But I'm not a stranger.'

'That's what a stranger would say. We've never met you before,' said the girl with unanswerable logic.

The lower lips of two of the boys started to wobble. Farrell was twisting like a fish on a hook. Suddenly, he had it. Rummaging about in his wallet he produced an old photograph of him, Laura, and John taken when they were around eighteen. He showed it to the girl, who solemnly inspected it.

'It's you, mummy and daddy. Daddy's got hair!' she said, sounding surprised.

'Can we play with him, now, Molly?' asked one of the little boys.

Molly nodded decisively and with a loud whoop the boys launched themselves at him.

'Let's play wrestling,' they shouted, catching Farrell off balance.

He was then run ragged for the next hour until he received a polite tap on the shoulder from Molly, who had been reading a book, holding herself aloof from the boys' antics.

'Excuse me, what's for tea?'

Farrell foraged in the freezer and discovered some pizza and chips. He sat the kids together on the couch while it was heating in the oven. The eldest child, Molly, had such a look of Laura about her it made his breath catch in his throat. The same dark brown curls, solemn blue eyes, and dimpled chin. Already she was like a little mother hen: soothing baby Adam on her knee and silencing the two boys, Luke and Hugh, who had started to argue over a toy car.

The microwave interrupted his reverie with a ping, and he was then run off his feet for what felt like hours; shovelling food into a reluctant mouth, a stinky nappy, baths, and story time. Eventually, come 8 p.m., the kids were all settled in bed, and Farrell collapsed into a chair, more tired than he'd been for years.

Keeping his voice low, he telephoned the station and was put through to DS Stirling.

'Just checking in. Any developments?'

'Sod all,' said Stirling, sounding frustrated. 'Door-to-door enquiries revealed diddly-squat. Nobody seems to have seen or heard a thing.'

Farrell could picture the scene only too well. Everybody pumped up on caffeine and adrenalin ready to charge out the door and catch a killer. How could such a violent murderer have retained sufficient self-control to slip away leaving no obvious clues behind him? The trail was already starting to go cold, which didn't bode well. He couldn't share his worries with Stirling though; it was important to keep morale and energy high.

'Early days, yet. Once we get forensics back I'm sure that will open up a few lines of enquiry.'

'Any word on how John's wife is doing? She's a lovely lass, doesn't seem fair,' said Stirling.

'Nothing yet. Keep me posted.' He terminated the call and listened carefully. Not a sound from upstairs.

After a while the silence started to feel oppressive, and Farrell took out the rosary he carried everywhere and began to pray for Laura and the baby, lips moving silently as he repeated the soothing incantations. Such was his concentration he failed to notice that John had slipped in and was regarding him with troubled eyes. A polite cough had him stuffing the rosary in his pocket and leaping up out of the chair like he'd been caught doing something illicit.

'How is she?' he asked.

'She'll be fine,' said Lind wearily.

'And the baby?'

'Didn't make it,' Lind said. 'Stillborn. A girl …'

Farrell moved towards him, but Lind put his hands up creating a barrier. Farrell could now see that his friend's eyes were brimming with tears that threatened to spill.

'Don't,' said Lind, voice wavering.

'Would it help to talk?' Farrell steeled himself to ask.

'Not now,' said Lind. 'Look, Frank, I can't thank you enough for stepping into the breach like that …'

'Hey, what are friends for?' said Farrell. 'You sure you'll be OK here on your own?'

'I'll see you tomorrow, yeah?' said Lind.

'Right you are,' said Farrell.

As he glanced back at the house, now wrapped in shadow, Farrell felt the weight of his friend's sorrow pressing against his chest. He prayed for the soul of their stillborn child and that they be given the strength to bear it.

CHAPTER TEN

After a disturbed night's sleep, Farrell was hotfooting it down to the Major Crime Administration room after getting his usual caffeine fix when he saw Lind bearing down on him, his face set in an uncharacteristically grim expression. Immediately, Farrell tensed. Had Laura taken a turn for the worse? Lind halted in front of him, his personal anguish bricked up behind a brisk demeanour.

'Twin boys have been abducted from Happy Faces Nursery in Catherine Street. I'll coordinate the search from here. I've appointed DI Moore to head up the investigation. However, being a small force, we need all hands on deck for this one. I want you to drive to the nursery and see what you can get from the woman in charge. She didn't make much sense on the phone. Then get over to the parents. The kids are only three years old. What they must be going through …'

Lind spun on his heel, barking orders at the swarm of officers buzzing around him as he went.

Galvanized into action, Farrell grabbed his jacket and keys and took off down the corridor.

'McLeod,' he bellowed. 'You're with me.'

Mhairi emerged from the ladies at a brisk trot looking disgruntled.

'Is nothing sacred?' she grumbled as she trotted to keep up with her boss's loping stride.

'Two three-year-olds are missing from their nursery. It seems they've been abducted by some nutter.'

'Who's the Family Liaison Officer, Sir?'

Farrell thought for a moment.

'You are, if DI Moore has no objection. That's if you think you can handle it?'

'I'm sure I can, Sir.'

Their eyes met in sombre recognition. Dealing with relatives was hard enough at the best of times, but when there was a possibility that some sick creep might have killed two little kids the job would be harrowing in the extreme.

The nursery was located in a sandstone-terraced house near the Ewart Library. Cheerful pictures and smiley faces adorned the windows. As Farrell and McLeod pulled up into the adjacent kerb they had to dodge a stampede of hysterical mothers bearing their offspring away. The jungle drums had been beating in the manner of all small towns. Frightened by the commotion, the youngsters were bawling their eyes out. A crowd of onlookers were already starting to gather, ready to stake their claim in what might turn out to be a tragedy.

A slender middle-aged woman with red-rimmed eyes came to the door. Wordlessly she let them in and took them into a small tidy office. She gestured for them to sit opposite her.

'I'm DI Farrell and this is Detective Constable McLeod,' started Farrell. 'And you are?'

'Janet McDougall; I own the nursery.' Her eyes filled and she clasped her hands together to stop them shaking.

'Who else works here?'

'There were three of us on duty today: myself, and two nursery assistants, Fiona Thomson and Gill Brown. They didn't see anything as Fiona was settling the babies in another room and Gill was leading story-time in the quiet room.'

Farrell asked Mhairi to nip out and take preliminary statements from the two young women waiting outside the office, one of whom was weeping quietly while being comforted by the other. The last remaining children had now clearly left. He returned to his seat.

'Can you tell me exactly what happened when Mark and Jamie Summers were taken?'

'This man came,' she began. 'He said he was from the social work department, had an ID card with him.'

'Did you examine it carefully?' asked Farrell, holding her gaze.

Janet McDougall flushed but didn't look away.

'Of course, I did. It looked absolutely authentic. He was even wearing the same tie in the photo as he had on when he came here.'

'What time did he arrive?'

'It was shortly after nine; the boys had been dropped off by their mum at around 8.15. She works at that firm of accountants in Irish Street.'

'What exactly did he tell you?' asked Farrell.

'He told me the boys' father had been in a bad car accident on his way to Glasgow, might not even survive.'

'Go on.'

'The mother had gone on ahead to the hospital, he said. He'd been asked to take the boys to join her. He gave me this.'

With shaking hands, she pulled a letter out of her pocket. It was a handwritten note, apparently from the mother, asking the nursery to hand over the boys to David Nolan, social worker.

Farrell immediately radioed the station so that they could verify whether or not a David Nolan actually existed within the social work department.

He was careful to keep any note of censure out of his voice.

'Did you recognize the handwriting?'

'I hadn't had much in the way of letters from her before but

I did compare her signature with something I had on file. It matched, or I thought it did …' she added miserably.

Turning away from them she rummaged through a file with shaking hands and produced a consent form. Farrell scrutinized the two signatures. They looked alike, if not identical. The abductor had done his homework. His radio crackled into life.

'DS Byers here. There's a David Nolan all right. He's been off for months on the sick.'

'Put a call in to Cornwall Mount and request a firearms team be mobilized as soon as can be arranged to surround Nolan's house. He might or might not be armed but I'm not taking any chances where young kids are concerned. We'll also need uniformed backup. Bring Lind and DI Moore up to speed.'

'This man,' said Farrell, 'what did he look like? Tell me anything you can remember.'

'He was tall, very tall. About your height and build.'

'What colour were his eyes?'

'Green.'

'Are you certain?'

'Yes. He had glasses on, but at one point he took them off, gave them a wipe and put them on again. Now I think about it he had cold eyes. His mouth smiled but his eyes didn't. Oh God, what have I done?' she moaned.

'What colour was his hair?'

'Dark, very dark. He had a lot of it. And a large beard covering most of his face, but very tidy.'

'Any distinguishing marks? Scars, tattoos?'

'I can't remember anything like that but, thinking back, there wasn't all that much of his skin visible.'

'What was he wearing?'

'He looked very professional, had a suit on, navy I think, and a red tie over a white shirt. He looked … respectable.'

'What made you call the police if you had been satisfied he was genuine?'

'Their mother called to say that Jamie had forgotten his lunchbox. I knew then.' She started to sob again. 'If anything happens to those little boys, I'll never forgive myself. It was my job to keep them safe.'

Farrell placed his hand on her arm and gave it a squeeze. He said nothing. What was there to say?

'Do you have any recent photos of Mark and Jamie?'

Janet McDougall jumped up and walked over to a brightly coloured wall display.

'Here's one. They were playing at the sandpit out back.' She choked back a sob as she handed it over.

Farrell's throat tightened as he beheld the two toddlers grinning happily into the camera, each with wide blue eyes and blond hair flopping over their foreheads. They were dressed identically in shorts and T-shirts and could have been clones of each other.

'Can I see out the back where this was taken?' he asked.

So desperate to help that she almost overturned her chair, Janet MacDougall jumped up and showed him through the kitchen to the back door. A large tray of small milk bottles sat untouched beside a plate of home-baked biscuits.

The backyard was securely fenced, with a large sandpit area, a tree with a low-slung tyre attached to a rope, and a few ride-on toy tractors and cars. Behind the yard was a private lane opening into the gardens of adjacent sandstone houses. While the fence was too high for small children to climb out, a reasonably tall adult could see into the yard and see the children playing when walking by.

'Do you think he's been watching us for a while?' she asked, eyes darting everywhere.

'Very possibly,' answered Farrell. 'I must get going now but, if anything else occurs to you in the meantime, here's my card. Someone will be in touch to arrange for you to come into the station shortly to work with an identikit sketch artist.'

'Wait, there's one more thing,' Janet McDougall said. 'He left in a grey Primera car. I noticed the make because I've fancied one myself for ages.'

'I don't suppose you happened to notice any of the registration plate?' asked Farrell.

'No, sorry,' she whispered.

After obtaining a rough description of what the two little boys had been wearing that morning, Farrell sped back to Loreburn Street with Mhairi to deposit the photograph and descriptions with DI Moore. As expected the two nursery assistants hadn't had anything material to add.

DI Moore was sitting in a large room. Information was being fed to her from all directions. Calm and serene, she projected a quiet authority that was bringing out the best in the officers under her command.

'Have you any objections to appointing DC McLeod as Family Liaison Officer, Kate?' asked Farrell.

DI Moore turned to Mhairi.

'Have you been a FLO before, Mhairi?'

'No, Ma'am, but I am fully aware of all the duties and responsibilities that go with the position. I would like to be there for the family to help them through this.'

'You must guard against getting too emotionally involved though; don't lose your objectivity. Either or both parents could potentially be implicated.'

'No, Ma'am.'

'Even though I'm SIO on this one, Frank, I'd welcome your input as the case progresses. We're lucky to have an officer with your experience. Child abduction not linked to marital breakdown is a rarity down here.'

Her phone rang as three young constables marched into the room bearing documents and files.

Farrell told Mhairi to wait for him at the car and swung by Lind's office on the way out. He was worried about how his friend would be coping given his own recent tragedy. However, when he walked in to Lind's spacious office he came face to face with a wall of people to whom Lind was competently issuing orders. As the last officer ran out the door with Lind's instructions ringing in his ears Farrell updated him, each of them conscious of the clock ticking.

'I don't like it,' Lind said. 'Bastard has done his homework. Probably been planning this for some time.'

'Did the super sign off on the firearms team?' asked Farrell.

'Yes, we're going in at 12.30. I want you there, Farrell. There's just enough time for you and DC McLeod to get round to the parents first. The father should be back home by now. He'd been on the way to Glasgow when the kids were taken.'

CHAPTER ELEVEN

Farrell and McLeod drew up outside a detached redbrick house on the Lomax Estate out on the Edinburgh Road. There was a large grassy recreation area to one side with a sign saying 'NO BALL GAMES'.

'Must have a few bob,' said McLeod, taking in the gleaming red 4x4 in the driveway.

Farrell wondered what drove people to live in these fancy little boxes with their upwardly mobile neighbours breathing enviously down their necks. He didn't fancy it, that's for sure.

Two little bikes with round chubby wheels and stabilizers were propped up against the side of the house. Farrell glimpsed a state-of-the art climbing frame in the back garden, despite the fact they had passed a swing park not two hundred metres away.

They were ushered into the house by PC Thomson, who had been waiting with the parents until Farrell could get there. The first thing that met their eyes on going into the hall was a studio portrait of the family. Farrell paused to study it, allowing Mhairi to precede him into the lounge. An attractive woman with honey blonde hair and dimples had her arms resting on the shoulders of two mischievous-looking toddlers, who were dressed alike and had an identical smattering of freckles across upturned noses.

Their eyes were sparkling with merriment as though the photographer had just made them laugh. Positioned slightly self-consciously to the rear was a short thickset man whose eyes rested on his family rather than on the camera.

Farrell walked into the lounge feeling a weight settle on his chest. Mhairi was sitting with her arm round a shaking woman, who Farrell took to be the mother. Despite the fact that she still had her work suit on she bore little resemblance to the confident immaculately groomed woman in the photograph. Her hair was straggly and unkempt and mascara ran down channels gouged by tears.

PC Thomson looked ill at ease and as if he wished he were someplace else. Tough, thought Farrell; there was more to being a copper than running around in panda cars, chasing baddies, and the sooner the lad realized it the better.

He walked over to the woman and sat beside her on the large couch, folding both her manicured hands inside his own.

'DI Farrell. I'm so sorry that this has happened to your family. You have my assurance that we will not rest until your little boys have been returned to you.'

Dead or alive, added Farrell grimly in his own head.

'Elspeth Summers,' she said, raising her eyes to meet his.

'Can you tell me exactly what each of the boys was wearing today? The nursery teacher wasn't completely sure.' He signalled to PC Thomson, who took out his notebook, pen at the ready.

'Mark had on red joggers, a white T-shirt, and navy cardigan with Thomas the Tank Engine on the pocket, and white trainers. Jamie had green joggers, a yellow T-shirt, and a cream knitted jumper. My mother knitted it. Oh God, my mother! She doesn't know yet.'

'All in good time,' soothed Farrell. 'Jamie's shoes?'

'Black trainers.'

'Are they identical twins or fraternal?'

'Identical.'

58

Farrell heard the sound of a car pulling into the driveway with a spurt of gravel and turned his head to see a man running to the front door. Gently, he disengaged himself from Elspeth and stood up.

A red-faced man burst into the room, causing the door to slam against the wall. His eyes were frantic with anxiety and flecks of spittle sprayed out when he spoke.

'Who's in charge here?'

'That would be me, DI Farrell.'

'Why are you here? Why aren't you out looking for my sons? Anything could be happening to them while you're here … anything.'

The man started to sway, and Farrell quickly grabbed an upright chair and caught him as his legs buckled, pushing his head down between his knees until the light-headedness went.

'Barry!' remonstrated his wife from the settee, getting to her feet unsteadily. 'My husband doesn't mean it, Inspector; he's just worried sick. We both are.'

Farrell looked them both in the eyes and spoke with quiet urgency.

'Be assured that right now we've got every available officer on the streets searching high and low for Mark and Jamie. Our press officer is liaising with the media to ensure as wide coverage as possible. By lunchtime today every library, post office, school, and the town centre will be plastered with pictures of your sons and offering a reward for any information leading to their safe return. We have experts in social media sending out alerts on every possible site. We know our business and we will stop at nothing to ensure a good outcome for you and your family. The reason I've come is to try and ascertain whether you can give us any additional information that might narrow the search.'

'Like what?' asked the father, quietly this time.

'Have you noticed anyone hanging around, looking suspicious?'

'No, no one,' they said in unison.

'Have you had any cold callers? Anyone on the doorstep trying to sell you anything? Any unfamiliar cars parked nearby, particularly grey Primera cars?'

They shook their heads helplessly.

'Have you had any contact with the social work department?'

The man bristled.

'No, of course not! What are you implying?'

'The man who took your sons produced a social work ID. Does the name David Nolan mean anything to you?'

'No, should it?' asked Elspeth, anxiously.

'Is he the bastard who did this? When I get my hands on him I'll—'

'Barry! Shut up, you're not helping. While you're shouting the odds, some nutter could be harming our children.'

'You're right. I'm sorry. It's just …' He tailed off into silence.

Farrell had seen this type of bluster a number of times in similar situations. The ungovernable frustration and rage of a man who feels he has failed to protect his family. He shot a sympathetic glance at the man, who had again simmered down.

'Have you had any unusual telephone calls?'

'A couple of wrong numbers, nothing out of the ordinary,' Elspeth answered.

'Anyone threatened you recently; anyone have a grudge against you?'

'I'm a car salesman, for God's sake …' Barry said. 'Just a regular bloke …'

Farrell put a finger under his collar, which suddenly felt too tight. He paused, reluctant to clobber them with more unpalatable information.

'It's possible there may be a ransom demand in a while.'

'Is that what this is about, money?' asked Barry, eyes wide with terror.

'It's a possibility,' replied Farrell.

'But we have no money. We're in debt up to our eyeballs,' said Elspeth in a low voice.

'It's the recession. Things haven't been so good of late …' said her husband.

So it wasn't about money, thought Farrell. That didn't bode well.

'They haven't got their comforters with them,' said Elspeth, on the verge of losing it.

'Someone will be round shortly to modify your phone so that we can try and trace the call should the abductor try and contact you for any reason. Try not to give up hope. It's early days yet.'

Farrell stood up, ready to leave.

'I've appointed DC McLeod here as your Family Liaison Officer. She'll stay here with you for a while in case the man makes contact and also fill you in on any developments. She can also deal with any members of the press that decide to make a nuisance of themselves. I'm taking the other officer with me to help with the search.'

'Can I come?' blurted out Barry. 'Anything's better than just sitting here … wondering.'

Farrell looked at him. If anything had happened to those two little boys this guy wasn't going to make it.

'I'm sorry, Sir,' he said. 'It's just not possible. In any event, I think your wife needs you here.'

He gestured to Mhairi to walk him out and when they were out of earshot he said to her, 'keep your eye on him. He's not thinking straight.'

'Don't worry, Sir. I'll keep on top of the situation,' McLeod answered, her determination belied just slightly by the worry lines snaking across her forehead.

CHAPTER TWELVE

Farrell's leg jiggled with impatience as he sat in the carpeted reception area of police headquarters at Cornwall Mount. Situated well out of the town centre the light-filled atrium and tasteful foliage creeping unobtrusively around it would not look amiss in a posh hotel. Gloria, the immaculately groomed civilian receptionist, suddenly turned a full-voltage smile on him and told him to go straight on down to the armoury in the basement.

As he rounded the corner, walking past the twenty-five metre firing range, Farrell saw the firearms sergeant briefing his men in quiet emphatic tones. The atmosphere was tense with none of the usual banter. The doors to both the weapons armoury and, across the corridor, the ammunitions armoury, were still open. As his men began to file out to their waiting vehicles Sergeant Forsythe turned his measured gaze on Farrell.

'Well, Sir, what can I do you for? You'll need a bulletproof vest for starters.'

'I'd like the bog standard one, not the heavy-duty version,' requested Farrell.

The vests that the firearms team wore were damn heavy and he wanted to be able to give chase if necessary. It was well known that the members of the firearms team were among the fittest on the force. They had to be.

'I believe you're authorized to carry a firearm, Sir?'

'Just give me a Taser,' said Farrell decisively. 'That'll do me. Has DS Stirling been down to get equipped?'

'He's waiting for you in the car park, Sir.'

By the time Farrell and Stirling had driven over to Hardacre Road, Sergeant Forsythe already had his men in place. A number of uniforms were dispersed around the perimeter of the property awaiting further instructions. A cordon had been set up to keep back members of the public in case things turned nasty. The bungalow looked uncared for, as did the small rectangular garden, which was choked with weeds. There was no sign of movement from within.

Farrell and Stirling approached through the rusty gate that screeched out a warning of their approach. Farrell noticed that Stirling was trembling and chalky white. He'd selected him because of his age and experience, but looking at him now Farrell suspected his backup wouldn't amount to much. Two of the firearms team took up position behind them on either side of the front door. Farrell knocked briskly, adrenalin flooding his system, causing his heart to pound. There was no response from inside the house.

After a few seconds, he was about to give the order to bust the door down when there was a sound of a bolt sliding back on the other side. A man put his head round the door then promptly ducked back in, trying to slam it shut. Farrell was having none of it. He blocked the door with his shoulder and flashed his warrant card.

'David Nolan, we are investigating the abduction of two boys and believe that you might have information pertinent to our inquiry.'

The man silently let go of the door and trudged into the

interior of the house, followed by Stirling and Farrell. As he turned to face them they could see beads of sweat gathered on his forehead. His sweat gave off a sour odour that Farrell had encountered many times: the smell of fear.

At a nod from Farrell, Stirling proceeded to methodically search the house. Farrell plonked himself down in an armchair and crossed his legs as though this were a social call. Nolan dithered for a few seconds, unsure of how to react, then sank into the chair opposite.

'You'll find nothing here,' he said. 'Them kiddies going missing has nothing to do with me.'

Farrell was inclined to agree. David Nolan was a sorry specimen of manhood. About five feet seven inches, his hair was sparse and speckled with grey. Flaccid and pale, he had on an old pair of baggy joggers and a khaki sweatshirt that bore traces of previous meals. Hardly credible that a man like him would have the balls to carry off a crime like this. So why did he look so nervous then? What did he have to hide? There was a computer in the corner of the room with a screensaver on and Farrell noticed that Nolan's eyes periodically slithered towards it and then flicked back to him. Interesting.

Stirling came back in looking disappointed.

'Nothing, Sir. No sign the boys have ever been here.'

Nolan looked smug. Farrell gave him a hard stare then walked purposefully towards the computer.

Nolan jumped to his feet and shouted, 'stay away from that, you've got no right. Leave it alone.'

'Oops,' said Farrell theatrically and stumbled.

As he put out his hands, ostensibly to save himself, he pressed the mouse on the computer and the screensaver vanished. Farrell blanched. Behind him he heard Stirling curse. Hardened as he'd had to become to the darker side of human nature, Farrell had rarely seen anything as horrific as the images of child pornography that dominated the screen. The suffering in the eyes of that small child would haunt him for a long time to come.

'It's not mine. Someone's trying to set me up,' whined Nolan as Farrell roughly snapped the handcuffs on and read him his rights, barely able to contain his fury.

Farrell left Stirling to supervise the seizure of the computer and search for further evidence then made his way back to the station. If it wasn't this creep was it possible that the abductor of the twins had flagged him deliberately? Or was it simply a convenient theft of identity? At any rate it would give the vice boys something to chew on and, with a bit of luck, Nolan would give up some other low-lives into the bargain. He didn't strike Farrell as the stoical type.

CHAPTER THIRTEEN

Back at the station, Farrell dodged into the washroom and soaped his face and arms up to the elbows then did it again for good measure. Sometimes this job made him feel so polluted he imagined the grime seeped right into his soul. As he rinsed off he caught a glimpse of his enraged face in the mirror and slammed his fist into the wall beside it, wishing it was Nolan's face. The pain would help to calm him. He didn't often lose his self-control, which had been hard won over the years, but right now he was spoiling for a fight. Anything to get those images elbowed out of his mind. Struggling for composure, he took a few deep breaths and gradually regained mastery over his emotions. Checking in the mirror that his face was once more cool and impassive, giving nothing away, he strode back out into the corridor.

As he passed the conference suite, he glanced through the glass door and saw Border TV setting up for a televised appeal. Mhairi was inside with DI Moore and the family. He caught her eye and beckoned to her and she excused herself and hurried over.

'How are they holding up?' Farrell asked, but really he wanted to see how she was holding up, since he had taken something of a gamble in having her appointed as FLO.

'Not so good, Sir,' she replied. 'But, I guess that's to be expected.

We had all been hoping that Nolan had them at the house so that was a massive blow. Do you think he knows the kidnapper, Sir?'

'I doubt it but he might know something that we can use. He's being interviewed shortly by DCI Lind and DS Byers. And how are you managing, Mhairi?'

'Fine, Sir. I mean it's challenging and exhausting but nothing compared to what the parents are going through.'

Farrell could see the parents, Elspeth and Barry, being led to the table by DI Moore and the reporter taking up her position in readiness.

'You'd better get back in there. I reckon they're about to start. Keep me posted.'

'Will do, Sir.'

Farrell's radio beeped. He'd asked Byers to let him know when Nolan was due to be questioned as he wanted to watch the interview take place from behind the one-way mirror in the adjacent room. There was nothing further he could do on the Boyd case for the time being and he wanted to keep up to speed on the missing boys just in case Lind needed backup. DI Moore seemed to have things well under control but he didn't yet fully have her measure. His old friend hadn't had an opportunity to grieve for his lost daughter yet, and a case of this sort was hard enough at the best of times. It would also give him an opportunity to observe Byers in action as he hadn't been all that impressed with what he had seen so far.

David Nolan cut a forlorn figure slumped in a plastic chair in the interview room, which, like the table, was bolted to the floor. He appeared to be sporting a few cuts and bruises more than the last time Farrell had clapped eyes on him, which he struggled to feel sorry about. Nolan's young solicitor was obviously a local man as Byers and Stirling seemed to know him and had been exchanging small talk while setting up the recording equipment.

The parties introduced themselves for the benefit of the tape, and Farrell learned the solicitor was called Brian Whitelaw. Stirling kicked off the questioning.

'I am reminding you that you are still under caution and that anything you say can be used against you in court, do you understand?'

Nolan nodded.

'For the tape, please?'

'Yes.'

'Is your full name David Henry Nolan?'

'Yes.'

'Date of birth?'

'Fourteenth of the first, seventy-three.'

'How long have you been a social worker with Dumfries and Galloway Council?'

'Ten years.'

'What department do you work in?'

There was a pause. Nolan stared at the table.

'Well?'

'Child protection,' he muttered.

From his vantage point, Farrell could see Stirling clench and then uncurl his fists under the table.

'Look!' burst out Nolan, shrugging off the restraining arm of his solicitor. 'I know how this looks but I would NEVER actually harm a child. I'm not even a bloody paedophile. At least, I don't think I am.'

Byers leaned across the table, his face reddening with fury.

'Those kids bloody happy to be photographed while those things are done to them, are they?'

'Byers!' snapped Stirling. 'I'll take it from here.'

Byers subsided, but fury still blazed in his eyes. Farrell wondered if he'd been the architect of the cuts and bruises.

'What do you mean?' asked Stirling.

'I've been depressed. Me and my wife got divorced. I went on a real downer. Had to go on the sick. Thought I was going mad staring at four walls all day. I started watching porn, just for something to do but I couldn't feel anything. I started to look at harder stuff. Still nothing. Then some random kid stuff came up. It repulsed me but it made me feel something. Breaking that taboo made me scared but it made me feel alive again. I know that sounds bloody crazy but I'm trying to be honest.'

Too bloody honest, said the annoyed expression on his solicitor's face.

'Did you tell anyone what you'd been doing?' asked Stirling.

'Of course not. I knew how people would react. A year ago I would most likely have been one of them.'

'Have you had any unusual phone calls recently?' asked Stirling.

'Human Resources phoned last week to check on how long I was intending to remain off on the sick. First time they've phoned since I went off a year ago. Probably gearing up to sack me, the bastards.'

Stirling glanced at Byers but he was already writing in his notebook. Not so slow on the uptake as Farrell had thought.

'Have you ordered any replacement credit cards, bank cards, driving licence, passport, anything like that?' asked Stirling.

'I ordered a new bank card,' Nolan said. 'Come to think of it, bloody thing never arrived. I haven't had a statement for a while either. It's like you cease to exist when you're on the sick,' Nolan said with a self-pitying whine in his voice.

'Have you had anyone at the door trying to sell you anything?' asked Byers.

'I thought the Jehovah's Witnesses were bad enough but last week I'd a Catholic priest round trying to get me to sign up for some missionary newsletter.'

Stirling and Byers looked indifferent to this information, but Farrell frowned. That was odd. The Catholic Church was old school and didn't cold call as far as he was aware. He waited to see if they asked Nolan for a description, but they didn't.

'Did you sign anything?' interjected Byers.

'Eventually, just to get rid of him. Took persistent to a whole new level. And you can't exactly roughhouse a priest, can you?'

Plenty have tried, thought Farrell.

'Anyone or anything else?' asked Stirling.

'That's all I can think of …' answered Nolan.

The interview was terminated, and Nolan was remanded in custody to appear before the Sheriff the next morning.

Farrell slipped quietly out of the room before they became aware he had been listening in.

Before he went home he stopped by the MCA room and had a word with the Duty Sergeant. Still nothing concrete had emerged from the investigation. As Lind and Moore appeared to be making all the right moves and coping as well as could be expected, he resolved to focus his complete attention on the Boyd case from now on.

CHAPTER FOURTEEN

Farrell breakfasted on a bacon roll and two caffeine tablets washed down with a strong cup of coffee from the canteen. Within a few minutes he could feel the fog in his brain lifting and started to feel more alert. Although it was only the back of six he popped his head round Lind's door on the way past, not really expecting to see him in this early after what had happened with Laura the other day. Somewhat to his surprise his friend was immersed in paperwork, looking like he'd been sitting there for some time.

'Any leads on the kids' whereabouts yet?' asked Farrell.

'Not a dickie bird,' replied Lind. 'There's been no ransom note either. Bastard has just spirited them into thin air.'

'What about the car? Nothing doing there?'

'Turns out it was stolen. Owner reported it missing when he got back from work last night. It was found torched in the early hours of the morning out the back of the Labour Club.'

'Anything I can do to help?' asked Farrell.

'I think we've got all bases covered. The boys' pictures are everywhere: in social media, the papers, on leaflets. Border News televised an appeal by the parents last night. Did you catch it?'

'Just the tail end,' said Farrell. 'I take it the phones have been ringing off the hook ever since?'

'We've got officers working round the clock on dedicated lines but nothing concrete yet. Right now I need you to prioritize the murder investigation. The bishop is demanding daily updates, and I don't need to tell you that the super would like nothing more than to dish your head up to him on a silver salver.'

'You got that right. Don't worry. I'm sure we'll catch a break in the case soon,' said Farrell, sounding more confident than he actually felt. He turned and left the room without sharing with Lind his plans for the later part of the day.

Farrell glanced at his watch. It was time to go to the railway station and meet his old friend and spiritual adviser, Father Joe Spinelli. Given that he was in Boyd's appointment diary, Farrell knew that he ought, by rights, to be conducting the interview at the station, to make things official, but no way was he going to put someone he revered so highly in a smelly interview room and have his soul polluted by the experience. Farrell had invited him to stay at Kelton, where he was sure he would be able to draw out any information that might be pertinent to the investigation.

Two hours later, as he served the elderly priest a modest helping of chilli, Farrell couldn't help but feel an anticipatory pang of loss. Joe was now in his late seventies and looking increasingly frail. He had retired from active work in his Edinburgh parish and had an almost ethereal look about him, as if he was not long for this world. After his friend had said grace and eaten a few mouthfuls his pale face relaxed a little.

'I see you still like your Gregorian chants, Frank,' he said with a wry smile. 'I thought that after all this time your tastes might have become a little more secular.'

'I like my music to transport me not thrash me over the head with an iron bar,' replied Farrell.

His friend looked troubled.

'Interesting metaphor,' he said. 'It must be a struggle to maintain your connection to the Divine when you are mired in such violence.'

'You're reading way too much into this. It was just the first random thing that came into my head,' protested Farrell.

'Exactly,' said Father Joe.

Farrell glared at him, exasperated.

'While we're on the subject of my job there's something I need to ask you, Joe.'

'I'll answer if I can,' the priest replied.

'Father Boyd was due to meet with you. Can you tell me what about?'

The elderly priest sighed and looked away.

'I was his spiritual adviser, just as I am yours.'

'For how long?' asked Farrell, trying hard to keep the feeling of betrayal out of his voice.

'Does it matter?' asked the priest. 'Long enough. Longer than you. Your paths didn't cross until afterwards. I thought you would get over it. I thought I could help you resolve the hatred and bitterness within your heart. I was wrong, I see that now.'

Farrell felt trapped in a maelstrom of emotion that threatened to overwhelm his carefully constructed defences. He had to focus, concentrate on the case rather than what this meant for him personally.

'I must bring his murderer to justice, Joe, don't you see? Maybe, in the process of doing so, I can finally begin to forgive him for what he put me through. I need to know if there was something in his past that might provide a motive for someone to kill him. You were his confessor, his spiritual adviser, maybe even his friend. Be his advocate. Tell me what I need to know,' begged Farrell, clasping the priest's hand.

Father Joe initially struggled, like his hand was a captive bird, but then the fight went out of him and he slumped in his seat.

'Very well,' he said. 'I don't have all the answers you're looking for. If I did, I would have been in touch before now. However, I can tell you there were a number of things troubling him shortly before his death.'

'When was the last time you saw him?' asked Farrell.

'I used to meet with him up in Edinburgh once every two months, more if required. The last time I saw him was the Friday before he died.'

Farrell leaned forward in his seat. 'Go on.'

'He was concerned about the young priest, Father Malone. He believed he was struggling to maintain a celibate lifestyle.'

'A woman?' asked Farrell.

'Would that it was that simple,' said the priest with a heavy sigh.

'You don't mean …?'

'Yes, I'm afraid so.'

'Was Boyd going to take the matter to the bishop?'

'I believe that was his intention, yes. He was going to give Father Malone one further opportunity to—'

'To what? Toe the party line or else?'

'I wouldn't put it quite like that, but in essence …'

'The housekeeper mentioned she'd overheard them arguing the night Boyd was murdered,' said Farrell.

Father Joe clutched the table.

'What are you saying? You don't think that …?'

'I don't know what to think,' replied Farrell. 'If Boyd had simply been hit over the head with a vase in the heat of the moment I might figure maybe it was Malone, but the way he was killed … that was real evil at work.'

'Unless it was calculated to throw you off the scent; convince you that you were dealing with something entirely different in character.'

Farrell sat back in his chair and regarded the elderly priest quizzically.

'I can't believe you just came out with that,' he said.

'I don't know why you find it surprising,' Father Joe said with a sad smile. 'After a lifetime of service in the Church I have seen how the human soul can transcend its existence and become a thing of beauty no matter what its earthly travail. I have also seen how easily a Godless soul can be polluted by evil until it is a scream of agony contaminating everything it touches.'

'And here's me thinking a man of the cloth like you just sits in his ivory tower counting rosary beads all day,' said Farrell, trying to lighten the atmosphere.

Father Joe laughed and the tension momentarily left his shoulders.

'Did Father Boyd know that he was running out of time?' asked Farrell.

'He was aware he had months rather than years left to live.'

The elderly priest paused and looked away.

Farrell leaned forward in his chair. 'What is it, Joe? What aren't you telling me? There's something else, isn't there?'

'He talked about you, that last Friday.'

'Me? What about me?' asked Farrell.

'The way he had behaved towards you in the past. I got the impression that it was weighing heavily upon him and that he wished to make amends. He also seemed to think he had wronged your mother.'

'My mother? What's she got to do with anything?'

'It's probably nothing. He'd had a couple of brandies after dinner, said it helped with the pain. I didn't like to press him.'

Farrell suddenly became aware that Father Joe was looking exhausted and felt a prickle of guilt. He poured two coffees and led the elderly priest upstairs to a comfortable seat in the lounge with panoramic views over the River Nith to the rolling hills beyond. In companionable silence they sat together enjoying the view to the uplifting strains of Bach.

CHAPTER FIFTEEN

The next morning, Farrell arrived at the Crichton Hospital and ducked into the men's room before announcing himself at reception. He splashed his face with cold water. The face that looked back at him out of the mirror gave nothing away. Good, that was how he wanted it.

Sitting in the waiting room, he remembered the last time he had been waiting here to see Dr Clare Yates. Mental illness was something he wouldn't wish on his worst enemy. It stripped you bare, turned you inside out for others to gawp at. A lot of what had happened to him was mercifully blank. He could still, however, remember the gut-wrenching terror afforded by the paranoid delusions. The episode of psychosis had never reoccurred although the fear that it might was like a persistent needle in the psyche that never let him alone.

He had had to submit to a stringent psychiatric evaluation when he joined the police and had to submit an annual report from his psychiatrist in Edinburgh to confirm that he was still of sound mind and cooperating with his treatment plan. He seriously doubted that there was any point in taking the tiny maintenance dose prescribed but he didn't feel inclined to make a fuss. He had been lucky to be taken on back then and he knew it.

Clare Yates had been like a cool drink of water to a man dying of thirst. Back then, still in her twenties, she had the effortless poise and confidence enjoyed by the alpha female at the top of her game. After years of depriving himself of female company he had fallen for her like a ton of bricks, mistaking clinical passion and concerned glances for something else. Recalling the moment when he had leaned across and kissed her on the mouth he remembered with shame the revulsion he had seen on her face. After that, he'd been referred to someone else, a senior male psychiatrist, who'd eventually stitched his shattered self back into something capable of masquerading as normality. Over time, the pretence became real.

Farrell gave himself a mental shake. He hadn't thought about Clare Yates for years. What was the matter with him? It must be being here in this room that had triggered all these unwanted memories. He was a police inspector now, a grown man in a position of authority not some broken-down washed-up priest. She'd better not try and stonewall him or she'd soon see he meant business.

Farrell determinedly squashed the small jolt of excitement he felt when she walked through the door. Her hair was different. The short cut that had framed her elfin features had gone and in its place were long tumbling dark curls. It suited the woman she had become. He stood up and approached her decisively. It gave him a huge measure of satisfaction to see that she looked even more ill at ease than he did. Determined to put matters on a formal footing and keep them there, Farrell spoke briskly.

'Doctor Yates, I'm hoping you can throw some light on an investigation I'm working on.'

She smiled warmly at him and he felt his defences begin to crumble.

'It's lovely to see you again. Come along to my room. We can talk there,' she said and set off along the corridor.

Farrell followed her, his eyes inscrutable. As they sat down in her comfortable office, more like a cosy sitting room than a consulting room, he was unable to stop his eyes sliding of their own volition to her left hand, to check out whether she was wearing a ring. She wasn't. The slight twitch of her mouth told him she'd seen him. Time to take control.

'Did you know a Catholic priest by the name of Father Boyd?' he asked.

Her eyes widened in recognition at both the name and his use of the past tense. She leaned forward in her chair.

'Yes, I knew him. Are you telling me he's …?'

'Dead. Yes, I'm afraid so.'

'But I only saw him two weeks ago. He looked absolutely fine,' she continued, trying to make sense of it.

Farrell pressed on. 'He was murdered,' he informed her.

Her hand flew to her mouth.

'I can't believe it,' she said. 'So you're …?'

'Senior Investigating Officer,' he filled in for her.

'I see,' she said. 'What do you want to know?'

'He was meant to see you today at twelve o'clock. I need to know why. It could be relevant to the investigation.'

'I'm sure you don't need me to tell you that patient confidentiality continues after death.'

'There are a number of exceptions to that rule. You could justify disclosure on the basis that it's in the public interest to catch this murderer before he kills again. Surely, it is also in the interest of his surviving sister that the police are given any relevant information that might directly or indirectly lead to the capture of his killer?'

'Fine, you win. Father Boyd had been referred to me by his GP as he'd been suffering from moderate depression, a symptom of which was alcoholism.'

Farrell had guessed as much.

'I need you to keep this to yourself,' he said. 'Before he was murdered he'd been sent a few anonymous letters. One of these contained the comment "I know what you did". In his sessions with you did he make any reference to the letters or who might have sent them?'

'No,' said Clare. 'Definitely not. We'd only had three sessions so I'd just scraped the surface really, barely got started; you know how long these things take.'

That's it, thought Farrell, twist the knife. Don't let me forget who's got the upper hand in this little exchange. He kept his countenance impassive.

She continued, 'I can tell you that he seemed deeply troubled. He mentioned he felt guilty about something he had done years ago; made one or two comments about the past starting to haunt him, stuff like that.'

'And you didn't think to probe any deeper?' asked Farrell.

'I was getting to it,' she said defensively. 'You can't rush these things; have to peel the layers away slowly.'

There was an awkward silence. Farrell's heart was hammering and he felt hot and sweaty. Was it wishful thinking on his part or was she feeling some kind of connection between them too? She had lowered her gaze and was studying her clasped hands intensely. Probably just remembering what a basket case he'd been in those days. Looking at her full lips he felt an unwelcome frisson of desire as he remembered with startling clarity the moment he had touched his own to them. Time to get out of here.

He stood up abruptly, ready to leave. She rose as well. They stared at each other for a long moment before Farrell broke the silence.

'Well, if you think of anything else, please get in touch.'

He passed her a card and their hands touched. He snatched his back as though it had been burnt, hoped she hadn't noticed.

'Frank ...' she said, moving closer.

Farrell had to fight the impulse to back away from her and render himself even more ridiculous in her eyes. He looked at her in what he hoped was a manner of cool enquiry: one eyebrow quizzically raised, just the ticket.

'Yes?'

'About before …'

The woman was a sadist. Surely she wasn't going to rub his nose in it after all these years?

'Go on,' he said.

'I owe you an apology.'

Farrell could feel the heat rise in his face and move down his whole body. He said nothing, having temporarily lost control of his tongue.

'I was young, just starting out,' she continued. 'I'm afraid I allowed my feelings to get the better of me. I must have been sending out mixed messages. I realized when you kissed me that I'd failed you professionally and just panicked, I guess.'

Farrell tried for a joke to lighten the atmosphere.

'Hey, with that amount of guilt you must be Catholic,' he quipped.

She smiled and the sun came out. Farrell could feel a rusty grin pushing against his cheeks.

'Now we've got that out of the way, maybe you'd like to join me for a drink some night? I'm writing a paper on the development of criminality in adolescents: the old nature versus nurture debate. I would welcome the insights of a serving police officer informed by your unique spiritual background.'

'Sure. Why not?' replied Farrell, the nonchalance of his response utterly belied by the colour creeping up his face.

They arranged to meet at the Swan, a quiet country pub, the following week.

CHAPTER SIXTEEN

Farrell jerked bolt upright in bed; the memory of his scream ringing in his ears. Heart pounding, he threw back the covers and swung his legs over the edge of the bed, waiting for the nightmare images to recede. As the mist cleared from his eyes, early morning country sounds filtered through the open window. House martins squabbled under the eaves. Farrell glanced at the clock and groaned. Five a.m.

Throwing on running shorts and a vest, he limbered up with a few practised stretches, turning towards the small mahogany crucifix above his bed. Blank wooden eyes stared impassively back at him. He knew he should really take it down and pack it away but it had been a present from his mother at ordination: the last thing she had ever given him. Taking it down would feel like another betrayal.

As he opened the front door the scent of honeysuckle wafted past. Gravel crunched under his trainers like muesli. He headed for the river, legs pumping rhythmically, drinking in the mist-clad beauty of the summer morning. The River Nith snaked towards the Solway Coast, its mud banks already covered by the incoming tide. Bovine faces turned towards him curiously.

By the time he was heading homewards the sun was rising. Lights were pinging on all over the tiny hamlet of Kelton. His muscles shrieked in protest but with the pain came a welcome feeling of calm.

Back in the cottage Farrell peeled off his running gear then stepped into a steaming hot shower. As he worked up a fragrant lather he pushed away the thoughts that hovered on the periphery of his conscious mind ready to assail him. He had to learn to live more in the moment.

Eventually, he was forced out of the shower by the water running cold and then obliged to boil a kettle for his shave. Tense blue eyes glared back at him from the mirror as the razor rasped over his stubble, taking no prisoners, and flashbacks of Boyd's murdered body slipped through his mind like an unwanted slide show. Desperate to get going now and lose himself in action, Farrell reached abstractedly into the wardrobe for something to wear. He selected one of four identical black suits and black shirts. Just for an instant, he reached back in for a clerical collar instead of the dark grey tie he habitually wore. He shrugged away the thought, exasperated with himself.

After making his single bed with military precision and washing the breakfast dishes, Farrell grabbed his keys and badge then folded his long body into the dumpy blue Citroen outside.

Driving into town he wondered again whether he had done the right thing in coming back to Dumfries. In some ways it had been like slipping on a favourite sweater. The Galloway hills and pine forests never failed to soothe and delight him. Dumfries itself had changed, grown older and not necessarily wiser, since he was a boy. John and him had had a blast growing up here, and the kind of freedom money couldn't buy these days. They'd be off early in the morning with their jammy pieces, and their mothers wouldn't see them until they fetched back home at sundown, tired, hungry, and filthy dirty. Aye, but it was good clean dirt in those days. Not like now.

He had thought it might give him a chance to unwind, even build some bridges with his mother, before slipping back to his fast-paced life in Edinburgh. Instead, the first thing to land on his desk was a murder, swiftly followed by the abduction of two little boys. He fervently hoped they were safe. DI Moore might be running the investigation into their disappearance, but a case like that got under everybody's skin.

As he drove past St Aidan's on his way to work his thoughts turned to what he had discussed with Father Joe. He felt some compassion for Father Malone. The Catholic Church demanded a lot from its priests. To expect them to shoulder the heavy burdens of their parish without a partner or children to console them was harsh, especially when it wasn't theologically necessary. The rule of celibacy is merely classed as a rule of discipline. Farrell had always felt it had more to do with political expediency than theology.

I KNOW WHAT YOU DID

What if the anonymous letter hadn't been intended for Father Boyd at all, but for Father Malone? If someone had got wind of his homosexuality and a fledgling relationship might they have intended to blackmail him? Farrell glanced in his mirror then did a nifty U-turn up the road he had just come down.

Ten minutes later he was being handed a cup of tea by Father Malone. Farrell noticed the cup rattling in the saucer as it was passed to him. He sat back, sipped his tea and stared at the young priest thoughtfully. Father Malone sat back as well, trying to but not quite succeeding in mimicking Farrell's relaxed demeanour.

The silence ballooned between them, pressing tightly against the margins of acceptable social intercourse. Farrell waited. Father Malone's complexion went from white to waxy. Still Farrell said nothing.

'Look, why are you here?' burst out the younger man finally.

'The letters Father Boyd received,' Farrell said.

'Yes, what about them?'

'When were they delivered? Was there any pattern?'

'They were there in the morning when we got up, just lying on the mat.'

'Were they in an envelope?'

'No, just a folded over sheet of paper. I only saw Father Boyd pick up one of them.'

'Who was usually up first?'

'It used to be me, but latterly Father Boyd was already up and dressed when I came down. I think he had difficulty sleeping.'

Farrell opened a folder and took out a photocopy of one of the letters. He handed it across to Father Malone.

'I want you to consider the wording of this letter very carefully and tell me if it is at all possible that it was intended for you rather than Father Boyd,' said Farrell.

The colour staining the priest's cheeks and the anguished expression in his eyes told Farrell all he needed to know.

'But, Father Boyd thought it was sent to him …'

'Two guilty consciences under the same roof,' said Farrell. 'Not as uncommon as you might think.'

'Do you know who sent the letters?' asked the stricken priest.

'Not yet,' said Farrell. 'But I aim to find out.'

'Do you need to know …?'

Farrell held up a hand to stop him saying any more. 'I have no intention of violating your privacy unless it proves necessary to the case.'

He stood up to leave.

'Tell me,' said Father Malone hesitantly. 'Do you ever miss being a practising priest?'

Farrell considered for a moment.

'It was a lot to give up but I've made my peace with it.'

'Peace is an underrated commodity,' the priest said with a sad smile.

Farrell gave a last lingering look round and headed for the door.

CHAPTER SEVENTEEN

Mhairi skidded into the car park at Loreburn Street and stopped the car so abruptly she burned the tyres. Leaping from her seat, she managed to snag her tights as she picked up her bag and ran. Heart pounding, she flew into the building, incurring a raised eyebrow from Emily in reception at her dishevelled state. That bitch probably doesn't even fart, she thought resentfully as she took the stairs two at a time. Whirling into the office, she threw her jacket over the back of her seat and spun out again to seek the sanctuary of the locker room. She collapsed onto the bench. Head thumping like a bass drum she knocked back three paracetamols, fighting the urge to gag. Right, time to repair the damage. She gave an exploratory sniff under her armpits and recoiled. A pity she hadn't made it back to her flat this morning, as intended. She took some deodorant out of her bag and sprayed it liberally.

The door to the locker room opened and in came DI Kate Moore. Oh, crap.

She surveyed Mhairi. 'This really won't do, you know.'

'Ma'am?' said Mhairi, tasting bile in her mouth.

'When you pitch in to work late and in yesterday's clothes you don't just do yourself a disservice, but all of us.'

'Yes, Ma'am,' muttered Mhairi.

'If you keep this up,' she continued, 'you'll end up back in uniform.'

DI Moore turned to her own locker and took out a pristine white blouse, a pair of expensive black slacks, and a set of white cotton underwear and handed them over.

'Shower and make yourself presentable,' she said. 'I expect you to make up the time at the end of the day, and I want these items returned in immaculate condition.'

'Yes, Ma'am. Thank you,' said Mhairi.

'You know, if you applied your mind to your job you could really be rather good,' said DI Moore and left the room.

Mhairi peeled off her stale clothes and stepped into the shower. The family had gone to stay with Elspeth's mother in Ayr for a couple of days to get away from all the media attention. She had taken the opportunity to blow off some steam. What was so wrong with that? The guilt twisting in her gut told her plenty.

Twenty minutes later she was at her desk, burrowing through a pile of paper work. DS Stirling wordlessly placed a cup of strong coffee at her elbow, and she flashed him a grateful smile. The older copper regarded her with a twinkle in his eyes.

'Nice outfit,' he said.

'Guess whose?'

'Let me see: expensive material, crease resistant, nice finish, elegant tailoring, I'm guessing DI Moore?'

'Got it in one.'

'Read you the riot act, did she?'

'And then some.'

'Good night was it?'

'I'd tell you if I could remember.'

'You ought to watch yourself, lass.'

'What are you, my mother?'

'Sorry I spoke,' Stirling said with a grin.

Byers came striding into the room and Mhairi immediately tensed up. There was something overtly predatory about Byers that she had never liked. He stared at her in a way that made her wish she had on a cardigan.

'Been playing with the dressing-up box, DC McLeod?' Byers asked.

Mhairi turned her head away from him and pointedly picked up her pen.

'If you don't mind, Sir, I've got work to be getting on with.'

Byers looked annoyed that she had rebuffed his attempt at humour.

'Right, if you're that keen you can come with me to do some more interviews. Pity St Aidan's isn't a Proddy church,' Byers moaned. 'It would only have taken us five minutes to interview one of their congregations. This church seems to have been stuffed to the gunnels. Just our bloody luck.'

Five hours later they were footsore and hungry. They had taken nine statements, none of which had revealed anything that they didn't already know. Father Boyd, it would seem, had been a good enough parish priest, though liked to keep himself to himself when he wasn't on parish business. They'd heard the odd subversive whisper that he could be a bit harsh but nothing that would give anyone a motive for wanting to kill him. Byers glanced at his watch.

'Right, time for one more before we knock off for lunch,' he said. 'What's the next name on the list?'

'Miss Agnes Brown,' McLeod replied.

A few minutes later they drew up outside the ground floor flat of a row of sandstone terraces. As they walked up the path McLeod noticed the net curtain give a compulsive twitch. The old woman who answered the door was dressed in black, which contrasted unfavourably with her pallor. Her face had collapsed in on itself like someone had let out too much air. She bared her teeth in a smile or it could have been a grimace of pain.

'I wondered when you lot were going to show up,' she rasped, turning to lead the way into a freezing cold parlour.

She smelled of stale urine and fleshy decay as if she was already half dead.

McLeod said gently, 'I know that this must all have been a terrible shock for you. Did you know Father Boyd well?'

'Since I was a girl,' the old woman said.

She doesn't look like she's ever been a girl, thought McLeod.

'In that time have you ever known of anyone to have a grudge against Father Boyd?' asked Byers.

The old woman paused a moment, sizing them up with her bright beady eyes. Her false teeth clicked and the sound of her hissing breath filled the room. Byers was about to repeat the question when she let out a cackle that made them both jump.

'Frank Farrell,' she said, rolling the words around her mouth with relish. 'You ought to be looking at Frank Farrell.'

McLeod and Byers stiffened in their seats, glanced at each other. Whatever they'd expected it hadn't been this.

'You don't mean Inspector Frank Farrell, do you?' asked Byers.

'The very same.' The beady eyes gleamed with mischief.

'But that's insane,' McLeod burst out.

Byers shot her a warning glance.

'Oh, it's insane I am now, is it?' the old woman grumbled.

'I didn't mean … that is to say … I'm sorry,' said McLeod.

'Got a thing for him, have you, lass?' asked Miss Brown.

'No! I mean, er …' McLeod retreated into silence, her cheeks burning. She didn't have a thing for Farrell, did she?

'Always was a good-looking lad. Used to turn all the lassies' heads, but he only had eyes for one.'

'What makes you think that Inspector Farrell had a grudge against Father Boyd?' asked Byers.

'It was Father Boyd who was behind him leaving the priesthood,' she said and sat back to watch their reaction.

'How do you know this?' asked Byers, his voice harder.

'When you've been around as long as I have you get to know a lot of things,' she retorted. 'Why don't you ask him, if you don't believe me?'

'Do you know why Boyd allegedly made Inspector Farrell leave the priesthood?'

Miss Brown looked defeated for the first time. 'No, I don't. But it must have been for something bad. Priests are like doctors and you lot. They tend to stick together. Frank Farrell turned up at Mass the day Father Boyd was murdered. It gave the priest a right turn, so it did. I turned round to see what he was staring at and there was Farrell sitting there, bold as brass.'

'Did they speak to each other afterwards?' asked Byers.

'Father Boyd went running out the church after him, shouting his name, but Farrell, he just kept right on walking though he must have heard him.' The old woman looked at them maliciously. 'Going to arrest him are you?'

'I hardly see that's any of your concern,' said Byers.

'Thought not,' she said.

Byers and McLeod walked back to the car in silence.

As they drew up to the station, McLeod turned to Byers.

'What are you going to do, Sarge?' she asked.

'I don't know yet,' he said. 'I'm going to have to run it by the DCI and take it from there.'

'You can't believe the ranting of a crazy old woman, Sarge. There's no way DI Farrell had anything to do with Boyd's death. It's just coincidence, that's all.'

'She was right about one thing though,' said Byers. 'I reckon you've got a soft spot for him.'

'Absolute bollocks, Sir.'

'But there again, who haven't you got a soft spot for, Mhairi? It's not exactly an exclusive club.'

McLeod reined herself in and answered him with icy composure.

'Will there be anything else, Sir?'

Byers looked disappointed she hadn't risen to the bait.

McLeod exited the car and walked stiffly into the station aware of his hot eyes following her. Jerk.

CHAPTER EIGHTEEN

DCI Lind listened impassively as DS Byers relayed the morning's events. After Byers had finished Lind thought for a moment before speaking.

'I'd take what she said with a pinch of salt. We're talking about a disagreement that happened around fifteen years ago. It's not as though she was even able to give you any specifics.'

'But, Sir …' interjected Byers

'I will of course speak to DI Farrell and get his take on events before drawing a line under the matter. Satisfied?'

'Yes, Sir.' said Byers, clearly not satisfied at all.

There was a rap on the door and Farrell poked his head round.

'Ah, Frank, come in, come in. Byers is just leaving.'

Byers brushed past Farrell, refusing to catch his eye. Farrell raised his eyebrows at Lind.

'Was it something I said?'

'No, something someone else said. Take a seat, Frank.'

Farrell sat down and regarded his boss steadily. Lind seemed to be having difficulty finding the right words.

'Come on, John, spit it out. We've known each other too long to beat about the bush.'

'Byers interviewed someone today who indicated you had a grudge against our dead priest.'

'And?' asked Farrell.

Lind looked disconcerted.

'Oh. So you admit it then.'

'Of course I admit it. Why wouldn't I?' The penny dropped. 'Wait a minute, you don't think …? Well, I'll be blowed. You must do or you wouldn't have—'

'Frank,' interrupted Lind. 'Get off your high horse. Of course I don't think you had anything to do with the murder but surely you can see why I had to ask?'

'You're right; I'm being an eejit,' said Frank. 'It was nearly fifteen years ago. I just didn't think it was relevant.'

'I never really asked what happened,' said Lind. 'You were in such a state, what with being ill and all, I just never got round to it.'

'Ancient history,' said Farrell. 'Some nutter was killing women in Glasgow. He got off on yanking my chain in the confessional.'

'Jesus, Frank, I'd no idea,' said Lind.

'The monster said all the right words, so I was forced to go on granting him absolution, time after time. Then he started telling me which one he was tempted to off next. I was powerless. The sanctity of the confessional is such that I knew I couldn't say anything while he pretended contrition. It would have meant automatic expulsion from the priesthood. Another woman was killed, just like he said. I was tortured by guilt. There was an anonymous tip off to the police. They never found out who it was. The killer himself believed it was me. He gave an interview to someone in the gutter press. They were going to run with it until the police legal team managed to get an interdict.'

'But how did Boyd . . .?'

'I left Glasgow after that, having asked for a move back down here. I was still pretty screwed up, made the mistake of confiding in him. He didn't believe me and told the bishop he thought I

92

had tipped off the police. The bishop was pretty good about it. Told me he believed me and that I had to work through what he considered to be my misplaced feelings of guilt with my spiritual adviser. Boyd, however, just wouldn't let it go. Eventually he pushed me too far. I just couldn't take it any more. I quit.'

'And then you ...'

'Became a basket case?'

'If I'd only known. Why didn't you come to us, Laura and me? We're your oldest friends, for God's sake.'

Farrell's mouth twisted. He and Laura used to be the 'us'. He pushed away that treacherous thought.

'It seemed easier to go it alone. You guys were up in Aberdeen at the time. Hey, like I said, ancient history. Anyhow, if there's nothing else ...'

'I'll keep what you told me to myself for now, Frank. However, if it becomes relevant in any way to the investigation ...'

'Sure, no worries,' replied Farrell. 'Any word on the missing kids yet?'

'We've got nothing. No leads and no contact from the kidnapper. It's not looking good, I'm afraid.'

Farrell dived into the gents on the way back to the MCA room and found Stirling and Byers there. From the way it went totally quiet he knew they'd been talking about him. Stuff them, he thought. He was going to have a drink with Clare Yates and he refused to let anyone or anything rain on his parade.

CHAPTER NINETEEN

Farrell had showered, changed, and was winging his way out the station with a spring in his step when he saw the diminutive figure of DC McLeod ahead of him. As he drew abreast of her, the expression of unguarded misery on her face brought him up short.

'DC McLeod, Mhairi, what's the matter?'

Startled, McLeod turned an anguished face towards him.

'Just thinking, Sir; you know how it is.'

'Come on, in here.'

Farrell sidestepped into an empty office, leaving her no option but to follow him. He sat down behind the desk and motioned for her to sit, which she did with evident reluctance.

'Right, Mhairi,' Farrell said, 'tell me what's wrong. I've been around a bit longer than you and I know that something is bothering you. Don't make me get the thumbscrews out.'

'Honestly, Sir, it's nothing.' Mhairi's face flushed.

'Hey come on, I'm a priest, I love hearing confession,' Farrell said, trying to lighten the mood.

To Farrell's horror his comment had the opposite effect. Mhairi's eyes brimmed with tears.

'Last night I went to meet someone,' she burst out. 'Someone

I was really keen on. Turns out … he was married. He didn't see fit to tell me till after we … we …'

'It's okay, Mhairi, I get the picture. Some men can be total pigs. Losers like him aren't worth all this grief.'

'It's just … I know what they all think of me but a married man … I would never have …'

Seeing her there with her face all crumpled Farrell had an insane urge to put his arms around her. He should never have started this. Standing up he patted her awkwardly on the shoulder.

'All the best lessons in life are learned the hard way. Sometimes we need to be broken down before we can become truly strong.'

Mhairi cracked a smile for the first time.

'Is this a sermon?'

'Sorry, I'm a bit rusty. I used to have them all quaking in their seats.'

'I doubt that,' said Mhairi. 'Look, you're right, I should be glad I'm not the one married to him. Sorry, Sir, it's just with the murder, the kids, and everything, I've been running on empty. You don't need to worry about me, I'll be fine.'

'I know it's none of my business …' said Farrell.

'So old, yet so perceptive,' muttered Mhairi under her breath.

'But don't sell yourself short,' said Farrell, starting to perspire. 'That's all I'm saying … Love tends to turn up when you least expect it.'

'Love,' snorted Mhairi, 'is a four letter word.'

'Er, right,' said Farrell. Why in God's name had he got into this?

'I'm glad we had this little talk,' said Mhairi.

'You are? Excellent!' said Farrell, exhaling with relief.

'Don't you have to be somewhere, Sir?' asked Mhairi, taking pity on him. 'You looked like you were in a hurry …'

Farrell glanced at his watch.

'Go on, Sir. I'm fine. If you keep me any longer, I'll miss the start of *EastEnders*.'

'See you tomorrow then, DC McLeod, bright and early,' Farrell said with mock severity.

As he drove along the quiet country lanes to meet Clare, Farrell felt increasingly nervous. Since he had left active service in the priesthood he had tended to avoid involvement with the opposite sex. The very few relationships he had tentatively embarked on had been short-lived, as the guilt had gnawed away at him like cancer until he ended it and laid himself bare in the confessional. Even though, if he met someone he wanted to marry he could apply for a papal dispensation, he still couldn't rid himself of the feeling deep down that he would be betraying his vows. It had been a good number of years since his last relationship. It's only a drink, he told himself.

The Solway Inn was a few miles out of Dumfries. As he walked towards the lounge entrance light spilled onto the pavement from the mullioned windows. Pulling open the heavy wooden door, he glanced around quickly, worried that she might not be there. His fears were groundless. She was sitting framed by the glowing log fire, perfectly composed.

The time flew by as they chatted about books, films, and music. Nice safe topics. Then she brought up the paper she was writing.

'So where do you stand on the nature versus nurture debate?' she asked, looking as though she wanted to take notes but thought that might be a breach of social protocol.

Farrell thought about it.

'Firmly on the fence, I would say. I've come across kids that have been dragged up with mothers on the game, fathers in prison, and the kind of poverty that eats into the soul yet they've struggled and strived and somehow come out on top. Equally, I've come across kids that have wanted for nothing; their every whim catered to by devoted parents, and they've got involved in drugs and spiralled downwards until all that's left of them is their addiction, like a big black hole sucking in everything around them.'

'So you don't think some people are simply born bad?'

'No. I like to think that we can all exercise choice to a greater or lesser degree but I admit that good choices are harder to make in certain environments.'

There was then a lull in the conversation and Farrell knew it was coming.

'So, Frank, how have you been?' she said.

'If I want to book a consult I'll contact your office,' he snapped.

She looked hurt and he hated himself for being so boorish but what did she expect?

'It's just that, if we're to see each other socially, I need to know if there are any issues that could complicate things ...' she said.

'Sorry,' he told her. 'I overreacted.'

'Are you still taking lithium?' she asked.

'No,' he said, sending a silent apology winging up to the Almighty. 'After a while I didn't seem to need it.' It was only a little lie. After all he'd been off it for the last few days and still felt fine. He'd only ever had that one episode and the circum-stances had been extreme, to say the least.

Clare seemed to relax again and turned the conversation away to other things. Farrell decided to sound her out about the murder. Maybe she could shed some light on the kind of mind that would dream up something so horrific. Clare listened attentively. She thought in silence for a few minutes after he had finished then turned towards him again.

'It sounds to me as though this murder was staged for effect, everything planned down to the tiniest detail, yet there's ferocity about it that contradicts that. I would hazard a guess that the killer knew Boyd and felt he'd a very real grievance against him,' she said.

The evening went a little flat after that and Farrell blamed himself for ruining the mood. As they took their leave in the car park, he wondered if he'd blown his chances. But as he reached down to kiss her goodnight on the cheek she turned her head and her lips touched his, sending a jolt of electricity through his body. Gently he pulled away and smiled at her.

'Call me,' she said as she slipped into her car and drove away.

Once home, he was asleep within minutes, the rigours of the last few days catching up with him. The phone woke him abruptly and he reached for it still half-asleep. His clock showed the time to be 3 a.m.

A strangely muffled voice said, 'what's yours is mine and what's mine will be yours.'

Farrell sat bolt upright.

'Who is this?'

The caller rang off. Just some fruit loop had one too many, Farrell thought. Uneasily, he fell asleep once more but his dreams were troubled.

CHAPTER TWENTY

Farrell woke with a start and lay there with the darkness pressed against him, blood roaring through his ears like an express train. He'd slept only fitfully, one nightmare image after another chasing through his mind. Galvanized into action, he leapt out of bed, peeled off his sweat-soaked T-shirt and dived into the shower. No time to waste.

Turning the radio up loud so he could catch the news in the bathroom, Farrell peered at his haggard complexion in the mirror, while wrapped in a towel. He needed a shave. Drat, no shaving foam; he'd have to make do with ordinary soap. He couldn't see his aftershave either. Lathering up as best as he could Farrell was oblivious to everything but the rasping and scraping of the razor over his face when all of a sudden he jumped, cutting himself in the process.

Someone was in the cottage. He could hear them. Stealthily he crept through the open door into the bedroom and turned the radio off so he could hear better. Stooping, he picked up the baseball bat that he kept under the bed. Maybe he could take the intruder by surprise. Another creak, this time on the stairs. Heart pounding, body tensed in anticipation, Farrell waited behind the open door, avoiding looking at the crucifix above his bed. He was dashed if he was going to turn the other cheek and let some loser beat him up in his own home. The steps were nearing the top of the stairs. Farrell coiled, ready to spring. Now. He leapt out, weapon held aloft, and beheld the wide-eyed stare of Clare Yates. Farrell froze.

'Wow, nice caveman routine,' she said. 'What do you do for an encore?'

Clare slowly looked him up and down, and to his intense chagrin Farrell felt himself blush. Time to go on the offensive.

'Clare, what are you doing here?'

'I brought you some light reading on the way to work. I thought it might help you with the case.'

She placed a couple of heavy-looking tomes and a number of journals on a low table.

Another thought occurred to him.

'How did you get in?'

'The door was open. I did knock but there was no answer. I called out as well, but figured you were maybe in the shower and couldn't hear me because of the radio. I didn't have you pegged for a Radio 4 listener, by the way.'

'Back in a minute, I've just got to get something,' muttered Farrell and took off downstairs.

That door had been locked. He was sure of it. As he stood in the hallway his heart thudded uncomfortably as he noticed the key sitting on the hall table. There was something underneath it. A playing card. The joker's grinning face leered up at him. Farrell felt the world tilt and staggered back against the wall. What did it mean?

Clare's face materialized in front of him. She was looking at him with concern but there was something else there behind her eyes. She thinks I'm losing it, thought Farrell. He made a monumental effort to pull himself together and act normal.

'Frank, what's wrong?' she asked. 'You're scaring me.'

'Sorry, just a bit dizzy. Need to eat something.'

The clouds lifted from her face and she smiled at him. He leaned in and kissed her. The intensity of her response both thrilled and terrified him. He pulled away, his head a riot of conflicting thoughts.

'I'm sorry, I've got to get going.'

'Already? It's only gone seven.'

'Those little boys are still missing. It's not looking good.'

'I'm sorry, I won't hold you back.' She turned to leave.

'I'll phone you later,' he called after her.

Driving in to work, Farrell could scarce recall a start to a morning that had left him feeling so rattled.

Nodding curtly at the constable on duty he made straight for the canteen and grabbed a coffee from the machine and a banana that looked as though someone had sat on it then made straight for his office on the second floor. He was about to enter when he caught a glimpse of a shadow moving about behind the opaque glass. Carefully placing his coffee on the floor he tensed then swung the door back causing it to crash against the filing cabinet to reveal a startled DCI Lind.

'Bloody Hell, Frank, what's your problem? I nearly shit a brick.'

'Sorry, don't know my own strength,' said Farrell, weak with relief. What was with him this morning? He picked up his coffee and moved to his desk, Lind staring at him all the while.

'How's Laura?'

'You know, putting a brave face on things.'

'And you?'

'Life goes on.'

Farrell made a decision. He extracted a plastic evidence envelope from his pocket and wordlessly pushed it across the desk.

Lind read it out loud:

'I'm tempted to confess again.

Your guilt will grow and grow.

Only you can stop me now.

101

Just like before.'

He looked at Farrell, his expression inscrutable.

'Where did you get this?'

'Some joker pushed it through my door a couple of days after Boyd was murdered. It meant nothing at the time. It was only when the boys went missing that I started to wonder if that was what it was referring to.'

'He seems to know a lot about you.'

'Perhaps,' said Farrell. 'On the other hand, it could just be a shot in the dark, a wind up ... There's no way of knowing for sure.'

Lind flopped into his seat like a sack of potatoes, brow furrowed as his analytical mind looked at this disturbing piece of information from all angles. Farrell paced up and down, muscles coiled tight as though trying to burst through the restraints of his skin. He said nothing, knowing Lind would not welcome any interruption to his train of thought. Finally, just when Farrell was about to crack, Lind looked up.

'How on earth did this geezer know about what happened to you back then? Christ, I'm one of your best friends and even I just got to hear about it. We're talking about something that happened over fifteen years ago.'

'Unless they're one and the same person,' said Farrell. 'He could be out by now if he kept his nose clean inside. I didn't follow his progress. I didn't want to know.'

'I suppose anything's possible,' said Lind, suddenly looking older and greyer at the thought of a deranged psychopath turning up on his patch.

'There's more,' said Farrell. Reluctantly, he pulled another evidence bag out of his pocket and slid it across to Lind, whose eyes were now on a collision course with his receding hairline.

'Anything else?' he managed, while gingerly reaching for the bag.

'That's the lot,' said Farrell.

'I take it this was put through your door with the note?' asked Lind.

Farrell shifted in his seat.

'Not exactly.'

'Spit it out man,' barked Lind.

'I found the card on my hall table this morning.'

'Right,' said Lind, decisively. 'That settles it. Bugger off down to the crime lab with these. I'm arranging twenty-four-hour surveillance on your property. A complete nut job has been inside your house. I can't ignore that. As to whether it has got any bearing on the abduction of the kids? That remains to be seen. It's a tenuous link at best.'

Lind reached for the phone but Farrell slammed his hand down on it before he had a chance to dial.

'Don't make me pull rank on you here, Frank,' Lind said.

'Look, John … Sir … none of this matters now. There are two wee boys out there that need to be found, and I don't want coppers wasting their efforts on me when they could be out pounding the streets. You know how these things go down as well as anyone. If they're not found soon …' Farrell punched the desk in impotent fury.

Lind looked at him.

'You'd better get out there then, hadn't you,' he said.

Farrell tore along to the briefing room, dropping the two evidence bags off at the crime lab en route after photocopying the contents. He was just leaving the lab when he bumped into the SOCO, Janet White.

'I don't know if you've heard, Sir,' she muttered, sounding embarrassed.

'What is it, Janet?' asked Farrell, giving her his full attention.

'We got the analysis of the DNA samples back from Dundee this morning.'

'And?' asked Farrell.

'No matches with known criminal profiles … although they did find some of your DNA on the note Boyd was holding.'

Farrell slapped his head in annoyance. Somehow he had managed to contaminate evidence at the crime scene. It must have been the shock had made him careless momentarily. Still, it was no excuse.

'Thanks for the head's up, Janet. I don't know how it could have happened.'

'It won't be the first time, Sir,' she said, walking away.

The increasing sophistication of DNA analysis was proving to be a double-edged sword, thought Farrell. Still annoyed with himself, he headed for DI Moore's office, hoping to intercept her before she made it along to the MCA room for the first briefing of the day.

'Wanted to give you a head's up,' he said, declining her offer of a seat. 'I received this anonymous note through my door before the boys were taken. Then a playing card, the joker, arrived on my hall table this morning. It might be linked to someone banged up a number of years ago in a case I was involved in as a priest rather than as a copper. Equally, it might have nothing to do with it.' He placed the copies on her desk.

Moore looked at them and frowned before looking up at him. 'Why on earth did you sit on the note for so long? It's tantamount to withholding evidence, Frank.'

He sighed and slumped into the seat opposite.

'You're right, of course. At the time, I was only concerned with Boyd's murder, and I didn't see how it could have any possible correlation with that. I also—'

'What, Frank? Spit it out.'

'I also didn't want to dredge up the past. Not unless it was absolutely necessary.'

Her expression softened.

'No one likes to feel exposed, Frank, but let's get this job done. I'm trusting you to be straight with me from now on.'

'You got it. Whatever it takes,' he said. 'Jason Baxter is his name. Last I heard he was in doing life for the murders of three young women. A total psychopath.'

'How's the Boyd investigation going?'

'Byers is trawling through the parishioners, hoping to open new lines of enquiry that way. But if we don't catch a break soon … his killer may never be caught.'

Moore stood up and gathered her papers.

'Sorry, Frank. I have to get along to the briefing. I'd like you there if you can spare the time, especially in light of this new information.'

It was nearly 8 a.m., and the Investigation Team were filing in with none of their usual banter. Cases involving kids were the worst and no one had a good feeling about this one.

Holding up her hand for silence, DI Moore began. 'Information received points to the possible involvement of one Jason Baxter in the abduction of the boys. However, he was banged-up around fifteen years ago for a number of murders so we have to ascertain whether he's still inside or whether he was subsequently released.'

She pointed to Stirling who immediately jumped up.

'I'm on it, Ma'am,' he fired over his shoulder as he left the room.

'Byers, any joy from the appeal by the parents on Border News?'

'We're still getting inundated with calls, Ma'am, but nothing concrete yet.'

'Did you get anywhere on the family trees?'

'Still working on it, Ma'am. I did discover one thing though. The twins were adopted at birth.'

'Who are their real parents?'

'Their adoptive parents don't know. It was all done through a Catholic adoption agency, and it's like pulling teeth trying to extract information out of that crowd.'

'Get on to legal. Tell them it's urgent.'

The door opened, and a young WPC approached DI Moore, blushing, as all eyes swivelled to follow her progress.

'The police artist thought you might want copies of this, Ma'am.'

Farrell took one of the sheets being passed around and studied it closely, heart ricocheting about his chest like a squash ball. The picture didn't mean anything to him. Was it or was it not Jason Baxter? Impossible to say: it had been so long and incarceration changed a man. The beard didn't help either. He certainly couldn't rule him out.

'Make sure this picture is widely circulated,' said Moore. 'I want it plastered everywhere so this man has no place to hide. Get it on the local news and get the editors of all the local papers to run it in their next editions.'

As he stared into the blank eyes of the identikit image Farrell wondered what kind of man could have had the daring to carry out such a meticulously planned abduction and vanish into thin air. There was something familiar about him. Nothing he could put his finger on, just a feeling he'd seen him before somewhere. His eyes lighted on Mhairi. She looked tired and drawn but ready for anything. She was proving herself to be an outstanding member of the team, he thought.

'How's it going with the family, Mhairi?' asked DI Moore.

'As you'd expect, Ma'am. They've been up all night waiting for the phone to ring.'

'No jarring notes?'

'None at all, Ma'am; at least, none that I've been able to detect. The boys do have an uncle that was convicted of indecent exposure two years ago but he looks nothing like the description we've been given for the suspect and has an alibi for the time in question.'

'Alibis can be broken. Bring him in for questioning anyway,' said Moore, obviously determined to leave no stone unturned. She glanced at the clock and said, 'right, everyone that hasn't been allocated a specific task should get out on the streets with pictures of Mark and Jamie to help with the search. No exceptions. Every hour that goes by without a result means those little boys might be an hour closer to death. I want to see maximum effort. Let's move it.'

Farrell strode out, pulling on his jacket as the room behind him erupted. He'd noticed from the search grids pinned to the wall that a number of coppers were due to search Burns Walk down by the river at 9 a.m. He used to play down there himself as a kid and knew it better than most so he'd added his name.

He felt a slight tug on his sleeve and turned around, frown already in place, and saw that it was DI Moore. He made a conscious effort to smile, the tension in his jaw making it more of a grimace.

'Frank, wonder if I might tag along? I see you're heading out to join the search at Burns Walk?'

He looked doubtfully at her immaculate attire and expensive-looking court shoes. How to put her off without giving offence? Before he had a chance to fob her off she piped up.

'I've got wellies and an anorak in the car. I'll drive.'

He was left with no alternative but to follow in her wake, lengthening his stride to keep up with her.

As she opened the back of the car to get her gear out he was amused to see she had a matching scarf, woolly hat, and gloves set as well as some sparkly chiffon number with matching shoes and purse. Talk about being well prepared.

'I used to walk my dog, Jasper, down here,' she said. 'He managed to get in all the nooks and crannies.'

Walking down to the river from Nunholm Road, Farrell got a sudden waft of perfume from the magnolia climbing over the stone wall of a shuttered Georgian house. Across the Nith, the sun was high in the sky, shooting warm tendrils into the mist rising off the fields.

Fanning out, the officers worked silently, poking and prodding the secret spaces where Burns had strolled and which J. M. Barrie had gazed upon from his handsome sandstone house. They sifted through the detritus of modern living grafted onto the beauty of the morning like some creeping disease: lager cans, fag ends, even condoms. Early birds on the adjacent golf course looked at them curiously, annoyed at being put off their stroke. He noticed that DI Moore didn't shrink from getting her manicured hands dirty.

Was the kidnapper really someone from his past or just one of those bampots who liked to play games with the police? Hearing a muffled curse behind him, he spun round to see DI Moore keel over, having caught her ankle in a rabbit hole. He turned round to help her up and was surprised when she slapped his hand away.

'I can manage,' she snapped.

'As you wish,' he replied.

She struggled painfully to her feet, drained of all colour. Seeing her lurch forward, Farrell put out a steadying hand before he could help himself and was rewarded with a glare.

'Come on, Kate, we need to get you away to the doctor. You'll be no use to man or beast till that ankle is strapped up. I reckon we're done here anyway. Time to check in with the rest of the team back at HQ.'

'Sorry', she said. 'I prefer to stand on my own two feet.'

'Looking at that ankle, I reckon that's going to be a problem,' he said.

Hesitantly, she put her arm through his and they hobbled back to the car in silence.

CHAPTER TWENTY-ONE

As soon as he was back at Loreburn Street Farrell went in search of Stirling.

'Well?' he demanded as soon as he clapped eyes on him. 'What's the score with Baxter?'

'He was released from Barlinnie on appeal five years ago. His conviction was ruled unsafe by the appeal court and he's since made a tidy packet through settling a civil action for wrongful imprisonment.'

'Unbelievable,' muttered Farrell in disgust.

'Apparently, he lived in Glasgow up until recently.'

'And now?' asked Farrell.

'Lives out at Lochside, Dalscairth Avenue.'

'Let's go,' said Farrell, turning on his heel.

Stirling grabbed a scuffed corduroy jacket and followed him out the door.

'Don't you think we should call for some backup?' asked Stirling. 'Maybe get the firearms team to meet us there? You did say he's a murderer, didn't you?'

'Take too long to mobilize. If he's got those kids they're living on borrowed time. That's if we're not already too late.'

'I don't like it,' said Stirling.

'You don't have to like it. Just get in the bloody car, man.'

Stirling's mouth tightened into a thin line but he got in beside Farrell and they took off for Lochside with squealing tyres. Farrell drove like a maniac, feeling sick to his stomach at the thought of the upcoming confrontation.

'What makes you so sure Jason Baxter is our guy?' asked Stirling. 'I did a bit of digging around and he only ever targeted young women before. Something like this would be completely atypical.'

'You don't think the timing's suspicious?'

'Could just be coincidence. He's a Doonhamer, you know. Still got family here.'

'I'd no idea,' said Farrell grimly, skin crawling at the thought that he and Jason Baxter had inhabited the same small world as they were growing up, might even have stood next to each other in the pub or supermarket.

They parked around the corner and approached on foot. The mid-terraced sandstone house looked immaculately maintained. The small lawn was manicured to perfection. Farrell slipped the catch off the gate and walked quickly up the path. No sign of activity within. He looked up and saw black storm clouds gathering: a portent of the evil within? Rapping firmly on the door he waited, adrenalin surging round his body.

The door opened and he was suddenly face to face with his tormentor from all those years ago. Except this man looked nothing like the virile monster that charged through his dreams with such menace. This was an old man, looked like somebody's granddad: all Marks and Sparks cardies and floppy white hair. More importantly he looked nothing like the description of the abductor.

Stirling glanced at Farrell, waiting for him to take the lead. Farrell said nothing, just stood there with the blood draining from his head to his feet like a receding tide. Stirling stepped forward. The man ignored him, face clouded with confusion; staring hard at Farrell as though trying to place him. Farrell stared back like one in a trance, fighting the urge to turn and run from the evil soul lurking behind that mild façade.

'DS Stirling and DI Farrell,' said Stirling, no doubt wondering what the blazes was going on.

'Can you confirm that you are Jason Baxter?'

'The one and only. What's this about, officers?'

'We'd like to ask you some questions in connection with the disappearance of two little boys,' Stirling continued.

Baxter laughed. The sound had an obscene quality to it that made Farrell's skin shudder. Moving so quickly that Baxter nearly fell backwards into the hall, Farrell towered above him like an avenging angel, though from Heaven or Hell it would have been hard to say.

'Easy boss,' muttered Stirling in his ear.

Farrell unclenched his fists and was gratified to see a flicker of fear in Baxter's eyes.

'I don't know anything about missing boys,' he smirked. 'The ladies were always more my style. Don't you remember?'

Stirling looked at him in confusion. Farrell grimaced inwardly. He was going to have some explaining to do later. It would be all round the station in no time.

'Of course,' continued Baxter, 'it was always a shame that someone didn't stop the killer sooner. Seemed a nice lass that Emily, although I only know what I read about her in the press, of course.'

This time Farrell didn't rise to the bait.

'Mind if we come in?' he said, nearly knocking Baxter off his feet as he strode past him.

'Search upstairs,' he barked.

Stirling took off at the double and Farrell took the rooms downstairs. Baxter stood in the hall watching him with something akin to glee in his eyes.

'If I'd known you had such a keen interest in decorating I'd have dropped off some swatches,' he said.

Farrell reached the room at the end of the hall and threw the door open. The sight within caused him to falter then stop, completely dumbfounded. There sat Father Malone, completely at home and drinking tea from a bone china cup and saucer. There was a plate of scones in front of him.

'You know me, *Father*,' said Baxter. 'Always had a bit of a soft spot for the clergy.'

Farrell and Stirling drove back to Loreburn Street in tight-lipped silence, the air exploding with things unsaid. As they drew into the car park, Stirling opened his mouth.

'Permission to speak freely, Sir?'

'Spit it out, Sergeant,' said Farrell.

'That was one helluva stunt you pulled back there.'

'Just doing my job, Sergeant.'

'Listen, you gung ho Fuck! We should have waited for backup.'

'Cops like you need backup in place before they're willing to wipe their own arse.'

'Listen up, pal, I've got a wife and kids at home. I'm due to retire next year. I don't intend to be one of those sad bastards that leave the force in a body bag. You don't just drop in unannounced on a serial killer, for Christ's sake. What's the matter with you? Have you got a death wish or something?'

'I don't have time for this,' said Farrell. He turned on his heel and strode off leaving Stirling staring after him, face contorted with fury.

CHAPTER TWENTY-TWO

Still badly shaken, Farrell had nearly reached the sanctity of his office when a whirlwind of energy coming round the corner crashed into him, rocking him on his heels. He should have guessed. DC Mhairi McLeod.

'Where are you off to in such a hurry?' he asked, patting himself down.

'I'm off to interview your mother, Sir.'

'Oh? In connection with the Boyd case?'

'Yes, she's turned up as being very involved in activities at St Aidan's. DS Byers and I were meant to go and interview her, but DI Moore has nabbed him to do something else. Everyone else is busy so I'm looking for PC Thomson, but he seems to have disappeared.'

Farrell froze. He should have seen this coming.

'I'll come,' he said quickly.

Mhairi looked uncomfortable.

'Oh, right, er … are you sure that's wise?'

'Is she a suspect?'

'No, of course not, it's just …'

'Good, then I'm coming along.'

Mhairi shrugged her acquiescence.

If he went along himself he might manage to needle more information out of her than they'd get otherwise. It would give her less opportunity to do him down as well. She was never one to wash her dirty laundry in public. The silence stretched between them. McLeod started to look puzzled. He made a decision.

'OK, DC McLeod. Let's get going. I take it you're driving?'

''Course, Sir. You know what they say about male drivers.'

As they drew up outside his mother's immaculate small bungalow Farrell was assailed by fresh doubts. It had been about thirteen years since they'd last spoken; her decision not his. How would she react? They rang the doorbell and the door opened. When she saw him standing there her face went slack with shock and she moved to slam the door. Farrell had his foot ready to stop her.

'I'm afraid we're here on police business. This is DC McLeod. We have a few questions for you in relation to the murder of Father Ignatius Boyd.'

Was it his imagination or had a twitch of fear shown in her face?

'You'd better come in, I suppose,' she said and made way for them to enter.

Farrell was shocked to see how thin his mother had become. She had always been paranoid about gaining weight but now she looked almost anorexic, as though she was trying to deny her own existence. Her hair was still scraped back in the severe bun that Farrell remembered though it was now shot through with flecks of grey.

DC McLeod looked at him curiously as they followed his mother into the front parlour. Goodness knows what she was making of all this, thought Farrell. He indicated to McLeod that she should kick off.

'Mrs Farrell, we understand that you knew Father Boyd very well. As one of his more active parishioners you were possibly his confidante at times?'

114

Attagirl, thought Farrell. Flattery works just the ticket on women like her.

'You could say that, I suppose,' said his mother, keeping her eyes fixed on DC McLeod at all times.

'Did he seem troubled about anything of late?'

The eyes slid away from McLeod, skidded in Farrell's direction and took off round the room.

'Mrs Farrell? Would you like me to repeat the question?'

'Certainly not. I'm still in possession of all my faculties, thank you very much.'

'I didn't mean to imply—'

'The answer is no,' she interrupted. 'There was nothing worrying him as far as I'm aware.'

'Were you aware that he had received anonymous letters?'

'Good Heavens! No, I wasn't.'

'Had you seen anyone strange hanging about the church of late: someone who maybe hadn't been there before?' McLeod persisted.

'No, no one, I can think of,' she said. Again her eyes slithered towards Farrell, again she pulled them back.

'Can you think of anyone who might have had a grudge against Father Boyd, past or present?'

His mother paused before answering then shook her head decisively.

'He could be somewhat blunt and I don't doubt his traditional views didn't sit well with some of the more … progressive … members of the congregation, but nothing likely to lead to his murder as far as I am aware.'

Farrell allowed his attention to wander. Looking round the immaculately buffed and polished room, he felt no connection with its pristine contents even though he had lived there until he was eighteen. There were no photos of him. It was as if he had ceased to exist for her. More surprisingly, there were no longer any photographs of his father on display either. That was odd. Although his father had died before he was born his mother had always seemed to idolize him. Maybe she had met someone else? He struggled to regain his focus and concentrate on the job in hand.

'Would you mind terribly if I used your bathroom?' asked Mhairi, standing up expectantly.

For a fleeting second his mother looked so horrified at the prospect of being alone with him that Farrell almost laughed out loud.

'If you must,' ground out his mother. 'Along the hall and turn left.'

'Thank you,' said Mhairi, spinning on her heel and managing to wink at him as she walked out the door.

The awkward silence lengthened.

'It doesn't have to be like this,' said Farrell.

His mother flinched and her back seemed to become even straighter.

'You made your bed, now you have to lie in it,' she said, still avoiding looking at him.

'What exactly did I do that was so wrong you can't find it in you to forgive me?' asked Farrell with an edge to his voice.

Suddenly she whipped round to face him, her eyes slit with anger.

'You left the priesthood, isn't that enough?'

'And you wanted a priest more than you wanted a son,' Farrell said.

'I didn't say that,' she snapped.

'You didn't have to,' replied Farrell.

'I'm only glad your father didn't live long enough to see how his son turned out,' she hissed.

Farrell rolled with the punch and shot out one of his own.

'So why have you taken down his photos then? Did you meet someone else?'

His mother turned brick red and opened and shut her mouth like a guppy.

'How dare you be so presumptuous! You have no right to come in here on the pretext of police business and ask intrusive personal questions. I want you to leave. Now!'

He became aware of DC McLeod standing in the doorway looking shocked. Farrell stood up. They were almost at the front door when his mother burst out.

'Father Boyd was a good man, you know. I won't hear a word said against him. He dedicated his life to the service of others and didn't deserve to meet his end like that. It's a travesty, that's what it is.'

'I know this must have been very distressing for you,' said McLeod. 'Thank you so much for your time. We'll be in touch if there's anything else.'

They walked to the car in silence.

'Family rift?' queried McLeod.

'You could say that,' Farrell replied.

'This is kind of tricky, Sir, what with her being your mother and all, but I got the feeling she was hiding something.'

'You and me both,' said Farrell. 'She'll need to be interviewed again, maybe without me present this time. Look, it's been a long day and you hardly got any sleep last night. Can I drop you off at home or someplace else?'

'I'm meeting someone at Wetherspoons, so there would be fine,' she said.

'A young man?'

'One of them,' she answered cheerily.

Farrell looked at her in concern. It was really none of his business how she lived her life but he had a feeling he could get quite fond of Miss Party Cop and didn't want to see her hurt.

'And the one you told me about before?'

'Kicked into touch,' she replied. 'I'll not be caught out again.'

'How can you be so sure if you don't take the time to get to know them properly?'

Mhairi glared at him.

'Who appointed you my moral guardian?' she snapped.

'Sorry', said Farrell. 'You're right. Forget I said anything.'

Mhairi's expression softened.

'Look, I get it. I know you're just trying to look out for me, Sir. It's fine. I'm a detective so I've got it all worked out. For example, a white band on his finger shows a wedding ring recently taken off. If he won't let me borrow his mobile or rushes out the room to take a call that's also dodgy. I'm done with being taken for a mug,' said Mhairi as she got out the car.

Farrell toyed with the idea of heading back to the station, but rejected it out of hand. He'd been going around in circles all day and his brain felt fried. What he needed was to clear his head. His stomach growled with hunger but he felt too restless to go home. On impulse he picked up a fish supper from a chip shop and headed out the New Abbey Road towards the coast.

The beach was deserted at this time of night. As he sat on a flat rock, the salt on his chips mingling with salt from the spray on his lips, he felt the tension slowly ebb from his body. Removing his socks and shoes he rolled up his trousers and strolled to the water's edge. The cool sand pushed up between his toes as he meandered along the shoreline, the sun falling inexorably into the sea.

What on earth had Boyd been up to? Clearly the man had had a guilty conscience or he would have involved the police when he first started getting the letters. Farrell thought back to when he had lived with Boyd in that same house as a young priest. Try as he might the images refused to come; the whole experience expunged by the mental illness that had later consumed him.

As a teenager, Boyd had always singled him out for special attention when he came to the school to give them religious instruction. He hadn't always been a dry old stick. Back then he made a life devoted to God sound like such an adventure: filling their impressionable young minds with stories of the martyrdom of the saints. Farrell had lapped it up. The priest even had a box of holy relics that he used to great effect. The girls had recoiled from the grisly contents, but Farrell's neck had prickled with excitement.

Farrell sighed and turned back to his car. Maybe the interviews tomorrow would offer up a lead. If they couldn't establish a motive it was going to be hard to flush out the killer.

By the time he arrived back in Dumfries it was already getting dark. With a heavy heart he drove past the church but there was no sign of life. What had Boyd been trying to tell him the day before he died? Guilt twisted his intestines into knots. If only he'd swallowed his pride and turned round at church that morning, then Boyd might still be alive.

CHAPTER TWENTY-THREE

The following morning, Farrell was about to enter the MCA room when a breathless DC McLeod caught up with him.

'Sir, it's the two boys. We've just had a call. One of them has been found.'

'Alive or dead?'

'Alive, Sir. There's no sign of the other one'.

'The locus?'

'An abandoned church out near Kirkton.'

'I know the one,' said Farrell. 'Who called it in?'

'A couple of kids planning to bunk off school. They got as far as busting a board from one of the rear windows when they heard a child crying and called it in.'

'Lucky break,' said Farrell.

'DCI Lind asked for you to nip out to the scene. He's already gone out there with DI Moore.'

'You'd better go and be with the family; we'll keep you apprised of developments by radio. That is, if you're up to it?' he said with a hint of sarcasm. It did the trick.

'Of course I'm up to it, Sir,' she flung at him and marched off with her head held high.

Farrell tore to the crime scene, which was a few miles out of town. As he waited impatiently at the lights in St Mary's Street the sky seemed to develop an ominous tinge with the clouds swirling to make a demonic image. He averted his eyes. It's not real. Not enough sleep. He fumbled around in his pocket. No pills. He'd been getting careless. The lights changed. He'd sort things later. Right now he needed to focus on the job.

Drawing up outside the abandoned church Farrell could see that the crumbling sandstone masonry was well on the way to becoming a ruin. Set well back from the road, there were bushes poking out through the walls and it had clearly been a number of years since anyone had tended the forlorn graves. Moss covered the stone flags that led to the open wooden door, which was hanging off its hinges. The doorway resembled a gaping mouth, and Farrell shuddered at the thought of entering. To his fevered mind the place reeked of evil. Get a grip, he told himself. It's only mildew and dry rot.

An incident van arrived, and SOCOs spilled out already suited up and carrying with them the usual paraphernalia of their trade. The local news teams arrived hot on their heels.

PC Thomson stood guard at the outer cordon, looking as intimidating as he knew how. Farrell lifted the tape and patted him on the shoulder in passing.

'Good lad,' he muttered. 'Don't let anyone past, except on my say so.'

Inside the church, Farrell sucked in a deep breath then wished that he hadn't. The air was fetid and reeked of decay. As his eyes grew accustomed to the gloom, Farrell began to take in his surroundings. He heard some scuttling and scraping sounds and beamed his torch into the red eyes of a rat with an empty crisp packet hanging from its mouth. Around the walls, where the altar would have been, were slogans sprayed in red: 'SATAN LIVES', being among the most literate offerings. He moved on down the aisle to the inner cordon, which seemed a hub of activity. Farrell donned the obligatory plastic suit and passed through. Lind greeted him, sounding strained beneath his professional demeanour.

Forcing himself to remain objective he examined the first separately cordoned-off scene beside the left-hand wall from every angle. An old-fashioned book of fairy tales that looked vaguely familiar lay beside a makeshift bed on the floor. Farrell picked it up and opened it, noticing the corner turned down at *Sleeping Beauty*. As he was replacing the book he noticed something poking out from under a blanket. His jaw tightened when he saw that it was a playing card: the Queen of Hearts. He left it untouched, wanting the SOCO to extract it first.

'Where's the child?' he asked tersely.

'Over there with DI Moore and DS Byers,' answered Lind. 'Poor little chap hasn't said a word since we found him.'

Farrell strode over to the small group on the other side of the church, removing his plastic coveralls as he did so. As he approached the officers parted to let him through. He recognized that it was Mark from the description of his clothes: red joggers, a white T-shirt, and a navy cardigan, all looking a bit grubby now. The little boy looked up, and the instant his big blue eyes met Farrell's he started to scream, hiding his face in DI Moore's skirt. She glared at him.

He had never been good with kids this age. Squatting down to the boy's level he gave his most winning smile but it was no use. The hysterical toddler was having none of it. Farrell struggled to make himself heard above the din.

'Where was Mark found?'

'Lying on that bed beside the far wall.'

'Is there another bed for the other boy anywhere?'

'Over there, inside that alcove.'

Farrell followed her finger and realized that she was pointing to where the crib would normally have been erected at Christmas. As his feet marched across the tiled floor he could smell a faint whiff of something familiar. Incense. That's what it was. This church had been lying empty for close on ten years. Not to mention the fact that incense was a dirty word to most self-respecting Church of Scotland types. This stuff was the real article, not just some hippy joss sticks.

As he walked towards the alcove he saw that the space was littered with chip papers that still stank of vinegar. At least he'd fed the poor mites. The SOCOs, Phil Tait and Janet White, were busy bagging evidence.

Farrell probed with his eyes until he saw what he was looking for. He signalled to Janet.

'Pull that piece of card out for me. It's sticking out from under the blanket.'

She carefully extracted it using a pair of tweezers and held it up for inspection. Farrell took a step back as he realized the implications of what he was seeing.

'Bastard,' he hissed.

'Sir?' asked Janet, not following.

Farrell ignored her, lost in his own thoughts. Clearly the murderer had made the little boys select a card to determine their fate. The card that he was looking at was the three of spades. Highest wins.

The SOCO put it in an evidence bag and Farrell, forcing his thoughts back into the moment, co-signed the tag. He had learned very early on in his career that sloppy police work plus good defence lawyer equalled bad guy out on the street. Maybe that was what had happened with Baxter, resulting in his get out of jail free card.

'There's another card underneath the bed over there,' he pointed.

Comprehension dawned in Janet's eyes, and she nodded but carried on processing the scene in front of her: the consummate professional. Phil gathered up his case and moved in the direction indicated by Farrell.

Farrell turned on his heel to leave, but Janet stopped him.

'Wait, there's something else. Just give me a minute …'

Farrell looked on with ill-concealed impatience as she slowly peeled off a piece of white-backed card from the underside of the blanket then rotated it so he could see that it was a piece of a black-and-white photo of some age.

Just then he heard an excited exclamation.

'Sir! You'd better get over here and look at this,' yelled Byers.

Farrell picked his way up the central aisle to a set of stone stairs leading up to where the altar would have been. Another, smaller, set of stairs led up to the pulpit on one side, where the minister would have addressed the congregation. On the adjacent wall was an old-fashioned gilt-edged mirror. Farrell stared at it in surprise. He'd never seen the likes of it. There was a small notice above the mirror crudely attached to the wall with tape. It read:

'WATCHING YOU WATCHING ME'

Farrell rubbed his eyes, which felt like they'd glass in them. What did it all mean? This set-up had all the hallmarks of an elaborate production in which the abductor was trying to convey some kind of a message. But what was it and who was the intended recipient? He thought back to the murder of Father Boyd. That too had been staged for maximum impact. Farrell left instructions with Byers to alert the SOCOs and cordon off this additional area, then picked his way back down the stairs to the main body of the kirk.

The female police surgeon had just finished examining the little boy in DI Moore's arms and pronounced him fit and well. As Farrell approached he turned his head away and cuddled in to his protector. Farrell tousled his curls gently but Mark shrank from his touch. Poor little mite probably had a downer on most men after what he'd been through.

DCI Lind came across.

'This little lad needs to get home to his mum,' he said. 'He seems to have taken to you, Kate, so why don't you and Farrell take him back where he belongs. I'll stay here to make sure everything is done by the book.'

As he looked at her cradling the child in her arms, uncaring of the fact that her tights were laddered and her fancy suit covered in dust, Farrell wondered whether it had been choice or circumstance that had resulted in her not having children of her own to care for.

He strode out of the church, grateful for the cool air fanning his face. DI Moore got into the back of his car, snuggling the boy on her knees minus a seatbelt. Farrell said nothing. To heck with the law.

CHAPTER TWENTY-FOUR

As they drew up outside the house where the family lived Farrell's stomach lurched with dread. He glanced at DI Moore in the mirror and saw the same anguished look in her eyes. It was never easy being the bearer of bad news. The local press was in attendance but before long would be getting elbowed to the back of the crowd by journalists from the nationals, who were meaner and hungrier for a good story to pick over.

Farrell exited the car and looked as threatening as he knew how at the assembled posse. It didn't stop the flash bulbs popping as they hurried to the front door to be let in by a grim DC McLeod.

'Have they no decency, Sir?' she asked.

'Not part of the job description, I'm afraid, DC McLeod.'

The boy's mother came bursting through a door, followed by the father. She snatched her son out of DI Moore's arms and fell to the floor with him, smothering him in kisses.

'Mark, thank God; I've been so worried.'

'Elspeth, come away in here with him where it's warmer. He looks frozen,' said her husband, his voice coarse with emotion.

She allowed herself to be led into the comfortable lounge, where a log fire blazed in the grate. Having been bid to sit, Farrell perched awkwardly on the edge of a floral print chair. The woman turned to DI Moore, hope briefly kindling in her eyes.

'My other son, Jamie, Officer?'

'I'm so sorry. There was no sign of him and no indication as to what might have happened to him.'

Elspeth's face crumpled as she turned into her husband. Her joy had been short-lived. DC McLeod took the little boy by the hand and went into the kitchen for some juice.

'So he might still be alive then?' asked Barry, who seemed somehow to have reduced in stature since they'd first met.

'Anything's possible,' replied Farrell, sounding more positive than he felt.

Just because a body hadn't been found yet it didn't necessarily mean that the other boy was still alive. DI Moore didn't share the information that they were awaiting the arrival of a specialist dog team, trained to sniff out cadavers, to cover the area around the church and the small wood behind it.

'He'd clearly fed them chips for tea and there was a book of fairy tales with the page turned down at *Sleeping Beauty*,' said DI Moore.

'That was always Jamie's favourite story,' said his mother, smiling through her tears.

Farrell felt suddenly uneasy. The book had been beside Mark's bed, not Jamie's.

'Mrs Sullivan, can you confirm again what Mark was wearing the last time you saw him?'

Farrell cursed himself for not having checked this out before. What was wrong with him? DI Moore's level grey eyes met his, uncomprehending. Mr Sullivan glanced at his tearful wife.

'Look, is this really necessary? Can't it wait until tomorrow? Hasn't she been through enough?'

'No argument there, Sir,' said Farrell with feeling. He looked into the father's eyes.

'It was something your wife said; I have my reasons for needing

127

to know,' he continued doggedly, hating himself for what he suspected might be yet another blow he'd have to inflict on this tortured couple.

'What he's wearing now: red joggers, a white T-shirt, and a navy cardigan,' she replied, sounding puzzled but not yet alarmed.

'Thank you, ma'am. Do either of your sons have any birthmarks that enable you to tell them apart?'

Farrell saw the horror flare in DI Moore's eyes. She got it.

'Well, Jamie has a strawberry mark under his hair at the base of his neck. Mark has a mole on his left anklebone.'

'DI Moore, do you think I could have a cup of tea?' asked Farrell.

She got up immediately and went to the kitchen. Moments later she returned with the little boy and DC McLeod and shook her head. Farrell rubbed his hand over his eyes. No easy way to say this; he just had to launch straight in.

'Mr and Mrs Sullivan, DI Moore has just had a look at your little boy in the kitchen. It appears that for some reason unknown to us the killer made the children swap clothes. I'm almost positive that it is Jamie who we brought back with us and not Mark.'

Both parents sat there as though hit by a thunderbolt then dived at the son they had thought might be dead before weeping afresh for the other son they had now lost.

DI Moore stood up and beckoned to DC McLeod and Farrell to join her in the kitchen. She spoke to Mhairi first.

'DC McLeod, I gather that you have come off a night shift. Do you want someone to relieve you?'

'No, Ma'am, I'll be fine. They've got to know me. I think it would be best if I stayed, provided some continuity.'

'I'll send an officer round with some supplies and an overnight case,' said DI Moore, giving her a brief hug.

'Nothing too stylish, Ma'am, or no one will recognize me,' said Mhairi in a weak attempt at humour.

'Just hang on in there, McLeod,' said Farrell. 'You're doing sterling work.'

'Thank you, Sir,' said Mhairi.

Farrell envied women their ease with each other. He always felt so clumsy when the emotional stakes got high. Best to keep a professional distance.

Before they left he asked the parents one more question.

'Are you members of any particular church in the town?'

'Yes, St Aidan's. I wouldn't say we make it along every single Sunday or anything but we were married there and the kids are baptized in the faith,' said Mr Sullivan.

Mrs Sullivan was sitting staring into space. Her son was clambering over her knee trying to get her attention, but she was unresponsive. Mhairi gently lifted him off her knee and took him upstairs. It had been a long day for the little chap.

The doorbell rang and an elderly gentleman with an avuncular manner was admitted. Fortunately, DC McLeod had called the family doctor earlier as poor Mrs Sullivan seemed to be sinking fast. On their way out, DI Moore pressed a card with her personal numbers into Mr Sullivan's hand.

'If you think of anything, anything at all, no matter how trivial it might have a bearing on the case, call me day or night. I want you to know that I will not rest until we know what has happened to Mark.'

Mr Sullivan pressed her hand, too overcome to speak.

As Farrell was pulling away from the kerb he saw Father Malone turn the corner looking like he had the weight of the world on his shoulders. He waited to be sure and saw him turn into the gateway of the house they had just left. Farrell wondered what reception he would get from the parents.

Later that night as he drove home a murderous rage filled Farrell. What kind of warped individual could have played such sick games with those little boys?

Once back at Kelton, he was too wired to sleep and prowled around the cottage like a caged tiger. He tried to pray to calm himself but the words wouldn't come. Instead he sought solace in a bottle of malt whisky. However, far from placating the angry beast within him the whisky seemed to embolden it. Swaying in the open doorway to his room he yelled at the wooden crucifix.

'Why did you let this happen? They're only little boys. Why didn't you stop him?'

Fiendish laughter filled the room. Farrell stood transfixed with horror as the crude wooden head on the crucifix slowly turned to face him. The eyes glowed red and the lips parted. A forked tongue darted out; at which point Farrell slammed the door shut and retreated to the living room, where he remained with his back to the wall, lights blazing all night, muttering, over and over.

'It isn't real. It isn't real. It isn't real.'

CHAPTER TWENTY-FIVE

Farrell woke with a sour taste in his mouth and a thumping headache. Stumbling, he rooted about in the washing basket for some running gear. Only after a few stretches did he dare open his bedroom door and look at the crucifix. Wooden eyes stared impassively back at him. Excellent.

He took his lithium with some orange juice straight from the carton then ran out into the rain, aware that he must cut a somewhat ridiculous figure but knowing that the exercise would help stabilize his mood.

As his feet squelched along the mud flats the fine drizzle seemed to permeate his very bones. The lonely cry of an oystercatcher escaped the dampening effect of the mist rolling inland from the Solway estuary. Body now on autopilot, Farrell's mind churned over the events of yesterday. St Aidan's seemed to be a common denominator; yet, considering the large size of the parish relative to the population of Dumfries as a whole, was that necessarily significant? What about Father Malone? He'd worked with the dead priest but clearly knew the boys' family as well. Then there was that day he'd been sitting having tea and biscuits with Jason Baxter. Sure, it could have been nothing more than a pastoral visit or it could have been something more sinister. And where did Baxter fit into the equation? Another coincidence? He wasn't buying it.

Back at the cottage Farrell traipsed wet feet up the wooden stairs. After a scalding hot shower and vigorous rub with a rough towel he felt closer to human than he had for a while. He came out the shower room ready for anything … except this.

Standing at the top of the stairs he could see there were now two sets of wet footprints going up the stairs, not just one. Blood pumping, he crept into the adjacent bedroom, nudging the door against the wall with his bare foot in case there was anyone behind it. He then charged through to the living room. The plaintive beauty of a Gregorian chant suddenly swelled to fill the silence. He'd forgotten to switch off his CD alarm. As he made his way round the austerely furnished room he suddenly became aware of a draught. Racing downstairs he found the front door swinging open. Still clad in his towel he raced outside and looked up and down the lane. Two schoolgirls clocked him and ran off giggling.

Back inside, with the door locked behind him, Farrell pondered. The wet footprints had long evaporated. Had he imagined the whole thing? He'd been briefly delusional last night, courtesy of the whisky, he hoped. Maybe he'd nipped back downstairs for something and forgotten. It happens. Working a case like this it was no wonder he was spooked. Throwing on the first black suit that came to hand he quickly dressed before heading into work. Maybe today they'd get the breakthrough in the Boyd case they'd been waiting for.

DCI Lind was already over at Cornwall Mount briefing the Chief Constable and other senior officers by conference call. DI Moore was at Glasgow meeting with a child psychologist, specializing in trauma, and had left a message asking Farrell to take her morning briefing in relation to the child abduction case. There was some crossover of personnel already due to the relatively small number of available officers in a force this size. Farrell decided to hold a combined briefing in the lecture theatre at Loreburn Street, which was large enough to hold both investigating teams. Glancing around at the assorted members of his team, Farrell knew that their morale must be at low ebb. He'd picked up the morning papers on the way in and the headlines had made him wince.

'POLICE OUT OF THEIR DEPTH IN LOCAL MURDER'

'LOCAL BOOBIES FLOUNDER IN LOCAL CRIME WAVE'

Unless they picked up their game and started to get results they would be vilified nationwide. He had to seem positive, look like he was in control of the situation. He cleared his throat and the room fell quiet.

'Yesterday was a tough day for all of us. I want to congratulate you all on a job well done under difficult circumstances. We still don't know what has happened to young Mark. An examination of the grounds and wood around the church has revealed nothing sinister so far. A specialist dog team will be arriving from the Central Belt this afternoon and if they strike out then this will remain an open case to which we devote maximum effort and attention. The stakes don't come much higher than a missing child.'

'Do you think it's likely we'll find him alive?' asked Byers.

'Statistically, it's more likely that he is dead than alive at this stage but statistics are not facts. The abductor is intelligent and plans his crimes meticulously down to the last detail. That does not mean he is infallible. The fact that he appears to have made some effort to cater to the needs of the boys in terms of food, bedding, even a storybook, I believe gives some grounds for optimism.'

A hand shot up.

'Yes, DC McLeod?'

'Sir, do you think he's done here or is he likely to strike again?'

'My gut tells me he'll strike again,' said Farrell. 'Clare Yates, a local forensic psychiatrist, has been called in to consult on the case, and I'm meeting her tomorrow morning. I'm hoping she might be able to give us something additional to go on.'

'Has any thought been given to questioning Jamie?' asked DS Stirling.

'DCI Lind has put out feelers to child services and the Council legal team to ascertain whether sufficient safeguards could be put in place to make that a possibility. Right now, DI Moore is in Glasgow meeting with a psychologist specializing in the forensic examination of children. While it would have very little evidentiary weight in terms of court proceedings it could give some limited indication of the abductor's intentions.' Farrell paused. 'Moving on now to the unsolved murder of Father Boyd. DS Stirling?'

'Sir?'

Farrell regarded the man closely but there was no trace of the animosity he'd displayed towards him before. Missing kids had a way of putting things into perspective.

'I want you to organize twenty-four hour tails on Jason Baxter and Father Malone. Use the most experienced men on Baxter. It won't be the first time he's been followed and he knows all the dodges.'

'McLeod.'

'Sir?'

'Are you available to come to Father Boyd's funeral with me later this morning?'

'Yes, Sir. Elspeth's mother arrived this morning. She said she'll take care of the family meantime, pending further developments.'

'In that case, I want you to review the footage of Father Boyd's funeral this afternoon. I want a complete list of who was there, together with their addresses and who talked to whom at the graveside or anywhere else. Look for anything out of the ordinary. Also, I want you to chase up the various forensic reports we're waiting on. Say that DSup Walker will be all over them if they don't drop everything they're doing to concentrate on these two inquiries.'

'Yes sir,' said DC McLeod.

'The rest of you have been allocated actions by DI Moore or myself, so what are you waiting for?'

Galvanized into action, the rest of the men and women assembled sprang to their feet and filed out. Farrell applied himself to making notes for DI Moore on where they were at so she could press on when she returned later that morning.

After a few minutes he felt the hair on the back of his neck prickle a warning. He spun round. DSup Walker was standing with his back against the closed door. The expression on his blowsy face was even more ugly than usual.

'Sir?' Farrell asked, careful not to rile the man.

Walker approached slowly. Farrell resisted the impulse to back away from him and stood his ground. Everything in the older man's stance was suggestive of barely contained aggression. When he stopped he was so close Farrell could see the broken veins on his nose and smell last night's whisky on his breath.

'I knew you were trouble as soon as you walked in the door,' Walker hissed.

'Sir?' said Farrell.

'Everything was chugging along nicely; the odd domestic murder every couple of years, just to spice things up a little, give us some respect. Then you show up. All of a sudden everything's gone to Hell.'

'That's hardly my fault, Sir,' protested Farrell.

'Think about it,' Walker continued relentlessly. 'You're a Catholic priest with a history of dodgy past shenanigans, like exorcisms. All of a sudden we've got a murdered priest, a little boy turning up in a church, and another one missing. I'm telling you I don't like it. Something smells bad and I'm hoping it's not you, Farrell. Do I make myself clear?'

'Abundantly, Sir,' snapped Farrell, seriously riled himself now.

'Word is we've got all the national press on the way. I don't need to tell you that the police usually get a rough deal from these bastards. I want the investigations wrapped up and someone in the frame pronto.'

'Anyone particular spring to mind, Sir,' asked Farrell.

'I'll be watching you, Farrell, make no mistake about it. And if I need to hang out anyone's arse to dry …'

'I'm guessing that would be mine, Sir.'

'*Now* we understand each other,' said Walker, and stomped heavily off.

'Always a pleasure,' muttered Farrell after his departing back.

After work, Farrell forced himself to go along to Wetherspoons for a quick drink with Sergeants Byers and Stirling and a bunch of others, detectives and civilians alike. He'd never been into the ritualistic piss up but politics dictated he fake it now and then. Recent events had been harrowing for everyone and he reckoned they all needed to blow off steam. As he looked around the cavernous interior of the pub he couldn't help but marvel. Last time he'd lived in the town it had been a hollowed out ruin of an old church; the remaining fluted columns a defiant last stand against secular indifference.

Just then, Farrell's eyes were drawn across the crowded bar. Mhairi was with a young man who looked somewhat the worse for wear and was trying to get a little too friendly.

Byers nudged Stirling.

'Well if it isn't the tart with a heart,' he sneered.

'Don't talk about the lass like that,' admonished Stirling.

'Look at her! She's asking for it, isn't she?' continued Byers, undaunted.

Farrell turned on Byers, causing him to take a step backwards in surprise.

'Watch your mouth, Byers,' he snapped. DC McLeod is part of this team and I won't have her spoken about like that.'

Byers glared at him but said nothing further.

There was an awkward silence. Farrell tossed three tenners on the bar top.

'Have a round on me.'

As he was turning to leave he glanced over again at DC McLeod and their eyes locked. She flushed and turned away.

CHAPTER TWENTY-SIX

Mhairi didn't know what to expect as she entered St Aidan's alongside Farrell on the morning of the funeral. Awkwardly she copied Farrell as he genuflected while making the sign of the cross. She had never been to a Requiem Mass before and felt the sombre atmosphere permeate her bones as she sat down. Stealing a sideways glance at her boss, she saw that he was chalk white. His eyes were downcast and he appeared to be praying. Crikey, looked like the observations were down to her. As subtly as she could manage she slowly glanced around, seeing members of the team in all directions. They had paired into couples to draw less attention and drafted some uniforms in as well. She saw Byers lean towards a female constable, no doubt intending to make some wisecrack, and saw him quelled with a look. The church was absolutely mobbed and everyone was dressed in black and sat with heads bowed, or whispering quietly to each other.

The ornate coffin was at the top of the centre aisle, close to the altar, with one large wreath of lilies on top of it discharging their intense sweet scent into the mourners. The sight of it made Mhairi shudder. Ever since she had read *The Ka of Gifford Hillary* by Dennis Wheatley at the age of twelve she had been terrified of being buried alive. Not much chance of that in this case.

Suddenly the organ struck up and with a collective rustle everyone stood and began to sing 'Amazing Grace'. To her horror, Mhairi felt the first pricking of inappropriate tears. She hadn't thought it would happen here because she was on the job but it seemed to make no difference. Every time she was at any event with stirring music she could not stop herself blubbing. Oh no, this was bad, very bad. She would be a laughing stock if anyone clocked her. By the time the last strains of the music had faded away her face was drenched with tears and snot. As they sat down she felt an ironed handkerchief being pressed into her hand by Farrell and surreptitiously repaired the damage.

She noticed an elderly woman, who she took to be Boyd's sister, sitting at the front with her head tilted back as though she had a bad smell under her nose. With a jolt she also recognized Elspeth and Barry sitting with little Jamie off to one side, near the rear door.

The Mass was being conducted by an elderly priest. Father Malone was assisting. Proceedings seemed to go on forever with the congregation kneeling, standing, and sitting in patterns Mhairi could not anticipate. As the priests circled the coffin uttering the immortal words 'ashes to ashes, dust to dust ...', while swinging a heavy gold contraption wafting incense, she found her emotions veering wildly out of control again. It was all just so sad. She could see why people became drawn to religion. There was a bleak kind of comfort in these rituals of farewell.

Finally, the coffin was processed out of the church to the stirring music of 'How Great Thou Art'. There had been no scenes, no drama, just a regular funeral.

As they left the church all the mourners were funnelled into a line, forcing them to pass through a team of uniformed officers taking names, addresses, and digital images. Most people were accommodating but a few got a bit uppity and had to be leaned on. As instructed, Mhairi had taken up a position beside the doors in case anyone tried to make a run for it. A minor scuffle broke out and she took a step forward, craning her neck to see what was going on. Suddenly she received an almighty shove that pitched her forward onto her knees. She turned angrily to see a flame-haired woman legging it across the car park and disappearing round the corner. Radioing to one of the uniforms to come cover her position she tore off in pursuit but there was no sign of the woman anywhere. She hadn't been the only one trying to slither out the side and escape the queue but she had been the only one who cared enough about getting away to assault a police officer. Unfortunately, Mhairi hadn't got a good enough look at her to issue a description or even to hazard a guess at her age. Redheads in Scotland weren't exactly a rare occurrence.

Once her breathing had returned to normal she radioed Farrell, who was on his way to the graveside, then headed back to the station, annoyed with herself for letting the woman slip through her fingers like some probationer. Maybe she would get a better look at her when the video footage came in this afternoon.

Back at the station she chased up the outstanding forensic reports, trying to inject the maximum amount of urgency into her voice. Then she sat back in her chair, temporarily overwhelmed. The amount of work she'd had to do since Farrell burst on the scene was unprecedented in all her time in the force. Never had she had to deal with two such complex and sinister investigations. Her stomach lurched with dread as she thought about the dog team arriving that afternoon to search for signs of little Mark in the woods. Barry and Elspeth must be out of their minds with worry yet they had taken the trouble to go to Father Boyd's funeral this morning, all the while having to live with the uncertainty of whether they would be having one of their own soon for a much-loved child.

With renewed determination she opened up the digital footage from this morning and began the laborious process of cross-matching photos to names and addresses and ticking those off the list of names on the parishioner database they had constructed from the book given to them by Father Malone.

The bishop had prohibited the use of cameras inside the church so, to her intense frustration, there were no images of the redhead anywhere. Mhairi's gut told her that the woman had information pertinent to the investigation but there was simply no way she could think of to track her down.

CHAPTER TWENTY-SEVEN

Farrell slipped away from the graveyard in advance of the mourners. As expected, only a small number of those in the church had made it out here to this serene resting place in an elevated position overlooking the hurly burly of the town below. Boyd's sister had stood with a countenance carved from granite throughout. Farrell was unable to determine whether her stony features spoke to her upbringing or to her relationship with her brother.

Father Joe Spinelli had been there, leaning heavily on the arm of a younger priest unknown to Farrell. By tacit agreement they had given each other a wide berth under the circumstances.

Glancing at his watch he figured he had time to drive out to the woods, where the police dog team would shortly be arriving. Although, strictly speaking, it wasn't his investigation, he figured that DI Moore could do with his support and experience at what could turn out to be a particularly distressing scene.

He turned into the small muddy area adjacent to the woods where a handful of sombre SOCOs conversed in low voices with DI Moore and DS Stirling. The police dog van pulled in just as Farrell was exiting the car and he saw it was Michael Patmore at the wheel; a consummate professional he had worked with before.

Farrell quickly introduced Michael and his partner, Pam Kelly, to those assembled before DI Moore brought them up to speed on the missing boy. With a grimace, she produced a sealed bag with Mark's comforter and a worn teddy and handed them over.

'His mother tells me these were the items he had on him most of the time. I've also brought one of his trainers.'

'Excellent. We'll see what Barney makes of these,' said Michael. 'Barney is trained to find missing persons. The other dog, Charlie, is trained to sniff out cadavers.'

The Alsatians that bounded out the back of the van were so huge that Farrell took an involuntary step back. He needn't have worried. The dogs' intelligent brown eyes never left their handlers as they went through a well-rehearsed sequence of commands.

Finally, the items were presented one at a time and Barney was let off the leash into the woods with Michael jogging after him. Pam and Charlie followed at a more sedate and rambling pace. Everyone else remained where they were, too tense for small talk.

A tremendous barking rent the air followed by a whistle. Hearts sank. They'd found something.

DI Moore and the two SOCOs suited up and walked off in single file into the woods. After what seemed like an eternity Moore came back on her own, her face ashen, and clutching a number of evidence bags.

'No body, as far as we can determine. The only hot spot was a shallow pit covered by leaves and sticks in which we found these.'

She held out the bags so that the others could see the contents through the clear plastic. A small pair of green joggers, a yellow T-shirt, cream jumper, and a pair of black trainers with socks stuffed inside.

'He's messing with us,' said Farrell. 'It's almost as if he wanted us to find these items.'

'Does that make it more or less likely he's killed the kid, though?' asked DS Stirling.

'I wish I knew,' replied Farrell.

CHAPTER TWENTY-EIGHT

The next morning Farrell was shown into the comfortable consulting room as soon as he arrived. Instead of remaining behind her desk, Clare came round and gestured for him to take one of a number of easy chairs grouped round a small table. When they were seated she reached over and took his hand.

'How are you holding up?'

The warmth and understanding in her voice almost did for him. Gently, he pulled his hand away and cleared his throat. She took her cue from him and sat back in her chair, once again the cool professional.

He ran both cases by her in their entirety, well, almost. He left out the bit about the potential intruder at Kelton and the personal stuff. No point in muddying the waters. She might think he was imagining things, becoming ill again. After he had stopped talking she continued making notes then pulled out a pair of glasses to study the crime scene photos relating to the murder and also those taken in the church where the boy was found.

'There are some broad similarities between the two cases,' she said. 'Both have been carefully planned and executed down to the smallest detail. The perpetrator in both cases could arguably be making a point, several points actually. It's as if he's left us signposts. Either he's playing with us or deep down he wants to be caught. There's deferred gratification in the case of the boys, which suggests the person who took them is highly intelligent and still very much in control.'

'What do you make of the fact that one of the boys was found in a church?' asked Farrell.

'Could be coincidence,' Clare mused. 'After all, it was no longer consecrated, was it?'

'Been deserted for ten years.'

'Could have simply been a good place to stash the boys unde-tected or could have had resonance with his underlying theme.'

'There was a faint smell of incense,' offered Farrell, feeling faintly embarrassed.

'Did anyone else notice that?' asked Clare, subjecting him to intense scrutiny.

'Not that they can recall,' he answered. That look again. Was his former illness always going to stand between them? 'Then there was the mirror in the church with the note on it.'

'Do you know for certain that it wasn't there before?'

'We can't say for sure but I would have thought that was highly unlikely. When was the last time you saw a clergyman comb his hair before delivering a sermon? Besides the frame of the mirror would have been tarnished by now in such a damp place,' said Farrell

'Maybe he told the boys it was a magic mirror to make them feel under constant surveillance and so render them more compliant?'

'I hadn't thought of that. Makes sense, I suppose,' said Farrell.

'It would be a consistent frame of reference with the book of fairy tales,' said Clare.

'The level of aggression is entirely different in the two cases,' Farrell said. 'In the case of Boyd the murder is a violent one.'

'The little boy that was recovered, on the other hand, didn't have a mark on him. Although we don't know whether that is the case with Mark. Both boys seem to have been fed and given bedding,' said Clare. 'Also, the whole bedtime story thing is very strange. Why go to such lengths to care for the children?'

'My gut feeling is that it might be the same person behind the murder of Boyd and the abduction of the kids,' said Farrell. 'What do you think?'

'I hear what you're saying but it doesn't fit any crime pathology that I'm aware of,' Clare replied. 'In my opinion there would need to be a link between Boyd and the kids or their family for that to be a plausible theory. If the choice of victims was entirely random and we were dealing with your run-of-the-mill serial killer, then I would expect to see a pattern in victim choice and also in the way the victims were killed. Most pathological killers wouldn't switch from killing an adult to abducting, maybe killing, a child. It would be one or the other. Also, we still have no idea what his intentions are in relation to Mark. Whether he intends to kill him, hang onto him, or let him go.'

Farrell slumped in his seat. She was right, dammit.

'Look,' Clare said gently, 'why don't I cook you dinner tonight? We can chill out afterwards, watch a DVD. No pressure. After the last few days I reckon that's just what you need. Doctor's orders.'

Despite himself, Farrell stiffened. Clare looked exasperated.

'For goodness' sake, stop being so touchy. I meant it as a joke,' she said.

'Sorry, dinner sounds wonderful. Around eight OK?'

'Perfect. And I promise to leave my stethoscope at the office,' she said.

As he left the building Farrell felt his jaw start to ache and realized that he was smiling. Almost immediately, the smile was replaced by a frown. What had possessed him to agree to go round to her place? He should have just made an excuse. He was getting way too old and set in his ways for this carry-on. What would she expect from him? What if she tried to ... *stop right there!*

Farrell reined himself in with effort and refocused his mind on the case. Where did his old nemesis Baxter fit in? Was he the murderer or had he really come back to the town simply because it was where he had grown up? Apparently he had a rock solid alibi for the night Boyd was killed, but rocks have been known to split apart with the right tools. Maybe he'd been working in concert with the killer, manipulating him behind the scenes? That was certainly a possibility. Farrell knew that when it came to Baxter he was ready to bark at shadows, but whether those shadows were real or imaginary it was impossible yet to say.

Back at the station, he checked in to the MCA room to see what his team had come up with in his absence.

'Stirling? Any feedback on how the tails are doing?'

'Nothing interesting so far, Sir. Baxter is moving up the food chain. Seems to have taken up golf, would you believe? He apparently had lunch in the clubhouse with some flash bird from Edinburgh, name of Moira Sharkey.'

Farrell felt the colour drain from his face and sat down more abruptly than he had intended. Faces swam back into focus. DC McLeod thrust a Mars bar into his face.

'Low blood sugar, Sir, bet you've forgotten to eat in all the stramash.'

He took it from her, playing along.

'The Mars Bar Diet. Now that's one I've always fancied trying.'

'What about Father Malone?' he asked Stirling.

'Clean as a whistle so far, Sir. Seems to spend an awful lot of time in church. Apparently, he's been in there three hours.'

Farrell smelled a rat.

'There are three doors into St Aidan's: the main entrance at the front, a side door, and a small fire door at the rear. I take it all three are covered?'

Farrell could tell by the stricken look on Stirling's face that he hadn't thought to check.

'Right, let's go,' he said to the sergeant decisively and headed out.

They got to the church in record time and found two shamefaced constables waiting on them. Both looked to be barely out of college so Farrell went easy on them.

He walked up to the closed church door. It yielded under his weight, opening with a creak. Inside, he observed Father Malone praying on his knees at the altar steps. The young priest continued his silent devotions, seemingly oblivious to Farrell's approach. Farrell took in the fresh mud on the shoes poking out from under his surplice and also the ragged edge to the man's breathing. Interesting. He genuflected and kneeled down beside the priest, hands clasped, deliberately invading his space. Malone kept his eyes closed and head bent but, sneaking a glance through his peripheral vision, Farrell could see a faint sheen of sweat starting to form on his forehead. An unmistakable tang of sweat mingled with the salty odour of fear began to manifest itself. Farrell remained as still as the adjacent statue of the Virgin Mary. Eventually, just as his knees were beginning to give out, the younger man cracked.

'Detective Inspector Farrell, how can I help you?' Father Malone said, from between clenched teeth.

'By telling me the truth,' said Farrell.

'I don't know what you mean.'

'Well, for starters, where have you been for the last three hours?'

'I've been here all the time, praying,' said the priest.

Farrell leapt to his feet and towered over the young man. He cast around before he found what he was looking for. A bible. Roughly he held it up to Father Malone.

'Swear on this bible that you haven't been out of the church in the past three hours and maybe, just maybe, I'll believe you.'

'I haven't …' faltered the priest.

'Swear it,' insisted Farrell angrily. 'Perjure yourself in a house of God under the body of Our Lord Jesus Christ who died for our sins. Swear it!'

'I can't,' the priest muttered close to tears. 'I can't tell you where I've been. I won't.'

Farrell grabbed Malone by the arm, intending to force him to his feet, but Malone resisted. He paused. This wouldn't do. Two priests brawling in a church? He would deal with Malone later. He wasn't going anywhere.

Forcing down his temper, Farrell turned on his heel and walked out the door.

CHAPTER TWENTY-NINE

Farrell strode through the swing doors at Loreburn Street and stopped dead, wondering whether the woman sitting in the waiting area would clock him if he spun round on his heel and pushed his way back out. Too late. She was on her feet and advancing towards him. Her stooped posture, hooded lids, and hooked nose put him in mind of a vulture; an image enhanced by her greasy dark curls and shaggy black coat. Gritting his teeth, he held out his hand in greeting, pressing the cool slightly scaly flesh on her bony hand.

'I'd been praying you'd stop by,' she drawled, looking up at him with heavy-lidded insolence.

'It's been a long time, Ms Sharkey,' he countered. 'Is this a social call?'

She bared her teeth in what passed for a smile.

'Hardly.'

Farrell escorted her reluctantly to his office. She was a piece of work this one. He'd have to be on his guard. Years ago, during a murder trial in Edinburgh, she'd vilified him, the arresting officer, in the press, almost going so far as to suggest that they'd got the wrong man and that Farrell had more to do with the murder of a gangland boss than he was letting on. His background had been dragged up and she had made out as though he was on a moral crusade fuelled by religious fanaticism rather than following police procedures. She'd been blatantly out to make a name for herself. It had worked.

They sat facing each other, old adversaries. Farrell resisted the urge to fill the silence that stretched between them. He was older and wiser now.

'So,' she said in a voice coarsened by years of cigarettes. 'Heard any good confessions lately?'

'Why? Need to make one?'

Sharkey looked shifty all of a sudden.

'What is it? Why have you come? Have you heard anything pertaining to our investigations?'

She still wouldn't meet his eyes as though engaged in some internal battle. Farrell hardened his voice.

'A little boy is missing and may have been murdered. This nutter is likely to strike again. Do you really want that on your conscience? To know that, if you had only spoken out earlier, a life might have been saved?'

Despite himself his voice had grown ragged. Her eyes flicked towards him, enjoying his discomfort while pondering her own.

'I know nothing about the missing boy. This concerns the murdered priest.'

'Go on', said Farrell, leaning forward, despite himself.

'I'd want an exclusive interview, something that no one else in the press has got.'

'If your information leads to a break in the case that could be arranged,' said Farrell, mouth dry with anticipation.

Sharkey's cold black eyes glittered with malice as she strung out the tension between them. Farrell felt an unholy urge to slap her. Finally, she spoke.

'The priest's housekeeper is a drunk. I caught her on the razzle one night and she spilled her guts. Turns out, Father Boyd wasn't so holy after all.'

'What do you mean?' demanded Farrell.

'He had a secret love child.'

'No way,' said Farrell. 'I don't believe it.'

'Apparently she was a local woman, married the first poor sucker who asked her and passed the kid off as his.'

'I assume you have proof,' said Farrell.

'I'm working on it.'

Manufacturing it, more likely, thought Farrell.

'You have a name, something I can work with?'

'Not yet,' she conceded reluctantly.

Farrell stood up, terminating the interview.

'I'll be in touch, Inspector,' she flung over her shoulder as he escorted her from the premises.

More of a threat than a promise, he decided, as he watched her picking her way down the street.

DC McLeod came bursting through the door and was brought up short by the savage look on the face of her boss.

'Sir, anything wrong?'

Farrell quickly brought her up to speed on the morning's developments.

'Do you think there's anything in it, Sir?'

'Hard to say. I know it goes on a lot more than people realize. The celibate state is an unnatural one. But Boyd? I never had him down for shenanigans of that sort.'

'People change, though, don't they, Sir. You never knew him as a young man. I'd never have had you down for a priest either,' she said incautiously, her hand flying to her mouth as though to stuff the words back in.

'I meant it as a compliment, Sir,' she said blushing.

Farrell raised an eyebrow. McLeod squirmed.

'It at least gives us another line of enquiry,' he said. 'If we can establish the identity of the woman he had the child with then that gives us a whole raft of additional suspects.'

'There's the woman herself,' said McLeod.

'Unlikely,' replied Farrell. 'She'd have to be fairly old by now. Also, why wait all these years? No, my money's on the kid or the husband.'

'Do we know if it was a boy or a girl?'

'No, could be either,' said Farrell.

'Not a lot to go on, Sir, is it?'

'That's why we need to question the housekeeper again. I'll bet she knows more than she's letting on. When she was interviewed with her lawyer in custody we got nothing worth having out of her at all. The whole charade was a complete waste of time.'

'I'll get uniforms to bring her in.'

'No, given that she's still got a pending charge against her for attempting to pervert the course of justice, I reckon that might cause us problems. Apparently she likes a tipple. Do some digging. Find out where she drinks and we can contrive to bump into her there,' said Farrell.

McLeod sped off.

Farrell decided to pay his mother a visit. He felt a stab of sadness that he had to have the excuse of police business to get him past the threshold. Why couldn't they be like other mothers and sons, with her trying to feed him up and him putting up her shelves? Why did everything have to still be so fraught even after all these years? Why did being a Roman Catholic priest matter more than his happiness, even his sanity? As usual, his thoughts threw up more questions than answers.

As he drew up at her neat semi he observed a shadow flit across the curtain. He rang the doorbell. No reply. Fine. If that was the way she wanted to play it. Farrell banged hard on the door.

'Police business; open up.'

He was gratified to see other curtains pulled back to enjoy the show. The door flew open and his mother stood there quivering with rage. Playing to the gallery, he produced his warrant card with a flourish. Without a word she turned on her heel and walked back into the house. He followed her into the front room. She didn't invite him to sit and glared at him with eyes like flint.

He felt his bravado melt away, no match for the coldness of her gaze. Focus, he told himself fiercely. Uninvited, he sat down. Her lips tightened but she said nothing. After a few moments of silence, she sank onto an upright chair, as though the strength had left her legs. Farrell felt ashamed at the small jolt of triumph that shot through him at her capitulation. He should be bigger than this.

'What do you want?' she asked.

Now there was a loaded question, thought Farrell. He kept his voice neutral as he replied.

'How well did you really know Father Boyd?'

His mother looked startled.

'Fairly well, as you know. He was our parish priest for a great number of years.'

'Did you ever hear any talk of him seeing anyone, a woman?'

His mother shot upright like someone had given her an electric shock.

'How dare you. He was a priest, a man of the cloth. Hasn't he suffered enough without you trying to sully his reputation after his death? You, of all people, should know how hard it is to keep such vows. He was a better man than you'll ever be.'

There she goes again, sticking the boot in, thought Farrell.

'Who was he close to back then? Who were his friends?'

'I'm afraid I can't help you,' she replied.

Can't or won't, wondered Farrell? He knew it was brutal but she left him no choice. He took out a colour crime scene photo and stuck it under her nose. She flinched and looked away.

'Don't you want to see his killer caught?'

'Of course I do. I just don't see how raking over the past is going to achieve that. What possible bearing could events that happened over twenty years ago have on his murder now?'

'That's what we're trying to find out.'

'Probably some yob high on drugs, wanting a soft target.'

'And the little boys?'

His mother paled.

'I don't understand?'

'There is a possibility that the same person who murdered Boyd could be behind the abduction of three-year-old twin boys, one of whom is still missing, maybe dead.'

'What kind of a monster would do something like that to a helpless child?' his mother whispered.

Farrell worried that he was perhaps being too tough on her. She was getting on in years.

'Don't hold out on me, mother.'

'There was a woman,' she said in a low voice. 'A long time ago.'

'What was her name?'

'I can't remember.'

'Think!'

'It was all very hushed up. She went away. There were rumours of a child. No one knew for sure. I certainly never believed it.'

'Can you remember anything about her? Anything at all?'

'Her name was … Rosalie … MacFarlane.'

'Where did she live?'

'I think she may have lived in Primrose Street.'

'Has she any family still living in the town?'

'Nobody that I know of. I think she came over from Ireland to work here in one of the local hotels.'

'Do you know which one?'

'No. Even if I did the odds are that it would have closed down by now anyway.'

'Is there anything else at all you can tell me? I promise I'll be as discreet as possible.'

'That's it. I've told you all I know. I'd like you to leave now.'

His mother stood up and moved to the door, her back ramrod straight. Farrell longed to give those bony shoulders a squeeze as he went past her but knew it was a familiarity she would not forgive.

CHAPTER THIRTY

Farrell headed straight back to his office and instigated a search of parish records for any mention of a woman called Rosalie MacFarlane. He also fired off a search to the Registrar at the Mid Steeple for all births and marriages in relation to the same name. Thankfully MacFarlane wasn't that common a name so he was hopeful something would turn up.

He was just raising a welcome cup of coffee to his mouth when the door burst open, causing the scalding coffee to spill down his chest. DC McLeod looked on in horror as he hastily ripped off his shirt to reveal already reddening flesh. Farrell turned on her in exasperation.

'DC McLeod, is it too much to ask that you knock at the door like a regular person instead of storming in here like the SAS, giving me heart failure in the process?'

Sergeant Byers had to pick that exact moment to poke his head round the door.

'Yes?' barked Farrell.

'Er, it'll wait, Sir,' smirked Byers and took off.

McLeod looked at her boss aghast. She had never seen him look so wild.

'Er, sorry, Sir,' she said.

Farrell turned his back to her to get another shirt from the cupboard and spun round again when he heard her involuntary intake of breath. What was wrong with him today? He'd forgotten the raised scars criss-crossing his back.

'Sir, how did you ...?'

Farrell quelled her with a look and flung his shirt on.

'Right, DC McLeod. What's so important?'

'It's the housekeeper, Sir. PC Thomson just phoned to let us know she's in the Drover's Arms, down at the bottom of English Street.'

'I know the one,' said Farrell. 'Anyone with her?'

'She's alone, Sir.'

'Right, let's get down there.'

Farrell took off down the corridor with McLeod in hot pursuit.

'We'll take my car,' he informed her.

Rummaging round in the boot he pulled out a scuffed brown leather jacket, a crumpled white T-shirt, and a pair of Levis. He looked McLeod over critically.

'Haven't you got anything better to wear than that?'

'Sir?' she asked, black affronted.

'That get-up you're wearing. It's too smart. I want us to go in there as if we were off duty, a bit pissed.'

'I've got just the thing in my locker, Sir,' she said cottoning on. 'Back in a jiffy.'

Twenty-five minutes later they were sitting squashed together at a small table in the pub. Although it was a bright sunny day the interior of the pub was dark and gloomy. There were about fifteen customers dotted about the place with only a couple of the clientele being women. For the most part people sat alone nursing their drinks along with their resentments.

The housekeeper, Mary Flannigan, was ensconced at a table against a wall between them and the bar. There were three empty gin glasses on the adjacent table and, from the way she was almost missing her mouth every time she took a sip from the glass in front of her, Farrell guessed they belonged to her. He twisted in his seat so he could keep her in view with his peripheral vision and saw that she had clocked them, shooting baleful glances in their direction.

McLeod shrugged off her jacket, and Farrell, caught unawares, was treated to an eyeful of cleavage that made his hair stand on end. Immediately, he dragged his eyes upwards but not before she'd caught him looking. Bang goes the moral high ground, he thought. She winked at him and, remembering their purpose there, he roughened his voice, slurring his words a little.

'Come on, let's push the boat out, we're not on duty now.'

'Another Bacardi and Coke then. Make it a double,' said Mhairi loudly.

'What's it worth?' asked Farrell, lurching clumsily to his feet.

'That's for me to know and you to find out,' said Mhairi, flicking her hair back from her face.

Turning away from the housekeeper Farrell muttered to Mhairi, 'I feel ridiculous, like we're in some B-movie.'

'Speak for yourself,' said Mhairi. 'I'm strictly A-list myself.'

As he weaved to the bar on slightly unsteady feet Farrell contrived to bump into the wooden table the housekeeper was sitting at, causing her drink to spill slightly. She stared at him with loathing.

'Be careful,' she hissed.

'Hey relax, lady, it was an accident,' he said, affecting not to recognize her.

'Father Boyd would be turning in his grave if he could see you with that floozy,' she said.

Farrell crashed into the seat beside her and stuck his face right up to hers.

'Oh, I don't think so. From what I hear he was partial to a bit of skirt.'

'How dare you! That's a wicked lie!'

'Or was he just not partial to you, Mary, was that the problem?'

She tried to stand up but he anchored her by leaning on a meaty hand.

'He was worth ten of you. Don't you dare speak ill of him.'

'Get jealous of her, did you? Want a piece of him yourself?'

'You don't know what you're talking about. Father Boyd was a man of the cloth. I would never have ...'

'And what about the child? How did he manage to sweep that under the carpet?'

'There was no child.'

'Arranged an abortion, did he?'

'Of course not! Father Boyd would never have murdered his ...'

'So there was a child. Boy or girl?'

'Stop twisting things. You've got me all confused.'

'What was the name of the woman?'

The shaven-headed barman started in their direction, rolling up his sleeves. Mhairi quickly flashed her warrant card and shook her head. He didn't look happy but retreated back behind the bar.

The housekeeper cringed but remained silent.

'Was it Rosalie MacFarlane?' demanded Farrell.

The housekeeper sucked in a breath then bent over coughing.

'Who told you that?'

'Never you mind,' said Farrell, remembering to slur his words.

'I never knew her name. I caught a glimpse of her once, from a distance.'

'How did you know it was her?'

'He had a photo of her. I stumbled upon it accidentally,' the housekeeper said, looking shifty.

'Oh yeah?' said Farrell, injecting a note of scepticism into his voice. 'What did she look like then?'

'She had long red hair and looked barely old enough to be out of school. Sent by the devil to tempt him, she was. He succumbed in a moment of weakness. That's all it was.'

'What happened to the baby?'

161

'I didn't say there was a baby,' she sneered.

'Come on, Mary,' cajoled Farrell. 'What does it matter now? He's dead. There's nothing more you can do for him except help us find his killer. Don't you think he'd want justice? An eye for an eye, a tooth for a tooth. Wasn't that one of his favourite quotes from the Bible?'

'He wouldn't like you of all people poking around into his life. He never trusted you, said you were a lightweight and that you should never have been ordained in the first place.'

'Did he now?' slurred Farrell. 'And I suppose his own son is a pillar of rectitude is he?'

'I'm sure that he is,' she said defiantly.

A boy then. Farrell decided to chance his arm further.

'You couldn't have thought that highly of Father Boyd if you sent him those letters,' he said.

'They weren't meant for him,' she shot back, clamping a hand over her mouth as she realized what she had said.

'Thank you, you've been most helpful,' Farrell said, straightening up. She knew then that she'd been tricked, and the look she gave him would have curdled milk.

Driving back to the station, Farrell's thoughts were in turmoil. Boyd had been so hard on him when he thought he had breached the sanctity of the confessional, yet all along Boyd had been harbouring an even bigger secret in the shape of a lover and child. Not for the first time, Farrell wondered if you could ever really know someone.

'So who killed Boyd then, Sir?' McLeod's voice broke into his reverie.

'Could be the old flame, though I doubt it, given the manner of the killing.'

'What about the child?'

'Maybe. He'll be a man now. Could even be the housekeeper. Don't reckon it would take much to push her over the edge.'

'I can't see her killing a priest, though,' said McLeod.

'She's a bit of a zealot,' said Farrell. 'I could see her doing almost anything if she felt it was God's will.'

'What about this woman's husband? If he suddenly found out after all these years, he might have snapped.'

'No way of finding out who he was until we positively identify the woman.'

Farrell suddenly executed an emergency stop, missing Father Malone by inches. The young priest had run right across the road from the church. He didn't stop, but ran on, looking as if the devil himself was after him.

Farrell turned to McLeod, who was looking shaken and rubbing her neck where the seatbelt had dug into her skin. He could smell burning rubber from the tyres.

'Are you all right, Mhairi?'

'Yes, Sir. Never a dull moment when you're around,' she quipped, her shaking hands belying the bold words.

'Do you feel up to a little more surveillance work before we pack it in for the night?'

'Father Malone?'

'He looked terrified out of his wits. I want to know where he's going in such a hurry.'

Farrell turned at the roundabout and cruised along, looking for his quarry. He soon caught sight of the priest hurrying along looking neither to left or right and followed at a discreet distance. Soon his suspicions were confirmed. Father Malone was paying a visit to Jason Baxter.

Parking further down the road, Farrell bade McLeod wait in the car while he crept up the garden path, keeping just below the level of the front window, shielded by a well-placed bush. He heard raised voices, but couldn't make out what was being said.

He had just returned to the car when the door was flung open and Father Malone came loping down the road towards them.

'He'll see us,' said McLeod, panicking.

'I have a plan,' said Farrell.

'What?' asked McLeod.

'This.'

Farrell turned to McLeod and gathered her into his arms, planting his lips firmly on hers thus hiding both their faces. The priest didn't give them a second glance as he carried on by. They broke apart, and Farrell could feel the heat of embarrassment staining his cheeks. McLeod looked like she didn't know whether to laugh or cry.

'I … er … sorry for leaping on you like that, McLeod. I didn't feel there was any other way we could avoid detection. Please don't think … I mean I'm not that …'

'No problem, Sir,' she said. 'Anytime. I mean er, in the line of duty.'

They drove back to the station in awkward silence.

After dropping Mhairi off, Farrell changed back into his suit. He touched base with DS Byers in the MCA room, updating him on what had transpired. Then, he walked into town to pick up a bunch of flowers and a good bottle of Australian red wine for Clare. The address she had given him was not one he was familiar with and turned out to be an exclusive apartment block overlooking the River Nith. He rang the doorbell and seconds later Clare stood framed in the doorway. She was wearing black linen trousers with a red fitted blouse and her hair was pinned up in a loose chignon, which exposed the back of her graceful neck. She welcomed him with a brief kiss and he followed her inside.

The interior of the flat looked like it had been styled for a magazine shoot. Everything was cream with honeyed pine stripped floors. There was no clutter, just the odd carefully chosen splash of colour or piece of expensive-looking art. He couldn't imagine children living here and for a moment caught himself comparing it unfavourably with the lived-in clutter of the Lind family home.

'Something smells good,' he commented, handing over the wine and flowers with a smile.

She had clearly gone to a lot of trouble. The glass dining table was beautifully set with a tasteful flower arrangement in the centre. Farrell was glad he hadn't had a chance to go home and change into fresh clothes or he'd have probably turned up in jeans and disgraced himself.

As she served up steaming plates of beef Wellington Farrell poured the wine and could feel himself starting to relax. He really must train himself to be less solitary in his habits.

Suddenly there was a lull in the conversation. Farrell looked up and saw Clare's brow was furrowed. Clearly there was something on her mind. He sat back in his chair and looked at her.

'Right then out with it,' he said.

She laughed nervously.

'I'm an atheist. Given that you're not only Catholic but a priest to boot I'm guessing that might cause us some problems further down the line?'

Farrell didn't reply right away. He was a great believer in respecting other faiths and ways of looking at the world, but to have no faith at all? He looked at her heart-shaped face studying him so earnestly across the table and knew that he owed her the truth.

'Your lack of faith does bother me but only because I feel like you're missing out. I'm drawn to you and want to see where this leads. Maybe it will lead you to God or to me finally renouncing my vocation, maybe neither of these things.'

'I'm sorry, Frank. I'm overthinking stuff. Call it an occupational hazard. Let's just take it a day at a time. Agreed?'

'Agreed,' Farrell replied.

After a delicious meal they cleared the dishes and washed up before settling down to watch a DVD.

'I got us *The Exorcist*,' said Clare, bursting out laughing at Farrell's horrified expression.

'Just kidding. How about *Music and Lyrics*?'

'Perfect,' said Farrell.

Clare inserted the DVD, then, with an almost imperceptible hesitation, joined him on the sofa. Wordlessly, he put his arm around her and she rested her head on his shoulder.

CHAPTER THIRTY-ONE

Farrell pounded relentlessly along the mud flats sucking in great gulps of briny air, feet slapping down on the wiry tufts of grass that tried to survive in this inhospitable environment. Eventually he could force his aching limbs on no further and collapsed onto a broken-down wall to rest. Immediately, nightmare images from last night's dream crowded into his mind.

He could hear Clare screaming, begging him to save her as he ran into St Aidan's graveyard. It was dark and a full moon lit up the swirling mist, making it look like phantom spirits. As he rounded the corner he saw them. Clare was lying spread-eagled on a huge tombstone on which the words 'JASON BAXTER' were etched. Above her was a man intent on rape. As he struggled to reach them he had felt as though his limbs were wading through treacle; Clare's pitiful screams spurring him on. At last he had reached the man and grabbed his shoulder, spinning him round. The shock had made his hair stand on end. He was staring at a bestial version of himself.

'It was only a dream,' Farrell muttered. 'It was only a dream!' he yelled, the words echoing round the deserted expanse. A gaggle of geese honked overhead, almost as if they were laughing at this ridiculous human and his posturing.

'Get a grip Farrell,' he told himself. 'You're losing it.'

Back at the cottage after his run he soothed his stiffening limbs with a steaming hot shower then fried up a mound of bacon and French toast and had it while listening to Westsound radio. The news started just as he was about to leave the cottage, causing him to freeze in disbelief.

Another pair of twins had been abducted this morning. Why had no one called him? He reached for the phone. The line was dead. He took the stairs two at a time to get his mobile from his bedside table. It wasn't there. He could have sworn it had been there when he went to bed. No matter, it would turn up. He ran downstairs and grabbed his keys, then hurriedly locking up, he threw himself into the Citroen and left in a flurry of gravel.

Bursting into the MCA room eight minutes later he groaned inwardly. The super was there, black eyes glinting with malice at his late arrival.

'Nice of you to join us, DI Farrell,' he intoned. 'I do hope we're not putting you out?'

'I didn't know, Sir,' Farrell said through gritted teeth.

'What, no tip off from the Almighty? You do disappoint me.'

Farrell ignored the jibe and sat down beside DI Moore. DCI Lind was at the front with the super, looking grave, as well he might.

'So, to recap,' continued Lind, 'we have the same modus operandi as before, give or take a few details: a man presents at Head Start Nursery at 8 a.m., the kids having been dropped off by the mother at 7.30. He produces social work ID and a piece of paper purporting to be a place of safety order from the Children's Panel. The senior member of staff on duty phones the number on the order and is assured the papers are genuine and the person is who he says he is. The man waltzes out with the kids, gets into a blue Ford Mondeo this time, and disappears.'

'Any known link between the family in this case and the last family?' asked Farrell.

'None that we know of,' replied Lind. 'Nothing beyond the fact it's identical twins again and they were taken from a nursery. These kids have wealthy parents. The father's some big commercial lawyer in Edinburgh; the mother owns a beauty parlour in the town.'

'Do you think there might be a ransom demand this time then, Sir?' asked McLeod.

'Time will tell,' said Lind. 'Personally, I doubt it.'

'I agree,' said Farrell. 'Whatever is driving this nutter, I doubt it's money.'

The super got up and cleared his throat. 'I'm sure I don't need to remind you that this case is going to generate media frenzy. This police force is going to be on trial in a way it has never been before. I want results and I want them FAST.' He glared at them all belligerently before popping an antacid and departing to deal with the press.

Lind hurriedly assigned actions for the day. Every available uniform had been dispatched on door-to-door enquiries in the vicinity of the nursery and the children's family home. DI Moore and DS Stirling went off to interview the mother at her home, and Byers was dispatched to the incident van. That left Farrell and McLeod to take the nursery.

Head Start Nursery was situated in an impressive Georgian mansion house set in its own extensive area of grounds on the outskirts of town, just past the bypass. A red-eyed security guard examined their warrant card with shaking hands and then buzzed them through the massive wrought iron security gates.

'Probably wishing he'd never been born, poor chap,' said Farrell.

As they drew closer they could see a flurry of small kids being frogmarched out the building by worried parents. The cars would not have looked out of place in a suburban area of Edinburgh. The idyllic surroundings, with state-of-the-art adventure playground and chubby Shetland ponies looking over a paddock fence, only served to remind those present that the dream had turned into a nightmare.

A young woman in her twenties opened the door, showing clear signs of strain. She too scrutinized their ID carefully: something that Farrell found irritating in the circumstances but refrained from commenting on.

Farrell introduced himself and McLeod and learned that the woman's name was Maura and she had been working in the baby room so hadn't seen anything.

'It's Mrs Mitchell you need to talk to,' the girl said, inclining her head towards a door from behind which raised voices could be heard.

Farrell had to hammer on the door to be heard over the commotion. There was a moment of silence then an imperious voice bade him enter.

Farrell found himself confronted by an imposing perfectly groomed woman who looked to be in her early forties. She held out her hand to him in greeting. Before he could step forward and shake it the other occupant of the room, a bull-headed man in his forties with an impressive physique and an expensive suit, rudely inserted himself between them. Farrell could feel his hackles rise.

'How exactly do you plan to save my boys from this maniac?'

'Mr Frew,' interjected the woman, 'the police have to …'

'Quiet, woman!' he hissed.

Farrell glanced at McLeod to indicate she should take the lead here. The last thing this guy needed was to add a charge of assault to his list of woes. She stepped forward at once.

'Time is of the essence, Sir. Now let's get to it. If we go through here you can tell me, for starters, exactly what your sons were wearing.'

She placed her hand under his elbow and steered him out the room, talking firmly to him all the while. He went quietly; all the fight draining out of him.

Left alone with Mrs Mitchell, Farrell gestured for her to take a seat. She perched reluctantly on the edge of an upright chair, and Farrell sat opposite her.

'I feel such a fool,' she burst out.

'You weren't to know,' Farrell said.

'The paperwork was spot on. It's happened before, you see. One of the children we had last year. Turned out the father was abusing the little girl. The mother refused to believe it. Social services got a place of safety order, turned up here out of the blue and took the child away.'

Farrell leaned forward, pulse quickening.

'Do you still have the earlier paperwork?'

'Of course.'

The woman went over to an immaculately ordered mahogany filing cabinet and extracted a slim file. She handed it to Farrell.

'This is what I was given when I handed over Melanie Thomson. This is what the man gave me this morning when he took the little boys. I compared what I was given with last year's paperwork, which I knew to be genuine. I phoned the number at the top of the page, just to double check. I wanted to be sure,' she said.

'Did the person answering the phone identify themselves?'

'Yes, he said he was Brian Scott, duty social worker. I noted it down.'

'The telephone numbers don't match but everything else is the same,' said Farrell.

'What do you mean? I checked the numbers. They were the same.'

'Not quite, I'm afraid. One digit was different.'

171

'I freely admit I was a bit flustered but I was so sure it all checked out. That I'd done everything I could …'

Farrell threw her a lifeline to cling onto.

'You mustn't blame yourself. This man is clever. Everything is planned down to the finest detail. He leaves nothing to chance. What alerted you to the fact that the twins had been abducted?'

'The mother phoned in not long after they'd gone to say she would be picking them up earlier than usual as they had dental appointments. The way she reacted when I told her I knew immediately that something was terribly wrong. She told me there had been no Children's Panel.'

'Had you ever had reason to believe that the children were at risk within the family?'

Mrs Mitchell hesitated.

'The mother … she's very young, fragile, I suppose you might say. And well, you've met the father …'

'Go on,' said Farrell.

'I might be speaking totally out of turn but the mother, Kerry … I've seen bruises on a number of occasions. I tried to talk to her but she insisted everything was fine.'

'And the boys?'

'Never a mark on them,' she replied. 'Or at least, nothing out of the ordinary for two active toddlers.'

'We'll place a Family Liaison Officer with the family. I'll make sure she keeps a watchful eye out for the mother meantime.'

'Those little boys, Paul and Andy, do you think …?' she broke off, too choked to continue.

'There's no way of knowing at this stage,' said Farrell.

Farrell produced an identikit photo of the man believed to have been behind the abduction of the first twins.

'Is that the man?'

The woman scrutinized it carefully.

'I don't know. It could be. He had a moustache though, not

172

a beard, and he was wearing different glasses. His hair was shorter, though the colour's the same.'

'What about his height?' asked Farrell. 'Was he taller or shorter than me?'

'About the same, I would say.'

She gazed at Farrell, a strange expression on her face, then shook her head as though she were punch drunk and tried to refocus.

'Did you notice the colour of his eyes?'

'Brown,' she said.

'Is there anything else you can remember about him?'

'He had a tattoo on his right forearm; I saw it when he lifted up Paul.'

'Can you describe it?'

'I can, as it happens. It was a sign of the zodiac.'

'Which sign?' asked Farrell

'Gemini.'

'Would you be willing to come down to the station and work with a sketch artist?'

'Of course, I'll come as soon as the last child leaves.'

'Thank you,' said Farrell. 'You've been most helpful.'

He spun on his heel and raced out to speak to McLeod, who was seeing off the father in a uniformed police car.

'Well?'

'I got a full description of the boys that has gone out to all units.'

She handed over a snapshot of two dark-haired little boys in identical navy shorts and striped T-shirts smiling happily for the camera.

'No known enemies, crank calls, or anything suspicious before today. Guy's loaded, but no ransom note, as of yet.'

'The abductor has a tattoo,' Farrell said. 'Gemini, a zodiac sign.'

'The twins, Sir?'

'So it would seem. I want you to nip back and see the woman

at the first nursery, see if she can remember anything about a tattoo. He's also changed his appearance but I'm fairly sure we're dealing with the same guy. I don't like it. I don't like it at all. What did you make of the father?'

'He's frustrated as Hell; the type that's used to solving problems by throwing money around. He's desperate for a ransom note, ready to write a cheque to buy back his kids.'

'If only it were that simple,' said Farrell. 'Any information about the mother?'

'He wasn't very forthcoming on that score, Sir. We'll know more when we hear from DI Moore.'

'Phone DI Moore and tell her to tread carefully. This guy's got a temper and might be in the habit of taking it out on his wife.'

CHAPTER THIRTY-TWO

Back in his office at Loreburn Street, having ascertained that there were no new developments in the Boyd case, Farrell buried himself in the files relating to the missing kids. They were severely under-staffed in Dumfries compared to the manpower and resources available in the Central Belt. It was going to be all hands to the pump until further notice if these kids were to stand a chance. It might even be already too late. Patterns were starting to emerge. It was also clear that the abductor had an accomplice. Mrs Mitchell from Head Start had phoned and spoken to someone who confirmed the man's identity while he was there. It had transpired that there was someone at the social work department who went by the name of Brian Scott but he was currently sunning himself in Ibiza.

Farrell compared the fake child protection order with the genuine article from last year. The only discrepancy was the phone number. He tried it, not expecting an answer. Someone picked up after the third ring. Farrell froze. What had he done?

'Inspector Farrell here, who am I speaking to?'

'Well, hello, Inspector Farrell, this is a surprise,' said the voice on the phone.

'What should I call you?' asked Farrell, trying to keep his voice as even as his pounding heart would allow.

'What's in a name? Names are just accidents of birth; don't you agree?'

'Perhaps,' said Farrell neutrally. 'The little boys, Mark, Paul, and Andy, are they still alive?'

'So many questions. It's really not polite, Frank.'

'What do you want to talk about then?'

'Are you a gambling man, Frank?'

'Can't say that I am,' answered Farrell, keen to keep him on the phone for as long as possible.

'Well if I were you I wouldn't bet on Andy coming back home. Two aren't always better than one. You've got until midnight on Friday to save me from myself, Frank.'

'Turn yourself in,' urged Farrell. 'We can do a deal. Anything is possible if you let those little boys walk out of this unharmed.'

'Be great, wouldn't it, Frank? Life isn't like that.'

'Make it like that,' urged Farrell. 'You're the one holding all the cards.'

'And Andy just drew the two of clubs. Life's a bitch.'

'It's not too late to turn back. Tell me where those boys are.'

'Do you believe in a bountiful God, Father Frank?'

Farrell stiffened. 'Why did you kill Boyd? It was you, wasn't it?'

'Now why did you have to go and ruin the ambience, Frank? I was just starting to enjoy our little chat.'

'Wait! We can talk about something else.'

'Bye Frank. Give my regards to Clare.'

'How do you …'

The phone went dead.

'Dammit!' Farrell yelled and sent his chair crashing backwards as he leapt up and tore down the corridor to the MCA room. He flung the door back against its hinges, startling the occupants.

'The abductor. I've just spoken to him. Get technical support in my room to set up a trace in case he calls me back.'

Lind walked over to him, looking worried.

'What, you mean he called the station?'

'No,' said Farrell, grimly. 'I called him.'

'From your *room*?' asked Lind.

'Yes, from my room,' snapped Farrell, already aware that he'd blown it big time.

If he'd only had the sense to call from the MCA room, they could have maybe traced the call, got a lead on where he was keeping the kids.

'Jesus, Frank. Wait until the super hears about this,' murmured Lind, worriedly.

'Hears about *what* exactly,' boomed a voice from the open doorway.

Everyone except Lind and Farrell became totally engrossed in what they were doing.

'Well, Sir ...' began Lind.

Farrell stepped in front of the super and eyeballed him. Better to go out with a bang than a whimper.

'I've just spoken to the abductor, Sir.'

'Get a trace?' barked the super.

'No, Sir. I dialled the number on the place of safety order. Never thought I'd get through to anyone.'

'Well, isn't this just fine and dandy,' hissed the super, so angry he looked on the verge of stroking out.

'Sorry, Sir,' said Farrell, uncomfortably aware that this time he deserved the wrath of the man in front of him.

'We have a deranged kidnapper loose on our patch and you didn't think to start a trace before you phoned him for a little chat?'

'No, Sir,' said Farrell.

Walker suddenly slumped as though the fight had gone out of him. In a more reasonable tone of voice he asked, 'did he say anything about the kids, anything to help us find them?'

'Just that Andy had drawn the two of clubs, and we have until midnight on Friday to save him from himself.'

'That gives us four days to nail the bastard,' yelled the super to the room at large. 'I want every available body on this investigation and I want RESULTS!'

As he was walking out the door he stuck his face right in Farrell's, so close Farrell could smell the stale odour of his last fag.

'No more cock-ups, Farrell?'

'No, Sir.'

Once the super had left there was a collective exhalation of air by all those present. Farrell quickly briefed them on the details of his conversation, this time holding nothing back. Lind looked worried.

'This guy seems to know a helluva lot about you, Frank. I don't like it.'

'It's not uncommon for a perpetrator to fixate on one of the main investigating officers. Everything he said about me is a matter of public record,' said Farrell.

'Then who's Clare?' piped up the irrepressible Byers, earning a frown from Lind.

'A forensic psychiatrist who's been helping me with the Boyd case,' replied Farrell, not batting an eyelid.

Byers looked disappointed.

'Right folks, listen up,' said Lind. 'We have several new lines of enquiry. The abductor obviously has an accomplice. He waltzed into that nursery this morning with paperwork he knew would be subject to scrutiny. While he was there, Mrs Mitchell phoned a number purporting to be social services and spoke to someone who verified the documents were genuine. The name he gave was Brian Scott, duty social worker, but we've already established the real Brian Scott is out of the country therefore couldn't have made the call. Our accomplice may work in social services or for Dumfries and Galloway Council in some capacity. We need to get onto BT and get a location for the phone number and officers out there right away. The abductor is targeting identical twin boys. Find out who has information on their database about twins living in this area. I want all empty churches and church halls within a thirty-mile radius of Dumfries identified and searched. Given the fact that the first boys were found in an abandoned church he may have picked a hideaway again, either for some as yet undisclosed religious significance or simply for convenience. There are three scared toddlers out there relying on us to find some answers. Let's get to it.'

Farrell turned on his heel to leave.

'Frank, what about Clare?' asked Lind. 'The killer mentioned her by name. You'd better warn her to be careful.'

'Don't worry,' replied Farrell. 'I've already thought of that.'

CHAPTER THIRTY-THREE

Clare looked up from her notes and stretched her arms above her head to relieve the tension in her neck. To her surprise she noticed that it was already getting dark and her room was pooled with shadows from the light thrown by her desk lamp. She had a cheek to moan about Frank being wedded to his job when she was just as bad. No one in her Department knew that he used to be a patient here all those years ago. She knew that some of her colleagues might disapprove and consider she was being unethical if they got wind of the fact she had once had a fleeting involvement in his treatment. It had been a while since she had been in a serious relationship. Her career was demanding and most men still seemed ill-equipped to deal with that. She packed up her briefcase with a file for a case conference tomorrow and a few journal articles she still had to read. There really weren't enough hours in the day.

Her steps quickened as she headed for the main hospital car park. She glanced round nervously as a slight breeze rustled through the bushes bordering the lush landscaped gardens. Hadn't there been some gossip in the canteen about a prowler having been spotted lurking in the grounds? Her heels wobbled and made a clacking sound over the slightly uneven surface. She wrapped her scarf around her tightly to ward off the evening chill. As her thoughts turned to the lonely evening ahead she wished that Frank had been free this evening.

Suddenly she was enveloped in an embrace from behind. Frank! She leaned her head back against his broad chest. He'd managed to get away after all. She smelled the familiar tang of his aftershave as he nuzzled her ear. She tried to wriggle round to face him but was being held too tightly to manoeuvre. His hands started to roam over her body, his tongue in her ear. She squirmed awkwardly.

'Frank, don't! Someone might see.'

The mauling continued. She became annoyed.

'Frank, knock it off. I'm not kidding.'

Suddenly, he shoved her violently, sending her flying forward onto her knees, ripping her tights in the process. By the time she scrambled to her feet, ready to give him a bollocking, he was a distant figure, running away from her, his head down.

Hurt and confused she made her way to her car, her knees stinging. What on earth had got into him? Was he ill? Having some kind of breakdown? Whatever was going on the one thing she knew for certain was that she wanted no part of it.

CHAPTER THIRTY-FOUR

Farrell woke up with a pounding headache and the sour taste of whisky at the back of his throat. Then he realized that the sound of banging wasn't entirely in his head but was being reinforced by an insistent knocking at the front door. Groaning, he threw back the covers and lurched to his feet. He was stunned to see that he was still wearing his suit from yesterday. What on earth was going on?

With unsteady legs he staggered down the stairs and flung open the front door, wincing at the bright sunlight. There in front of him stood DC McLeod with her arms folded.

'DCI Lind sent me out to check you were OK as he couldn't get through on your landline and you weren't answering your mobile.'

She looked him up and down with disdain.

'Heavy night, Sir?'

'I wish I knew,' he answered.

McLeod looked at him through narrowed eyes.

'No offence, Sir, but you look like shit. What happened?'

Farrell rubbed his eyes and swallowed. His tongue felt thick and rubbery and his mouth was dry and tacky. He was still feeling disorientated and confused.

'It's the weirdest thing. I can remember coming home quite late, pouring myself a nightcap, then nothing. The next thing I remember is hearing you knocking on the door.'

Farrell threw the door open and McLeod followed him in. He lurched upstairs to the lounge, still unsteady on his feet. Walking across the room he threw open the door to a cupboard and produced an almost full bottle of Macallan.

'I knew it!' he expostulated.

'What are you saying, Sir?'

'I've been drugged. Somebody's been in here and slipped something in my whisky.'

'Are you sure, Sir?' asked McLeod, eyes darting around in alarm. 'Could whoever it is still be here?'

Farrell snorted. 'Not if they know what's good for them.'

'Shouldn't you see someone, Sir, get checked out?'

'There are three wee boys missing. Anything else will have to wait,' Farrell muttered. 'Stick a pot of strong coffee on, there's a good lass. It's nothing a hot shower won't cure. I'll be down in a tick.'

Mhairi waited until he was out of sight, zoomed downstairs to stick the coffee on, then carefully bagged up the bottle of whisky to take it to the lab for analysis. She slipped out and stashed it in the boot of her car. Had Farrell really been drugged or had he been on a bender and blacked out and was now trying to cover his tracks? Either way it might be important. The way this investigation was going she wasn't inclined to take chances.

Hearing the sound of the shower being turned on she crept back up the stairs and poked her head round Farrell's bedroom door, taking in the single bed with raised eyebrows. Her eyes were drawn to the small crucifix above the bed and a well-thumbed leather bible beside it. Scarcely daring to breathe, she tiptoed over to the wardrobe and gently tugged the door open.

Hanging in one corner in a transparent bag was a black suit with a white clerical collar. On the bottom, beneath the hanging rail, was an old intricately carved wooden box. Nervously McLeod glanced towards the door leading to the shower room. The shower was still running. She reached over and opened the box and drew in her breath sharply at the contents. That might explain the old scars on his back. And yet, he didn't come over like some religious fanatic. Maybe it was some kind of self-harming thing? There were definitely some things it was better not to know. Shit. The shower had stopped. With the speed borne of true panic Mhairi leapt to the door and managed to appear to be popping her head round it as Farrell emerged in a cloud of steam from the shower room. Although clad in a dressing gown he still looked embarrassed to see her standing there.

'Coffee's ready,' she blurted, still out of breath.

'I'll be down in a minute,' he replied.

Mhairi charged downstairs and along the hall to the kitchen, where she poured out the coffee and rustled up some toast. As she was opening cupboards looking for some marmalade she saw a box of tablets pushed to the back of the shelf. Conscious that she had invaded her boss's privacy enough for one morning she still couldn't resist sliding them out to have a look. Lithium.

'What do you think you're playing at?' thundered a voice behind her.

Mhairi spun round, shaking. Farrell looked furious.

'I was just looking for some marmalade when I came across these. I'm sorry. I had no right.'

Her boss ran his hands through his hair and suddenly looked so bone weary that Mhairi had to resist the impulse to throw her arms round him. He sank into a chair at the table and she brought over the pot of coffee and toast.

'Are you sick?' she asked.

'I used to be. I had a breakdown many years ago. The pills help to keep me on an even keel. End of story.'

'I won't say anything to anyone.'

'For a price?' Farrell asked.

'You obviously don't know me very well,' snapped Mhairi.

Farrell drained his cup and stood up.

'Come on. We've got work to do,' he said in a flat voice.

Mhairi drove Farrell's car as he wasn't yet fit to drive. McLeod couldn't help stealing a sideways glance at her boss every so often. His face remained inscrutable. Talk about baggage. No wonder he had never married. What with the pills and what she had seen in that box she was a bit freaked out. Get over it, McLeod, she told herself.

Then, Farrell's police radio crackled into life. He picked up the hand piece and put it to his ear.

'Farrell,' he growled, 'we're coming up to St Michael's Bridge … Be there in five … Maintain radio silence.'

'Well?' demanded Mhairi. 'Have they found them?'

'Step on it, McLeod. Uniform has been told to give us a wide berth. An anonymous caller phoned. He was walking his dogs in the grounds of the old Benedictine convent on Maxwell Street when he heard a child crying. The firearms team is mobilizing.'

Mhairi put her foot down, cursing the fact that she was driving Farrell's clapped-out Citroen and not her own little Cleo, which was much nippier. They flew through the junction at the Dock Park as the lights were changing and reared like an ageing bronco up the steep hill that followed. Turning into Maxwell Street with squealing tyres she rode to the summit of the long hill in second gear and parked outside the grounds where Farrell indicated. There was no sign of any other police presence. Shit, thought Mhairi, heart pounding. This is it. She reached for the door handle but Farrell grabbed her arm. Surprised, she spun round to face him.

'Wait here,' he commanded. 'I'm going in alone. Backup will be here shortly.'

'What is this, the Dark Ages?' she snapped. 'I'm coming. There's no time to waste so let's get on with it.'

He gave her a long look then nodded abruptly and released her arm.

CHAPTER THIRTY-FIVE

The convent had been abandoned back in 1990 when the few remaining elderly nuns moved back to their sister house in Largs. The impressive sandstone façade could be glimpsed behind the towering beech trees that lined the drive. There was an ominous quiet about the place as though it existed in a vacuum, disconnected from the hurly burly of the town below.

Mhairi felt her skin prickle with unease as she crept through the undergrowth with Farrell, her breath becoming more laboured. She was scared shitless but she was damned if she was going to play it by the book when there were kids' lives at stake.

The building was divided into two parts, the chapel and the school, connected by a network of corridors. Following Farrell's lead she slunk round the back bypassing the chapel until they reached a boarded-up window with rotting planks leading into the basement of the abandoned school.

'My money's on them being in the chapel,' Farrell whispered. 'The only way in is through the front door, which will be locked. If we go in through the school we can maybe take them by surprise.'

The rotten planks yielded without too much protest, though to Mhairi's fevered imagination it sounded like the death throes of an Amazonian rainforest. They crept inside and found themselves in what must have been the former cloakroom. The air was heavy as though it hadn't been disturbed for years and still reeked of sweaty feet. Hugging the wall, they quietly climbed the stairs and made their way along empty corridors where nuns' feet used to whisper along under long black robes. The brown and cream tiles felt cool under her feet. The arches overhead resembled hands held together in prayer.

A rat suddenly scurried across her path and it was all she could do to choke off the scream that rose in her throat. Farrell turned and grinned at her. Ha, bloody ha!

Motioning to her to follow him he crossed the corridor and paused in front of a wooden door, listening intently. Turning the handle, he opened the door and went into a large bright room. Holding his finger fiercely to his lips he crept across to what Mhairi thought looked like a cupboard. He sank to his knees and gently turned the handle, signalling to Mhairi to do likewise to the adjacent door. What the Hell was he playing at, she wondered?

Reflexively, she ducked down, heart racing as she realized she was looking down over the interior of the chapel below. She carefully closed the door behind her as Farrell had done in case it banged shut alerting those below to their presence. Carefully, she knelt down on the padded leather kneeler in the small cubicle and peered down into the chapel. Her stomach clenched as she saw two toddlers wandering around, half-heartedly playing with a couple of Action Men. They were each tethered by the wrist to an intricate wrought iron grille that had previously divided the enclosed nuns from lay members of the congregation. Mhairi could feel tears start to spurt at their plight and angrily dashed them away. What kind of a monster could do this to kids that age?

A man spoke into the silence, causing Mhairi to flinch. She peered over the rail but he must have been standing under the overhang as she couldn't get a glimpse of him. His voice was pleasant, vaguely familiar, and with a definite Glasgow twang.

'Time for a picnic,' he announced.

The little boys flinched and huddled together trying to get as far away from their abductor as possible.

'Come on, now, don't be like that,' he coaxed. 'We're playing this grand game of Hide and Seek, and in a little while one of you will go back to Mummy and the other will go and play with the angels.'

One of the toddlers yelled forcefully, 'Want Mummy now. Bad Man.'

'Mummy, want Mummy,' wailed the other child, hiding behind his brother.

A carrier bag was tossed by the unseen man across to the bolshier of the twins.

'There's food and drink in there. Take it or leave it,' he said, all pretence at jollity gone.

After some initial hesitation the bolder of the two boys peered into the bag and with chubby fingers pulled out sandwiches, chocolate, and juice, which he and his brother devoured.

Just as her knees were starting to go numb Mhairi saw the handle turning on the door behind her. That had better be Farrell, she thought, bracing herself just in case. To her relief his familiar face appeared round the door. He put a finger to his lips and gestured to her to follow him.

Silently, scarcely daring to breathe, Mhairi and Farrell retreated back down the stairs until they were well out of earshot of those in the chapel.

'I think I can take him,' Farrell said.

'He might have a gun,' hissed Mhairi.

'Unlikely,' said Farrell. 'There aren't many guns in this neck of the woods. The plan is for me to storm in from the priest's robing chamber, behind the altar. That gives him the option of running out the front door; hopefully, into the arms of the Armed Response Unit. As soon as we're out of sight I want you to hustle the kids back out through the door of the robing chamber and find somewhere else to hide with them till the All Clear sounds. Got it?'

'I don't like it,' said Mhairi, knowing nonetheless that there was no other way.

'Here, take this,' said Farrell as an afterthought, pulling a flick knife from out of his sock.

'You can use this to cut the boys loose.'

He set off determinedly with Mhairi trotting to keep up with his loping stride. As they reached the tiny robing room, Mhairi smiled brightly and gave him the thumbs-up sign. He smiled back at her, clearly not fooled for an instant. As he turned the handle slowly, Mhairi's nerves shrieked in protest. Then he was gone from sight.

Farrell crept up on the man who was sitting on a chair reading a paper. He looked tall and angular with dark hair. As he drew closer the children stopped eating and stared at him. The man glanced at the children then stiffened, leaping to his feet and turning round to face Farrell in one fluid movement. With a jolt, Farrell saw that he was wearing a Mickey Mouse mask. Yelling as loudly as he could, Farrell lunged at him. They grappled furiously; Farrell trying without success to dislodge the grinning mask.

Suddenly, he felt white heat pierce his shoulder and realized he'd been stabbed. As he fell back, his adversary took off for the door. Farrell picked himself up and staggered after him, shouting to Mhairi to come out and get the boys.

Mhairi rushed forward, cut the ropes tethering the two toddlers and, grabbing their hot little hands, she ran back into the interior of the building. Seeing a set of stone spiral steps on her right she rushed down them to find herself in the old kitchens of the convent. She scouted round until she found a pantry with a small window to the rear courtyard through which the boys could be lifted if necessary. She sank to the floor and cuddled them into her. And waited.

Farrell charged after the man like a raging bull, summoning up every last scrap of aggression in him to override the growing pain and dizziness. He had hoped that he would be flushing the killer out into the midst of the ARU but there was no sign of them. No sign of anyone. Where were they? Legs pumping, he forced himself through the woods bordering the driveway, unkempt branches whipping his face relentlessly. He started to gain on his assailant. Suddenly the man stopped some way ahead and turned to face him. Farrell juddered to a halt, preparing to square up to him. A fine drizzle of rain made the blood from a cut on his forehead run into his eyes, giving the now shadowy form of the killer an ominous red tinge. Suddenly, the killer removed his mask and the sound of maniacal laughter seemed to echo all round Farrell as he sank to the ground, his body finally betraying him. He strained forward, trying to imprint the man's face on his memory before he lost consciousness but all he could see was a dark bushy beard and wild blue eyes. Those eyes, where had he seen them before …?

CHAPTER THIRTY-SIX

Farrell came round to discover he was in an ambulance. The sound of the sirens filled his ears and a burly paramedic was writing on a clipboard. A second later the pain sliced through him like cheese wire, causing a moan to escape from between his teeth. The paramedic injected something into the venflon on his hand.

'Easy, mate. I've given you something to take the edge off.'

'Sir, are you all right? Did you get a good look at him?' asked a disembodied voice.

Farrell turned his head and DC McLeod swam into view.

'Blue eyes, bushy dark beard, my height, give or take an inch,' he managed before losing consciousness.

As he slipped under he could hear DC McLeod on her radio crisply imparting the information to Control.

An hour later at Loreburn Street, Mhairi sat quaking in the conference room in front of a grim-faced Superintendent and an equally grim-faced DCI Lind. The third person present was DI Moore, whose expression was carefully neutral.

'Did you enter the convent on DI Farrell's orders, DC McLeod?' barked the super.

'No, Sir,' answered McLeod, lifting her chin. 'He wanted me to wait for backup, but I decided to accompany him as I figured that someone would need to look after the boys if he engaged the assailant.'

'Are you saying you disobeyed a direct order?' asked the super.

'No, Sir, it wasn't like that, Sir.' Mhairi shot a desperate look at DI Moore, who interceded on her behalf.

'I believe what DC McLeod is trying to convey, Sir, is that DI Farrell made a judgement call to risk his own neck in order to take the killer by surprise to try and save the lives of those two little boys. He appears to have tried to protect DC McLeod by ordering her to stay put but she then volunteered to put herself into danger as time was of the essence. Had they both not performed so heroically under difficult circumstances the outcome might have been very different.'

'Hear hear,' interjected DCI Lind.

Walker was outmanoeuvred and he knew it. He got to his feet and shook hands with DC McLeod.

'Well done, DC McLeod. That will be all for now.' He turned to DCI Lind and DI Moore. 'Keep me apprised of all further developments.'

'Yes, Sir,' they chorused as Walker swept out the room, brass jangling. Lind hurried out after him.

Once Mhairi was alone with DI Moore she collapsed back into her chair, shaking.

'I thought I was for the chop there,' she said.

'It wasn't you he was after,' said DI Moore.

'You mean …?'

'Forget I said anything. Now DC McLeod I want you to clear off and get some rest. We can spare you for a couple of days. Perhaps I should arrange some counselling?'

'No thanks, Ma'am,' replied Mhairi. 'I've got a self-help library to rival Oprah's. I'll be fine.'

Mhairi grabbed her bag and left the station. Who would have thought DI Moore could be such a star?

On her way home she decided to drop in at the Infirmary to see how Farrell was doing. She found him sitting up in bed, struggling to put his shirt on, his face drained of all colour.

'What the bloody hell do you think you're doing?' she spluttered.

'I'm discharging myself, what does it look like?'

'But you've been stabbed,' Mhairi protested.

'It was just a flesh wound. I'm going home.'

'Come on then, you big dope,' she sighed. 'Let me help you get dressed.'

'A dope, eh?' He shot back. 'I don't recall that form of address being in the manual.'

'I'm off duty,' she replied, helping him carefully into his shirt.

Mhairi didn't know whether to be upset or relieved when the door to the ward opened and a tired-looking doctor came towards them looking stern, eyebrows climbing high in disbelief.

'What's this? *The Great Escape*?' he asked.

'Look, I'm grateful for all you've done for me, Doctor, but I'll recover much quicker at home. My colleague, DC McLeod, is a trained first aider and will make sure I'm comfortable before leaving.'

Mhairi glared at Farrell in response to a none-too-gentle poke in the back. He really was the giddy limit. Did he *ever* do what he was told?

'Don't worry, Doctor,' she said. 'I'll look after him.'

'Rather you than me,' the doctor replied.

It took a further hour before they were cleared to go. They left clutching a carrier bag bursting with prescription drugs and having signed every waiver under the sun; absolving the hospital from liability in the event of an untimely demise.

Having manhandled Farrell from the mandatory wheelchair into the front seat of her car, Mhairi was suddenly assailed by doubt as she looked at his bloodless complexion. He looked barely conscious for goodness' sake.

Turning the key in the ignition she set off, crawling along like an old granny and nudging the Citroen over each speed bump like it was the edge of a cliff. Despite her precautions, stifled moans of pain still squeezed out of her wounded passenger.

Finally, she reached the cottage at Kelton. It seemed almost impossible to believe that it had been only twelve hours since they had set off this morning. She could feel her own knees going weak as the reaction set in.

Hauling Farrell upstairs, Mhairi helped him lie down under the quilt after removing his shoes and socks. She hovered anxiously until he fell asleep, lulled by the pain meds, and then she slipped out into the night.

CHAPTER THIRTY-SEVEN

Pain sliced through Farrell's shoulder as he turned round in bed, causing him to groan out loud. Eyes still screwed shut against the onslaught of the sun flooding his bedroom, he groped for his clock like a blind man. Struggling into a sitting position he decided to pop some more happy pills before trying to get back to sleep. Still only half awake, he registered that Mhairi had left his pills and a glass of water beside the bed.

As he was turning back round he caught a movement out of the side of his eye. Tensing, he turned to hurtle out of bed and floor the intruder. However, the thought had barely formed when he realized it was Lind sitting in a chair at the foot of his bed. He slumped back on the pillows, heart pounding like a samba drum.

'Take it easy, Frank. Mhairi phoned me. She was worried about you. You should have stayed in hospital, you daft bugger.'

'How's Laura bearing up? You should be at home with her, not running round after me.'

Lind looked sheepish.

'Well, to be honest, she insisted I came. There's a whole load of supplies in your fridge. Worrying about you gave her something else to focus on, other than ... well, you know.'

'The little boys, how are they?'

196

'Recovering well. There wasn't a scratch on them. It could so easily have gone down differently had it not been for you and Mhairi ... It was still one helluva risk.'

'If we let the Health and Safety boys dictate our policing we'll all be running around with chocolate truncheons in no time,' muttered Farrell. 'I take it you haven't apprehended him yet?'

'He's disappeared into thin air,' said Lind.

Farrell winced as he delicately prodded his bandaged shoulder.

'No sign of the missing boy? He wasn't with the other two?'

'No indication he was ever there. It's not looking good, poor wee mite.' Lind sighed heavily and got up to leave.

Farrell looked up at him, calculating the pain of his wound against the pain of inertia, and flung back the bedclothes.

'Wait for me. I'm coming in.'

'The Hell you are!' said Lind, looking wildly around as though for backup.

'I need to get all the stuff that happened out of my head before it goes fuzzy round the edges. We got lucky this time. We don't want there to be a next time.'

'All right,' said Lind. 'But if Laura finds out about this you're on your own.'

'Wimp,' said Farrell.

An hour later, Farrell was ensconced in his office with a strong cup of coffee. He'd had a steady stream of visitors including the SOCO, Janet White, who indicated that she'd taken scrapings from under his fingernails while he was unconscious, but that no useful DNA had been recovered. The sketch artist had been in to see him but he was unable to add anything significant to the existing image. He still had a nagging feeling of recognition but put it down to the fact he'd been staring at the identikit image for so long in the course of the case. It didn't help that he was floating high on painkillers either. Those were definitely going down on his Santa list this year.

There was a quiet knock at his door and DI Moore entered, her forehead wrinkled with concern.

'Frank, how are you? When I heard you'd been stabbed …'

'Och, it's just a scratch,' he shrugged and then wished he hadn't as the pain caused him to grit his teeth.

'I tried to give Mhairi a couple of days off, but she was having none of it. She's really shown her mettle since you took her under your wing.'

'She's got her head screwed on where it matters,' said Farrell.

'DS Byers managed to trace Rosalie MacFarlane. She's downstairs now in an interview room but he's out chasing down another lead. Mhairi asked me to see if you were fit enough to conduct the interview with her?'

Farrell struggled to his feet, embarrassed to be appearing at such a disadvantage.

'Let's go,' he said, trying to sound full of vim and vigour, but falling well short.

'I don't know that I'm entirely convinced,' she said. 'Why don't I do it?'

'Nonsense! It's not as though you don't have enough on your plate as it is, Kate.'

'I suppose I'm wasting my breath,' she said with a sigh. 'Come on then. I'd better see you get down there in one piece, at least.'

They progressed down to the interview room like two pensioners out for a Sunday stroll with DI Moore matching her stride to his, still not fully recovered from her sprained ankle.

Rosalie MacFarlane looked to be in her early forties. Her clothes were elegant and looked expensive even to Farrell's untutored eye. A curtain of dark red hair framed her pale face. She was sitting across the table from a stroppy-looking McLeod.

McLeod introduced them and then with a nod of his head he indicated to her that she should kick off the questioning. He then sat back in his seat the better to observe the woman's reactions.

'You were at Father Boyd's funeral, weren't you?'

The woman looked at her more closely.

'Yes. I pushed you, I'm sorry. I just needed to get away without being seen. I shouldn't have gone there. I don't know what I was thinking.'

'Information received has led us to believe that you had or were having a relationship with Father Ignatius Boyd, now deceased,' said McLeod.

The woman's cheeks flushed like she'd been slapped but she simply averted her eyes and said nothing. The silence lengthened. McLeod looked at Farrell, unsure how to proceed.

'Look,' he said, leaning forward, 'I know how difficult this must be for you.'

Abruptly, she turned on him, green eyes sparking with emotion.

'No, you don't. How could you? I'm married to a devout Catholic. If this ever came out, he would never forgive me. Having an affair with a Catholic priest ... it's totally ...'

'Taboo,' Farrell finished for her.

'Yes,' she whispered. 'And if he knew that our son ...'

'You didn't tell him?' asked Farrell, trying to keep any note of censure out of his voice.

'No,' she said, her eyes downcast. 'I was very young. When I told Father Boyd he said he would deny everything. He said I was a whore sent by the devil to tempt him. I was terrified. I didn't know what to do or where to turn. I even contemplated taking my own life. I was truly desperate. Then along came Stephen. He was handsome, well off, and he adored me. I knew what I was doing was wrong but I was fighting for survival.'

'He never suspected that the boy wasn't his?'

'He is tall and dark like Stephen but he has my eyes and mouth. God saw fit to protect us.'

'What age is your son?'

'He is twenty-three.'

'Have you told him that Father Boyd was his biological father?' asked Farrell.

'Of course not. It would destroy him.'

'Could he have found out accidentally?' asked DC McLeod.

'I don't see how,' said the woman, her brow creased with worry. 'I've been so careful. I kept no souvenir of my relationship with Father Boyd, not a thing except—'

'The baby?' interjected Farrell.

'Yes,' she replied with a sigh.

'What is your husband's full name?' DI Moore asked.

'Stephen Mark Edwards.'

'And his occupation?'

'He's a consultant neurologist at the Southern General in Glasgow.'

'We need to confirm you and your husband's whereabouts on the night of seventh June this year,' interjected DC McLeod.

The woman lifted up a seriously expensive green leather bag and rummaged about for a few moments before extracting a slim dairy. She opened it and flicked through the pages until she came to June.

'Well?' asked Farrell, unable to hide his impatience.

'I was at the cinema with my friend, Maria, in Glasgow. We went out for a late supper afterwards. Here is her number,' Rosalie said, tearing a page out of a notebook.

'My husband was at a medical conference in New York, presenting a paper. That is why I had made plans, to avoid feeling lonely while he was away. Here is his secretary's number. She will be able to give you the conference organizer's number but please, I beg you, be discreet. A lot is at stake for me here,' she said, fighting back tears.

'Can you tell us your son's name?' asked DI Moore.

'Joseph Murray Edwards.'

'And his present whereabouts?' asked Farrell.

The woman put her head in her hands and said nothing.

'Rosalie? Where is your son?' he repeated.

'He's at a Catholic seminary in Rome,' she said. 'And, before you ask, yes: I did try and talk him out of it.'

'I'll still need to verify his exact whereabouts on the night of the murder,' said Farrell. 'But I'll do my level best not to reveal the truth about his paternity if he can establish an alibi for the night in question.'

'Thank you,' she whispered.

DC McLeod escorted her out. Farrell remained seated; his face an impassive mask but his brain filled with a riot of conflicting thoughts. How Boyd could have thought he had the right to sit in judgement over anyone when his own personal life was such a shambles was beyond him.

McLeod came back into the interview room just as Farrell was struggling to his feet.

'I'll verify the alibis. I'm only really fit to be chained to a desk today anyhow.'

'Do you reckon they'll all check out?' she asked.

'I'd put money on it,' said Farrell. 'She landed on her feet despite, and maybe even because of, what Boyd did to her. If her husband hadn't thought she was pregnant with his child, he might not have been in such a hurry to wed. They might never have married. She's got no motive to kill Boyd at this stage. It's all too far in the past now, too remote from their current lives. Even if the husband did find out about his son's paternity it would more likely end up in divorce than murder. And as for the son … the mind boggles. I just don't see it. I'll make the calls though and get back to you.'

Two hours later and, after a great number of phone calls, Farrell despondently scratched the three names off his list of suspects. Were they never going to catch a break in this case? It was time to go home. His wound was aching and his eyes were scratchy with fatigue.

He stopped by the locker room on his way out and was washing his hands still deep in thought. Glancing into the mirror above the sink it suddenly hit him like a grenade exploding in his chest where he had seen the killer's eyes before. His world tilted then went black.

Farrell woke up as the paramedics were lifting him into the ambulance.

'What are you doing? Leave me, I'm fine,' he protested, his voice sounding smaller and thinner than normal.

'Not this time, Frank,' said DCI Lind in his ear. 'I should never have let you con me into letting you come in. You're off sick for at least a week and that's an order. Your wound has opened up and is showing signs of infection. No one's indispensable, not even you. Give it up.'

Farrell sank back on the stretcher, knowing he was beat. Knowing that he needed time to figure out just what in Hell's name was going on.

They kept him in for two days, re-suturing the wound that had burst open when he fainted and dosing him with strong IV antibiotics to treat the infection. Was that all it had been? That moment of recognition when he had glanced in the mirror and saw the eyes of the man at the church staring back at him. Was it simply a hallucination down to an infection raging out of control? Or had it been as real as it felt? If so, what were the implications? His mind slid around a third, even more unpalatable, option: could it be possible? Was he losing his mind?

CHAPTER THIRTY-EIGHT

Three days later, Farrell walked stiffly into the reception area at Nithbank. He was in no mood to brook interference. He placed his warrant card face down on the desk.

'I need to speak with Dr Yates.'

'I'll just check if she's available,' the receptionist said, eying him warily.

After a brief exchange on the phone she motioned to him to go through.

He walked through and opened her door. Clare jumped up from her desk and backed away from him. He approached her, concerned.

'Clare, what's wrong? Why haven't you returned my calls?'

'I should have thought that would be perfectly obvious,' she replied.

'I've no idea what you're talking about,' he countered.

'I don't take kindly to men jumping out of bushes and mauling me.'

'Why would you? But what does this have to do with me?'

Clare stared at him through narrowed eyes.

An iron fist squeezed Farrell's entrails. Struggling to keep his voice level, he asked, 'this incident, when exactly did it happen?'

'As if you don't know,' she scoffed.

'Humour me,' he said.

'Wednesday, around 9 p.m.'

Farrell's legs felt weak. He slumped into a chair. The night he had blacked out or been drugged; he still didn't know which.

'It wasn't me,' he protested.

'You left this behind,' she said, producing his mobile phone from her pocket.

Farrell looked at it in horror. He slowly took it from her.

'I wouldn't do that. That's not who I am.'

'I didn't think so either,' she said, her voice softer. 'Look, Frank. Tell me what's going on with you. Are you getting sick again, is that it? Has the stress of these cases triggered a relapse?'

Farrell's head was all over the place. He didn't know what to think. If he levelled with her, she might have him carted off to the funny farm. However, on the other hand, there was no one else so uniquely placed to help him. To heck with it, he thought. Here goes.

'You asked if I'm getting sick again? Truthfully I don't know. Lately, I've been a bit lax about the lithium ...'

'You're still on lithium?' she interjected. 'But you said ... why didn't you tell me?'

'Why do you think?' he said. 'Because you would have written me off as a broken-down whack job.'

'Give me a little credit,' she said.

Farrell looked at her. She turned away, gnawing her lip.

'All right! I admit it might have made me a little twitchy. Satisfied?'

'Anyway,' said Farrell. 'None of that matters now. The night you thought I was hiding in the bushes is the night I either had a blackout or was drugged. He could have stolen my mobile phone. It went missing sometime before that night and hasn't turned up since. I know he's been in my house before.'

Farrell quickly brought her up to speed on the investigation, including his dramatic encounter with the abductor.

'You were actually stabbed?'

'It was nothing, just a flesh wound. Didn't hit anything vital,' said Farrell.

'Why didn't you tell me? I would have …'

'What Clare? You would have done what exactly? I did try to phone, several times, but you wouldn't even take my calls.'

Clare couldn't meet his eyes.

'I'm sorry. I was confused. I didn't know what to think. You scared me.'

'It wasn't me!' shouted Farrell louder than he had intended.

Clare's eyes filled with tears.

'You're scaring me now,' she said in a low voice.

Farrell took a deep breath and forced himself to calm down. He was handling this all wrong.

'The thing is, Clare, when I looked in the mirror a few days ago it suddenly hit me where I had seen the killer's eyes before.'

'Where?' demanded Clare.

'In the mirror.'

'What do you mean? I don't understand.'

'That makes two of us,' countered Farrell.

Clare stared at Farrell. He stared back.

'That night,' she began, 'I didn't see the man head on as he approached me from behind. When he put his arms round me I thought it was you. He was the same height and build. I even got a whiff of that aftershave you wear. It was you and yet it wasn't you. I'm not making any sense, am I?'

'Join the club,' said Farrell. 'Although, for what it's worth, the aftershave disappeared around the same time as the phone.'

'I suppose it's possible you're having some kind of psychotic episode,' said Clare slowly, 'but that would mean …'

'That I'm the one who assaulted you the other night,' finished Farrell.

'You mentioned DC McLeod was with you up at the convent. Did she see you and the abductor at the same time?'

Farrell thought back, replaying the whole terrifying scene in his mind. He shook his head decisively.

'She only heard his voice. She didn't get a look at him. I think she said he had a Glaswegian accent.'

Another uncomfortable thought occurred to him.

'Wait a minute, I've remembered something. She said there was something familiar about the voice but she couldn't place it.'

Farrell jumped up and started to pace round the room.

'Clare, I don't suppose, you don't think … ?'

Farrell's breath became ragged and the room began to recede. All he could hear was the sound of his own blood pounding in his ears like a river in spate. He felt a cool hand take hold of his hot one and gently lead him to the chair he'd recently vacated. Feeling like a fool he obeyed her instructions to place his head between his knees. Gradually the room swam back into focus. He pushed himself upright. Their eyes met and his slid away in confusion.

'I'll be honest, Frank. I don't know what to think,' Clare said carefully. 'You've certainly had a psychotic episode in the past but after all this time a recurrence is unlikely. I don't like the fact that you've been haphazard with your lithium. It muddies the water a little,' she said looking worried.

'There's no way I'm behind these abductions,' said Farrell. 'I know myself better than that. Plus, I would have to have stabbed myself as well. That's a whole different level of crazy. There's got to be another explanation.'

'Like what?' asked Clare.

'Hell, I don't know!' exploded Farrell. 'Some kind of doppelganger? The whole thing's ridiculous. Forget I said anything. I'll figure it out,' he said as he got to his feet and turned towards the door.

'Could someone be deliberately impersonating you?'

Farrell paused and looked at her like he thought she'd taken leave of her senses.

'To what end?'

'Trying to frame you, exact revenge for a past grievance?'

'Jason Baxter is the only person I can think of down this neck of the woods that has a grudge against me.'

'Well?'

'Well, nothing! He's an old guy with a big belly, not to mention the wrong height. You'd have sussed the difference immediately.'

'I don't know …' she said, the corners of her mouth twitching.

'Very funny.'

'I don't know what else to suggest,' said Clare. 'To all intents and purposes it was you but not you.'

'If it was just your experience alone I would be more likely to think it was someone pretending to be me, but you're forgetting I looked into his eyes. They were my eyes, I know it!'

'Frank, you have blue eyes. The person who abducted the boys has been variously described as having green or brown eyes.'

'Coloured contact lenses, probably, so we don't really know.'

'Let's just put it behind us and move on. Whether it was you or not, it doesn't matter. I'm fine and you seem your normal self now. Either it was you or it was someone with the same physical build trying to impersonate you. There are no other possibilities.'

'Unless I've got a twin brother, a mirror image?'

'Frank,' Clare said, looking concerned. 'I don't think …'

'I can't be adopted. I've got my mother's eyes and she also gave me these dimples, for my sins.'

'And your father?' she asked, clearly trying to humour him.

Farrell paused before answering, feeling a familiar emptiness. How could he continue to mourn someone he had never known?

'My father died when I was a baby,' he said. 'He was a fireman and suffered smoke inhalation after rescuing a family from a burning tenement in Glasgow.'

'It can be tough having a parent die so heroically. People around you place them on a pedestal. It makes it harder to gain a realistic sense of who they were, warts and all.'

'I'm pretty sure my father was wart free judging by the way my mother used to go on about him when I was growing up.'

'Wait a minute, I thought you grew up in Dumfries?'

'We moved not long after the funeral. Too many memories, my mother said. Maybe I had a twin that was adopted?'

'That wouldn't make any sense,' said Clare.

'Nothing about this makes sense. A twin brother makes a lot more sense to me than that I assaulted you the other night. That just couldn't have happened, mad or not.'

'If you were ill, your normal parameters of behaviour wouldn't apply. You might have been disinhibited, in an altered state. I know that's hard to accept.'

'What? It's more likely that I'm off my rocker than had a brother that was adopted?'

Clare said nothing, which in itself spoke volumes.

Farrell stood up to leave.

'Look, why don't you have a word with your mother, broach the subject, solely to put your mind at rest?'

'Not an option,' said Farrell. 'We're not on the best of terms right now. Maybe I got it wrong anyway. When I came face to face with the abductor I was close to passing out from the stabbing. Maybe my brain got a bit scrambled in the process.'

There was an awkward pause.

Farrell stood up to go. Best to get it over with.

'I guess, given the circumstances, you and I probably shouldn't continue seeing each other?'

'If you think that's best,' she replied with composure.

Farrell scanned her expression and was dismayed to see a flicker of relief. What had he expected? That she would collapse into hysterics and beg him to reconsider? At least he could exit her life with dignity. He owed her that at least.

'Frank, wait. Don't go!'

Farrell turned round, scarcely daring to hope.

Clare walked towards him and took both his hands in hers.

'I don't want us to stop seeing each other but I need you to promise me that you'll keep taking your medication. I'm worried about you.'

'I promise,' Farrell said. 'I won't let you down.'

'The reason I became a psychiatrist was that my mother was mentally ill. She ended up killing herself.'

'I'm sorry,' said Farrell, squeezing her hands. 'I had no idea.'

'I was driven to help others like her but it gave me a fear of ever being tangled up with something like that in my personal life. If I didn't like you so much things would never even have got this far.'

'Let's just take things one day at a time,' said Farrell.

'There's something else,' said Clare. 'A condition, if you like.'

'Go on.'

'I want you to see a psychiatrist, just to be on the safe side. I assume you have someone you see in Edinburgh?'

'I do. And I will,' said Farrell. 'I promise. But in the meantime, I'm still signed off sick so at least it gives me a bit of free time to start digging around.'

'Be careful,' Clare said.

As Farrell drove back to Kelton his thoughts whirled like an erratic fairground ride, trying to make sense of all the information whizzing by. Could he really have a twin? How could that be possible? With a jolt he remembered the first crime scene. His DNA had been found there. He'd put it down to the shock, kicked himself for being sloppy. Suppose it hadn't been his after all? A bark of mirth squeezed from his lips as he imagined how the super would take it if it turned out he had a twin running amok. He had to keep even the remote possibility to himself for the time being. The only person who would know for sure was his mother and she'd cut out her tongue rather than tell him any—

That's it! Suddenly Farrell knew what he had to do. You can

always rely on the Bible to point the way. Time for a visit from the prodigal son. He needed help; someone else in the loop. Someone who could reel him in if he really was going off his rocker. Who to trust?

CHAPTER THIRTY-NINE

Fresh from the gym, DS Byers walked into the MCA room with a smile on his face. While Farrell was off sick, Lind had put him in charge of the investigation into Boyd's murder and he was determined to crack open the case before he got back. Showing him up would be the icing on the cake. He didn't understand why the guy was so popular. He for one thought he was completely overrated. Probably only slumming it down here because he couldn't hack it in Edinburgh.

The Boyd case had started to stagnate as Farrell had become more and more distracted by the missing kids. Not that there had been much to follow by way of leads.

PC Thomson came up to him at once, looking eager.

'Sarge, I've been going through Boyd's phone records. They took their time getting here. It looks as though he called the police station the day that he was murdered.'

'Who did he speak to?' asked Byers.

'There's no record of that. All I know is that he called Town Office.'

'Go and speak to Marjorie downstairs; she'll be able to show you where they log all the calls. Report back to me as soon as you pin it down.'

'Right away, Sarge.'

PC Thomson left the room, and Byers pondered, why hadn't this come up before? Surely someone at the station would have piped up by now if they'd spoken to the murder victim the day before he was killed? He still felt that more weight should have been given to the statement of the old biddy, Agnes Brown. They ought to be looking at Farrell, given he may have had a long-standing grudge against Boyd. If she'd said that about him, he thought bitterly, Lind would have had the team all over his ass for weeks until he was satisfied he was in the clear. It was like a poor man's version of the old school tie system. From what he could gather, Farrell and Lind hadn't seen each other for years. People change, and Lind had been bang out of order to dismiss a potential line of enquiry like that. Maybe he could chase it down himself?

Another thing, hadn't Mhairi said the mother seemed like she was hiding something? Farrell should never have gone along with McLeod to question her. Totally unprofessional. She was another one that seemed blind to reason where Farrell was concerned. For all she knew Farrell could have been trying to intimidate his mother to prevent her revealing the extent of the bad blood between him and the dead priest. Either way, she should be questioned again. He would take along PC Thomson. The lad was proving himself to be useful and wasn't likely to blab if he told him to zip it. And as for the housekeeper? There was obviously no love lost between her and Farrell. She would probably be happy to stick the boot in if she knew the source of any ill feeling between the two men. Farrell hadn't even mentioned to the team that he had known her previously. Nor, for that matter, had he volunteered that when he had been a priest he had lived with the deceased. Individually, it was all neither here nor there, but taken as a whole it was starting to look incriminating.

He was heading downstairs to intercept PC Thomson when he saw him walking towards him, looking serious.

'Well?' he said. 'Spit it out. Who was he put through to?'

'No one, Sarge. He asked for DI Farrell by name and left a message for him to call back. He didn't start work until the next day but the message was definitely left on his desk. Didn't DI Farrell mention it, Sir?'

'It would seem not,' said Byers. 'Come on, we've got work to do. We need to re-interview Yvonne Farrell and Mary Flannigan.'

CHAPTER FORTY

DCI Lind gestured for Clare to take a seat opposite him. He noticed that she was very pale, with dark shadows under her eyes. No wonder in her line of work. And he thought his job was hard.

'Clare, come away in and have a seat. I've heard great things about you from Frank. In fact, I was hoping you would agree to formally consult with us on the abduction cases?'

She swallowed hard.

'About that. I don't know if you are aware but Frank and I have been seeing each other.'

'Oh,' said Lind. 'I see.'

'The thing is … I'm not entirely sure how well he is.'

'Well, he has been stabbed, of course.'

Claire closed her eyes and took a deep breath.

'I wasn't talking about his physical health. The things he's been saying …'

'Such as?'

'Don't get me wrong. Most of the time he seems completely fine, but lately …'

'He's certainly been under a lot of stress.'

'Last Wednesday, I was assaulted on my way home from work. A man of Frank's build and height put his hands round me from behind. He was wearing the same aftershave. He started groping me from behind and when I told him to stop he pushed me over and fled.'

'You think Frank did this? It doesn't sound like him.'

'When I got to my feet I noticed a mobile phone on the ground. It was Frank's.'

'I see.'

'I confronted him about it and he denied it was him. He said his phone and aftershave had gone missing.'

'I do vaguely remember him complaining about his mobile going missing. Are you here to make a formal complaint?'

'No, that's not what this is about.'

Lind looked puzzled.

'There's more. He told me he saw the abductor's eyes looking back at him out of the mirror.'

'He said *what*? When was this?'

'Yesterday. He came to see me yesterday.'

'Bloody Hell! Is he having some kind of a breakdown?'

'Honestly? I don't know. He's recently been stabbed. Maybe his mind is bending under the stress? He was going on and on about how the only explanation is that he has a twin brother, like he was developing some kind of paranoid fantasy.'

'And what do you think? Was it Farrell who assaulted you? Could it have been someone trying to frame him?'

'I wish I knew. If it was him, he must have been in an altered state.'

'I have no right to ask, but would you consider keeping this quiet for the time being? He's off recovering for a few days. It'll give me time to make a few discreet enquiries and see if there's any cause for concern in relation to his work, which might provide some insight into how he's coping.'

Clare stood up to go.

'I only want what's best for him.'

'You and me both. Leave it with me.'

CHAPTER FORTY-ONE

It had been a long day. Mhairi peered at her haggard reflection in the staff toilets and reckoned it was going to take more than make-up to make that face fit for human consumption. The last few weeks had been gruelling. She was still haunted by the sight of those two little boys in the church. It could all have gone so terribly wrong. If it hadn't been for Farrell who knows what might have happened? He might have his foibles but when push came to shove she could think of no one else she would rather have in her corner.

She should probably have agreed to take a few days off afterwards but Mark was still missing and she felt she owed it to the parents to keep going. When she'd been round at the house this afternoon, Elspeth had just sat listlessly in a chair while Barry talked to her. Her eyes looked like nobody was home. Jamie had seemed very subdued, which was hardly surprising, given that the room conveyed all the joy of a funeral parlour. Not a healthy atmosphere for the youngster.

Mhairi looked in on DI Moore to see if she could help her with anything else and noticed that even her well-groomed boss was looking somewhat wispy and dishevelled. How long could they keep this up?

'Any further developments, Ma'am?'

DI Moore shook her head, closing her eyes in frustration.

'Nothing so far. The only meaningful DNA recovered was that of the two boys and Farrell himself. His blood was all over the place. The abductor was canny enough to wear gloves, so no prints either. Not even on that damned Mickey Mouse mask. We didn't find any DNA in relation to young Mark so he's almost certainly never been held at that location. That's if he's still alive, poor mite,' she said with a sigh.

'I've been through the data so many times but I still can't work out how he is selecting his victims. There are no points of intersection, apart from St Aidan's, and that congregation is huge,' said Mhairi with a sigh.

'If only DI Farrell hadn't rung that number before we had a chance to set up a trace. I still can't believe he did that. With his years of experience to boot!'

'Are Paul and Andy able to be questioned, Ma'am?'

'No, given their age and the danger of re-traumatizing them the child psychologist felt it would be too risky; same with Jamie.'

'Are you sure there's nothing else I can do before knocking off for the night, Ma'am?'

'Away home, Mhairi, get some rest.'

On her way out she popped into the MCA room to pick up her briefcase. Byers, DS Stirling, and PC Thomson were huddled together talking in low voices. They stopped as soon as she opened the door, looking unaccountably furtive.

What was all that about, she wondered?

The tension still hovered in the air as the three men split apart and went their separate ways.

Casually, she sauntered after PC Thomson, then picked up speed once she was through the door. She caught up with him at the end of the corridor and dragged him into a nearby interview room.

'OK, Dave, spill! What the hell is going on?'

'Mhairi, it's more than my job's worth. I'm not allowed to say anything. They said the consequences would be dire.'

Mhairi thought for a minute, her body blocking the door. Whatever it was they were deliberately leaving her out of the loop. Suddenly she had it.

'This is about DI Farrell, isn't it?'

His guilty expression told her all she needed to know.

'At first I didn't believe it, but now I'm not so sure,' he muttered.

'They're fingering him for something, aren't they? Well?'

He knew her well enough to know she wasn't going to let it go.

'DS Byers and DS Stirling reckon he might have murdered Boyd. They've been gathering evidence to present to DCI Lind.'

Mhairi was stunned into silence. This couldn't be happening.

'Promise you won't tip him off, Mhairi. If this gets out they'll blame me and bang goes any chance of making detective.'

'Relax, I won't let on. And don't you blab that you told me. It won't do either of us any good.'

Mhairi left the room and walked to her car. Her head felt like it was buzzing with bees. Just how far was she prepared to stick her neck out for Farrell? And what about DCI Lind? Surely she owed him some loyalty too? If she tipped off Farrell she could be compromising a murder investigation.

She would sleep on it, she decided.

CHAPTER FORTY-TWO

Mhairi settled down on the couch with Oscar purring on her knee, his sides going in and out like bagpipes. Reaching for her glass of chardonnay, she snuggled deeper into her fluffy dressing gown. She had eschewed the temptations of the pub in favour of a TV dinner and an early night. Flicking the remote, she relaxed as the opening strains of *EastEnders* were heard.

A persistent knocking interrupted. Damn! She slid Oscar to the floor and padded to the door with a scowl on her face. As she flung it open her jaw dropped in surprise. What the Hell?

'Hello, Mhairi,' said Farrell.

'Sir, er, what are you doing here?'

'Call me Frank, we're both off duty.'

'You look …'

'Different? That's the whole idea. Let me in and I'll explain.'

Wordlessly, she opened the door and followed him in, affronted to have been caught in her old dressing gown without a scrap of make-up on. And also more than a little wary, given what she had just heard at work today. She gestured to a chair and sank back down onto the couch. Oscar returned to her knee looking peeved. The man who sat in front of her looked nothing like the Farrell she knew, who was a bit of a neat freak. His hair was spiked up with gel and he had a scruffy beard. He was wearing baggy jeans, cool trainers, and a leather jacket. Chunky gold jewellery hung from his neck and wrists.

'Jesus, Frank, you look like a pimp,' Mhairi blurted out. 'Tell me you're working undercover or something?'

'I suppose I am in a manner of speaking,' he said.

Mhairi felt a further prickle of unease.

'Frank what's going on?'

He spoke quickly, sounding almost feverish.

'I've been working on the abduction case while I've been off. What I've got to tell you may seem a bit strange but hear me out.'

'Go on,' said Mhairi.

'That day when I collapsed at work I was looking in the mirror when I saw him.'

'The abductor? He was in the station? Why didn't you ...?'

'He has my eyes.'

'Frank, this is crazy talk. You're not making any sense.'

'You didn't see him at the convent. He's my height and build and has got the same blue eyes. It didn't hit me at the time; too much was going on. It was only at work when I glanced in the mirror ... when for a split second I saw him looking back at me ... that I knew.'

'Knew what?'

'That he's connected to me. We're twins.'

'Maybe I should call someone, a medical someone. You've been under a lot of strain.'

'You thought there was something familiar about his voice. Did he sound like me?'

'No of course he didn't. He had a strong Glasgow twang. You sound nothing like him.'

Farrell grabbed today's paper from the coffee table and started reading from it, borrowing heavily from the accent of one of his old informants in Edinburgh who hailed from Glasgow.

220

Mhairi felt a flicker of doubt. Maybe he had something after all. The voice. It did sound quite familiar, so familiar in fact it sent a shiver up her spine. Her brain raced as she thought it through until the realization hit her like an express train. Either it was like Farrell said and he had a twin, or … else … he was the abductor and she was in terrible danger. Not to mention the fact that Byers clearly thought he was a murderer to boot. Shit! Meet rock and a hard place.

Farrell looked up. She froze, trying to act natural. All of a sudden she seemed to have a golf ball lodged in her throat. He ran his hands through his hair and glared at her.

'Tell me you're not thinking what I think you're thinking,' he sighed.

Mhairi considered him carefully. He looked mad, but normal mad, not psycho mad. She sighed wearily. So much for a relaxing night.

'For what it's worth, Frank, I don't have you pegged as a child abductor or a murderer …'

'Whoa, a murderer, where did that come from? Has Mark been found?'

'No, never mind that for now. What if you were … you know … sick … and didn't know what you'd done?'

'Might as well accuse me of being possessed by the devil and have done with it.'

'SO not helping!' fired back Mhairi.

'You're right, I'm sorry. We can't discount it as a possibility. I shouldn't be churlish about you considering that I might be insane … not in the circumstances anyway.'

'Now you're making me feel bad,' she chided.

'Mission accomplished,' he said.

They grinned at each other and the atmosphere lightened.

'We can hopefully prove it's not me,' said Farrell.

'How?' asked Mhairi.

'By cross-referencing the abductor's known movements with

mine. No one can be in two places at once. With a bit of luck, I'll have an alibi for some or all of the times he was known to be interacting with others.'

'Like at the nursery,' Mhairi chipped in.

'Exactly,' said Farrell.

'I'll get cracking on that tomorrow,' said Mhairi.

'Now what was that about murder?'

Mhairi waged war within herself for a few seconds then decided to tell him.

'Byers and Stirling have been gathering evidence to implicate you in Boyd's murder.'

'Does Lind know about this?'

'No, not yet, but I think they're going to try and get him on board soon.'

Farrell's jaw tightened.

She stood up, expecting him to leave.

'There's something else,' he said.

Mhairi sank back onto the cushions with a groan.

'Now what? Do the words off duty not mean anything to you?'

'I need to pay my mother a surprise visit, encourage her to take a trip down memory lane.'

'You're going to pretend to be *him*, aren't you?'

'I'll need a witness; in case she makes an admission.'

'I don't believe this. You want me to go and get dressed NOW?'

'For all we know he could be planning another abduction. It's vital we leave no stone unturned. It may be my last shot anyway given what you've just told me.'

Mhairi got to her feet and held up her hands in surrender.

'All right, I'll come! Enough with the guilt trip.'

'What do you expect? I'm Catholic.'

'I take it from your get-up I should be going for the gangster's moll look?'

'Something like that. We don't want her to recognize you so the more make-up and whatnot the better.'

Mhairi sloped off to get ready and Farrell was left on his own with Oscar, who treated him to a disdainful look. Curious, he browsed round the small sitting room that was furnished with a comfy sofa, a couple of chairs, and lots of scatter cushions. There were a number of photos and knick-knacks dotted round. One was of a handsome young man in an army uniform. He could see the family resemblance. Tucked away in a corner he found an old school photo of a shy self-conscious Mhairi trying to hide her braces from the camera and peering out from under a curtain of hair. He turned round guiltily as he heard her coming back into the room.

'This isn't *Through the Keyhole*,' she said crossly as she marched over and stuck her childhood self in the cupboard.

Farrell looked at her and immediately slid his eyes away. The short leather skirt and plunging neckline showed off Mhairi's hourglass figure to devastating effect. The red stilettos were so high she was almost as tall as he was.

'Too conservative?' she said impishly, sensing his embarrassment.

'Hardly, but perfect for the job in hand. Let's hope vice aren't out on patrol or we'll have some explaining to do,' said Farrell.

'That's not very gentlemanly,' she sniffed.

'Come on, let's go before I dig myself an even deeper hole.'

CHAPTER FORTY-THREE

They parked the car round the corner and approached his mother's house on foot, Mhairi's heels clacking on the pavement. The neighbourhood was mainly composed of retirement bungalows, and curtains were drawn to ward off the chill of the night. Lawns were trimmed to perfection although the flaking paint on a few of the exteriors disclosed that some of the elderly residents had already begun an inexorable descent into poverty.

Farrell's steps slowed as they neared his mother's house, an involuntary shiver rustling though his body. They paused. The curtains were drawn here too, though the flicker of a television could be detected behind them.

'Are you sure you want to go through with this?' asked Mhairi.

'Too much at stake not to,' replied Farrell as he opened the gate and marched up to the front door. He rang the bell. Getting into character, Mhairi popped a stick of gum in her mouth and lounged against the doorjamb looking bored.

The door finally opened, and his mother stood there erect and unyielding, until he spoke in the Glasgow twang he had practised earlier.

'Hello, Mother. Aren't you going to invite your son in?'

His mother sagged against the door; her mouth opening and

closing soundlessly; her breath tearing from her chest in gulps.

Farrell smoothly passed through and propelled her into the lounge, followed by Mhairi, who stifled her natural urge to console and flung herself sulkily into an armchair instead. Farrell's mother sank into the other chair as though her legs could no longer support her weight. He remained standing, assuming a position of dominance.

'How did you find me?' his mother quavered.

Farrell turned his face to Mhairi and she saw the jubilance flare in his eyes.

'How do you think?' he snarled at her.

'But they promised,' she said, her voice getting stronger, struggling for mastery over the situation.

Farrell considered her with narrowed eyes. She was a tough old bird, he'd give her that. He was going to have to keep pulling the rug from under her to get the information he was looking for. Hardening his heart, he pressed on.

'Think closer to home,' he said, his voice harsh and tinged with menace.

'Father Boyd wouldn't. He told me he'd take it to the grave with him.'

Farrell didn't really know what he was digging for but he pressed on.

'Father Boyd, eh? You're getting warmer.'

The colour drained from his mother's face and she collapsed back against the cushions, her breath coming in short gasps.

'No, it couldn't have been him,' she cried.

Mhairi shot him a warning look, as though she was itching to call the whole thing off. Farrell shored up his own resolve. Just one more push, Mother dearest, he said to himself.

'Not your father?' she asked, her voice cracked with anguish.

Farrell straightened up and spoke in his normal voice.

'Most illuminating.'

Realizing that she'd been tricked, his mother sprang at him, thin arms flailing against his chest like the wings of an angry sparrow.

When her rage was spent, Mhairi led her gently back to her chair and pressed a glass of water into her trembling hands.

Farrell struggled to control his own anger as he spoke.

'You told me my father was dead. That he was killed in a fire when I was a baby.'

'I did you a favour,' she replied.

'Are you telling me he's still alive?'

'He's dead to me,' snapped his mother.

'Where is he?'

'Barlinnie, last I heard.'

'What's he in for?'

His mother looked away, determined not to yield.

'Tell me,' he shouted.

Mhairi put a restraining hand on his arm. Angrily he shrugged her off. Suddenly, his mother stood up and gazed into his eyes defiantly. Farrell realized he was holding his breath.

'Fine,' she said. 'Have it your way, Mr Big Shot Detective. Your father was a rapist. You and your brother are the devil's spawn.'

Farrell felt his stomach contents rise up and swallowed hard. Whatever he had expected it hadn't been this.

'Me and my brother?'

His mother sighed and leaned back in the chair, her lips chalk white.

'I was coming home from work. It was dark. I was tired. I'd been on my feet all day. I decided to take a shortcut. He was in there ... waiting ...'

Farrell couldn't bear to think about it but he had to get the information he needed. Lives depended on it.

'Why did you give him away and keep me?'

'I hadn't realized I was expecting twins until I gave birth. Things were different then. There were no fancy scans like you have nowadays. It was a shock. Especially given the circumstances.'

226

'So you gave your son away as ruthlessly as you cut me out your life years later?'

'Don't you dare presume to judge me,' snapped his mother, colour storming into her cheeks again. 'I was a single mother with no support. My own parents disowned me. If it hadn't been for Father Boyd—'

'What does he have to do with any of this?'

'He was my parish priest in Glasgow and arranged a private adoption to a good Catholic family. He even helped us move down to Dumfries and start a new life here. I owed him everything. We both do.'

'Tell me my father's name,' demanded Farrell.

'I have no intention of saying another word on the subject,' said his mother. 'I'd like you to leave now.'

A red mist descended. Farrell grabbed a glass ornament from the table and pulled back his arm to throw it against the wall. The anger he was feeling was too strong to be contained. Dimly he heard Mhairi screaming at him.

'Frank, stop it! It's not worth it, come on!'

With trembling hands he put the vase back down. He felt Mhairi dragging him out the house. The last thing he saw was the fear in his mother's eyes.

Farrell tore up the road as though the flames of Hell were already licking at his heels.

Mhairi clacked after him, losing ground rapidly in her ridiculous shoes. Sod it, she thought. Reaching down, she pulled them off and tore after him in her bare feet, grimacing in pain as she sped over the uneven ground. As she drew level with him she grabbed his sleeve, forcing him to spin round and face her. The naked savagery in his eyes made her quail, but she stood her ground.

'I want to be alone,' he shouted.

'NO, you DON'T!' she yelled.

For an insane moment she thought he was going to hit her

but he got himself under control, and when he turned to face her again the terrifying stranger was gone.

'Sorry, Mhairi. I'm being a right headbanger.'

'Don't be so hard on yourself. You've had a shock.'

They drove back to her place in silence. As the car drew up to her flat, Mhairi made a snap decision.

'Look, you shouldn't be on your own tonight. Can I call Clare, get her to come over?'

Farrell grimaced.

'No, she's already worried I'm a basket case. No point gift wrapping it for her.'

'Well, stay the night with me then.'

Farrell's eyebrows shot up to greet his hair.

Mhairi sighed.

'Don't flatter yourself, Frank Farrell.'

She hustled him inside and in a voice that brooked no argument she told him to have a bath while she fixed them an omelette. She thrust denim jeans and a cotton chambray shirt at him.

'These should fit you.'

Farrell took them from her.

'Old boyfriend's?' he queried.

Mhairi turned away and glanced at the photograph he'd seen before of the soldier but not before he saw tears well up.

'They belonged to my brother,' she said.

Farrell cursed himself for being an insensitive fool but decided not to go there. They'd had enough upset for one night.

Lying in the bath, he began to discern some patterns in his swirling thoughts. This whole miserable chain of events had been triggered by one event: the moment of his conception. The thought of some monster defiling his mother made him bare his teeth in anger and punch the water in impotent fury. A mini tsunami sloshed over the side, drenching the fluffy pink bath mat. He glared at his reflection in the mirror beside the bath and felt like he beheld a stranger. Had his mother given him away instead of his twin would he be the psycho running about hurting people and his twin be about to share supper with Mhairi? Did he really have the same capacity for evil at his core?

Farrell erupted from the bath determined to push away the feelings that threatened to overwhelm him. He surveyed the cheerful clutter around him. As he was towelling himself dry, he shuddered at what he thought was a rather large spider but turned out to be a pair of false eyelashes.

He consciously tried to empty his mind as he opened the door onto the tiny hall and moved into the small kitchen where Mhairi was dishing up their omelettes. A green salad was on the table along with an open bottle of red wine. Mhairi had ditched the revealing outfit in favour of trackie bottoms and a T-shirt. Her face was scrubbed of make-up and her hair caught up in a ponytail. She looked younger and more vulnerable somehow.

He squeezed into the tiny space at the table and Mhairi sat across from him. Their knees bumped awkwardly and the tension heightened until suddenly Mhairi burst out laughing.

'You smell of roses.'

'Well it was either that or honeysuckle. Talk about Hobson's choice,' Farrell replied.

He suddenly realized he was starving and tucked in with gusto.

After they'd eaten he helped Mhairi clear up in companionable silence and then they plonked themselves down with some coffee. It was nearly midnight.

'I'll need to brief DCI Lind first thing. He's going to think I've taken leave of my senses,' said Farrell.

'You'd better try and get to him before DS Byers does.'

'I need to get all this squared away so it doesn't divert resources from finding that wee boy. Nothing matters more than that.'

'Try not to think about it till the morning,' replied Mhairi.

She left the room and came back with a duvet and a couple of pillows, stifling a yawn.

'Time to hit the sack. I have a feeling tomorrow is going to be yet another long day,' she said.

CHAPTER FORTY-FOUR

Farrell got up early and slipped out without disturbing Mhairi. Driving home to the cottage the dawn chorus was deafening and the world smelled brand new. He inhaled great lungfuls of air through the open window, trying to cleanse himself of the stench of human nature. The new knowledge of where he had come from settled like a brick in his psyche, and he knew that things would never be the same again.

Once home he showered and shaved then selected his usual sober work attire. He checked his messages in the hope there would be one from Clare. Nothing. After a light breakfast and his medication, he locked the door behind him. It was still only 6 a.m.

He turned towards his car and froze. Leaning against it were DS Stirling and DS Byers. He was too late. They had already got to Lind. He remembered to act surprised so that Mhairi wouldn't get in trouble for tipping him off.

'What brings you two out here?'

'DI Farrell, we'd like you to accompany us voluntarily to the station to answer some questions in relation to the murder of Ignatius Boyd.'

'I see,' he said. 'Well, I was heading there anyway. You can follow me in. I'm sure your car can outgun mine if you think I've got any funny business in mind.'

Byers and Stirling looked at each other and looked at his car. Stirling nodded imperceptibly. Byers looked annoyed.

They drove in convoy with Farrell further winding Byers up by driving slowly and with exaggerated care. Part of him was raging and humiliated but he knew that he had brought it on himself by playing his cards too close to his chest.

There was no small talk. Minutes after they reached the station Farrell found himself seated across the table from Byers and Stirling, having been cautioned and declined representation. He was fairly sure that Lind was on the other side of the one-way mirror but had no way of knowing for sure.

'Why did you not reveal that you had a message from the victim waiting for you when you started work?'

'I threw it away,' said Farrell. 'I had no intention of phoning him back and, at that stage, I hadn't realized anything was amiss. I didn't mention it because it couldn't add anything to the weight of the investigation.'

'How do you account for the fact that your DNA was recovered at the scene?'

'Two possibilities,' said Farrell. 'Either I was sloppy or it belonged to my identical twin.'

'Your what?' spluttered Byers, leaning forward in his seat. 'Are you taking the piss?'

'My mother admitted to his existence last night in the presence of DC McLeod. And for the record, I ordered her to come with me.'

'Name? Address?' asked Stirling, taking over the questioning and warning Byers to pipe down with a look.

'She doesn't know. He was adopted shortly after birth.'

'Do you deny that there was bad blood between you and the victim?'

'Not at all. I despised the man but not enough to kill him.'

'Why?'

'He forced me into leaving the priesthood fifteen years ago.'

'Do you have an alibi for the night of the murder?'

'No.'

'Why did you not let on that you knew Mary Flannigan?'

'I hadn't seen her for close on fifteen years. As far as I was concerned it added nothing to the case.'

Byers and Stirling looked at each other. It wasn't enough to hold him and they knew it. Farrell could see Stirling wavering but he doubted Byers would want to let it go.

They stopped the tape and left the room for a few minutes. Farrell waited motionless for their return.

'You're free to go but you've to go and see DCI Lind. He's expecting you,' said Stirling, avoiding eye contact.

Farrell sat in the chair in front of Lind's desk and tried not to look defensive. He had just brought the DCI bang up to date with the latest developments and was waiting for the fallout. As anticipated his normally mild-mannered friend went nuclear.

'Jesus Christ, Frank!'

Farrell tried not to wince.

Lind noticed. 'And fuck your delicate sensibilities.'

Farrell tried to look neutral as Lind exploded round the room like a firecracker before eventually collapsing back into his chair.

He glared at Farrell.

'I honestly don't know whether to lock you up or pat you on the back,' he said finally.

'I got results,' said Farrell.

'You got lucky,' fired back Lind. 'I've never heard of such gung ho policing in all my puff.'

'The ends justified the means,' said Farrell.

'You took a young police officer on an unsanctioned undercover operation.'

'We went to visit my mother, not a drugs baron,' said Farrell.

233

Lind glared at him.

'Did it ever occur to you that if your mother is involved somehow the abductor may have been in the vicinity? That you could have put Mhairi at risk to gratify your own whim?'

Ouch, that one hit home, thought Farrell. He remained silent.

Lind stared at him and his expression softened slightly.

'Look, Frank, I know it's been tough, all this family shenanigans rearing its head but let's not jump to conclusions. I don't want to close off any avenues of investigation yet. All this stuff about you having a brother might seem a possible fit for the facts on one level, but it might not stand up to closer scrutiny. It might even have nothing to do with the case at all.'

'I feel it in my water,' said Farrell.

'What are you, my Aunt Bridget?' scoffed Lind.

'Look, Frank, blue eyes are fairly common. In fact, the woman at the first nursery was clear that the abductor had green eyes, in any event.'

'Coloured contact lenses, most probably,' muttered Farrell.

'When you confronted him you were in a heightened physical and emotional state, having just been stabbed. If the resemblance was that dramatic don't you think any of the witnesses would have cottoned on?'

'Not if he was well enough disguised,' said Farrell. 'Anyway, now that I think of it, the first boy we found, Jamie, he was afraid to come anywhere near me.'

'Before this you were certain Jason Baxter was involved,' said Lind. 'There's also the fact that Father Malone's behaviour has been extremely suspicious of late. Didn't you say earlier that Boyd was giving him a hard time about his sexuality? It's as good a motive as any.'

'For killing Boyd though, not for abducting the little boys,' countered Farrell.

'I'm still not convinced that the two investigations are linked,' said Lind.

Farrell said nothing.

There was a tap on the door. DC McLeod entered and laid a piece of paper on Lind's desk.

'Results of the drugs test on the whisky, Sir. It tested positive for benzodiazepines.'

'Thanks, McLeod. Good work,' said Lind.

Farrell exhaled in relief.

'There's a combined briefing down for 8 a.m. What I've got to say should blow away the cobwebs. If you'd rather give this one a miss, Frank, that's fine by me.'

'Thanks, but I've got to face them all sometime. Might as well get it over with.'

At 8 a.m. Farrell took his preferred seat at the back of the lecture hall as Lind motioned for silence and took them through all the latest developments in both cases, holding nothing back. You could have heard a pin drop. When Lind got to the rape of his mother the bile rose in his throat. The product of a rape. His skin crawled with revulsion, not just for what had been done to his mother but also for the fact that his own DNA was lousy with that animal's. He felt a lesser man. There was a soft squeeze on his shoulder. DI Moore was behind him. He shot her a grateful look. Mhairi was seated near the front, notebook in hand. Despite their intimacy last night, she had greeted him coolly this morning in front of the others. Sensible lass. Lind got to the end of his spiel and started firing out actions for the day.

'Stirling and Byers, go bring Mrs Farrell in. Get a name. Then patch it through to me right away and I can get the fiscal to dig out the papers. If she doesn't cooperate charge her with attempting to pervert the course of justice. See how that goes down in the sewing circle. Lean on her hard about the connection with the priest. What that woman's been hiding would fill a suitcase. Was he bartering babies for cash or doing it out the goodness of his heart?'

'DI Farrell, I want you to bring Father Malone down to the station. From what you were saying earlier I reckon he's holding something back too. Make it as public as you like. Apply maximum pressure.'

'DI Moore, I want you to get together with Andy Moran and concoct an article for the local paper. Make it something provocative about twins separated at birth. Get Clare Yates on board; she'll give you some pointers but I don't want her to front it. Too dangerous. Use a false expert name. It's time to go on the attack and flush this bastard out from the undergrowth.'

'DC McLeod, I want you to compile an exhaustive list of every conceivable local organization that might hold records of twins. Concentrate on pre-schoolers, both public and private sector. Check the background of both sets of twins through HOLMES. If there's a point of intersection I want to know about it. He must be getting his information from somewhere. Fax all the nurseries and childcare agencies again. Warn them to be on high alert and to release no child into the care of someone they don't personally know without reference to us first. I have a feeling he's not done playing out his sick fantasies yet.'

Lind strode out and Farrell was quick to follow on his heels. Behind them bursts of excited chatter broke out all over the room. Mhairi rushed out the room behind them; her shirt hanging out of her skirt as though the various factions had each been trying to claim her as their own.

'Sirs,' she said formally and marched off down the corridor, head held high.

Farrell looked at his watch. He could just catch the morning Mass at St Aidan's. It would give him an opportunity to observe Malone's demeanour before bringing him in.

As Farrell sat surreptitiously studying the twenty or so members of the Catholic faithful, he marvelled at how their white pinched faces all resembled each other. Was it some universal badge of holiness and piety or merely the pallor of those for whom living in this world was a mere prelude to the real life beyond? He became aware that the congregation were becoming restless and shifting in their seats. A few coughs broke out and he heard a loud tut. Where was Father Malone? With a lurch of foreboding, Farrell leapt from his seat and ran lightly up the aisle to the sacristy door. He rapped firmly. No reply. He opened the door. There was nobody there.

CHAPTER FORTY-FIVE

Farrell exited the back door of the chapel and ran across the grass and up the lane to the priest's house. There was no sign of life. He pushed hard on the door and it swung open. The place smelled rank. In the kitchen dirty dishes were piled high in the sink. He soon ascertained that there was nobody downstairs.

Still without announcing himself, Farrell crept upstairs, trying to avoid the creaking treads from memory. Quietly opening one of the bedroom doors, he came upon Father Malone throwing things into a case on the bed. The priest spun round, a look of abject terror on his face, which only abated slightly when he realized it was Farrell.

Farrell leaned against the wall with folded arms and regarded the young priest sternly.

'Doing a runner?' he asked.

'I'm ... I'm ... just going on a little holiday, taking a break,' Father Malone faltered.

'With a church full of parishioners waiting for you? I don't think so,' said Farrell.

The priest sank onto the bed, refusing to meet Farrell's gaze. He was unshaven and had developed a nervous tic at the side of his mouth. His fingers moved compulsively as though threading an imaginary rosary. Farrell considered him closely, weighing up the best approach to take. If he came down too hard the priest might blow apart, and they'd never get anything worthwhile out of him. Relaxing his stance, he crossed the room to the bed and sat down beside the trembling man.

'Look,' he said. 'I'm on your side. Put me in the picture and I can make all this go away. Tell me what you know.'

'I can't,' Father Malone replied.

'What are you running from?'

The priest remained silent.

'Did you kill Father Boyd?'

The surprise and anger in Malone's face looked genuine.

'No, of course not! How can you think that I would do something like that?'

Farrell's eyes went to the open suitcase and back to Malone.

'Well, if you didn't kill him you must know or suspect who did?'

'I don't know his identity.'

'Has he communicated with you?'

The priest was silent.

'By letter? Phone? What?' snapped Farrell, beginning to lose patience.

Still no reply. A horrible thought occurred to him. He looked at the priest.

'In the confessional?' he asked.

Father Malone jerked like a puppet. He nodded dumbly, raising tormented eyes at last to meet Farrell's gaze.

Chilled to the soul, Farrell forced himself to ask a question to which he felt he already knew the answer.

'Has Boyd's killer confessed his sins to you?'

'I can't say,' the priest replied in a wooden voice.

'He's been asking you to grant him absolution, hasn't he?'

There was a long pause.

The priest nodded almost imperceptibly.

Farrell felt sick to the stomach. Unable to contain his emotion he rose to his feet and paced around the room.

Securing himself a 'Get out of Hell' card. Talk about forward planning.

'How long has this been going on?'

'A few weeks.'

'He told you all about Boyd's murder?'

'Yes, in sickening detail,' shuddered the priest.

'Did he say anything about the boy that's still missing?'

'I didn't know that was anything to do with him at first. After he'd confessed to killing Boyd, I thought that was it. Then he came back. Every time I begged him to tell me where the missing boy was being kept.'

'He's alive then?'

'I believe that he was a week ago. Beyond that I couldn't say. He would hint at particular places: abandoned churches, derelict buildings; say he couldn't quite remember which place he'd hidden the boy.'

'The mud on your shoes that day. You'd been out looking for the boy?'

'Yes. I didn't know what else to do. Every day I've been searching. Praying and searching.'

'If you had only said something,' sighed Farrell. 'We could have surrounded the church; maybe caught him before he abducted the other boys.'

'There are rules for a reason,' said Father Malone. 'If people felt their priest was liable to go running to the police they would never confess their sins. All those lost souls dying with the stain of sin. Not to mention automatic excommunication for the priest.'

'So why let on now?' asked Farrell. 'Because you're scared witless? So much for lofty ideals.'

'Because I don't think his penitence is sincere. And yes, I'm terrified that if I keep refusing to grant him absolution I'll meet the same fate as Father Boyd.'

'Running away won't solve anything. You need to stay and fight, be worthy of the cloth you wear. Help me stop this!' pleaded Farrell.

'What do you want me to do?'

'For a start, get yourself over to the chapel for Mass. Tell those that are still there that you had to administer the last rites to a parishioner. Stick to your normal routine as much as possible.'

'What if he's out there, watching me?'

'I'll be in the congregation. After Mass is over there will be an unmarked police car to meet you at the back door driven by a man and woman in plain clothes. They'll bring you to me. I don't want you at the station in Dumfries. Too risky.'

'I don't think I can go out there, connect with God.'

'Fake it.'

'What?'

'You heard,' retorted Farrell. 'Now get out there before they all leave. Hurry!'

Father Malone lurched to his feet and left the room. Farrell wasn't all that sure he'd be able to carry it off but hoped for the best. He radioed in to HQ, set up the car, and arranged the meeting place. Then he made his way over to the chapel; entering by the front so as not to arouse suspicion. Letting the familiar words and phrases wash over him he felt more disconnected from God than he could ever remember feeling before. He felt like a crude impostor; a million miles away from the devout young priest he used to be. A tarnished soul.

The Mass finally drew to its conclusion. Farrell took care to leave first and drew away in his car having first checked in with HQ who confirmed DS Stirling and PC Thomson had picked up the priest and were taking him to the police station at Lockerbie. Farrell went to Lockerbie by a different route, pushing the Citroen as far as it would go, which still wasn't fast enough to raise any eyebrows. For once he was indifferent to the soft undulations of the hills around him: his brain thinking tangentially about the case; ideas exploding round his head like bullets looking for a way out.

Twenty minutes later, Farrell arrived in the small bustling town of Lockerbie and parked in the supermarket car park before walking round to the back of the police station.

DS Stirling was pacing up and down the small reception area watched by an avid young constable, who was fairly agog with excitement; Lockerbie not being exactly the crime capital of Europe.

'Everything is set up,' said Stirling. 'We're ready to go.'

They moved into the adjacent interview room where Father Malone was sitting, gnawing miserably on his nails.

'I'm going to go to Hell for this, you know,' he said to Farrell while the recording equipment was being checked.

'You're going to go to Hell if you don't,' returned Farrell.

'We're good to go when you're ready, Sir,' said Stirling.

Farrell nodded his approval. Nowadays when they were interviewing a suspect or an important witness two tapes would run simultaneously, leaving no room for allegations of a stitch up. It was a lot safer for everybody: police and suspects alike.

After cautioning Father Malone, just in case, they took him through it all – right from the beginning.

Farrell struggled to keep his face impassive as the grisly details of how Boyd had been tortured and killed were narrated in a faltering voice by the young priest.

The killer had come right at the end of the confessions, when there was no one left in the church and Father Malone was readying himself to leave.

'Did you try and get a look at him?' asked Farrell.

'No, I was too afraid,' Father Malone replied in a low voice. 'After all, I knew better than anyone what he was capable of.'

'What about Baxter? Where does he fit in?'

'Jason Baxter? He's got nothing to do with it. I'm aware of his past. He was very candid about it. As far as I'm concerned he's just a new parishioner who wanted a bit of help settling in.'

I'll bet, thought Farrell. There had to be a connection. He just wasn't sure what it was yet.

'Did the man say why he had killed Boyd?'

'I did ask him that,' said Father Malone. 'His reply was that the Lord said we were meant to do as we were done by.'

'It's "do as you would be done by",' said Farrell.

'Of course it is. I told him that but he wouldn't be swayed from his point of view. He said God's true meaning had been corrupted by translation and that the correct meaning had been revealed to him in a dream.'

'What about the kids? Did he say why they had been taken?'

'He said he was taking them to a better place where they could play with the angels. In his last confession a week ago he said it was nearly time. That's when I panicked.'

'I want you to sit back and close your eyes,' said Farrell. 'I'm going to conduct a little experiment.'

'You're not going to rough me up, are you?' mumbled the priest.

Farrell and Stirling rolled the whites of their eyes at each other.

'For the record,' said DS Stirling formally, 'we are NOT going to rough you up.'

'Bless me, Father, for I have sinned,' said Farrell in the Glaswegian accent he'd been practising on the way over.

Father Malone's eyes flew open and he rushed for the door, overturning his chair. It was locked. He turned terrified eyes on Farrell, who had remained sitting.

'It was you all along; you're the killer!' he shouted, rattling the door handle.

Farrell stopped the tape and Stirling led the now shaking young priest back to the table.

'I'm sorry to give you a scare like that,' said Farrell. 'If I'd told you what I was intending to do it may have affected the result.'

'I don't understand,' muttered Father Malone. 'How did you manage to sound like that monster?'

'We have reason to believe that I may be closely related to him. We also need you to keep that information to yourself for the time being,' said Farrell.

'What's one more secret?' replied Father Malone.

'For what it's worth, no one outside the investigating team needs to know what you told us today.'

'I can't simply ignore the fact that I have broken the sanctity of the confessional and carry on as normal.'

'Think it over,' urged Farrell. 'Don't do anything rash. In the meantime, we're going to arrange for protection. Any time you hear confessions there will be at least six plain clothes detectives posing as parishioners so that the church is never empty while you are in it. Two of these will accompany you home now and stay with you until all of this is over.'

Farrell walked back to the car feeling fairly satisfied with the outcome of the interview. Pity the killer hadn't told Father Malone anything they hadn't already worked out for themselves at this stage.

A shame it hadn't thrown up a link with Jason Baxter. This whole confession thing threw up uncomfortable associations with the way Baxter had manipulated him in the past. He would love to pin something on that evil toe-rag and have him shunted back inside where he belonged. Farrell firmly squashed the inevitable pang of guilt that accompanied his vengeful musings.

While on the subject of uncharitable thoughts he wondered how his mother had fared earlier.

CHAPTER FORTY-SIX

Farrell got back to the station later than he'd hoped due to being stuck behind a tractor pulling a huge trailer. Impatient to hear of any progress made in the case, he swung by the HOLMES room to see how Mhairi was faring with her investigation.

'Nothing yet, Sir,' she informed him. 'The amount of organizations that hold information relating to twins is huge. There's the hospital, GP surgeries, Dumfries and Galloway Council, Registry of Births, Deaths, and Marriages, to name but a few. Potentially thousands of people could have access to this information, particularly if they're nifty with computers.'

'Prepare a detailed questionnaire and send a couple of PCs round to speak to both lots of parents again. Maybe there's something we've missed. It might just be random selection but if we could narrow the potential victims down it would be easier to take protective measures.'

Farrell left Mhairi buried in piles of computer printouts and headed downstairs to the interview rooms. The usual stench of body odour overlaid with air freshener and pine disinfectant assailed his senses. For obvious reasons he couldn't sit in on the interview, nor did he want to. He thought he might catch a fleeting glimpse through the window on the way past. Too late. As he rounded the corner he clocked his mother approaching him flanked by two police officers. Heart pounding, he stood to one side to let them pass. She stalked past, head held high, not acknowledging him. Fine, if that's the way she wants to play it. He poked his head round the door his mother had just vacated. Inside, DI Moore and DS Byers were bent over their notes at the small table.

'Well?' he asked.

They both looked up, and DI Moore's lovely grey eyes regarded him sympathetically.

Now she thought he was a ruddy charity case.

'Come away in, Frank,' she said. 'How are you bearing up?'

'Fine,' he replied, fooling no one.

'We got a name,' she said.

Farrell's stomach clenched. His legs felt weak.

'Gerald McWhirter.'

The name rang no bells with Farrell. No surprises there.

DI Moore turned to Byers, who had steadfastly avoided Farrell's gaze.

'DS Byers, contact the fiscal's office, get them to do a trace on this name, see if he's presently in custody anywhere. He must be a fair age by now.'

After he had left she motioned for Farrell to join her at the table.

'She cooperated. Eventually.'

'That's my mother. Ever the pragmatist,' countered Farrell.

'She confirmed she had been raped when she was sixteen, on her way home from work.'

'Did she tell the police at the time?'

'Apparently she told no one, just tried to block it out. He'd threatened to kill her if she breathed a word. She believed him. Still believes him.'

'When did she realize she was pregnant?'

'Not until she was six months gone. Just thought she was putting on weight.'

'Sex education wasn't exactly high on the agenda at Catholic schools in those days,' said Farrell.

'Even in my day it consisted of a book covered in brown paper given to the sixth year on their last day of school,' said DI Moore.

'You're Catholic?' asked Farrell.

'Lapsed,' she said, looking embarrassed. 'Anyway, her parents reacted badly. Didn't believe her about the rape and called in the parish priest, who was—'

'Father Boyd,' said Farrell.

'They leaned on her to put the baby up for adoption, which Father Boyd said he could arrange through private channels to a good Catholic family.'

'For a tidy sum?' asked Farrell.

'She didn't know anything about that, was shocked at the very idea.'

'She had no idea she was having twins?'

'Not a clue,' said DI Moore. 'She decided to give one baby away as planned but insisted on keeping the other.'

'Any idea why?' asked Farrell.

'She said she wanted it to become a priest and atone for the sins of its father.'

'Had it all thought out, didn't she?'

'Frank, she was very young. I'm sure she did the best she could under difficult circumstances.'

Farrell stood up abruptly. He had to get out of this confined space. With a muttered farewell he left the room and exited the station. He needed some air.

After a few minutes' walk he found himself at the Dock Park and strode along the tree-lined avenue bordered on the left by a children's play park and the fast-flowing waters of the River Nith on the right. As he looked at the massive gnarled trunks of the ancient beech trees he felt comforted by his insignificance in the wider scheme of things. So he hailed from a dysfunctional family. He wasn't the first and he wouldn't be the last.

As Farrell passed by the bandstand he remembered his hormone-fuelled youth. He used to sneak off early from choir practice, and Laura would be waiting for him there. Happy days. He wondered if he would ever have become a priest in the first place if he hadn't been so relentlessly forced in that direction by his mother. Hard to say. What was done was done. As he listened to the screams and laughter from the park, he felt a recurring pang of regret that he had never had children. A little boy in a stripy jumper with tousled hair toddled into his path in pursuit of a ball. Farrell stooped to pick it up and handed it to him, looking round for his mother. She was engrossed in conversation with a friend, didn't even notice the exchange.

Had the abductor already killed Mark or had he stashed him away somewhere for some foul purpose? He thought about how Boyd had died, and his stomach churned. His brother was a monster. What did that say about him? Did he have the same dark impulses coursing in his veins? Was there a difference between mad and bad or was it all just a question of semantics and perception?

His radio crackled into life. It was Mhairi to tell him the fiscal had confirmed Gerald McWhirter was currently banged-up in Barlinnie. He told her to pick him up in the car park and quickened his pace on the loop round the green where the large windows of elevated sandstone buildings stared sightlessly towards the river, remembering better times.

He reached the car park as Mhairi arrived in her Renault Clio complete with pink fluffy dice bouncing above the windscreen.

Farrell folded himself into the front seat, trying to find a toehold among all the clutter on the floor.

'I've been busy,' she said with a pre-emptive glare.

'Did I say anything?' protested Farrell, peeling a facial wipe off his shoe.

'DCI Lind wants us to head straight up to Barlinnie and see McWhirter. He said you are free to decline but he figured you might be able to get more out of him, Sir. Catch him on the back foot.'

'Can't beat family reunions for loosening the tongue,' said Farrell. 'Not like Lind to abandon protocol.'

'He said he was willing to do whatever it took to find that wee boy and worry about the consequences later.'

'What's McWhirter in for?'

Mhairi looked stricken, as though she couldn't bear to tell him.

'Come on, out with it,' he snapped.

'Multiple rapes. He's serving a life sentence,' said Mhairi, keeping her eyes on the road ahead as she gave Farrell time to assimilate the information.

CHAPTER FORTY-SEVEN

Nearly two hours later they pulled into the visitor's car park at Barlinnie, on the outskirts of Glasgow, where the dregs of society were left to fester behind high brick walls topped with coils of barbed wire. Most of the souls inside were damaged beyond repair: brutalized by what they had had done to them and what they themselves had meted out.

Farrell recalled the stir that the Barlinnie Special Unit had caused. It had been a bold experiment in its day. They had taken a number of hardcore offenders that were causing problems within the jail and put them away from the other inmates. They tore up the rule book and started giving them intensive art lessons; the opportunity to create something good out of all the mayhem. Jimmy Boyle was a graduate of the Unit; carved out a whole new life for himself as a sculptor and writer. He had gone to hear him speak once and been impressed. Some had said he was just working the system and that beneath that polished presentation there still lurked a black heart. Farrell had chosen to believe otherwise.

As they were buzzed through to the reception area Farrell noticed Mhairi was looking pale.

'Have you been here before?' he asked.

'Never.'

'Don't worry. Maximum security means just that. It's perfectly safe,' said Farrell, omitting to tell her about the time he had briefly been taken hostage there five years ago.

'Here I am worrying about how I feel,' said Mhairi. 'And you're going to meet your ...'

'Whatever else he may be, he's not THAT.'

'Sorry, I didn't mean ...'

'Forget it,' he said. 'I'm just a bit on edge.'

They passed over their warrant cards and explained the purpose of their visit. Ten minutes later they were cleared to enter the visitors' room. With a dull hiss of hydraulics the doors slid apart and then closed behind them with an air of finality. A jangle of keys heralded the arrival of another blank-faced prison officer. He led them further into the bowels of the prison; opening and locking doors behind them as they moved along featureless beige corridors with strip lighting. A smell of sweat mingled with disinfectant seemed to become stronger as they pressed deeper into the interior. Eventually, they were shown into a small room with a plastic table and four orange chairs, all bolted to the floor.

Farrell glanced out the small window with its thick metal bars and tensed as he saw a powerfully built man in handcuffs being escorted across the yard between two prison officers. As he passed the outside of the window the man turned and their eyes met. Farrell's skin crawled and he had to exert every ounce of willpower he possessed not to look away.

The door was unlocked and the man in handcuffs was escorted in by two grim-faced prison officers. The man had a feral presence that expanded to fill the room,

'Sit down, Mr McWhirter,' Farrell said.

'Well, well,' sneered McWhirter. 'To what do I owe the honour?'

'We're here to ask you some questions about the murder of a priest.'

'And here's me thinking it was a social call,' drawled McWhirter.

'Put a clean pair of boxers on in honour of the occasion,' he said, leering at Mhairi.

Mhairi glanced at her watch and stifled a yawn. Farrell saw the annoyance flare in McWhirter's eyes.

Farrell cautioned McWhirter then leaned back in his seat, studiedly nonchalant.

'I'd like to ask you some questions relating to the rape of Yvonne Farrell in Dumfries over forty years ago.'

'That was no rape,' said McWhirter. 'She was gagging for it that one. Like a bitch on heat. Is it details you're after?'

Farrell felt nauseous but strived to keep his expression neutral.

'Have you ever been visited by someone claiming to be a product of that rape?'

'What? Before today, you mean?'

Farrell intercepted a worried look from Mhairi. He fought for self-control: clenching his jaw and balling his hands into tight fists under the table. 'You just answered my question,' Farrell replied. 'How else would you have known what I looked like? You deliberately weren't given my name in advance of our meeting.'

'Think you're so bloody clever, don't you, Mr high and mighty fucking copper.'

'Give us a name,' snapped Farrell, thumping his fist on the table, causing Mhairi to flinch.

'Or you'll what? Rattle your rosary beads? I'm so scared I'm crapping my pants.'

'He told you that I was a priest?'

'Laughed myself silly when I heard. Gonnae put in a good word for me at the pearlies?'

'How did you find him?' asked Farrell.

'He found me. Social worker stuck her neb in. Wee bastard had such a shite life he thought if he could only meet me everything would be fine and dandy. The nutter heid genes must come from that slag mother of yours.'

'How long have you been seeing him?'

'For about a year on and off,' said McWhirter. 'You jealous … son?'

He reached out to stroke Farrell's hand in a parody of parental affection. Farrell removed his hand and pressed on.

'Did you put him up to the murder of a Catholic priest?'

'The only good priest is a dead priest as far as I'm concerned,' McWhirter hissed. 'Present company *not* excepted. However, much as I would like to take the credit it was nothing to do with me. He had an old score to settle there. Why would I stand in his way?'

Farrell decided to take a shot in the dark.

'And what about the three-year-old kid?' said Farrell grimly. 'Was he an old score as well?'

McWhirter dropped his eyes and looked uncomfortable for the first time.

'Aye well, that's a different kettle of fish. That's where him and I had a parting of the ways.'

'You messed with his head,' said Farrell. 'Tipped him over the edge.'

'Hey, don't try and pin this one on me,' shouted McWhirter. 'How was I supposed to know he was gonnae start taking weans? I'm no' fucking psychic. He's a complete nut job.'

'When was the last time you saw him?' asked Farrell.

The fight seemed to go out of McWhirter. His shoulders sagged.

'Two months ago. He told me what he was planning wi' the weans.'

'And what exactly was that?'

'He said one gets to live; one gets to die. He said God decides which one goes home and which goes wi' him tae the pearlies.'

'What else did he say? Think man!'

'Nothing, 'cos I telt him tae get the fuck away from me. A bit o' slap and tickle is one thing but I wouldn'ae take a wean. No fucking danger.'

'Prove it,' said Farrell with a hard edge to his voice. 'Give us

253

the name he operates under and the last address you had for him.'

'On yer bike,' sneered McWhirter.

'He's not done, you know. If you don't help us out here, the next kid he takes will be down to you.'

'What's in it for me?' asked McWhirter.

'The knowledge that for once in your miserable existence you did the right thing?'

McWhirter leaned forward close enough for Farrell to smell his fetid breath.

'Suppose we say that you'll owe me one, be in my debt like?' offered McWhirter with an evil grin.

Mhairi tugged at his arm, but Farrell ignored her. It cost him dear to owe this monster that had created him but he had to hold on to the bigger picture. Lives were at stake.

'As long as it doesn't involve breaking the law I think we can agree on that,' said Farrell, hiding his repugnance as best he could.

McWhirter stared at him then. A long hard stare. Farrell stared coolly back.

'Well?' he said. 'What's it to be?'

'He goes by the name of Michael Black,' said McWhirter, as though the words were stuck in his throat. 'The last address I have for him is 21 Harrison Road, Dumfries.'

Wordlessly, Farrell got up and left the room with Mhairi close behind.

'Don't forget you owe me!' yelled McWhirter. The sound of his mirthless laughter followed them down the corridor.

CHAPTER FORTY-EIGHT

Mhairi had to break into a trot to keep up with Farrell as he loped back across the car park, barking orders into his mobile phone. As soon as they were in the car Mhairi started the engine.

'Now we wait,' he said.

'Do you think he was on the level, Sir?' asked Mhairi.

Farrell laughed. Mhairi stole a sideways glance at him. A nervous tic was blinking at the side of his eye, and his face was deathly white. Given his medical history she wondered how much more of this strain he could take.

'Do I think he's a lying sociopath? Too right,' he answered his own question. 'Do I think he's spinning us a yarn about that name and address? Funnily enough, I don't. He wants to mess with us. OK he wants to mess with me in particular. If he tells us something completely without foundation he's going to have no further opportunity to play his sick head games.'

'Do you think that Michael Black chose to abduct identical twins as some kind of twisted revenge on you or your mother?'

'Possibly,' said Farrell. 'However, just because we share the same DNA doesn't mean we inhabit the same mind.'

'I didn't mean to imply …'

'Relax, Mhairi, I'm just saying that we're not the same. Your guess is as good as mine.'

Mhairi squealed out of the car park.

'Didn't have you down for a girl racer,' Farrell said.

'I'm dying to get back and crack on with things,' said Mhairi.

'You and me both.'

Mhairi flicked on a CD, figuring it would help her beleaguered boss relax. The sound of Girls Aloud filled the car and Mhairi lost herself in the music. After a few tracks she stole a glance at Farrell, whose face was twisted up into an expression of agony.

'Toothache, Sir?'

'Something like that,' he muttered.

Mhairi flicked a button and the soothing strains of Classic FM filled the car. Now it's my turn to grin and bear it, she thought. Halfway down the M74 motorway she stole another sideways glance at Farrell and was gratified to see the lines of tension had slackened. She, on the other hand, had the mother of a headache building up.

Farrell looked sideways at her.

'Thanks,' he said. 'I guess this music isn't quite up your street.'

'Actually,' she said, 'I've got a very catholic taste in music.'

'Hidden depths eh?' asked Farrell.

Hidden shallows more like, thought Mhairi, contenting herself with what she hoped was an enigmatic smile.

Back at the station, Mhairi sped off to continue her research into those having access to databases with twins.

Farrell took the stairs two at a time; bursting into Lind's room after a peremptory knock without waiting for an answer. On the other side of the door he came face to face with Detective Superintendent Walker. Lind shot him a warning look. Cave Canem. Too late.

'Sorry, Sir,' Farrell said. 'I didn't realize you were busy. I'll drop by later.'

Farrell spun round in a pirouette that would have done Darcey Bussell proud and was almost out the door when the super snapped, lips drawn back from nicotine-stained teeth.

'Farrell, get back in here.'

'Sir?'

'Sit down, man, sit down.'

Farrell sat and steeled himself for the inevitable onslaught. He shot a glance at Lind, whose expression was unreadable.

'By rights you shouldn't be in on this investigation,' said Walker. 'If this wasn't such a small force and I didn't need your expertise I'd have kicked you into touch long since. To say you're personally involved is an understatement. It seems you returning to Dumfries acted as some damn catalyst, setting this whole lamentable chain of events off.'

'I'm sorry about that, Sir,' said Farrell in as restrained a tone as he could manage.

'If it's any consolation it's not been exactly a barrel of laughs for me either.'

The super stared at him for a few long moments then his expression softened somewhat and he subsided into the chair beside Farrell with a sigh.

'Aye, it's an awful business, altogether. Tell me this, Farrell. Is blood thicker than water?'

'The only person I feel at all emotionally connected to in this investigation, Sir, is my mother, and we're not exactly what you'd call close. As for my brother? Until recently, I didn't even know he existed. Other than an accident of birth he means no more to me than any other nutter that needs locking up for his own good and the good of others. The man responsible for my conception is already incarcerated so no problems there.'

'Brave words, Farrell. You'll forgive me if I'm not entirely convinced? Here's the deal. You get to remain on the Boyd investigation but not as SIO. From now on myself and Lind will be completely running the show and you're just another plod that does what he's told. I imagine that DI Moore will also be happy to avail herself of your expertise in relation to that missing child as from what Lind tells me it looks increasingly likely that Michael Black is behind both cases.'

'But Sir …'

'That's the deal. Take it or leave it. Furthermore, if I get even the faintest whiff of a suggestion that you've withheld information or gone off half-cocked against orders I'll have you transferred to the Port Authority at Stranraer. Is that clear?'

'As a bell, Sir,' said Farrell.

'There's something else,' said Walker. 'DI Moore has been speaking to that psychiatrist up at Nithbank, what's her name?'

'Clare Yates,' supplied DI Lind.

'That's it. You know that we're putting a series of articles into the local press calculated to inflame Boyd's killer and prod him into making contact with you? I want to make sure that this is with your consent?'

'Of course, Sir,' said Farrell.

'You do realize there's no telling how he might respond. It could cause you to be placed in considerable danger?'

'Bring it on, Sir,' replied Farrell. 'We need to catch him before he strikes again.'

'That's the spirit,' said Walker. 'Good to see an officer step up to the plate when the occasion demands it. Too many youngsters these days are liable to melt into a puddle with stress if someone so much as says "boo" to them. Stress! Everybody's scared shitless to say what they mean and mean what they say. Might as well cut off our bollocks and string them up in a bloody necklace for all the use they are these days.'

Farrell risked a sideways glance at Lind and saw that he was slack jawed with astonishment at the super's outburst.

'Keep me posted, Farrell,' said Walker, getting heavily to his feet. He gave Farrell's shoulder a rough squeeze on the way past, slamming the door behind him.

Farrell and Lind looked at each other.

'OK,' said Farrell. 'He touched me. Now I know I've really entered the twilight zone.'

'He's right about one thing though,' said Lind. 'What they're planning to do might send the killer—'

'You mean my evil twin,' said Farrell.

'I was trying to be diplomatic, you moron,' said Lind. 'If these articles push his buttons, he'll come after you, and it might not just be idle chit-chat he has in mind.'

'Look, the sooner we flush him out into the open the sooner we can get him banged up and life can get back to normal,' said Farrell.

'I wish it was that simple,' said Lind, gnawing his lip.

Farrell sat up straight, cursing himself for being a self-absorbed fool.

'Is it Laura?'

Lind said nothing, which was all the reply Farrell needed.

'I thought you said she had been feeling a bit brighter. Getting back on top of things?'

'I lied,' said Lind. 'I figured with all the shit you had flying around the last thing you needed was to be burdened with my personal problems.'

'We're supposed to be friends.'

'Since we lost the baby she's been very low; not herself at all.'

'Hardly surprising,' said Farrell. 'It'll take her time to grieve, accept what's happened. I take it she's been to the doctor?'

'He gave her some tablets. Can't say it's made a difference. She's down to see a psychologist but it could take upwards of a year before she gets an appointment. I miss her,' Lind said. 'The kids miss her. It's as though she's somewhere we can't reach.'

'Is there anything I can do?' asked Farrell.

Lind looked at him blankly, lost in his own private Hell. Suddenly the mist cleared from his countenance.

'Come to dinner,' he said. 'Tonight.'

Farrell froze.

'Tonight? Actually, I'm fairly sure I need to—'

'Eight o'clock,' Lind interrupted. 'It'll bring her out of herself. You know you and she used to be close. It'll remind her of happier times. Say you'll come.'

Farrell couldn't ignore the naked look of entreaty in the other man's eyes. Used to be close? That was an understatement. He wondered if Laura had ever told her husband that in a last desperate attempt to prevent him leaving for the seminary in the morning she had stolen into his room and made love to him all night. Even now the thought of that hot sultry night was enough to curl his toes.

'Eight o'clock it is then,' he said, as heartily as he could manage.

CHAPTER FORTY-NINE

DS Stirling stuck his head round the door after a peremptory knock. He nodded to Farrell.

'Yes?' said Lind.

'The firearms team have got the house surrounded, Sir. There's been no sign of activity since surveillance commenced.'

'Right,' said Lind, jumping to his feet and grabbing his jacket. 'Let's get over there and see what we've got.'

Farrell parked his car in a nearby cul-de-sac from which he could observe the façade of the rundown semi. The elderly couple in the immaculate adjoining dwelling had been spirited away to Loreburn Street, in a right old tizz, for tea and chit-chat with DC McLeod. Lind pulled in behind him and got out of the car. Farrell made to do likewise but Lind shook his head, motioning for him to stay put as he walked swiftly by with DS Stirling. Farrell watched them closely as they marched up the weed-encrusted driveway. A curtain twitched within the property. Someone was there. Farrell sat bolt upright. It was at times like this that he wished he smoked. Sweat prickled under his arms and an iron fist squeezed his gut. It was always the same when something big was going down. Every cell in his body flooded with adrenalin.

He heard Lind rap firmly on the door; Stirling right beside him. No response. Lind stepped aside and motioned to a member of the armed response team, who burst the lock and charged inside. Farrell knew they would have entered the back door simultaneously. This was it. They would surely catch him now. Farrell tensed at the thought of being confronted with this brother he had never known: spawned, as he himself had been, from evil, and who had lain with him in his mother's womb. Now it was time to stop regarding this whole mess as an academic exercise and get real.

Two burly officers wearing bulletproof vests erupted from the front door and waved them forward.

Lind stepped past the door, now hanging from its hinges, and motioned for Farrell to follow him. The first thing that he noticed was the smell of incense. As they moved into the tiny living room it became intermingled with the rank smell of stale body odour and unwashed clothes. There was something else? Farrell wrinkled his nose and sniffed like a bloodhound, following the sweet sickly smell into the kitchen where he found the remains of what looked like cannabis resin on the worktop. He left the kitchen. At the bottom of the stairs there was a crucifix on the wall. Farrell barely glanced at it but Lind, hot on his heels, halted in front of it.

'Frank, you'd better see this.'

Farrell slowly turned and looked hard at the crucifix. His eyes widened in shock as he saw that the head of Christ had been removed and a near perfectly proportioned facsimile of his own head substituted. He could feel his skin crawl with revulsion.

'This is some kind of crude message,' Farrell said.

'What do you think he's trying to get across to you?'

'How would I know?' snapped Farrell. 'You honestly expect me to be able to crawl inside a mind as sick as his?'

'Frank, I didn't mean …'

'Just leave it,' said Farrell, turning to walk upstairs. 'If anything occurs to me you'll be the first to know.'

Turning the corner onto the upstairs landing, Farrell identified another familiar smell. Beeswax. The faint strains of a Gregorian chant wafted towards them. A door at the end of the passage was standing open. Farrell and Lind exchanged glances and moved cautiously towards it.

Standing on the threshold, Farrell stiffened, his heart pounding. The room was lit only by candlelight, and a shadowy figure with his back to them stood by the ruby velvet drapes wearing a long black cassock.

'Police, put your hands in the air,' yelled Lind, reaching for his baton.

There was no response.

Farrell strode over to the figure, grabbing it roughly by the shoulder, and felt his heart leap into his mouth as it toppled backwards into his arms.

'A dummy. Would you believe it?' he said to his boss.

Lind did not respond but was looking across the room at something behind him. Farrell swung round and beheld the words dripping in red down the back wall of the bedroom. Lind wordlessly hit the light switch.

FORGIVE ME FATHER FOR I HAVE SINNED

Farrell involuntarily crossed himself. There had been evil in this room. He could sense it. Lind was examining the dummy.

'You're not going to like this,' he said in a voice laced with foreboding.

'Tell me something I don't know,' Farrell said.

'These robes are yours,' said Lind.

Farrell slowly walked over to examine the collar. The name tag was blue stitching on cream linen. *Father Frank Farrell*, in his mother's painstaking embroidery stitch. The wooden cross around the dummy's neck was also his, given to him by his mentor, Father Spinelli, on ordination. Beside himself with fury,

Farrell lifted it, intent on removing it from this most unholy of rooms. Lind placed a hand on his arm to stop him.

'Sorry, Frank. It's evidence. Have to leave it where it is I'm afraid.'

Farrell reluctantly let his hand drop back.

'He's closing in,' said Farrell. 'It's as if he's inside my head.'

'No, he's not.' replied Lind. 'Listen to me, Frank. That's what he wants you to think. He's just a sick son of a bitch who's getting off on jerking us around. Sooner or later he'll make a mistake and we'll nail him.'

'I pray to God that you're right,' said Farrell.

CHAPTER FIFTY

Farrell buried himself in the ever-increasing mountain of paper-work surrounding the investigation. Attention to detail. That's what always caught them in the end. Not some eureka moment. Charts covered every wall of his small office. HOLMES was all very well and definitely had its place in modern policing, but the downside was that it could spew out so much meaningless infor-mation that it was like looking for a single snowflake in an avalanche.

He had reached the stage where he was trawling through all the statements and distilling facts he considered relevant onto index cards. Give him a pen and paper any day of the week. Say that to any bright young copper nowadays and they looked at you like you were an exhibit in a museum with a label saying 'PAST IT'. He'd just missed out on the whole computer thing. In his last year at school the first computer had arrived. It had sat in a tiny room next to the headmaster's office, cordoned off behind a rope like some squat nameless monster. The only kids allowed past the rope had been a handful of maths geeks who were excited to the point of frenzy. The seminary had also had little use for technology. During his career in the police he had been forced to undergo periodic training on computers but always under protest and never a pixel more than he had to. Computers couldn't do your thinking for you, no matter what hype surrounded them. Those sci-fi films with humans lying wasted and inert, living their lives in cyber space, weren't that far wide of the mark he reckoned. After all, look at the average teenager. Farrell snorted and cleared his throat. Concentrate, man.

Two hours passed with nothing but the rustling of papers and the scratch of Farrell's fountain pen on the cards. Finally, he tossed his pen down on the desk and sucked in his cheeks like he was eating a sour plum. So much for good old-fashioned police work, he thought. There was a firm knock on the door.

'Come in,' he sighed.

Mhairi popped her head round the door, bearing a steaming mug of coffee.

'My accomplice in crime,' Farrell greeted her.

'Thought you could do with a pick-me-up, Sir,' Mhairi said, placing the coffee down in front of him.

'You're a star,' he replied, taking a sip of the scalding liquid and gesturing for her to sit down opposite him.

Accomplice? In one of the abductions the man had had an accomplice, though at the time they'd drawn a blank. Farrell started frantically rifling through the files. He'd been so consumed with finding Boyd's killer and then the missing boys that he'd not focused on the person on the end of the phone. Where the heck were the details of that phone conversation?

'What is it, Sir? Have you got something?' asked Mhairi.

'The second abduction at that posh nursery ...'

'Head Start?'

'That's it. The woman in charge, Mrs Mitchell, said she'd phoned and spoken to someone, a male, who verified the abductor's story. The same number I phoned myself later.'

'Well, he couldn't have been in two places at once,' said Mhairi.

'Exactly, so he's got an accomplice, someone who was helping him.'

'But what good does that do us when we don't know who he is?' asked Mhairi.

'Maybe it was Jason Baxter.'

'I still don't get it,' said Mhairi, looking at him as though he was a sandwich short of a picnic. 'Where's the connection?'

'Find out if Baxter and Gerald McWhirter were ever cellmates in the pokey.'

'I'll get onto the Scottish Prison Service right away,' said Mhairi whirling from the room, leaving a vapour trail of perfume behind.

Farrell glanced at the clock. It was past six. Better get a move on if he was to turn up for dinner with the Linds looking halfway presentable. He didn't want to look like a total loser when he met the love of his life again. Who was he kidding? She'd picked the better man. It was all water under the bridge and if it wasn't then it should be.

Back at Kelton Farrell slipped on some shorts and a vest and took off along the estuary, feeling his muscles lengthen and unwind as his running shoes pounded along the coarse, springy grass on the riverbank. He filled his lungs with the tangy smell of the mud, tasting salty air on his tongue. A fine smirr of rain cleansed his soul and mingled with the sweat running off his body. He could feel dark forces gathering around him as the case gathered momentum, and he prayed he would have the cunning and tenacity to stop his brother before he took another life. It was snatched moments like this when his thoughts were subdued by the pain of physical exertion that gave him the strength to go on.

Returning to the cottage, he eased his aching muscles in a steaming hot shower then towelled himself dry to the soothing strains of Bach. Finally, feeling ridiculously adolescent he slapped on some aftershave and pulled out his best suit. Too formal? No. The occasion demanded a degree of formality given that he hadn't seen Laura for over a decade. He reached for his usual black shirt but then, mindful of its connotations of mourning, he chose a cobalt blue one instead. Finally, he selected a tie and was ready.

CHAPTER FIFTY-ONE

On the stroke of eight Farrell was standing on the doorstep of Lind's detached Victorian house, nervously clutching a large bunch of white carnations and a bottle of red wine. The garden was filled with the casual debris of childhood including a red-and-yellow pedal car, a ball, and an Action Man. A fat tabby cat wrapped itself round his legs, mewing plaintively up at the squabbling sparrows under the eaves. He breathed in deeply, steeling himself to face the evening ahead, then rang the doorbell.

Lind flung the door open wide, holding a cherubic-looking baby in his arms, and looking harassed in the extreme. A bang was heard from inside the house that set off a chorus of wails.

'Welcome to the madhouse,' said Lind.

'Here, take Adam for a minute, will you?' asked his friend. 'I've got to go and bang a few heads together. This is the only one that's behaving tonight.'

Farrell took the sleepy baby and awkwardly laid him against his shoulder. He had blue Winnie the Pooh pyjamas on and snuggled into him contentedly. Following the sounds of the commotion, he walked through into the living room. Lind was pursuing the remaining three children round and round the sofa, sounding increasingly severe. The children were hyper and paid him no mind.

Suddenly, Laura appeared from the door leading into the kitchen. The door banged behind her.

'Shut up!' she yelled. 'I can't stand this racket. Just shut up and get to bed before I beat the living daylights out of you!'

The boys came to a standstill and started to cry. Adam whimpered and Farrell handed him back to his father. There was an awkward pause when no one really knew what to say.

'Shock tactics,' said Farrell, trying to lighten the atmosphere. 'Works every time.'

Laura spun round on hearing his voice and, after a searching look that lasted a bit too long for comfort, she rushed over and flung her arms round his neck, clinging to him like she never wanted to let go. Farrell glanced awkwardly over at Lind, who shrugged helplessly and left the room with the two boys, motioning to his daughter to follow them upstairs. Whatever Farrell had expected it wasn't this. Off balance and not sure entirely how to react, he patted her awkwardly with his free hand; the other stuck out at an angle, still hanging on to the flowers and wine. She felt frail and brittle in his arms, almost impossibly fragile. He'd dreamt of holding her so many times over the years but never in circumstances like these. Fearful of Lind coming back downstairs and finding them still locked together, Farrell tossed the flowers and wine onto the chair beside him and gently prised her away from him. He led her by the hand to the couch and sat down with her. She averted her eyes from his.

'I'm sorry,' she said. 'Seeing you there, after all these years, I couldn't help it.'

'John told me you've been having a tough time lately,' said Farrell.

'I can't seem to come to terms with it.'

'Maybe you feel the grief is keeping her close to you and you're not ready to let her go yet.'

'John thinks I'm losing my mind; I know he does.'

'Hey, you're entitled. But don't forget he's grieving too. Don't push him away. You need to pull together on this one.'

'Will you pray for me, for us?'

'Your family has been included in my prayers ever since I heard.'

'I came to see you once. It was not long after you were ordained. I snuck in at the back of the chapel and heard you say Mass.'

'I saw you,' said Farrell, gently releasing her hand.

'Why didn't you come over to me at the end?'

'You know why,' he replied, looking directly into her eyes.

Farrell felt rather than saw Lind hovering in the doorway. He stood up and retrieved the bottle of wine.

'I'm guessing you'd rather have this than the flowers?' he said.

Lind took his cue and poured the wine. Farrell tried his best to jolly them both along, but it was hard going at first. It pained him to see Laura looking so broken instead of the exuberant girl that he remembered.

As they sat down to a simple pasta supper he felt a wave of gratitude that he had managed to find his way back to these old friends. He was about to start eating when Lind put a hand on his arm.

'Frank, would you like to say grace?'

Farrell nodded assent. 'For what we are about to receive, may the Lord make us truly thankful.'

The atmosphere inexplicably lightened after that. The men hammed it up for Laura with tall tales of their exploits as younger men, and Farrell was gratified to see some colour creep back into her cheeks; the dullness in her eyes relieved now and then by a spark of humour. She's still in there, he thought. They're going to make it through this.

After a pleasant evening tinged with nostalgia he bade them farewell. Laura gave him a brief hug as he was leaving.

'You're a tonic, Frank. Don't leave it so long next time.'

'I won't,' he promised, feeling a pang of emptiness at leaving her company.

Lind followed him out to the car. The air was electric with things unsaid.

'Thanks for coming over, Frank. You brightened Laura up no end.'

'Hey, it was my pleasure,' Farrell said. 'You two are good together.'

'You and her were good together once,' said Lind, glancing off into the middle distance.

'Ancient history,' said Farrell. 'I'd better head off. I promised Clare I'd swing by if it wasn't too late,' he lied.

After leaving his old friend, Farrell drove round aimlessly for a while. Seeing Laura had unsettled him more than he cared to admit. He'd been right to give them a wide berth all these years. He wondered, not for the first time, what would have happened if he'd defied his mother and not entered the priesthood. Would he be married to Laura instead of Lind? That one decision seemed to have led him by the nose his whole life. Yet had it been so wrong? Again, fate had intervened. Had Jason Baxter not enacted his sick fantasies in his confessional he might still be a priest.

His head bursting with unanswerable questions, Farrell suddenly made a U-turn and headed back into town. This was the hand he'd been dealt, and it was high time he made the most of it.

Boldly he decided to have a quick drink in Beau Jangles night-club, as most of the other pubs would have called last orders by now. He hadn't set foot in the place for years, but Farrell was determined: he would people watch and celebrate his newfound zest for life with a pint of Eighty Shilling. He walked past the doorman, who gave him a strange look. Must have me clocked as an off-duty copper, thought Farrell. As he emerged into the glare of the strobe lighting he stood for a second looking around him. Some things never changed. It was the same tacky place he remembered from his youth: a right cattle market. The flesh on display gyrated in what appeared to be pelmets rather than skirts, with much hair flicking, atop impossibly pointy shoes. They looked barely old enough to be allowed out to the corner shop. The youths ogling them huddled in groups, swaying to the rhythm of the liquor rather than the music, destroying brain cells they couldn't afford to lose. Farrell suddenly felt depressed. He didn't belong here. Who was he kidding?

Suddenly, a wall of muscle loomed in front of him. A bouncer sporting a mullet and tattoos was glaring at him with ferocious intensity. Out from his shadow stepped a nervous, acne-scarred youth, wearing a pink shirt and tie.

'You're not welcome here, Sir. We'd like you to leave at once,' said the youth.

'Any particular reason?' asked Farrell.

'You heard the man, sling yer hook,' grunted the muscle, cracking his knuckles.

The youth put a tentative hand on the bouncer's arm as though trying to control a pet gorilla.

'We're not obliged to give a reason. We'd simply like you to leave.'

'Look,' Farrell said. 'I came in for a quiet drink. There's obviously been some misunderstanding.'

Farrell reached inside his pocket to produce his warrant card. Big mistake. Quick as a flash, muscle man had him in an armlock.

'Release me at once, I'm a police officer,' ground out Farrell, face contorted in agony.

A small crowd began to gather. He could hear pink shirt calling the police. Terrific, the uniforms would be making a meal of this for weeks.

The girls on the dance floor sashayed over to stick their noses in. One of them, a pretty brunette of around sixteen, suddenly clutched the arm of her friend for support.

'That's him!' she screamed. 'That's the creep who assaulted me!'

CHAPTER FIFTY-TWO

Farrell sat in the back of the panda car with a face like a thundercloud. This was just fine and dandy. The whole station would have him down as some closet sexual predator. The mere idea would have normally raised a wry chuckle, but he was most definitely *not* amused. For this to have happened to *him*, of all people. Only those working on the investigation knew that there was someone else running amok wearing his face. An impostor with a black hole where his heart should be. At least the two young officers escorting him to the station had wordlessly uncuffed him before he got into the car.

As they drove through the town centre the car's headlights picked out the flotsam and jetsam of humanity swirling around the sink hole of their existence. He heartily wished he had gone straight home after dinner. What had he been thinking? It frustrated him that once more he had been wrongly identified as his brother, as if to the outside world they were interchangeable, cut from the same cloth. Even though Michael couldn't possibly have known he would pitch up in Beau Jangles, he had still managed to land him in a whole heap of trouble.

Farrell kept his head held high at Loreburn Street as he was escorted by the unsmiling officers to the Custody Sergeant, but couldn't avoid his face burning with humiliation at the curious glances the strange trio evinced.

The Custody Sergeant, Donald Sloan, who with his narrow face and ginger beard resembled a wily fox, intercepted them smoothly.

'Right, Constables, thanks for your assistance. I'll take it from here.'

The two youngsters exchanged relieved glances and shot off. The Custody Sergeant gave him a hard look. He looked right back at him.

'Step this way, Sir,' Sloan said, briskly showing him into an interview room.

He folded his long body onto the plastic chair and waited.

The door opened and in walked Byers and McLeod. Farrell had an insane urge to wipe the smile off Byers's face with the back of his hand.

'Well, well, Sir,' said Byers. 'I didn't think you had it in you.'

Farrell snapped to his feet.

'I don't, you moron. I never touched her! She's only a kid. It must have been him.'

'Assuming there *is* a him. You have heard of Jekyll and Hyde?'

Farrell swallowed a retort and sat back down.

'When is this alleged assault supposed to have taken place?'

'Saturday, fourteenth June,' replied Byers. 'Around midnight.'

Farrell racked his brains, reeling back through the cluttered memories of the last few weeks. Suddenly he had it. He glanced at Mhairi and saw the realization in her eyes too.

'Sorry,' he replied. 'Guess I was home alone.'

'He was with me,' Mhairi burst out.

Byers turned towards her. The penny dropped. He glanced from one to the other.

'Takes "open all hours" to a whole new dimension.'

In one fluid movement Farrell was out of the chair. He slammed Byers against the wall so hard some plaster fell to the floor. Mhairi's hand flew to her mouth in horror.

'We were working late. That's all there was to it.'

Byers, eyes bulging, attempted to nod vigorously.

'Now, I think you owe the lady an apology,' Farrell said, releasing his grip.

'Sorry, DC McLeod. I didn't mean anything by it. Just kidding around,' said Byers, eyes bouncing around like ping pong balls as he tried not to look at either of them.

'Apology accepted,' said Mhairi.

'Now, either let me out of here or charge me,' said Farrell.

'I guess you can go,' said Byers, 'seeing as how your alibi checks out.'

Farrell wordlessly got up and walked straight out the room and then out of the station into the cool fresh air. A raucous crowd of youths staggered by on the opposite pavement, one of them pausing to retch into the roadway. Obscenities rose from their midst like a mushroom cloud. He had to get home, clear his head.

Back at the cottage he poured himself a whisky and wandered out into the small walled garden. It was a clear night and, away from the town, the stars sprawled luxuriantly across the sky displaying their beauty for all to see. As Farrell sat down on the garden seat the scent of blowsy crimson roses and honeysuckle soothed him, chasing away the stench of human nature.

Looking around him Farrell realized that he could not simply enjoy the fruits of the previous tenant's labour forever. The garden had a faintly neglected air, a creeping malaise. Already he could see tendrils of bindweed edging tentatively around the precious blooms that did not yet realize they were under attack.

An emerald glint caught his eye. A large ginger tom stood motionless, every muscle tensed. His rear end began to wiggle as he prepared to launch himself onto a tiny field mouse that was sniffing the air anxiously, sensing danger but not sure where it was coming from.

Farrell erupted from his seat hissing loudly and the predatory moggy took off, yowling in anger. He looked round but the mouse had already made good his escape. You had to take your victories where you could find them. Feeling slightly comforted he went back inside.

CHAPTER FIFTY-THREE

The next morning Farrell awoke feeling refreshed. After his morning run he pulled sausage, bacon, and eggs out of the fridge and fried up a storm. Later, as he wiped the last morsel of fried bread round his plate and knocked back freshly squeezed orange juice chased down by a strong coffee, he felt unusually content.

Suddenly a brick came flying through the kitchen window. He leapt up in time to see a lean figure in jeans and a hoodie racing down the lane. In hot pursuit he sped out the door after him, already regretting his heavy breakfast. He slid to a halt at the top of the lane. Which way had he gone? To the left was the road into Dumfries. Farrell saw the hooded figure watching him, just before the bend. He roared in anger and charged after him. Just as suddenly he stopped dead. Wait a minute. Why did hoodie man pause on this side of the bend in clear view? Farrell smelled a rat. He executed an about turn and loped back home in long easy strides. Slipping round the side of the cottage Farrell paused, listening. He could hear someone in the house. The brick through the window had been a decoy, and he had fallen for it.

Creeping in the back door he picked up a carving knife from the wooden block in the kitchen. Heart banging against his ribs he crept up the stairs to the lounge. He could hear the sound of cupboards being opened and shut. Bracing himself, he stood in the doorway, knife held out in front of him. His skin crawled in revulsion. Jason Baxter! As his old adversary spun round, Farrell glimpsed a look of such feral savagery he almost took a step backwards. It was gone so suddenly that, had he not known what lurked underneath the now amiable façade, he might have thought he had imagined it.

'Detective Inspector Farrell,' Baxter said. 'How lovely to see you! I did knock but no one answered so I took the liberty of making myself comfortable until your return.'

'Since when has breaking and entering been classed as a social call?' asked Farrell.

'Isn't it an offence to brandish one of those things?' asked Baxter.

'This is a private place,' said Farrell, wondering how best to play this.

He needed backup for starters. Pulling out his mobile he carefully positioned the knife on the windowsill, still blocking the door. As he spoke quietly to Force Control he saw Baxter weighing up his options: to charge past him and risk getting stabbed through the heart by an enraged copper who hated his guts, or to take his chances with the local constabulary? No contest. Baxter sank down into an armchair and crossed his legs.

'Good decision,' snapped Farrell.

'Well, isn't this cosy?' said Baxter, baring his nicotine-stained teeth. 'Aren't you going to offer me a coffee? Milk and two sugars.'

Farrell tensed. Don't let him get to you. He wants you to take a pop at him so you'll finally get booted off the case.

'Sorry. No can do,' he replied. 'It's the maid's day off, unless, you'd like to invite your accomplice to join us?'

'Accomplice?' queried Baxter, wrinkling his pallid face in a parody of concentration. 'There was no one with me. I was merely partaking of the morning air when I found myself in the neighbourhood. I noticed the brick in the kitchen, by the way. Kids these days.'

'Still keep up with your mates from the pokie?' asked Farrell, a hard edge to his voice.

'Anyone in particular?' asked Baxter, peering at him with his cold reptilian eyes.

He knows, thought Farrell. The creep knows. He bit back an angry retort sensible of the fact that he was the wrong person to interrogate this particular lowlife. Also, anything he got out of him now would be ruled as inadmissible in a court of law and Baxter knew it.

After a few tense minutes Farrell heard the sound of a police siren, followed by the crunch of gravel and the sound of slamming doors.

'Up here,' he yelled as two burly uniforms rushed past him and cuffed Baxter, reading him his rights.

As the sound of the siren receded into the distance, Farrell felt the reaction set in. He sunk into the chair opposite where Baxter had sat and allowed his head to flop back. The thought that that psychopath had invaded his personal space, the place he had come to think of as home, made him feel sick to the stomach. Had the accomplice been his brother? For a moment Farrell closed his eyes as he imagined gaining on the fleeing hooded figure, then grabbing him by the shoulder and spinning him around only to gaze upon a mirror image of himself. Would he feel any reluctant affinity with this man made in his likeness or simply repelled by the outward manifestation of a darker alter ego? Time would tell. The confrontation was coming. Farrell could feel it building like an electric current through his body.

He needed an antidote to push away the blackness. Before he got cold feet he pulled out his mobile and arranged to meet Clare for dinner that evening. Just the sound of her voice lifted his spirits. It was time he evicted Laura from the space she had always occupied in his heart. Clare was gorgeous, intelligent, and available. She had everything going for her apart from the slightly dubious fact that she seemed to like him. He was done with messing around. Maybe the time had come to put matters in hand to release him from his vows. He boarded up the kitchen window as best as he could and then set off for the station.

His first port of call was Mhairi's desk. She jumped to her feet when she saw him, looking worried.

'Are you all right, Sir?'

'Never better,' he said. 'Any joy with the prison service?'

'They confirmed your er ... I mean Gerald McWhirter and Baxter were cellmates for a number of years. They also checked the visitor logs and discovered Baxter has been visiting McWhirter on and off since his release. I passed the information to DI Moore who's conducting the interview along with DS Stirling.'

'Has the report on the brick come back from the lab yet?'

'Not yet, Sir.'

'I'll go and chivvy them along,' he said. 'In the meantime, I want the old identity suite set up for an aural ID test. Get Mrs Mitchell in from Head Start Nursery and round up as many men as you can of around Baxter's age. Time spent in Glasgow would be an advantage. To make it stick we have to be seen to make it as fair as possible.'

Without waiting for a reply, Farrell spun round on his heels and left the room. To get to the tiny lab he had to enter a device affectionately known as the TARDIS in the fine tradition of *Doctor Who*. Being mildly claustrophobic Farrell hated the darned thing. It was covered by a black curtain and he had to stoop to enter. He then flicked a switch and was spun round to emerge into a rabbit warren of small labs with different purposes. Donning his most ingratiating smile he entered the door with a picture of a skull and crossbones and a snarling Rottweiler. He knew that what was waiting inside for him would be far worse.

A fierce pair of grey eyes glared at him out of a thin wrinkled face. Irene MacTaggart did not like being interrupted and ruled her small kingdom with an iron fist. It was rumoured even Walker, the big man himself, was scared to come down here and face her ire. She drew herself up to her full height of five foot nothing and Farrell could feel the smile slipping off his face like ice cream melting on a sunny day.

'You needn't think flashing those white teeth at me is going to buy you preferential treatment, DI Farrell.'

'No, er, of course not,' said Farrell, feeling like he was fifteen again and getting a roasting from the headmistress. 'It's just that it's really important, Irene. I'm desperate to catch this man before he snatches any more little boys.'

Wordlessly she pulled up some films, put them in an envelope with a sheet of paper, and handed it to him.

'Don't presume again, DI Farrell,' she scowled.

He thanked her profusely. As he entered the TARDIS again he risked a quick glance over his shoulder and saw the amused smirk on her face. So the Rottweiler had a sense of humour?

Once in his room he tore open the envelope. The prints were similar but not identical to his. He'd been incredibly careful not to touch the brick at all and it hadn't come from his garden. So he'd been right. It had been his brother working with Baxter.

What had they been after though? It didn't make any sense. Why risk everything just for a snoop round his home. What had they been looking for?

CHAPTER FIFTY-FOUR

Farrell couldn't contain himself any longer. He charged down the stairs to the custody suite only to meet a pained-looking DI Moore emerging from the interview room. The reason for her lack of exuberance soon became apparent. Behind him, accompanying Baxter, was Sergio Bertucci: the most feared defence attorney in Glasgow. He was getting on in years now, silver hair thinning on top, but he still had the kind of presence that hushed a room when he entered. Farrell had often thought he could have been a star of the big screen. He'd seen him in action in trials a number of times and the jury had been putty in his hands. Farrell tried to carry on past them as though he had urgent business elsewhere but Bertucci didn't buy it for a minute. He paused, blocking his way; a man mountain.

'DI Farrell, it's been a while.'

'Feels like only yesterday.'

'I see you're still harassing my unfortunate client.'

'He broke into my house,' said Farrell. 'What would you have me do? Offer to fill his swag bag?'

'The door was open. My client was merely paying a social call. There's really no need for all this ... hysteria.'

Farrell clenched his fist then swiftly unclenched it. The small movement did not go undetected, and the corners of Bertucci's mouth turned up slightly.

'Always a pleasure, DI Farrell,' he said, holding out his hand.

Farrell looked at him with loathing, reluctant to shake hands with the man but, given that DI Moore was staring at him, he felt he had no choice.

A few minutes later he swung by DI Moore's office. Without waiting for an invitation he sat down opposite her. She regarded him coolly and waited for him to speak.

'Well?' he demanded. 'Did you get anything out of him?'

'Sorry, Frank. Bertucci arrived before the interview even started.'

'But he's based in Glasgow. How did he get here in time?'

'That's down to bad luck, I'm afraid. He was already here for another client: someone vice brought in last night.'

'Did he admit to having an accomplice?'

'No, he stuck to his story. We've still got enough to charge him though.'

'I suppose that's something.'

'I'm hoping to get a voice ID set up during the six-hour window before I have to charge and release him on bail. Would you mind overseeing that for me?'

'No problem. Anything else I can help you with, Kate?'

'While you're here you may as well look over that bogus article we're going to place in the local paper,' said DI Moore, pushing a piece of paper across the desk.

Farrell scanned it, sucking in his breath.

'This is going to get a reaction.'

'That's the idea,' she said. 'Clare Yates supplied some of the material, though we've given the name of a fictitious expert to avoid her becoming a target. I'll need to show her the finished article so it can go in for the end of the week.'

'Actually, I'm going to be seeing her tonight,' said Farrell. 'I'll give it to her then.'

'Oh, are you and she …?'

'Sort of … early days yet,' said Farrell. 'Anyway, stick the article on my desk when you're done,' he said as he walked out the door.

He swung by Mhairi's desk.

'How's that voice ID coming along?' he asked. 'Can we do it while he's still in custody?'

'All organized,' she said. 'Two uniforms are picking up Mrs Mitchell at the moment. We should be good to go in half an hour or so, Sir.'

'Remember, make sure it's conducted by a uniform sergeant who has had no prior involvement with either of the investigations.'

'That'll take some doing, Sir. I reckon I might need to scare up someone from the mobile support unit at this rate.'

'Just do it. If we get a positive ID, I don't want Bertucci getting it ruled as inadmissible on a technicality.'

Mhairi nodded acquiescence.

'Give me a shout when you're ready to proceed.'

'Will do, Sir.'

His next stop was the HOLMES room.

'Any points of commonality between the abducted children yet?' he asked the Duty Sergeant.

'Nothing, as of yet. Different doctors, dentists, nurseries, health visitors.'

'Were they all born in the local hospital?' asked Farrell.

'Them and every other kid in Dumfries. There's still only one maternity hospital. We've interviewed everyone in the hospital records department. They all check out,' said the sergeant.

'Have you checked the social work employee records for the last year for the name Michael Black?' asked Farrell.

'No, Sir, I'll get right on it,' he said.

'Both sets of twins were abducted using the names of real social workers and credible paperwork,' said Farrell. 'It would make sense if he has a connection there. Check casual workers and cleaners as well. Look for something that would let him snoop about the building when no one else is there.'

'Makes sense,' said the sergeant, fingers tapping fast on the screen. Farrell turned to go. He stopped in his tracks.

'So far, the only point of commonality is the fact they are identical male twins. Neither family had any previous social work involvement. Check into whether there are any associations in the town that provide support to parents with twins. The local health visitors should know.'

'Is that it, Sir?' asked the sergeant with an expression on his face that said it was going to be a long night.

'One more thing,' said Farrell. 'What were the names of the two sets of twins again?'

'Mark and Jamie were the first twins taken and Paul and Andy were the second set,' replied the sergeant after consulting a sheaf of papers.

'Mark, James, Paul, and Andrew ... all names of the apostles,' said Farrell, feeling his stomach lurch.

'There's been other religious symbolism in this case. It would make perfect sense for the killer to select his victims based on such a criterion.'

Farrell grabbed a pad and paper and scribbled down the names of the twelve apostles.

'Feed this into the twin database you've built up. It may help us predict where he's likely to strike again. Surely there can't be that many pre-school sets of twin boys in a town this size who both have names of an apostle?'

'It's worth a try, Sir,' said the sergeant, settling down in front of the screen.

Farrell glanced at his watch, then, after grabbing a cup of coffee from the canteen, made his way down to the aural ID suite. He slipped into an interview room nearby when he saw a uniform sergeant, whose name escaped him, heading down the corridor with the woman from Head Start Nursery. She looked sick with anxiety and appeared even thinner than when he had last clapped eyes on her.

The sergeant escorted the woman into the viewing gallery, although she would not be able to see the twelve men below. Each of them would have to read words from a card that reflected what Mrs Mitchell could remember of the brief phone conversation when she had phoned to check the authenticity of the paperwork. Farrell was joined by Mhairi ten minutes later and they waited in silence for the result.

After around twenty minutes they heard the door to the identity suite open, and Mhairi popped out to escort the witness from the station and ensure she had no contact with Baxter. Farrell waited until they had passed and popped his head round the door to catch the sergeant.

'Well?' he demanded.

'We got a result, Sir. No hesitation. As soon as he read from the card she knew it was the voice she had heard.'

Farrell punched the air in triumph. Finally, some good news.

'Is he going to be charged, Sir?'

'No, he'll be processed for release. There isn't enough evidence to charge him as an accomplice to abduction yet. The attempted burglary is just a summary matter so he'll be released on police bail pending an appearance at the sheriff court in the morning.'

Farrell thanked the man for helping him out and went upstairs. The idea of Baxter waltzing out of here made his blood boil, but he knew he had no option if he wished to ever see him brought successfully to trial. Baxter wasn't going to worm his way out of this one.

CHAPTER FIFTY-FIVE

Laura barely recognized the face that stared back at her from the bathroom mirror. Her once sparkling brown eyes looked empty, as though the woman she used to be had gone on vacation, leaving behind an empty shell. Standing there, without a hint of make-up, she looked old and worn out. Greasy hair hung down in lank strips to her shoulders. This was the woman her husband came home to every night after a hard day's work. This was the face of the mother that held her children. God, she was even starting to think of herself in the third person. She had to get a grip. Maybe if she could force herself to look normal on the outside she would come back to life on the inside.

She had an hour to herself while the kids watched the Disney video she had put on for them. Still moving slowly, as though she had to conserve enough energy to get through the remainder of the day, she picked up some expensive shower gel and blew the dust off it. A single step, she told herself, a single step to get back onto the path that was her life. Then she turned on the shower and stepped into the steam.

The fresh fragrance of the shower gel lifted her in the manner of someone getting a whiff of bougainvillea and being transported back to their holiday villa. She caressed her empty belly, allowing healing tears to flow. The agony was less sharp now and she wept for the knowledge that her sorrow had swelled to its peak and was starting to recede.

As she sat at her dressing table applying tinted moisturiser, mascara, and a slick of lipstick she felt that she at least looked more in control of herself now. She swept her hair up into a loose knot the way her husband liked it and slipped into a peasant blouse and skirt. Transformation complete.

Exhausted now, she went downstairs to the children. The DVD must have finished as she could hear the twins starting to bounce off the walls again. She glanced at her watch. It was gone six o'clock. The kids should have had their tea an hour ago. She could feel her new resolve start to melt under the onslaught of the baby yelling and the twins starting to knock lumps out of each other. She became aware of the implacable glare of her small daughter, standing to one side with her arms folded.

'Mummy, do something!'

'I will in a minute, pet,' Laura said, feeling her heart start to race as tears threatened to spill over.

Abruptly she turned her back on the family life imploding before her and rushed into the kitchen. With trembling hands she opened a bottle of white wine and, only using a glass for propriety's sake, drank deeply until she thought she would never come up for air.

Momentarily fortified by the alcohol Laura managed to dish up pizza, sweetcorn, and chips within thirty minutes. Sitting on the squashy sofa, catastrophe averted for the time being, she closed her eyes and let her mind wander. An image of Frank Farrell swam into focus. Usually she pushed him resolutely away, but tonight she didn't fight it. His deep blue eyes looked into hers with such warmth and compassion that she could feel tears squeeze out from under her eyelids. Hating herself but unable to stop she watched in slow motion as his lips bent to hers and felt her treacherous body begin to respond …

The doorbell rang, jolting her out of her reverie. Guilt washed through her like a tidal wave. What had she been thinking? She loved John, didn't she? As she opened the door her legs nearly went from under her. Frank Farrell stood on the threshold.

Rain was running down in rivulets from the hood of his waterproof jacket. As she stood staring at him he blew noisily into a large white handkerchief and sneezed.

'Frank, what are you doing here?'

'John sent me. The children are in danger. Can I come in?'

Laura swung the door wide.

'Yes of course, but I don't understand. What do you mean?'

Laura looked into his eyes but was startled to see they were hard and cold. His voice sounded strange …

'Are you all right, Frank? You don't seem yourself.'

He drew the white handkerchief out his pocket again and coughed into it.

'Sorry, I've got a bit of a cold. We're so overstretched with this case I can't take time off.'

'You said the children are in danger. What did you mean?'

'Your kids are called Luke and Matthew, right?'

'Yes?'

'Well the man we're looking for is abducting identical twin boys with the names of the twelve apostles.'

'Oh my God,' whispered Laura, her face draining of colour.

'John sent me to remove the kids to a safe location. They're closing in on him now. It won't be for long.'

'But why didn't John come himself?'

'He was too busy. You want him to catch this guy, don't you?'

'Well of course I do. I'll just go pack their things.'

'There's no time. I need to take them right now. John was most insistent. He can bring their things along later.'

Laura felt tired and confused. She zipped the twins into their anoraks and gave them each a toy car to take with them. As she hugged their hot little bodies to her she silently prayed that they would be safe.

CHAPTER FIFTY-SIX

Farrell was due to meet Clare at the new Italian restaurant in less than an hour. He'd never make it back to Kelton and back in again now. He'd have to shower and change at the station. Who could he scrounge a shirt from? It would have to be Lind as he was around his build. Farrell took the stairs to Lind's office three at a time he felt so pumped up on adrenalin. Lind wasn't there so Farrell made a beeline for his cupboard, which fortunately yielded an immaculately laundered cream linen shirt with a ruby silk tie. He also made off with his friend's expensive aftershave. Needs must.

As he passed Lind's desk he scrutinized a picture of the family taken in happier times. Laura looked radiant with her arms round the boys. He picked up the photo to look at it more closely and felt a prickle of unease. He had assumed that the twins weren't identical as they had different hairstyles and weren't dressed alike. Looking at this image of them he was no longer completely sure. What were their names again? Luke and … Hugh? That was it. He sighed with relief. Well, there was no apostle called Hugh, so even if his theory of victim selection was correct, the twins should be fine. Still, better safe than sorry. He dialled Lind and reached his answerphone.

'John, Hi, I've just realized our abductor may be targeting identical twins with the same names as the apostles. Your boys should be fine, as one of them is called Hugh, but it might be an idea to keep a closer eye on them than usual, just in case. They're not even identical, right?'

As Farrell hung up he felt his misgivings return but he was already running late. He would ring Lind again in the morning. He set off for the restaurant.

Farrell watched Clare make her way across the crowded restaurant to his table, causing more than a few heads to turn. She was dressed in a simple red silk dress which set off her long chestnut locks to perfection. Farrell wondered what she could possibly see in him. He greeted her warmly with a kiss, happy to be in her company. He wasn't going to blow it this time. Being with Lind and Laura had made him realize that he craved a settled family life. It was time to stop clinging onto the tattered remnants of his life as a priest. Sitting down, he noticed that she was looking a little subdued.

'What's up?' he asked, reaching for her hand.

'I'm so sorry I doubted you. Did Lind tell you I'd been in …?'

'No, as it happens, but I can hardly blame you. I was starting to doubt myself.'

'Even so, I should have been straight with you and not run off behind your back. An identical twin, how crazy is that?'

'You don't have to tell me. Anyway, apology accepted. Let's move on.'

'Why are you smiling like that?' Clare asked.

'Just happy to be here,' he said. For once his guard was down and it felt good.

As they ordered from the extensive menu Farrell felt his mouth watering in anticipation. Normally someone who ate to live rather than lived to eat he ordered the biggest steak on the menu with all the trimmings. No wonder he was starving. Since he came back to Dumfries he had practically been living on the emaciated offerings provided by the staff canteen. For too long he had let his job rule his life and it was time to reclaim some ground. Further throwing caution to the wind he ordered an expensive bottle of red wine. As the rich ruby liquid swirled round his mouth like velvet he felt himself relax into a depth of content-ment that he hadn't felt for some time.

'So then,' Clare said. 'I'll bet you were a right goody-goody at school. Priest in training and all that?'

'Not as good as you might think. I used to bunk off school with John Lind and his now wife, Laura. We'd cycle off to Mabie Forest with a bottle of cheap cider, sure that we were living on the edge.'

'It must have been good hooking up with your old friends when you came back to the town. And they got married too?'

'Yes,' said Farrell. How to change the subject? He became aware that Clare was looking at him with a question in her eyes. 'They belong together,' he said quickly and moved on. 'What about you? Have you ever been married? Had children? Done jail time?'

He wanted to know every last thing about this woman.

'Yes, No, and Not yet,' she smiled, but not before he had noticed the tightening around her mouth when he mentioned children.

'Divorced?'

'No. Widowed.'

'I'm sorry.'

'It was a few years ago. I got through it.'

Farrell cast about with increasing desperation for a safe topic but she got there ahead of him.

'Do you ever go running?'

'All the time. This honed physique didn't happen all by itself,' he said mock seriously but was pleased to notice she sent an appreciative glance his way.

'I'm registered for the London marathon,' she said. 'Amateur.'

After that they both laughed and relaxed, the conversation becoming easier and more natural. The food was so good that he felt in danger of popping a button. He should cook more. He was pleased to see that Clare ate with gusto. It worried him when women treated food as an enemy.

After Farrell had paid the bill they left the restaurant. He wanted Clare so much he could hardly think straight. She turned towards him and raised her lips up to his.

'Come back with me,' she said, eyes huge in her shadowy face.

Farrell didn't need to be asked twice. It was only a five-minute walk to Clare's riverside apartment but it felt like an eternity. As soon as they were inside, Clare led him through to the lounge, kissing him with an urgency that matched his own. She kicked off her high heels and sank gracefully onto a sofa piled high with cream suede cushions, her scarlet dress fanning out around her. Farrell sank down beside her and enfolded her in his arms, breathing in her heady scent. Before he surrendered himself completely he switched off his mobile. What difference could a few minutes make?

Sunshine flooded the room as Farrell slowly woke up. For a split second he felt confused by the strange bed and unfamiliar surroundings, then it all came back to him. Slowly, so as not to wake her, he turned his head on the pillow. The duvet had slipped from her in the night and as he took in the sight of her sleeping he felt a pang of tenderness. He waited for guilt to pierce his happy bubble. Nothing.

A few minutes later, tucking into warm croissants, fresh orange, and coffee, Farrell felt a slow burning contentment nourish his soul. He wasn't due at work for over an hour. His mobile? Where was it? He had forgotten to switch it back on.

Suddenly they both jumped as there was a loud banging at the door.

'Police, open up!'

Farrell strode to the door and flung it open. Byers, Stirling, and McLeod were standing outside, their expressions stony.

'What the blazes—?' began Farrell.

'It's the twins, Sir,' interrupted Mhairi. 'DCI Lind's twins. He's got them.'

Farrell blanched. He glanced back at Clare, whose eyes were wide with shock. Then he picked up his jacket and ran out the door.

CHAPTER FIFTY-SEVEN

Farrell exited the car before it had stopped moving and sprinted up the stairs to the MCA room, his whole body charged with adrenalin. As the door swung open, his eyes sought out Lind, who was barking out orders with a ferocity Farrell had never heard before. The other occupants in the room were hunched over computer terminals. The tension in the room was palpable.

Lind spun round at the intrusion. Normally immaculately presented, he looked like a tramp. His shirt was stained and his face was covered with a film of grease. A rank odour emanated from him.

'Where the fuck were you last night?' he yelled at Farrell, oblivious to the presence of the junior officers, who were clearly wishing themselves a million miles away.

'I was off duty, John,' replied Farrell. 'If I'd known, I would've been here in a flash, you know that.'

'You're in the middle of a murder investigation and you switch your bloody mobile off? Christ, I hope she was worth it.'

Farrell remained silent, biting his tongue. Now wasn't the time and it certainly wasn't the place. Anyway, Lind couldn't make him feel any worse than he did already.

One of the other men turned round and addressed Farrell.

'Sir, I fed the names of the twelve apostles into our twin data-base and only two other matches came up. One was a set of twins out in Georgetown and one was ... DCI Lind's twins. We've relocated the family in Georgetown but by the time we got to DCI Lind's house, we were too late ...'

'Great theory, Farrell,' spat Lind. 'Pity you didn't see fit to share it with me before you clocked off last night.'

'I left you a voicemail,' said Farrell.

'I was in a meeting,' snapped Lind. 'By the time I got out it was too late.'

'I didn't know your twins were identical. They looked so different from each other.'

'It was Laura that always insisted on making them look different. She wanted them to be seen as individuals in their own right, not just as twins, like some novelty act.'

'But I thought one of them was called Hugh? There are no apostles with that name.'

'His name is Matthew,' said Lind, with a catch in his voice. 'Molly couldn't pronounce it and shortened it to "Hew" and the name just stuck.'

It was obvious to Farrell that Lind was on the verge of collapse and should not be working. It was equally obvious that he was determined to stay. Farrell deliberated for a moment then had a brainwave.

'Where's DI Moore?' he asked.

'With Laura,' Lind answered with a combative gleam in his eyes. Farrell gave up. It was beyond him.

'If you're intending to stay, Sir, can I suggest we step into your office so you can bring me up to speed? Everyone in here has a job to do and is hell-bent on getting your boys returned. That right?'

Vigorous nods from everyone. Lind looked round at them and his face sagged. He was starting to get in the way and he knew it. They walked in silence to Lind's room, picking up a couple of coffees en route. Everywhere they went they were subjected to covert glances, people shying away from them as though misery was contagious. Lind didn't even notice, so caught up was he in his own private Hell.

As soon as the door closed behind them Farrell turned to his old friend.

'I'm sorry I wasn't around when you needed me. I'm here now and I'm going to make sure that I nail the bastard this time. You'll get your boys back. I won't rest until they're safe. You have my word on that.'

'I'm sorry I blew up at you,' said Lind.

'I could kick myself, John, I really could. I should have come over; I should have—'

'Stop,' said Lind. 'This won't get my sons back. I need your help, Frank.'

'Right,' said Farrell, pulling himself together. 'You're right. Take me through it from the beginning. Firstly, how did he get hold of the kids in the first place?'

Lind emitted a harsh guttural sound.

'I was working last night. Around seven o'clock you arrived at the house and told Laura I'd sent you to pick up the twins and take them to a place of safety.'

'Me?'

'The spitting image, according to Laura. She did say the voice sounded a bit different but he kept coughing into a handkerchief, told her he had a cold.'

Farrell sucked in his breath. Better to get it out of the way.

'Did you ever wonder if it actually was me?' he asked.

Lind looked at him.

'If I thought that for one minute, you'd be dead already,' he replied. 'Just as well for once in your sorry life you decide to get it together and actually get laid.'

'What did he tell her?'

'He told her the twins were at risk of being snatched because of their names being the same as the apostles.'

'But I only came up with that before clocking off yesterday,' said Farrell.

'This bastard has been one step ahead of us for some time. It makes you wonder,' said Lind.

'If he can pass for me sufficiently well to fool Laura then maybe he's been able to access the station. He might even have planted the odd bug here and there.'

'I'll get the surveillance team on to that,' said Lind.

'How's Laura?'

'Out of her mind with worry,' said Lind. 'Maybe you could …?'

'I'm going to pop round later this morning, go over every detail with her, make sure nothing has been missed.'

Farrell took his leave and sprang into action, determined to leave no stone unturned. He put a team of officers on determining possible locations from the Ordnance Survey map and liaising with Council departments. A local Church of Scotland minister was hauled in to advise on any disused churches and halls that might have been utilized by the killer. Traces were set up on incoming calls to CMS and Farrell's home and mobile numbers, as well as Lind's. SOCOs had been round to Lind's house last night but had found no prints other than those belonging to the usual occupants. It seemed likely that the handkerchief used by the killer to muffle his voice had had a dual purpose.

Farrell knew that he was going to have to be at the top of his game to find the killer before one of the twins disappeared for good. Failure wasn't an option.

CHAPTER FIFTY-EIGHT

An hour later Farrell walked up the driveway of the Linds' family home. He didn't know how he was going to face Laura. If he hadn't spent the night with Clare, then he might have followed up on his hunch last night and the twins might still be safe.

Ringing the doorbell he braced himself. However, it was DI Moore who answered the door; her calm demeanour no doubt exactly what Laura needed right now.

'She's in the kitchen,' said DI Moore. 'Take it easy, she's only just holding it together.'

Farrell nodded his acquiescence and made his way through the house. He stood in the doorway to the kitchen. Laura was slumped at the kitchen table, an expression of undiluted agony on her fine-boned face. Farrell longed to comfort her by folding her in his arms, but didn't want to overstep the mark. He cleared his throat before speaking.

Laura jerked upright as though someone had slapped her. As she saw Farrell framed by the doorway she sprang up from the chair with such violence her chair overturned with a crash. Her lips drew back from her teeth in a snarl.

'You bastard!' she screamed. 'What have you done with them?'

Before Farrell could react she launched herself at him, flailing with her arms and managing to rake his cheek with her fingernails before he managed to pinion her arms to her side. He stared at her in consternation.

'Laura, it's me, Frank. You do know that I had nothing to do with the abduction of the boys? It was someone pretending to be me.'

She pulled away from him and sat back down at the table, her expression still hostile. DI Moore stuck her head round the door to see what all the commotion was about, but he signalled to her to leave them be and she silently slipped away again.

'I don't know what to think,' Laura shouted. 'How can I trust my own judgement any more? I believed it was you last night, not some monster intent on abducting my kids.'

'It wasn't your fault,' Farrell said. 'He's my identical twin. No wonder you were fooled.'

'Bollocks,' she yelled. 'You haven't got a twin. I think I'd have remembered.'

Quickly, he gave her the main facts of what he had uncovered. Her expression started to soften but then hardened again.

'Why wouldn't John have said anything?'

'Only the immediate investigative team know. We couldn't risk it getting out into the public domain. Not at this stage.'

'Even if all this crap is true, how do I know it's really you this time and not that maniac back to mess with my head?'

Farrell thought hard. He had to win her trust and fast. Time was running out.

'I know that you have a mole on your left hip bone and that you lost your virginity on 30 September 1988 at about ten o'clock, to a young fool who didn't deserve you,' he said.

Laura's face flamed, and she ran into his arms. Behind him DI Moore suddenly cleared her throat, making them both jump. How much had she heard, wondered Farrell? He led Laura over to the table, sat her down then pulled out the chair opposite, taking out his notebook.

'I don't understand. Why didn't John tell me any of this? He's not normally so secretive.'

'He probably didn't want to worry you. After everything you've been through recently.'

'So, if I hadn't been such a self-absorbed cow he might have told me and I would never have handed my kids over to that nutter?'

'Laura, that's not what I meant …'

'If anything happens to them, I will never forgive myself. Never.'

'I know this is the last thing you feel like doing right now,' Farrell said, 'but we've got very little time and I need to know every tiny detail you can remember.'

Slowly and painstakingly, he took her through the events of the preceding night. She admitted that a few things had seemed a bit off. His voice had sounded a bit different and his eyes were the same but very cold.

'Did you notice any tattoos?'

'None that I could see.'

'Could you see his forearms? He's supposed to have a Gemini tattoo there?'

'Yes, but I don't recall any tattoo. Mind you, I doubt I would have noticed one way or the other.'

'He really looked so like me you couldn't tell us apart?'

'I'd only met you once since you were back. He was so convincing. I can't believe I handed my poor boys into the hands of that monster. Promise me you'll catch him before he hurts them. Promise me!'

His empty promises ringing in his ears Farrell tore back to the station and tracked down the SOCO team that had attended in the early hours of the morning. Despite the fact that they should have been off duty hours ago they were still hard at it. These crimes had everyone on edge at the best of times but now the lives of DCI Lind's kids were at stake. It was personal.

'What have you got for me, Janet?' he asked a grey-haired woman in her fifties who was peering over some fibres with a magnifying glass.

'Not a lot. No prints whatsoever. Bastard must have wiped the door handles when she wasn't looking. He was smart enough to refuse her offer of coffee as well.'

'That's it? There's nothing else?'

Janet glowered at him.

'I didn't say that,' she snapped.

'What then?'

'It was raining last night. We managed to lift a print from the path to the front door, where the gravel had worn away. But the most interesting thing is the soil residue both outside and in the front porch where he must have wiped his feet. It had an unusual composition, which I fed into the national database. Interesting that he was so meticulous with everything else but not with his feet,' she pondered.

'This guy does nothing by chance,' said Farrell. 'I'm guessing either this is a false trail or he wants to be found.'

'The clay came from a quarry out at Locharbriggs,' she said. 'It's the only match locally I've been able to find.'

'Thanks, Janet, you're the business,' said Farrell over his shoulder as he sped away up to the MCA room.

Up on the wall were large-scale Ordnance Survey maps with pins showing the locations of all empty buildings with religious significance. Farrell briefly updated them on the lead on a possible locality and he and DS Stirling stared at the relevant sections with deep concentration. Farrell saw it first.

'There! A disused church beyond the quarry. Get on to the Council. I need the specs of that building. Hurry!'

DS Stirling got on the phone right away while Farrell quickly touched base with the rest of the investigators. The phone rang. Farrell snatched it up.

'DI Farrell speaking,' he snapped.

'Now, now, Frank, what's got you sounding so tetchy?' said a voice that sent shivers up his spine.

Farrell froze and signalled frantically to Stirling to start a trace. A deathly hush fell on the room as all eyes turned his way.

'Who's speaking?' Farrell asked.

A mirthless laugh grated in his ear.

'Oh, I think you know,' the voice said.

Farrell betrayed no sign of the rage engulfing him as he spoke calmly into the mouthpiece.

'How are those little boys? Are they well?'

'You mean are they both alive? Well they are at the minute. How long they stay that way depends on you.'

'Go on,' said Farrell.

'Any preference by the way?'

'What do you mean?'

'Any preference for which one lives and which one dies?'

Farrell was close to losing it by this time. He glanced over at Stirling, whose fingers were dancing over the keyboard.

'My preference is that neither dies, that everyone walks away from this, including you. Help me make that happen,' urged Farrell.

'And wipe the slate clean?' asked the voice, with a hard edge. 'I think you're full of shit, Frank. That's what I think.'

'What about a straight exchange: me for the boys? How about it?' asked Farrell.

'It's tempting, Frank. Let me get back to you on that one. Got to go, got little mouths to feed.'

'Wait!' yelled Farrell.

Too late. The connection was terminated. Farrell rounded on Stirling.

'Did you get a location?'

'Sorry, he broke the connection with a couple of seconds to spare. Bastard knows what he's doing.'

'We've still got a possible location from the clay residue,' said Farrell, desperate to be doing something.

He glanced at his watch. It was still only ten thirty. He was damned if he was going to waste a single second.

'Listen up,' he commanded. 'Unless I get information to dictate otherwise, we're going to launch a covert surveillance operation on the church out by Locharbriggs quarry. I want the area completely surrounded from all sides but the emphasis is on covert. I don't want him to know we're there. Complete radio silence must be maintained once everyone is locked in position. I also want roadblocks set up at all possible entrances and exits but again these must be far enough back as to be completely invisible from the church. Leave for all available personnel is cancelled until further notice. We'll need uniforms as well. Bring out their best and brightest. Notify Firearms; they need a team on standby at the location ready to respond when I give the signal. We'll need an ambulance and a doctor specializing in emergency medicine standing by, just in case. I want DI Moore replaced with a uniform and a meeting in the conference room at eleven thirty with her and the super, to sign off on the operation and offer their input.'

'DCI Lind, Sir?' asked Mhairi, who had furiously been taking notes.

'I reckon he's going to have to sit this one out,' said Farrell. 'His place is with his family. Assuming we get the go-ahead from the super I want all involved officers to attend a briefing in the conference room at noon. Remember one thing: failure is not an option.'

CHAPTER FIFTY-NINE

Farrell paced up and down the front of the briefing room waiting for the last few stragglers to squash into their seats. The room was packed to the gunnels and the heat generated by so many closely packed bodies was becoming oppressive. The officers chatted quietly in subdued tones. DCI Lind was a popular officer and everyone was devastated by this latest development in what was already a fraught case. Farrell glanced at his watch and was about to start the briefing when the double doors swung back. Detective Superintendent Walker marched in, closely followed by DI Moore, who looked positively agitated in contrast to her normal calm demeanour. However, as they drew closer, he noticed a third person bringing up the rear. Clare looked like she wanted to be anywhere in the world other than this room. Her face was bleached of colour, and the look she shot him was faintly hostile.

'I've been briefing Dr Yates on our situation,' boomed Walker.

'She feels she may be able to give us some insights on the kind of person we're dealing with.'

Farrell saw Byers snigger but was gratified to see Mhairi poking him hard in the ribs with her elbow.

Clare cleared her throat nervously. Walker gave her a glass of water. She shot a nervous glance in Farrell's direction and began.

'Everything I've learned about this case leads me to believe that we are dealing with someone who is highly intelligent but who might also be suffering from a severe mental health disorder. He may be delusional and feel he is following some higher calling with a strong compulsion to complete his fantasy. His motive may have been revenge insofar as Father Boyd was concerned, but that doesn't hold good for the little boys. He seems to have fed them, taken care of them, even to the extent of reading them bedtime stories. It would appear that he randomly selects the twin who is to go home by having the children select a card from a pack. The child with the highest card gets left behind and the one with the lowest card is taken somewhere else. We still don't know what he did with the missing boy, Mark. He could be dead or he could have him captive somewhere. He is clearly fixated on DI Farrell and that might give you an advantage you can use down the line. In short, you are dealing with an extremely capable, highly organized individual with a high probability of mental illness. This may make it less likely that you can resolve the situation by negotiation. His priority will be to complete his fantasy and he may well be careless of his own personal safety as a result. All of these factors make the situation highly volatile and dangerous. If you get the opportunity to engage with this man I would suggest you tread very carefully and attempt persuasion rather than confrontation. At present he is still functioning but if pushed too hard his fantasy world could crumble, causing him to either decompensate and become catatonic, or else become consumed with paranoia. At that stage he will be beyond the power of reason. A third less likely option is that he could come crashing back to reality again, shocked out of his altered state.'

'You mean regain his sanity?' queried Farrell.

'Yes. It's not always a one-way trip, DI Farrell,' she said, her eyes locked on his.

Farrell got to his feet and moved towards her. She looked at him with a guarded expression. Farrell wondered if their budding relationship would survive all these harsh intrusions.

'Thank you, Dr Yates,' he said. 'Feel free to remain for the rest of the briefing, if you wish.'

'Thank you, DI Farrell,' she replied. 'I regret I have an engagement elsewhere.'

He watched her exit the room, feeling a sensation of loss. Giving himself a mental shake he stepped up to address the room.

'Right, we're planning to move on the location near the quarry at 2 p.m. There will be an armed response unit backing us up, waiting on our orders at the perimeter. They've also drafted in a trained negotiator from Glasgow, who may attempt to engage the perpetrator in a dialogue. Our priority must be the safety of those little boys. I want no gung ho tactics. Is that absolutely clear?'

He intercepted a look from Mhairi that said *that's rich coming from you* and gave her a high-wattage glare, which sent her gaze veering off to the right.

'There are plans up on the wall that give the layout of the church. There are three entrances: one to the front, one to the rear, and one to the side. I want you all to familiarize yourselves with these. An ambulance will be standing by beyond the perimeter, just in case. Those of you who are attending the scene get yourselves to Cornwall Mount. They have instructions there to issue you with body armour and Tasers. We'll be split into three teams of six. I'll lead one team, DI Moore will lead the other, and the super will lead the third.'

At this a murmur of surprise rippled round the room.

'The lists are on the doors. I don't need to remind you of how high the stakes are here,' Farrell said.

'Be vigilant and good luck.'

As he strode out the briefing room and along the corridor, he heard Mhairi calling him. He kept walking, pretending he hadn't heard her, but undeterred she broke into a run and soon caught up with him.

'Sir, can we get together and discuss the operation?'

'Not now, DC McLeod. There's something I have to do first,' he answered.

Driving out the car park he headed through the town until he reached St Aidan's, where all this mess had begun. The car park was deserted. He went into the church. There he kneeled, bowed his head, and prayed as though his very soul depended on it.

Suddenly, behind closed eyes he sensed a change within and without. Startled, his eyes flew open and he beheld the figure on the cross bathed in the light from the midday sun streaming in through the stained glass window. As he gazed upon the embodiment of the son of God he could have sworn that he saw a smile flicker on the countenance of that suffering visage. A trick of the light or a sign of encouragement? Feeling comforted, Farrell made the sign of the cross and left as quietly as he had come.

CHAPTER SIXTY

Two hours later, Farrell was in position, flanked by Mhairi and Byers, lying flat on the underside of a small hillock and peering over the top with a rain-spattered pair of binoculars. The cold and wet had seeped into his bones but the adrenalin surging through his body kept him alert and on edge.

'Copy that,' said Mhairi quietly into her radio. 'All units in position, Sir,' she whispered.

'If I'd known this was the way today was going to pan out I'd never have worn these shoes,' grumbled Byers. 'Handmade Italian jobs they are.'

Farrell threw him a look that would stop a tank in its tracks and put a finger to his lips. Byers nodded nervously.

There were no signs of life. The old church looked stoically forlorn and closed-in on itself. Farrell hoped their intelligence was right and that this really was the place. The twins were surely living on borrowed time as it was.

Suddenly his mobile phone vibrated in his pocket. Mhairi looked at him disapprovingly as he fished it out. Then, as he moved to answer it, comprehension flared in her eyes. He held up a hand to silence her.

'I knew you would come,' said the voice on the phone.

Farrell felt a shiver run up and down his spine that had nothing to do with the cold.

'What can I say?' Farrell replied. 'I'm a sucker for family reunions. Talking of which, why don't you let those little boys go? Then you and I can get together, catch up all you want? What do you say, Michael?'

As he was talking Farrell began snaking forward on his belly through the long grass, motioning to his team to do likewise. Mhairi quietly brought the rest of them up to speed on her radio.

'Not going to happen, Frank. I have to finish what I started,' said the flat voice into his ear.

Farrell broke out in a sweat both from exertion and fear. Dammit, they were so close. If he could only keep him talking for a few minutes longer.

'Don't you want to meet me, meet our mother?' he asked, trying to keep the desperation from sounding in his voice.

'And do what exactly? Play happy families?'

'It doesn't have to be like that,' said Farrell. 'We can get you help, start over.'

'Goodbye, Frank,' said the voice.

Farrell charged at the front door yelling the activation code into his radio. He put his shoulder to the door and eventually it yielded. He could hear the sound of splintering wood at the other entrances as all three teams converged at once. Inside, the pervasive smell of incense crawled up his nose. He used to love that smell. Not any more. His eyes struggled to adjust to the gloom inside. He switched on his halogen torch and saw answering beams flare up all around. The super's voice sounded like a foghorn, issuing orders to the various teams. They searched the interior, terrified of what they might find lurking in the shadows. DI Moore found one small boy curled up in a ball inside the pulpit, sucking his thumb, and gently pulled him into her arms.

'You're safe now, little one,' she murmured, holding him close.

Farrell was able to confirm it was one of Lind's kids though he couldn't tell which one. The little boy wasn't for talking. That still left two boys missing.

'Ask him if he knows where his twin is, Kate,' he said. 'I don't want to scare the wee chap.'

DI Moore spoke softly to the little boy but he shook his head and buried his face against her neck.

They carried on searching, more methodically now. Inching forward slowly until they had covered the surface area of the church one more time.

'Bastard couldn't have got by us,' exploded the super. 'It's just not bloody possible. We had all the exits covered and there's nowt but grass to hide behind.'

'Quiet!' yelled Mhairi.

The super turned and stared at her as though she had taken leave of her senses. He was just drawing breath to give her a good rollicking when they all heard it: the keening sound of a young child crying.

'I don't understand it,' the super said. 'We've searched every nook and cranny of this place. Where's that noise coming from?'

'There must be an escape tunnel,' said Farrell. 'It wasn't on the plans but some old churches had hidden tunnels underground to allow the priests to escape their enemies. Look for a trapdoor concealed in the floor,' he urged.

They split into groups and combed every square inch of the dusty floors. Eventually, DS Stirling let out a shout.

'Over here.'

Farrell rushed over just in time to see him lifting up a trapdoor. A warm blast of fetid air struck him in the face as he shone his torch down into what could have passed for the mouth of Hell itself. The cries were louder now and without further ado Farrell swung himself over the edge and made his way down the rickety ladder. Landing with a thud on an earthen floor, he cautiously made his way along the narrow passageway, stooping to avoid banging his head. As he rounded a corner his heart leapt into his mouth as he saw two little bodies curled up, motionless, on the floor. As he approached, one of them came to life and started screaming, trying to shrink back into the wall away from him. The other remained motionless. An opened pack of playing cards lay beside them. Feeling sick to his stomach he felt for a pulse on the prone child and unashamedly wiped the tears from his face when he found a weak one.

'Thank God,' he murmured.

Mhairi arrived at his side looking anxious as she glanced down at the unconscious boy.

'The paramedics are waiting at the top of the hatch, Sir. If you can lift Mark, I'll help DI Lind's boy up the ladder. His twin will soon perk up when he sees he's OK.'

Farrell gently cradled Mark in his arms. His head lolled back and he was clammy; his breathing so shallow his chest barely moved. He's going to make it, said Farrell to himself, unable to countenance any alternative.

At the top of the hatch he wordlessly handed him over to the paramedics, who immediately hooked him up to oxygen and put him on a saline drip.

'Probably severely dehydrated,' ventured one of them.

They all watched the ambulance draw away in silence. Both twins were now cuddled into DI Moore and looking a lot brighter.

'Has someone told John they're OK?' he asked.

'Just off the blower,' said the super.

'DI Farrell, I think you should do the honours,' he said.

'DC McLeod, you'd better get over to Mark's family and take them to the hospital to be with their son.'

CHAPTER SIXTY-ONE

Farrell walked up the driveway and rang the bell, two little hands now folded trustingly in his big ones. He'd thought they might not want to go with him but, of course, they understood the concept of twins. The door flew open and Laura scooped both boys up into her arms, then the three of them were wrapped up in Lind's loving embrace like nesting dolls. Stuck awkwardly on the doorstep, Farrell felt a shard of loneliness pierce his soul. Would he ever have a family of his own? If his mother hadn't bowed to pressure all those years ago maybe he could have grown up with a brother who might have been whole instead of damaged beyond repair.

With typical sensitivity, Lind broke away from his family and flung the door open wide, inviting him to enter.

'Frank, how can I ever thank you?' he said, in a voice choked with emotion.

Laura snaked out a hand, pulled on his sleeve; her eyes filled with words unsaid. Farrell backed away, well out of his comfort zone.

'Happy to oblige,' he said. 'Can't stop, I'm afraid. Things to do. Paperwork and stuff, you know how it is.'

Lind looked at him, not fooled for a minute. Laura had already forgotten about him, smothering the boys' faces in kisses as she led them away down the hall.

Farrell sketched a wave and marched briskly down the drive to his car. As he reached the delimit sign and left the streetlights behind, he felt the energy drain from him as the reaction to the day's events set in. Images whirled through his mind like a kaleidoscope. Turning into the lane at Kelton he dipped his headlights as the gravel crunched under the tyres. Outside the cottage he turned off the ignition and slumped in his seat listening to the clicks of cooling metal.

As he let himself into the silent cottage he contrasted its sterile welcome with the warmth of the house he had just left. Picking up the phone he flopped into an easy chair and dialled Clare's number. No joy. Answering machine. He thought back to last night when they had been together. It felt like she had shone a lamp into the dark festering corners of his psyche. She had made him feel part of the human race again. A text pinged on his mobile. It was Mhairi. Mark was going to be fine. He closed his eyes in relief.

Farrell snapped awake, nerves jangling. He must have fallen asleep. The phone was ringing. Maybe it was Clare. He jumped out of the chair and snatched the phone up.

'Hello?'

The line crackled but nobody spoke. Farrell was about to hang up when he heard a soft mewl of pain.

'Hello, hello, who is this?' he demanded.

'It's your mother,' rasped a voice he hardly recognized.

'Mother, what's wrong? I can hardly hear you.'

Again a long pause.

'I've had a fall,' rasped the voice. 'I need your help.'

'I'll come over right away,' said Farrell, jumping to his feet.

'Wait. I'm not at home. I'm at St Aidan's.'

'What are you …?' began Farrell, only to have the connection broken.

Typical, thought Farrell. Cuts me dead at every opportunity then rings up out of the blue expecting me to bail her out, no questions asked. What was with the woman? It had started to drizzle, and Farrell pulled his collar up to ward off the evening chill. What was the daft old bat doing out at the church praying at this time of night?

When he arrived at St Aidan's it was in darkness. Farrell contemplated the blank façade of the building in exasperation. This was too much. Every fibre of his being was craving a hot bath and a generous measure of whisky. Leaving the car, he reluctantly trudged round the side of the building and tried the door there. It was locked. Rolling his eyes, he decided to try the Priest's door at the back, although he couldn't imagine his mother would have had the temerity to steal into the church that way. She had always been punctilious about observing rules. The round metal knob felt cool in his hand. To his surprise the door opened.

He stepped inside, closing the door quietly behind him. A familiar smell invaded his nose. Incense. Michael's signature scent. He tried to tell himself it was just a residue from the last Mass yet the hairs standing up on the back of his neck told him otherwise. It was a trap and his mother was the bait. For one craven moment he felt the impulse to turn and flee. Hastily, he texted Mhairi telling her his location and asking for backup. His mother was in there with a madman. A madman who had sent him an invitation. If he didn't go in and end this now there was no telling how many more victims there might be. He silently prayed for enough courage to see him through the coming ordeal.

As his eyes grew accustomed to the gloom he realized that the interior of the church beyond the small sacristy where he was standing was dimly lit by flickering candles. Stealthily, trying to quieten his rapid breathing, he crept towards the small door that opened onto the altar area. What he saw there caused his heart to miss a beat.

His mother was sitting in a chair in front of the altar wearing a blue dress. Her hair, which she normally wore scraped back from her face in a severe bun, was falling around her face in soft curls. Scarlet lipstick covered her trembling lips and rouge stained her cheeks. Mascara washed down from faded eyes following channels gouged by age. She looked like a hooker that had seen better days.

Heart pumping, Farrell scanned the interior of the church but it was hard to penetrate the shadows beyond the altar area. Where was he?

Just then he stiffened as he felt a soft breath on his neck. He started to spin round but then aborted the movement as he felt the unmistakable pressure of a gun thrust into the base of his spine. Slowly he put his hands in the air, deliberately relaxing the tension in his body. Things were not looking good.

'Glad you could join us,' said a flat voice in his ear.

Farrell's skin crawled.

'Why don't you tell me what it is you want? What do you stand to gain from this … charade?'

The man moved round to confront him, and Farrell sucked in his breath in disbelief as he witnessed a mirror image of himself.

The eyes that stared back at him were identical to his in every detail, except Farrell fancied there was a glint of something akin to madness lurking in their depths.

'I want revenge,' his brother said. 'Pure and simple. That bitch in there gave me to the devil himself.'

'Let her go,' pleaded Farrell. 'It's me you want. I'm the one who had the life you should have had.'

'Time to play happy families,' his brother said with a twisted grimace.

He prodded Farrell none too gently with the gun, and he stumbled forward until he was pushed into a seat beside his mother on the altar. Farrell tried to rally her with his eyes but she simply looked away, taking stubborn to a whole new dimension.

Farrell couldn't help himself. He let out a dry laugh. The gun immediately swung up but not before Farrell had noted the look of confusion on his brother's face.

'What the fuck is so funny?' spat Michael.

Farrell winced, in spite of himself, at the crude expletive in such a holy place.

'This,' he said, gesturing around him. 'All of this. We must be the most dysfunctional family in Christendom, don't you think? A guest appearance by the rapist who started all this and we're all set for an appearance on the Jerry Springer Show.'

'He didn't rape her. It was consensual. She was gagging for it. He told me.'

'That's a lie!' Burst out his mother. 'He forced himself on me. I was sixteen years old.'

Farrell tried to shush her with his eyes but she ignored him. Nothing new there, then.

'He was evil incarnate and you're the devil's spawn. Both of you!' she yelled, spittle flying out of her mouth.

'At least *he* didn't give me away like a bag of dirty washing,' Michael said, caressing her cheek with the gun.

'Father Boyd sold Michael, did you know that?' Farrell interjected.

'No! He wouldn't do that. I don't believe you,' his mother said.

'Nice little earner. Bought a few home comforts his stipend couldn't provide.'

'Sold to the highest bidder,' Michael snarled.

'You were meant to go to a good Catholic family,' his mother said with a catch in her voice. 'I didn't know there were going to be two of you until you were born. It was a shock. My family turned their back on me. I had to go to a Church hostel for unmarried mothers. I thought I would look at you and feel hatred. Yet when I held you both I felt nothing but love. I decided to keep one of you. I knew I couldn't raise two babies.'

'How did you choose?' Farrell asked, trying not to betray how much he cared about her answer.

His mother started to weep.

'Tell him!' shouted Michael.

'May God forgive me. In front of Father Boyd, I took a pack of cards, shuffled them and dealt you each a card.' She looked at Farrell. 'You lost.'

'I don't understand,' said Farrell. 'I'm the one you kept?'

His mother turned to Michael, her eyes pleading for understanding.

'Don't you see? It was you who got the highest card. I thought that you were going to a good Catholic couple who would be able to provide you with everything that I couldn't. I thought at the time that I was sending you off to have the better life.'

'Better life?' snarled Michael. 'The monster that raised me was a member of a paedophile ring.'

'No!' shouted Yvonne Farrell. 'Father Boyd would never have …'

'What? Looked the other way?' mocked Michael. 'He allowed himself to be convinced for thirty pieces of silver.'

'When did you find out you had a twin?' asked Farrell.

'I always knew,' said Michael, throwing down a faded black and white photo with one corner missing. It showed two identical babies lying beside each other on a bed, both sleeping and with their heads touching and limbs intertwined.

'It doesn't have to end like this,' said Farrell.

'It's too late and you know it,' said Michael. 'The only thing I have to live for is revenge.'

There was a loud banging noise on the heavy oak doors. That's torn it thought Farrell. He'd begun to feel he was making some headway. The banging started up again.

'Farrell, are you in there? Open up!'

CHAPTER SIXTY-TWO

Michael swung round to aim his gun at the door. The light of reason fading from his eyes to be replaced by a glint of mania. He looked excited, happy even.

'Today we're going to sample the fruits of eternal life.'

'I'll settle for a fish supper,' said Farrell, trying to jolt him out of his fantasy and back to reality. 'Look, Michael, there's been enough killing. End this now before anyone else gets hurt. You've found us now. It's not too late to have a real family; have what you've always craved. Is it, Mum?'

Farrell shot a glance at his mother, who had mumbled incoherently. Her eyes were round with fear as the strain of their desperate situation took its toll. He wondered which of his colleagues were outside with Mhairi, whose voice he had heard. His eyes flicked to the side door he had come in by. Mhairi's face peered out at him from the gloom and his eyes slithered quickly away lest he give away her position. The responsibility of his situation weighed heavily upon him. How to get everyone out safely without a bloodbath? Was it just his unarmed team outside or was there an armed response unit on its way?

Michael advanced on him and Farrell tensed in readiness.

'Give me your mobile phone,' he snarled.

Wordlessly Farrell handed it over after keying in the password. Michael flipped it open and looked at his contacts.

'Let's dial out for a bit of female company,' he drawled, hitting the speed dial.

The sound of a phone ringing in the sacristy made them all jump.

'Mhairi, why don't you come out here before I blow your pal's brains out?' Michael yelled, his voice thick with menace.

'No, Mhairi, don't do it,' Farrell yelled. 'Run! That's an order.'

'Did you say something, Sir?' asked Mhairi, sauntering over, like she was walking to the park instead of to almost certain death.

'Pull up a seat next to lover boy,' Michael said, waving his gun in her direction.

'Which one?' Mhairi asked, giving Michael a come-hither glance.

She was trying to play him, realized Farrell, marvelling at her bravery.

Michael regarded her coldly.

'Another whore to seek forgiveness in the House of God,' he said.

Farrell heard the ugliness creeping into his brother's voice. The expression in his eyes seemed even less rational somehow, as though the curtain of madness was about to fall. He had to try and reach him one last time.

'Michael, you're sick. You need help. These things that you've done are because you're ill. It's not too late. End this now.'

'It was too late the minute I was sold into slavery by that bastard priest!' his brother yelled; his voice amplified by the acoustics into a roar of thunder.

He walked slowly and deliberately over to the older woman and put the gun to her head.

'Wait!' yelled Farrell. 'At least allow her to confess her sins before she meets her maker. Please, I'm begging you.'

Michael considered Farrell for a long moment. Then he moved over to Mhairi, who tried not to flinch as he rammed the gun into the side of her head.

'Make it quick,' he snarled.

Farrell took out the small stole and rosary that he carried in his inside pocket. He approached his mother and kneeled down in front of her so his face was angled away from Michael.

'If you think I'm confessing my sins to you, you've got another think coming,' she hissed in his ear.

'Play along, dammit!' Farrell hissed back.

By now the building would surely be surrounded and the firearms unit in place. He had to buy them some time.

'Bless me, Father, for I have sinned. It has been one week since my last confession,' his mother said reluctantly.

As the words of the sacrament of penance slipped from his mouth like well-worn pebbles, Farrell was still assessing the situation from the corner of his eye. He noticed Mhairi had managed to hike up her already short skirt and unbuttoned her blouse to reveal some cleavage. She was trying to engage his brother in conversation and appeared to be making some headway. It was now or never. The gun had come away from Mhairi's head and fallen down against Michael's side.

Suddenly, Farrell pushed his mother off her chair and sprang at Michael with all the force he was capable of. A split second behind him, Mhairi flung herself down, knocking Michael off his feet in a rugby tackle that would have done Gavin Hastings proud. The three of them were grappling on the ground, trying to gain control of the gun, when there was a deafening explosion. Thick acrid smoke filled the altar area making it impossible to see. Shouts rent the air and the sound of running footsteps and harshly uttered commands seemed to be advancing in all directions. Farrell felt something sticky on his hand. Blood. But whose? With a last kick, Michael sent him flying. Farrell made a grab for him; his eyes streaming as he tried to pierce the gloom. His hands clutched at thin air.

In the midst of the ruckus he heard Lind's authoritative voice shouting out orders. Michael was getting away. Farrell lurched to his feet, dimly realizing that Mhairi and his mother were being taken care of. All the exits would be covered by now. He had to be hiding somewhere inside the church.

CHAPTER SIXTY-THREE

Cautiously, hugging the perimeter, Farrell made his way round the shadowy interior of the church. Even now, all these years later, he was still familiar with every nook and cranny. Reaching a recessed spiral staircase leading up to the balcony, he crept up the wooden stairs; the noise being made by his fellow officers now deadened by the thick wood panelling. Reaching the balcony, he probed the darkness with strained eyes. No sign of him. At the far end he glimpsed another set of stairs, roped off to the public, leading directly up to the bell tower. Climbing higher and higher, he wished he had had the sense to tell someone what he was up to. The stairs were narrower now, just wide enough for one person. Farrell's breath was forced out of him by exertion. Nearly at the top.

As he reached the last step he could see the bell hanging above him, secured by heavy-duty ropes. The weight would be enough to pulverize a man. A wooden door with a small toughened-glass panel opened out onto a panoramic viewing platform. He looked through the glass but saw no sign of Michael. Was he out there waiting for him or had he managed to slip round him and double back when he was on the balcony? Heart pumping, Farrell slowly turned the handle, took a deep breath and stepped across the threshold. It was a long way down. Hugging the wall, he slowly circled the platform. Where was he?

He got his answer soon enough. As he completed his circuit and returned to where he had started Michael was waiting for him with his back to the door and the gun pointed straight at him.

'Have you always been this stupid or did I just get lucky?' he asked, conversationally.

Frantically, Farrell cast about for an alternative means of escape. There was none. Those below would find their way up here eventually, but would it be in time?

'It's over, Michael,' Farrell said, sounding more confident than he felt. 'Give it up.'

'Take off your clothes,' snapped Michael.

'Come again?' said Farrell.

'You heard. Now get them off before I start shooting.'

Farrell slowly started unbuttoning his shirt. Michael was discarding his own clothes too; his aim never wavering. When they were both down to their underwear, Michael kicked his own pile over to Farrell.

'Put these on,' he demanded.

With a sinking heart, Farrell complied, taking as long as possible. The penny had dropped.

'You'll never get away with it,' Farrell blustered when they had both finished dressing. Actually, it was brilliant. Michael was going to push him over the edge then slip out dressed as Farrell and disappear in all the commotion. 'You'd kill me? Your own brother?' he asked.

'Don't act so surprised,' Michael said. 'Remember Cain and Abel?'

Farrell had his back against the parapet now; his body being forced backwards by the inexorable pressure of the gun against his head. He closed his eyes, ready to fall to his death; the words of a last act of contrition already forming on his lips.

A single retort rang out and Michael slumped at his feet, the gun clattering to the ground unfired. Farrell's legs went from under him with shock. The door onto the platform opened and what seemed like a torrent of people squeezed through. There was a single bullet hole from a high-performance rifle in the glass panel of the door.

'Nice shot,' croaked Farrell.

'Figured you didn't have a lot to lose,' shrugged the young firearms officer.

'How did you know which one to shoot?' asked Farrell.

The officer shrugged nonchalantly.

'I saw the tattoo on his arm.'

Farrell looked down at Michael. The tattoo was curling up at the edges. It was a fake.

His brother was being attended to by a paramedic. The woman grimly shook her head and radioed down for a stretcher.

'Give us a moment?' he said, turning to the firearms officer, who took in the situation at a glance.

'Sure thing,' he said motioning to his team to fall back.

The paramedic also moved away. The man was dying. There was nothing to be done.

'Why are you still here?'

'To make peace with my brother,' Farrell replied.

'I tried to kill you. It should be you lying here, not me,' Michael said, his voice growing fainter.

'Well, you know what they say about the best laid plans …' said Farrell.

Michael's face convulsed and he made a choking sound.

'Those little boys, I shouldn't have … I didn't want to … Something made me …'

'I know,' said Farrell.

He looked down at his dying brother and all the hatred that had been raging inside him just melted away, leaving only compassion in its place.

'The darkness is coming to take me,' Michael said, the life force continuing to ebb out of him.

'Don't be afraid. Say a genuine act of contrition and God will forgive your sins and welcome you into his family.'

'You really believe that?'

'With all my heart,' said Farrell, aware that time was running out.

'Bless me, Father, for I have sinned …'

Farrell leaned closer as Michael's voice grew fainter.

'I killed a man with hatred in my heart. I took little boys to save them, to bring them to You but got confused. I tried to kill my brother …' Michael coughed up blood. It wouldn't be long now. 'Forgive me, Father; I am sorry for my sins …'

Farrell closed his eyes in relief. 'May the Lord, who frees you from sin, save you and raise you up. May the Lord pardon you whatever sins you have committed. I hereby grant you a plenary indulgence and the remission of all your sins, and I bless you. In the name of the Father and of the Son and of the Holy Spirit. Amen.'

As Farrell finished, Michael took his last breath. Looking at the strangely familiar features relaxed in death Farrell prayed that his blighted soul was finally at peace.

CHAPTER SIXTY-FOUR

Farrell opened one bleary eye and glanced at the digital clock face. Ten a.m. With a sigh he rolled over in bed, pulling the duvet tightly around him. There was nothing to get up for so he might as well not bother.

The phone rang. Farrell gritted furry teeth in annoyance as he waited for the answerphone to kick in. It had better not be her again. She'd called every day for the last two weeks. Talk about not getting the message. He groaned in frustration as his mother's cool clipped tones intruded on his self-imposed exile.

'Frank, it's your mother. Again. I just need to know that you're all right. No one at the station will tell me anything. I want us to move forward from this terrible thing. I was wrong. I know that now. Call me.'

'Too little, too late,' grumbled Farrell trying to bully his conscience into submission.

He squeezed his eyes shut but sleep continued to elude him. Eventually he threw back the covers and stood up. His head was still thick from last night's whisky. Stumbling over to the mirror, he glared at himself belligerently then averted his eyes. He was a wreck and no mistake. A sour smell caused him to wrinkle his nose in distaste. He realized he need look no further for the

329

source than his own body. Slumping down on the edge of the mattress he realized he had a choice. He could keep going as he was until he ended up losing his job and maybe even the roof over his head or he could decide to rejoin the human race. It was the smell that clinched it. He stood up, straightened his shoulders and marched into the shower.

An hour later he had stripped the bed, thrown the windows open, and hoovered and dusted for good measure. Sitting at the kitchen table, nibbling half-heartedly on some toast, he felt completely spent. The rest of the day yawned before him like a black hole to fill. He felt absurdly reluctant to put a foot over the threshold of the cottage. Glancing through the door to the hallway he noticed that the postman had been again. He trudged along and picked up the various letters, putting them all in a wicker basket unopened. Some would be bills but most seemed to be cards and letters. Opening them would be allowing the world back in and he wasn't ready to do that quite yet. Daytime TV would be his saviour. Fill in some time until the clock struck six and he allowed himself the first shot of liquid oblivion. It was a life, of sorts.

Trudging upstairs, he flopped onto the couch and switched on the TV. He flicked through the channels before settling on *Teletubbies*. It made as much sense as anything else in his life of late. After an hour he decided it was rather appealing, and there was a lot to be said for being a teletubby whose main concerns seemed to be the consumption of adequate amounts of tubby toast and tubby custard.

The doorbell rang. He ignored it. It rang again. Scowling, Farrell crept over to the window and peered out. His heart quickened. It was Clare. The doorbell rang a third time. This time she bent down to the letterbox and shouted through it.

'Frank! I know you're in there. Let me in.'

Farrell swung the door wide.

'Clare, come in. It's great to see you,' he said, wincing at how

330

stilted and unnatural his voice sounded. It had been nearly three weeks since he'd talked to anyone.

He attempted to pull her into an embrace but she was stiff and unyielding. He offered her coffee and then they went upstairs to the lounge.

'How have you been?' she asked.

'Fine,' he replied, more testily than he had intended.

Well what did she expect? He had been holed up at Kelton for nearly three weeks and he hadn't heard a cheep out of her.

'I'm sorry, Frank. I know I've not been there for you.'

'Forget it,' he said.

'It all got so intense. I felt overwhelmed.'

'Yeah, me too,' he said dryly.

'Because of my work, I tend to be mired in people's private Hell a lot of the time. To be honest, it can be hard to cope with,' she said. 'It's hard to be detached, to keep my distance. That's why in my personal life I try and keep my relationships—'

'Light and frothy?' interjected Farrell.

'Something like that. I was … am … still attracted to you Frank, but you come with too much baggage. I can't deal with it. I'm sorry.'

Farrell stood up, anxious for her to leave now that she had said her piece. He didn't want her to know how much she had wounded him.

'No hard feelings,' he said with a smile. 'Now, if you don't mind I've got things I have to do,' he said, opening the front door.

This time, she flung her arms around him. As he folded her against him he closed his eyes trying to store the memory of her delicate form and the subtle notes of her perfume. He could feel her tears wet his cheek. After a few seconds it was done and he was alone again.

CHAPTER SIXTY-FIVE

As he approached Loreburn Street Farrell felt distinctly on edge. Walking through the corridors on the way to his office, he wondered whether it was his imagination or was everyone avoiding eye contact? Hardly surprising, mind you, he thought, given everything that had gone on. He pushed open the door to his office and stood there rooted to the spot.

'Surprise!' yelled a sea of faces.

It looked like he had stumbled onto the scene of a child's birthday party. There were balloons and streamers and a big banner saying 'WELCOME BACK' that was dripping with glitter glue.

Lind walked forward.

'The twins helped with the banner.'

'I guessed as much,' said Farrell.

His room appeared to have been feminized in his absence with a pink furry thing, flowers, and pictures.

Mhairi bounced forward, irrepressible as ever.

'I baked you a cake,' she announced, pushing Byers aside to reveal a towering edifice covered in chocolate and bearing more than a passing homage to the Leaning Tower of Pisa.

'Heart attack on a plate,' Farrell said. 'My favourite.'

From the back of the room, DI Moore picked her measured way towards him.

'Welcome back, Frank,' she said, handing over a slim leather-bound book of Psalms, exquisitely illustrated.

'It's beautiful,' he said. 'Thank you.'

As he leaned over to give her a peck on the cheek he was amused to notice Mhairi glaring. He immediately disengaged himself.

'Who's for chocolate cake?' he asked.

After half an hour everyone slowly dispersed until it was only Farrell and Lind left.

'So, how are you, really?' his friend asked.

'Turned the corner, I reckon,' replied Farrell. 'Ready to get back in the fray.'

'The super wants you on light duties for a couple of weeks. And er …'

'Out with it,' groaned Farrell.

'He asked me to convey that he will quite understand if you would like to apply for a transfer,' finished Lind, looking awkward.

Farrell laughed out loud.

'Tell him that God has revealed it is my vocation to serve the people of Dumfries and Galloway under his command.'

'Did he?' asked Lind, jaw dropping open.

''Course not, you pillock,' replied Farrell. 'Just can't resist the opportunity to wind up the super.'

'You'll have to tell him yourself,' said Lind on his way out the door. 'He might decide to shoot the messenger.'

Left alone at last, Farrell sank back into his chair and exhaled deeply. There was a vast amount of paperwork on his desk and he pulled some towards him and got stuck in.

After half an hour or so, he drew back in his chair. There it was again … a scratching noise. Where the blazes was it coming from? Could it be mice? A plaintive meow rent the air. Farrell followed the sound with a frown. It was coming from the cupboard. He flung open the cupboard door, bracing himself. A very irate black-and-white cat with impossibly green eyes arched its back and spat at him.

'Nice to meet you too,' murmured Farrell.

Not only was there a cat in his cupboard but it seemed to have come with a whole pile of accessories, he noted. It was the lilac fur in the basket that gave the game away. Gently closing the door again, he charged down the corridor, meeting a worried-looking Mhairi on the way up.

'Something you forgot to mention, DC McLeod?' he asked, folding his arms.

'Er, that depends, Sir.'

'On what?'

'On how what I might have forgotten to mention might be received?'

'A cat, Mhairi? Whatever possessed you?'

'Don't you like cats, Sir?'

'I've never really thought about it,' he said.

'I thought he would be company, something to come home to,' she said, shrugging helplessly and refusing to meet his eyes.

'Does he have a name?' asked Farrell.

'His name is Henry. He belonged to a really sweet old lady who died a few days ago. I couldn't bear to see him put down.'

'Relax, Mhairi,' Farrell replied. 'I'm sure that Henry and I are going to get along fine.'

That evening, as he drew the curtains and looked round the lamplit cottage, Farrell felt a rare feeling of peace steal over him. He poured himself a small drink, put on some classical guitar music, and sank into an easy chair by the crackling fire. After some hesitation, Henry leapt on his knee, turned himself around and settled down, purring contentedly. Farrell stroked him gently then came to a decision.

He picked up the phone from the table beside him and dialled a number from memory.

'Hello, Mother …' he said.

ACKNOWLEDGEMENTS

I would like to thank Jules Horne, a former writer-in-residence at Dumfries, who mentored me through the first draft with support and enthusiasm – I doubt I would have gone the distance without her; my sources within the local police who were so generous with their time; my fantastic editor, Lucy, who helped so much with insightful comments, and the team at Killer Reads. Thanks also to Cherie for my wonderful book design. A great big shout out to the supportive gang of writers from Crime and Publishment and Moffat Crime Writers for their friendship and encouragement. I would also like to thank the online twitter and blogging community, a world I have only recently discovered, for their helpfulness and generosity. In that regard, I am grateful to my son, Alex, for helping me to take my first faltering steps on social media. Finally, a big thank you to Guy, Alex and Jenny for encouraging me to keep going and supplying me with endless cups of coffee along the way.